LECARIAN'Ș
FANG

THE SHOLINDREAN TALES
YEAR: 9924

Anna McEwan

Lecarian's Fang
Sholindrean Tales
By
Anna McEwan

PUBLISHED BY:
Anna McEwan

Cover Image by Anna McEwan

ISBN: 979-8-9892546-0-6

Din
Shard

Sisho
Inmear
UNAH
Pryance Pass

Dragon racing
Roost
Linseen
Villa
Tribouin
Territory
Eila
Lynx
Territory

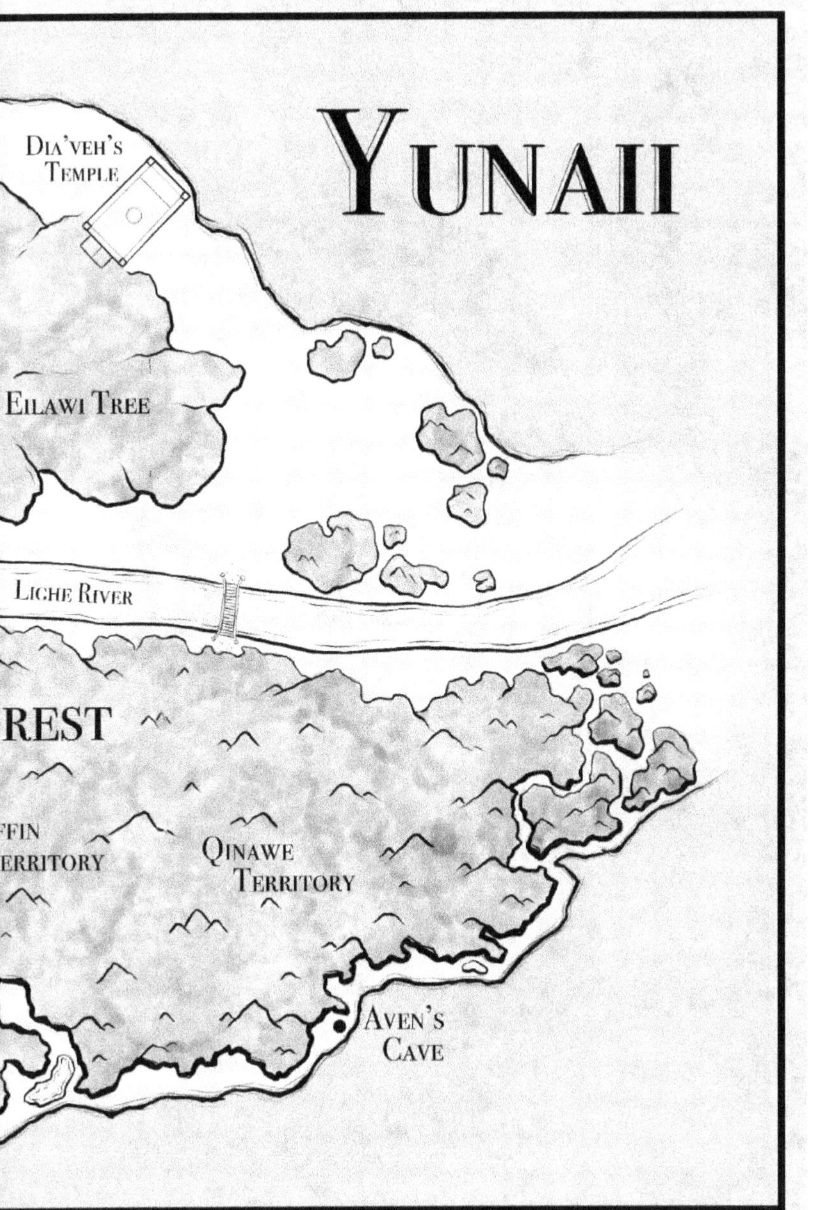

Yunaii
Dia'veh's Temple
Eilawi Tree
Lighe River
REST
FFIN ERRITORY
Qinawe Territory
Aven's Cave

Sholindrean
TALES

Sholindrean
TALES

TABLE OF CONTENTS

PRONUNCIATION GUIDE

Aven – Ah-ven
Mist – (I have faith in y'all with this one)
Kali – Kah-lee
Pryn – Pri-nn
Fennicks – Fen-nick-s
Ifera – I-feh-rah
Gaelin – Gay-lin
Dev – Deh-vv
Navya – Nah-vee-ya
Tomen – Toe-men
Rielnor – Ree-el-nor
Zoli – Zoe-lee
Ukila – U-kill-ah
Emriel – Em-ree-el
Thudan – Thu-dan
Anyvath – Ah-nee-vath
Dinon – Dee-none
Willela – Wih-lel-lah
Yliva – Yih-lee-vah
Kanai – Kah-nie
Hanawi – Hah-nah-wee
Yana – Yah-nah
Revari – Rev-are-ree
Yunaii – You-nie
Eilawi – Aye-lah-wee
Qinawe – Kee-nah-way
Tribouin – Tri-boo-in
Sholindrea – Sho-lin-dree-ah

CONTENT WARNING

This book is meant for ages 16+ and contains the following:

Descriptions of graphic violence
Descriptions of blood, death, and fatal injury
Explicit language
Graphic depictions of corpses
Mention of vomit and nausea
Mention of hunting animals
Mention of childhood neglect
Mention of religious/spiritual trauma
Mention of cultural trauma
Mention of broken bones
Mention of limb amputation

CHAPTER One

*A*ven clung to her dragon's saddle with sweaty hands. Almost through. The crowd was counting down. Their boos and cheers echoed through the gold-streaked sky.

Twenty seconds left.

She tightened her legs against Mist's sides, urging her on. The climb up the Eilawi tree always earned them a lead in the races. Despite the tree's vast canopy stretching so wide it blotted out the sky, the larger dragons still struggled to navigate between its branches. Mist was so much smaller than the others. They had to use that. Her lithe body coiled around the massive tree trunk like a serpent until only thinning foliage hung between them and the open sky.

This was it. They could win.

Nineteen, eighteen—

Mist's ribcage bulged before releasing a mighty roar. Triumph!

The last bit of green fell away. All their weight settled on a branch, shoving it down until their descent slowed and tension built. Then snap! Aven and Mist launched up into the blue, shooting free of the mighty tree they'd been climbing. Mist's neck arched, her feathered wings flapping around Aven's ears. Sweet music mingling with the crowd's boos and cheers.

Seventeen, sixteen—

The finish line hovered ahead. They just had to reach the flag flapping in the afternoon breeze.

A roar sounded behind them, and Aven flattened against Mist's back. No need to look. Fennicks, the black beast on their tail, had broken free as well.

Fifteen, fourteen—

Aven squeezed her eyes shut. "Go!"

Mist's wings beat hard, her forelegs pumping up and down as if she could claw her way to victory.

Thirteen, twelve, eleven—

They were going to make it. They had to make it. Aven glanced back.

Mistake.

Glittering black scales filled her vision as fire licked between Fennicks' bared teeth. Its heat seared her skin despite Aven's thick flying leathers. Farther below, more dragons burst from the tree, some covered in feathers, some with thick bat wings like Fennicks'. Their range of colors blazed like a sunset through the sea of swaying jade leaves. It wouldn't take them long to catch up.

Ten, nine—

"Faster!" Aven plastered herself to Mist's soft neck. These final moments relied on pure speed, leaving her a helpless passenger. Hopefully, Fennicks focused more on passing than knocking them out of the sky. One snap from the other dragon would take her leg clean off.

Eight, seven—

Fennicks' head pulled level with Mist's, black forelegs and wings working hard to pull ahead. From the other dragon's back, Pryn flashed a proud smirk as they passed.

They were going to win. Fennicks and that cheeky face-changer who whooped with delight. One more time Aven would watch them steal her victory. Steal any hope she had of leaving Yunaii in her dust. No winner's prize meant no transport across the desert. No boat across the ocean. With each flap of Fennicks' wings, whispered insults filled Aven's ears. She'd face her people's rejection again and again until the day she finally won.

Six, five—

Mist shot like a streak of light, but it wasn't enough. Aven had failed. Again. Jeers shouted from below; *runt dragon, nameless rider.* Roiling anger bubbled in her gut. They could all eat dragon fire.

The flag hung barely a wingbeat away. Mist strained, mouth opening to grab it. Her muscles tightened, body coated in sweat. *Flap, flap, flap.* Two dragons, neck and neck, one black as night and the other white as starlight. Fennicks bellowed as Mist crept ahead, bit by bit. Nearly there. Aven focused so hard on the flag, she barely noticed when Fennicks' neck curved back like a snake about to strike.

Four, three—

Snap! Teeth closed around Mist's neck, wrenching out an agonizing shriek. Time slowed. Aven's chest tightened as darkness edged around the sight of fangs clamped onto her friend. Cheers erupted below, booming like thunder. A scream ripped from her throat, tasting of bile. Raw and tearing. Her hand grabbed for the hatchet she'd given up at the beginning of the tournament. That filthy egg-breaker would pay!

Two, one!

But the world lurched and Fennicks slipped away. Down turned up. Left went right. They spun as they plummeted, Aven's vision blurring while Mist curled in on herself, howling in pain. This was it. No more races. There'd be no escaping Yunaii. Even worse, she never told Mist the truth. So much time wasted on dreaming about tomorrow.

Oh, Maker, what have I done?

Aven wrapped both arms around Mist, nuzzling into feathers and the scent of rose oil. Screams and cheers rang from the crowd. The heartless sacks of flesh. All of Yunaii would finally get what they wanted: no more nameless cub in their faces. No more walking reminder of how archaic their nonsense was. Horror flashed through her as she thought of Mama and Papa. Merciful Mother, please don't let them be watching. *Please no.* They didn't need to see her splatter on the ground.

The end raced for them. Any moment now. Wind whistled in Aven's ears, whipping against her exposed hands, leaving them stiff and raw. Her heart pounded as she braced for the inevitable crunch of bones hitting rock.

Instead, a bellow vibrated through Aven, drowning out the crowd with high-pitched ringing. Her head spun, vision blurring until vomit slid over her tongue. Did dying feel like this? Pain lanced down her spine as her body jerked upwards, head whipping back as if she'd collided with something. She could barely move. Something rock hard wrapped around her torso and leg, squeezing air from her lungs.

Aven blinked to clear her vision, to make sense of the blob of green peeking through white feathers. Slowly, shapes came into focus. Translucent wings, a golden belly, smooth emerald scales. Aven's shaking hand ran down the massive talon curled around her thigh, pinning her to Mist's body.

Another dragon held them tight. Had it caught them?

"Topaz?"

Incredible, leathery wings strained through a few heavy flaps as the much larger creature gained control of their descent. From the dragon's back, a familiar voice shouted encouragement. Aven strained her aching neck to catch a glimpse of Dev's tan face. He sounded angry. Dev *never* got angry.

Dirt and leaves shifted as Topaz laid them down, his talons unfurling so gently their razored tips didn't so much as nick her leathers. Aven barely settled against the ground before air whooshed, kicking up dust as Topaz launched back into the air. Was Dev hoping to finish the race? Fennicks and Pryn had definitely won by now.

Not that it mattered. She needed to check on Mist.

Aven willed herself to move, to jump up, to rush to her dragon's head, but her muscles only twitched. Everything hurt. Her head still spun. The force of being jerked out of a deadfall left her bones feeling smashed together. They must have been so close to splattering across the roots of the Eilawi tree.

Her stomach roiled at the thought, gut clenching as she rolled over, spilling her lunch from between her teeth. She heaved over and over, retching until bile bittered her tongue. That almost sent her gagging again, but Aven swallowed the feeling down.

Mist whined nearby, her torso expanding, trapping Aven's leg against the uneven ground.

She was alive!

Curses ripped from her lips as Aven pushed against her saddle, straining for freedom. Could Mist feel it? She called out, begging her to help, to move. *Something.* The struggle dragged on until muscles shifted, and for just a moment the pressure lifted from Aven's thigh.

"Yes, Mist! Good! I'm coming." Aven wiggled her ankle free and pushed onto all fours. She'd crawl if her strength failed her. And crawl she did, one shaking hand dragging forward, then a trembling knee. She slid along until her legs dragged through mud.

Only water wasn't what was mucked up the ground. A thick purple ooze dripped onto the dirt. Dragon's blood.

Curse Fennicks.

"I'm here, Mist. I'm here." Aven skimmed a hand along her friend's neck until eventually reaching her jaw. The feathery touch made Mist jerk away, another whine climbing from her throat.

"Easy, easy. It's just me." Aven caressed the tiny horns on Mist's head, then scratched her fluffy, deerlike ears. "Just breathe."

The bite gaped at the base of Mist's skull, but Aven couldn't tell how bad. Bloodstained feathers obscured the difference between wound and gore.

If the Maker ever heard any of her prayers, let it be this one: *Let Mist be okay.*

Aven searched for a glimpse of an approaching dragon. The judges carried medical supplies for moments just like this, but even those dung-kickers played favorites. She had no bandages on her racing saddle. The extra weight just slowed them down.

She cursed herself for making Mist pay the price for her foolishness. Riding leathers didn't hold a candle to dragonhide, so Aven had never worried about it until now. Cuts and burns made for interesting scars.

Another glance at the sky revealed Topaz herding a streak of gray her way. Good. Dev had fetched a judge. *Maker forbid the biased lemmings come on their own!* Probably too busy shaking Pryn's hand and clapping Fennicks' foreleg to care about the injured runt and her nameless rider.

"Just hang on." Aven swallowed down the bitterness. Mist needed her focus, not Pryn. "You'll be okay."

The bleeding had slowed to only gushing out when Mist rocked or coiled against the pain. Aven tried gently holding her down, but any pressure brought out whimpers and panting. Helplessness left her crooning as she stroked Mist's ears and ran fingers through her mane. Aven's experience with wounds consisted only of bringing down prey and ending life. Never treating, never healing.

The ground shook when Dev and the judge landed. Both of their dragons were more like the creatures of legend than Mist. The gray glittered with scales tough enough to repel most blades, and Topaz had the bulk to level a small village. Next to them, Aven felt like a child playing at dragon racing. Mist wasn't much larger than a massive draft horse.

A stocky man slid from the slate gray beast while Dev lingered by Topaz's side. His narrowed eyes undoubtedly took in every tiny detail: cataloging it all for later.

"Step back, step back," the judge huffed, more annoyance in his voice than concern. Black tattoos wrapped around his wrists and forearms, marking him as Tribouin. Another face-shifter like Pryn. Like Papa. He had the same coily dark hair as him, too, though his skin was sandy and freckled.

Aven considered ignoring his command. The look of shock on his face would be amazing, but she wouldn't risk Mist being left to bleed out on the grass. No one cared about a nameless and her pet. Especially the judges.

It took every scrap of willpower to placate the judge and shuffle to Mist's other side—to leave her even a moment. She wouldn't go through this alone. They'd done everything together since the day they met, and Maker willing, they would walk away from this together too.

As the judge crouched across from her, Aven searched his face. His brow didn't pinch. No sigh of discouragement came. He lazily stroked the bloody feathers, before producing a clean rag from his satchel, wet it with a foul-smelling liquid, then pressed it to the bite. Whatever it was ripped an awful hiss from Mist. Her tail thrashed as she raked claws through the dirt.

"It's going to be okay." Aven caressed her clenched jaw, coaxing Mist's head to rest on her thighs. Hopefully, the wobble in her voice was only obvious to her. The judge didn't need to hear the tears she fought to swallow down. "It's really not that bad."

Mist blinked fuchsia eyes once, twice, understanding flooding through her dilated pupils. A croon slipped free, the soft sound easing the tension in Aven's chest. There she was. Her best friend—her *only* friend. So wonderful and clever. She could have sobbed when Mist pressed her snout to Aven's stomach, breathing deep.

How did these fools convince themselves their dragons were mindless beasts? The intelligence in Mist's eyes rivaled most of the sheep in Yunaii.

The judge continued working, wiping away blood, plucking feathers. All with a disinterested look, as if he had better things to do than help the runt. Once he'd cleaned the wound, he applied a bitter-smelling liquid, eliciting another hiss from Mist. This time her talons only curled.

"She might need stitches but I've no supplies for that." The judge wiped his hands on his pants, not bothering to look at Aven. "Multiple puncture wounds and heavy bleeding. Blood loss most likely left her disoriented and in shock. The bite was just a bit too deep."

"A bit too deep." Aven clenched her fists. It was acceptable by the standard of racing rules. Dragons bit each other. It's what they did. As long as no one died, then no rules were broken.

Many of the dragons were covered in scars. Dev's Topaz had a swath of them across his face, down his long neck, and across his chest. Aven couldn't imagine the monster capable of ripping into such a massive dragon.

Fennicks would have some fresh ones if Aven got the chance. That filth would regret putting their mouth on Mist at all.

"Naught to do about it now," the judge said, snapping Aven from her murderous thoughts. He pulled out a few clean bandages and began wrapping Mist's neck, boredom etched into his sun-weathered face. "Keep the cuts cl—"

"Bites." Aven leaned towards him, a familiar itch slithering beneath her skin. "Fennicks *bit* her."

The judge clenched his teeth, staring her down like an impertinent child. If Papa was there, he'd say avert her eyes. Show respect. Tribouin were all about respect. But Aven wasn't Tribouin, even if Papa was. She was her mother's child and Qinawe women did not yield.

The judge's gaze dropped to the carved fang dangling around Aven's neck on a cord of beads. His nostrils flared, bursts of red exploding in his brown, face-changing eyes. "I see Tomen has allowed your ma to take more than just our ways from him."

Aven tightened her fists to keep from swiping claws across his smug face. Her nails lengthened into razors, their sharp pricks against her palm drawing blood. Not for the first time. Tiny scars speckled her hands. Reminders of all the times she'd drowned in a seething rage she could never act upon. Mama said guarding the souls of animals wasn't an excuse to act like one.

"Perhaps there's some Tribouin manners in you after all." A satisfied smirk stretched across the judge's face.

"Doubtful," Aven said with a feral smile of her own. Only the threat of Mama's disappointment kept her from showing the man his own severed tongue. "You helped my dragon so I'll refrain from teaching you some Qinawe manners."

The judge's eyes narrowed. "Keep the bites clean. Don't let her scratch or mess with them, or you'll be dealing with an infection on your hands and *no one* to treat it."

"Thanks," Aven forced through gritted teeth. Mist wasn't a fool. She wouldn't risk causing herself permanent damage. This tongue flapper only saw a fluffy lizard who'd gotten nipped by the competition. That's all anyone in Yunaii saw. So many had forgotten the secrets the dragons kept.

The judge retreated to his dragon without a glance back. No doubt he would run his mouth to anyone who would listen. *Tomen's nameless cub is exactly what everyone says!* Tribouin liked pretending they differed from the Qinawe because their men led instead of their women. As if that made a difference. She'd grown up an outcast from both, and found the Tribouin as stuck-up and senseless as they accused the Qinawe of being.

In a gust of wind, the gray dragon soared off to who knows where. Aven watched them go, before her attention fixed on the Eilawi tree's leaves shifting in the breeze, allowing cracks of golden light to slip through. She drew in a deep breath as she stroked the fang hanging around her neck, tracing the saber-toothed cat carved into its base. Every shape and bump so perfectly familiar. She imagined the cat the tooth once belonged to as she skimmed over the smooth length beneath the carving, to the pointed tip. The effort it took to beat back the rage, the urge to draw blood. It scared her sometimes. Mama made it seem so easy.

She only carried the soul of a wolf. A wonderful, beautiful creature, but still just an animal, unlike what Aven guarded. The power inside the fang rivaled all of her people's gifts.

Graceful footsteps drew her attention from the tree. She'd almost forgotten that Dev and his dragon still lingered. Even with all the training Mama pounded into her skull, Dev surpassed much of her skill. Confidence radiated from him, with his controlled movements and keen eyes. Even covered by flying leathers, what he'd once been still shone through. Klesian elves believed they were born for combat. Every one of them lived by the sword. Many of them died by it. One day Aven would find out how Dev ended up a dragon-riding tournament hound instead of some glory-winning warrior. So far, they'd only shared a few drinks to commiserate their many losses, but she'd pry it out of him, eventually.

"Do you need help moving her?" Dev asked, hooking a thumb through his belt. If he'd had a sword, she guessed he'd be resting a hand on the pommel instead. Another reminder of the warrior hidden beneath the tousled brown curls constantly falling into his eyes.

Aven looked to Mist, who had finally lifted her head. "Can you stand?"

An offended warble croaked as the dragon rolled onto her belly and strained to rise. Tremors shot through her legs, but eventually her stubbornness won out. She raised her tail high, mouth hanging open in an obvious dragon grin.

Dev's brows drew into a disapproving frown. "She should lean on Topaz. At least until she can get some water in her."

Mist growled in Topaz's direction, but the larger dragon didn't so much as glance her way. He lounged nearby, gold-streaked wings folded against his sides. The scars across his enormous head made him look even more dangerous despite him snoozing like a cat curled up in the sun.

"Thank you," Aven said, smiling at Mist's glowing eyes. "I think we've got it."

Dev's gaze cut to the cliffs, where the hammock seating normally dangled. As soon as the race ended, they were drawn up the reddish rock of the canyon wall, taking those seated there with them. Once the dragons were gone and all bets settled, the shapeshifters of Yunaii returned to their separate lives. No one would think about the little white dragon who almost died for their entertainment.

Aven glared at the pathways cut into the cliff. Those brave enough wound back and forth, moving slowly to avoid plummeting off the edge, while the rest took the easy way down. On dragonback. Any racer who didn't win had a chance at some lucrative trades. Quite profitable for those with bigger dragons.

No one ever asked for a ride down on Mist.

"That was a close call today." Dev's gaze traveled back to them. "Fennicks nearly splattered you two like melons in a fruit toss competition."

"Oh, I remember." Aven brushed dirt from her leathers when she rose. At least Mama's hard work remained intact.

"Of course." Dev almost looked embarrassed. If he felt that sort of emotion. The tips of his long ears flushed with the slightest bit of red. "My apologies."

"No need to apologize. You saved my life. I'm just—we were *so* close!" A screech died before escaping her throat. Fennicks had won. Pryn had received her prize. Another race lost, and nobody even cared to see if she and Mist were okay. Mindless mob.

Dev simply stood there staring, his pointed nose and sharp cheekbones almost like the sculptures around the market's Temple. If he didn't blink soon, she might think him made of stone.

"We're good, Dev." Aven ran a knuckle along Mist's furled wing. "She just needs rest."

He dipped his chin, sending a tumble of curls falling against his sweaty forehead. So impractical. Aven would have shaved the unruly mess off her own head. Thankfully, her sleek, brown hair remained tamed in a pair of tight braids Mama wove to keep it from her face.

Mama. Papa.

Aven whirled, searching the cliffs for anyone moving against the departing crowds. Had they been watching the race? Did they see her fall? The fright it would have given them! Papa would ask her not to race anymore.

"Do say so if you require further assistance," Dev called.

She waved distractedly, still searching for her parents. Only when Mist nudged her shoulder with an offended croak did Aven tear her gaze from the cliff. "What?"

Mist warbled before turning her nose at Dev's retreating back.

Ugh. A dramatic sigh slipped through Aven's lips. She hated speaking for Mist. Her manners rivaled even Dev's. Aven would rather throw herself from the Eilawi tree than thank anyone in Yunaii for anything, but this was a matter of dragon pride.

Through gritted teeth, she called out, "Hey Dev!"

He paused his climb into Topaz's saddle, perfectly poised as he looked over his shoulder. Aven pressed her lips together to keep from throwing some teasing jeer. Klesian elves weren't known for their sense of humor. But really. Did he even realize how he looked, perched on his dragon's leg as if having his portrait done? Honestly, elves could be so dramatic. Even more so than the Eilawi.

Mist nudged her again, so Aven rubbed the back of her neck. "Thank you. For catching us." Another rougher shove from the little white dragon. "For saving us."

Dev nodded, hand resting once more on his belt, his pointed nose, thin mouth, and wide eyes smoothed into the perfect picture of a humble soldier. "It was my duty and I am happy to aid."

Aven wrinkled her nose. Why did elves have to take everything so seriously? Even the Qinawe knew how to loosen up and have fun. *Sometimes.* Which was saying something for a clan run by matriarchs who took it as a challenge if you looked them in the eye.

As if he'd read her mind, a curve pulled at Dev's lips. "Topaz and I would hate to see Fennicks' only actual competition go out like that."

Mist crooned in agreement and Topaz rumbled back, something akin to a purr vibrating from his chest.

"One day," Aven said, rubbing Mist's side. The promise laid heavy in her heart. She *would* see Fennicks stomped into the ground. Just the thought of the black dragon sent heat flaring through her sore limbs.

Dev nodded in agreement and slid into his saddle. Then they were off, Topaz's wings beating so strong, Aven's two heavy braids flying back from her face.

"Let's go home," she said, heading for the dragon roost at the base of the cliff.

A hiss was her only warning before Mist's tail flicked her arm. Aven whirled around, fixing the dragon with a stubborn glare. "You must have lost more blood than I realized because I *know* you don't think we're flying anywhere."

This time the pearly dragon growled, feathers ruffling along her face and neck like an offended little owl. It took all of Aven's self-control to keep from smiling. She didn't feel like getting nipped for laughing out loud.

"Your legs work just fine."

Mist flapped her wings once, twice, shooting a look at them with one narrowed eye.

"I know your wings work too, but I don't feel like falling from the sky because you lost too much blood."

A loud huff escaped Mist as she stomped off, tail flicking back and forth. Just like the market cats who begged for Aven's food and looked so offended when she had nothing to give them.

She didn't know which comparison would irritate Mist more, the owl image or the angry kitty. Probably best she kept both to herself until a good teasing was in order. Dragon pride could certainly rival elven principles.

For now, Aven trailed behind Mist, watching for any reason to worry: a droop to her neck, weaving back and forth, or even just a clumsy stumble. If Mist couldn't make it home, they would rest in the safest place in Yunaii, beneath the glass ceiling of Dia'veh's Temple. Not ideal, but they would be together.

A short trek brought them to a line of boulders taller than any hut or house Aven had ever seen. Deep gouges scoured into their craggy sides, all from creatures like Topaz and Fennicks dragging them to create a vast ring stretched along the base of the cliff. A makeshift sanctuary for the riders. Behind the rocks, they stored gear, prepared their mounts before a race, even hung out from time to time. Aven's change of clothes awaited there, along with some food she'd packed for Mist, and of course all the other riders and their dragons, including Fennicks and Pryn.

She stood in a gap between two boulders, grinning from ear to ear as she regaled her flock of squawking fans with details of her and Fennicks' vicious win. The other riders didn't care she played dirty. She'd knocked the nameless and her runt out of the sky. Their excitement sizzled in the air.

Pryn's gaze swept over the heads of her sheep, and a grin spread across her lips. She'd set eyes on Aven and Mist.

That's when Aven knew her ex-girlfriend had stopped there to preen just so there'd be no avoiding her.

Oh, joy.

CHAPTER
Two

Aven

"I was wondering where you two had gone off to," Pryn called.

Aven froze when everyone turned. They'd seen Dev and Topaz go for the save, so their lack of surprise didn't shock her. The other riders had probably expected it of him. Elven honor and all that. What cut deeper than any blade were their disappointed looks. A few Qinawe riders sighed, one scowled, and a Tribouin who'd never come close to catching Mist or Fennicks had the audacity to grip the handle of his knife. As if he could finish what Pryn started. Aven would love for him to try. She didn't need her hatchet to lay him flat.

Mist's growl snapped her into motion. She wouldn't let these people see their venom sting. Aven walked straight into the hoard, shoulders thrown back, eyes fixed over Pryn's shoulder. *Bugs.* All of them. That's what Mama would say. Her lips curled as she imagined them sporting beady eyes, knobby limbs, and nasty, buzzing wings. If only shifters had to take the form of their own souls instead of the ones they desired. What an eye-opener that would be.

Pryn blocked the entrance, tension in her russet-brown shoulders and burgundy lips hidden behind a confident smile. Aven saw right through her.

"What in the Maker's name was that stunt back there? Fennicks nearly killed us."

"We didn't break the rules." Pryn's eyes shifted from brown to shimmering gold. "You're alive."

Oh, she was quite proud of herself. Pryn often shifted her eyes, her skin, her hair, as most Tribouin did, but Aven had learned long ago what different colors meant on her. She saved gold for special occasions. Seeing it streak through Pryn's eyes hurt more than Aven could explain. Once upon a time she'd have been horrified with herself.

"Well as long as you didn't break any rules." Aven shoved through the door, accepting the risk as she rammed her shoulder into Pryn's. That was all she dared. Slapping the satisfied smirk off Pryn's face was tempting but not worth the fit Mama would have if Aven struck another shifter. Even if they did deserve it.

Sometimes she loathed her people's pacifism.

Jeers and laughter trailed after Aven, even when Mist growled a warning. The other riders only saw a runt dragon. Nothing more dangerous than a yipping dog. If only they knew what Mist could do. Maybe Aven would let her show them right before they made their escape. If they ever won a race.

She huffed as they began the gauntlet of passing every other dragon to get to her things. Roofless stalls lined the cliff nearest the entrance, each holding one of the smaller dragons. They were still at least twice Mist's size, standing almost as tall as the Temple. They ranged in color like a spectrum of nature. Reds, yellows, browns, greens. Some sported feathers or scales like plate armor, while others had snakelike skin; each one unique in some way. Her favorites had luxurious manes like Mist's or were covered in enough spikes and horns to impale a clumsier rider. Beautiful, in a terrifying way.

She'd refused to build Mist a stall. The rough lumber boxes felt too much like a cage, even with the dragons' names lovingly etched into them. The larger dragons enjoyed the perk of long, flat sunning rocks to lounge on, a luxury Mist wasn't strong enough to afford.

Buckets, scrub brushes, soaps and combs lay strewn all around the roost, things Aven expected in a barn. She rolled her eyes every time she saw them. These people treated one of the most powerful creatures in Sholindrea like horses or housecats.

The dragons *did* let them, though, and Aven saw why.

They flourished in their riders' attention. Haunches of goat and boar were delivered to their stalls. Cool water filled their troughs, thanks to conjure stones from Shard's Port. The dragons had everything they wanted by playing at being simple beasts.

Aven and Mist snuck by unnoticed, until they reached the larger dragons, the older ones. A few bothered to stop gorging to hiss or growl. Fennicks' yellow eyes in particular bored into them, a low rumble vibrating from the black dragon like thunder on the horizon. The sound stopped Aven in her tracks.

She gazed up at Fennicks, skin itchy beneath her tight flying leathers. The beast didn't have the thick scaly plates like many of the others. How hard would it be to rip through the overlapping scales covering that black throat? Perhaps the smaller, softer patches of red running along Fennicks' belly would be easier. What would that purple blood taste like? It'd be worth it. Fennicks deserved to bleed. Only when her finger pricked the sharp tip of the fang dangling around her neck, did Aven realize she'd even grabbed it.

The coiling rage in her chest dampened when Mist crooned. With a grace the other dragons couldn't dream of, she slipped in between Fennicks and Aven, her feathery body blocking that yellow-eyed stare. She warbled a sad sound, nostrils quivering, her head bobbing softly. The sight of her wide, dilated eyes snapped Aven out of her reckless anger.

"Sorry," she whispered, stepping into the cover of Mist's raised wing. "Let's go."

A growl wafted against their retreating backs, but Aven didn't dare turn. The urge to dig claws into Fennicks' eyes or shred those massive wings left her quivering. She couldn't trust herself right now.

As soon as they finished their nerve-wracking walk, Aven ducked behind the shoulder height boulder where she stashed her things. A silent request to the Maker ran through her head. A prayer that her stuff was still there. She'd once returned from a race to find everything she owned strewn from the roost to the Eilawi tree without a culprit to be found. From then on, she left only the absolute essentials.

She must have paid enough dues for the other riders today. Everything was just as she left it. A relieved sigh escaped as she peeled off her riding leathers, barely remembering to step out of sight. She didn't really care if anyone saw her strip down to her undergarments. Qinawe didn't squeak and panic over nudity like Tribouin and humans did. That wasn't her people's way. Human flesh, wolf flesh, lizard flesh, it was all the same mess of meat, blood, and bones. Animals didn't quibble over such silly things, so why should the Qinawe?

She yanked at her tight riding pants, cursing as she wrestled her curvy bottom free. These leathers were such a blasted nuisance. Too often she hopped around, fighting to get her feet free without falling over like a Soulless cursed fool. She'd rather ride nude than in the uncomfortable clothes Mist insisted would keep her safe.

All they did was trap her in her own skin.

When Aven pulled apart the straps of her riding jacket, the weight of the fang she wore thumped against her chest. She caressed the ivory carving of Kali, the saber-toothed cat tethered to the fang, the soul she was responsible to guard in exchange for using Kali's form. Aven's eyes slipped shut as her breathing deepened. The lynx appeared in her mind, standing as tall as a man, covered in thick brown fur streaked with creamy silver stripes. So powerful and majestic, even in her last days of life. Kali had been one of the most beautiful creatures Aven had ever seen.

Being free of the leathers' cage set the great cat loose. She couldn't shift with them on. Not without shredding the expensive garments and possibly hurting herself. Would they give way if she let the cat explode from within? If her body shifted from fingers to claws, from teeth to fangs. In a few blinks of an eye, she could really be free. In a few more she could be on the other riders, could make them pay for calling Mist a runt.

For refusing to use her name.

Aven released a shaky breath and dropped the fang. *Foolish cub!* Kali's instincts almost took over. Again. It was one of the prices her people paid when they took in the souls they guarded. Sometimes the wildness of those creatures overpowered them. Kali's seemed especially strong, but she'd been especially powerful in life so Aven thought she deserved a little grace, all things considered.

She yanked on her favorite wrap dress, securing one side hem to the button stitched inside, then the other with a button on the outside before securing it with a coil of thin, golden rope. Mama had made the soft, green dress herself when Aven complained about tediously shedding layers of clothing before shifting. In this, she could be on all fours, bounding for the darkening forest in seconds. She could be free.

Aven shook off the urge to run and reached for her leather boots. It was time to go on a hunt. Kali's soul itched to take over for a while.

With the riding gear shoved into her pack, Aven threw it over one shoulder and stepped from behind the rock. Mist stood there, wings tight against her sides, and head up despite her pain. Her gaze followed anyone who came too close, and Aven couldn't help smiling. What did she need rocks to change behind for when her best friend would relieve anyone of their eyeballs if they tried for a peek?

Aven skimmed her fingertips over Mist's feathers as she passed, and they fell into step together. Dev passed them on their way out, carrying a pile of brushes with a bucket of water slung over his muscled forearm. He threw Aven a hasty nod as he went on his way, chattering to a Linseen elf walking beside him. He must have been about to give Topaz a bath.

Aven couldn't wait to dive into the bathing pool at home and then dig into whatever Papa cooked for dinner. Her stomach rumbled at the thought of his herbed thumper stew. A perfect way to end a horrible day.

"Taking your runt home?" Pryn asked, curled up against Fennicks' foreleg, scratching the ridges over their eyes.

Eyes fixed on Mist, their pupils thin slashes of black, like a cat on the prowl.

Aven met them glare for glare, without looking at Pryn. "She makes a great feather pillow. Too bad all you have is that monster to cuddle or has your father found someone new for you to hang on? I noticed your brother isn't around to sling barbs on your behalf."

Pryn's bottom lip pulled into a hurt, almost pouty look. "Maybe I have been Promised. What do you care?"

"I don't." A glance at the smooth brown skin beneath Pryn's fringe of short bangs confirmed what Aven should have noticed. All their lives, Pryn and her brother had worn the traditional ribbon of white lace signaling to other Tribouin that they had no Chosen. How had she not noticed it was gone? Not too long ago, Pryn being Promised would have been a kick to the gut.

"I hope for your brother's sake your Promised has a sister. What will he do now that he doesn't have to make sure no one looks at you the wrong way?"

Gold leached from Pryn's eyes as her brow furrowed. "Papa will find him a suitable match."

And Aven would pity the girl cursed with that burden. "Well at least the rest of us won't have to put up with his snake tongue anymore. When will the big day be?"

"I thought you didn't care." Pryn arched a thin brow.

"I don't. I just hope you've practiced your blade work since the last time. You wouldn't want to muck it up. *Again*." Regret hit as soon as the words left Aven's mouth. They weren't worth Pryn's widened eyes, their brown depths turning to deep blue. Aven was just so blasted tired and angry.

"At least I'm not slumming around like you. They say that girl you've been running with is a Tribouin, but Papa says she's not one of ours." Pryn leaned forward, eyes narrowing slightly. "Is she like you? Does your kind run in packs?"

A slap would have hurt worse than those words. "Don't spend all your winnings on something pointless. Maker knows there's people who actually need it."

With that, Aven hurried away, nostrils flaring against the reek of Pryn's hurt, Mist's sorrow, and the tang of anger she could only blame on Fennicks. All of it tightened her chest until she gasped for each breath. It shouldn't hurt anymore. Losing races. Seeing Pryn's face. So why was her vision blurred from traitorous tears?

Mist caught up by the exit of the roost, her soft warble nearly dropping Aven to her knees. Pryn would love that. The other racers, too. To finally see her broken. So, she pushed on, shoulders thrust back as she clenched her jaw. They had no right to her pain.

"It's okay," Aven whispered, even if it wasn't. She'd never get away from this place or those who left her a nameless amongst her people. It didn't have to be this way.

Kingdoms beyond their canyon cared little for traditions. If she'd been born in Estellias, like Mist, she might have never been singled out. Even their king had a blend of bloodlines, but he still held the confidence of his people. Mist said he had enough human in him that his skin wasn't the usual leafy green of the Eilawi, and no one cared. He ruled the most powerful kingdom in the world while Yunaii's shapeshifters hid themselves away, clinging to traditions that had meaning only in times of war.

Aven itched to shed the worries and sink into Kali's soul, to focus simply on her next meal and remaining clean and warm. If only Mist's steps weren't coming slow and stiff, her heavy-lidded eyes locked on the ground.

She wouldn't make it to the forest. Not like this.

Aven touched Mist's soft shoulder. "Let's go to the Temple."

A disgruntled growl came as her reply, but after swaying for a moment, Mist's pride dissolved beneath the look Aven gave her. "We'll see the Priestess. She can take another look at that bite. Make sure the judge didn't miss anything."

She got a little nod before Mist's steps veered towards the Eilawi tree. The Temple stood against the bottom of the canyon cliffs, its entrance stretching into the market place spanning the shady area shielded by the canopy.

There'd be no mad dash into the forest today. No shifting, running, or flying. Aven would be lucky if she got to see Mama and Papa before their sun, Sansia, yielded the sky.

Into the crowds they went, shifters and elves all heading for home. The forest across the river gave shelter to the Qinawe, Tribouin, lynx, and griffin, while the elves lived in the canopy of the Eilawi tree. All had to pass through the market though, creating a perfect opportunity for sellers of food and finery.

It was the worst time ever to be in the market.

Normally, Aven didn't mind the hustle. All the different traders, weavers, cooks, and weapon makers gathered around the base of the tree, shaded from the bright light of Sansia. They built stands and erected tents of tanned hide, set up benches and tables. Even the earth beneath the tree's roots had shifted away, leaving a cavern underneath where the more well-off traders preferred to sell.

She dipped into a fantasy world when winding around the coiled roots in that hollowed space. It was so different from the rest of Yunaii. The massive canopy crested over the cliffs and spanned the market space. The tree's branches were strong enough to hold creatures like Topaz and Fennicks without any strain, their pathways like those in the forest, leaves pressing in close and wind brushing against her skin. It was a world apart. Aven could forget about everything and bask in speckles of golden light as elven music drifted like bird song. The Forest elves lived up there, in a hidden oasis above Aven's rocky canyon home.

Whenever she made this walk, the tree's magnificence always left her wondering. No sapling could climb such heights and command this arid place on its own. That's how it earned its name. Only the Eilawi—the Elementals—could have brought Yunaii to life. Their ethereal creation watched over all the shifters, providing shade, softening the harsh air, cooling their dry climate. Aven wondered if an Earth Elemental had stood over a little twig and willed it to grow or had a Water Elemental guarded it through the decades, making sure it got the lifeblood it needed to thrive? What could she have done if the Maker Dia'veh had gifted her with such power instead of the ability to shift?

The Elementals had moved on from Yunaii long before the shifters arrived. The cataclysm forced them to abandon much of the world. Many had gone on to kingdoms like Estellias or disappeared to be with the old ones, where their power could no longer shape life or break continents. Aven had never seen one, but appreciated what they left behind. The Eilawi tree, the forest it seeded, even this canyon had been shaped by Earth and Water Elementals. Had it been for them to live here, or did they do it for the sheer act of creation? Aven was no artist herself, but having the power to shape Sholindrea's face had to be thrilling.

Her musings were interrupted by Mist's soft sigh, a sign that they had arrived at their destination. The Temple was her favorite place in Yunaii, a safe refuge from the other dragons, the tension between shifters, and all the politics.

The Temple's sand-colored walls stood out against the warm rock of the canyon's cliffs. Its existence and structure just another bit of proof of the Elementals' presence. It was the only building they had left behind, seamless and smooth, grown instead of built, thanks to their power and will. They shaped whatever they needed, from homes, to Temples, to the dam far down the river that kept this place unflooded during rainy seasons.

Mist dragged herself up the steps to the Temple with Aven on her heels. She couldn't help peering at the entrance, quaking beneath the sculptures of Elementals bursting from the stone. Only an Earth Elemental could have accomplished the feat. A figure of Fire and Water framed the archway, while Earth and Air hovered above with arms outstretched. Dia'veh's symbol was etched high above, a series of lines that almost looked like two hands cupped together, with a gem of starlight slipping from its fingers. The Maker's gifts falling from the sky to the world below.

Carvings decorated every bit of the walls. Dragons in flight, humans entwined in a dance, shifters mid-transition, and crits of all shapes and sizes hidden behind etchings of grass or soaring over clouds. No one knew just how many Sholi actually walked the Great Mother's lands, but the Elementals had done their best to capture as many as they could. Aven never knew whether to admire the flawless depictions or fear them. What could Eilawi do with such power when creation was not their goal?

The inside of the Temple matched its exterior. Sandy walls, smooth stone floors, pillars holding up a glass roof that allowed a perfect view of the Eilawi tree. Mist drew in a deep breath upon entering, no doubt inhaling deep the scent of flowers in the air. To Aven it was almost too sweet, too cool compared to the air outside, but it held significance for Mist. She had grown up in cold forests and plains of grass, where rivers and ponds cut through soft dirt instead of rock. Another fantasy world.

A crystalline pool sank into the center of the room, Sansia's light shining on its surface. Plants and flowers shimmered in the water, their blossoms the source of the scent in the air.

The Priestess knelt in the water, her long, black hair coiled into tight strands that cascaded past the small of her back. She had pinned some away from her face, keeping a small knot secure with two crisscrossed golden needles. The sight of her drew Aven up short, even as Mist continued her approach. The woman had always been kind, but that bred more questions than comfort. Was it fueled by pity, like the lynx's? Or obligation, like the elves?

"Do you seek communion or justice?" a male voice asked.

Aven nearly jumped out of her skin, Kali's hackles rising as she whirled on the elf beside her. She hadn't noticed a single tap of his boots or shift of his clothes. The truth elf moved like a wraith. He looked like a wraith, too, with skin paler than anyone in Yunaii, and long white hair that rivaled Mist's feathers.

He blinked his silver eyes, thin brows creeping up as she stared at him. "Do you—"

"I heard you, Truthseeker." Aven didn't mean for the bite in her voice, but her insides were still knotted. It wasn't often anyone could sneak up on her. "I don't need anything. I brought my dragon to the Priestess for healing."

His attention shifted towards the pool, moving with a grace even Dev didn't have. Were it not for his leather armor, smelling of oil and wax, and the blades crossed against his back, she could almost believe he was not of this world.

"Ah, young Mist," the Priestess said, stepping out of the water. She held out her hands, golden bangles clinking together as they cast gold hues over her cool brown skin. "I was hoping to put eyes on you after what happened. How are you, child?"

Mist dropped her nose into the Priestess's palm and blew out a deep breath. To anyone else, it probably looked like just a greeting, but Aven read the exhaustion in her friend's body. The day had been long and the ruse dragged out.

The Priestess glanced at the Truthseeker with shimmering golden eyes. "Dear one, might you guard the entrance to the Temple for a moment?"

He dipped his chin and moved away, his gliding steps unnervingly silent. Illieve were strange elves, sometimes creepy to talk to since they could see through any lie, even if one didn't know they were lying. Their power was a strange mystery Aven preferred avoiding more than facing.

The Priestess smiled softly at his retreating back before turning back to Mist. "Come, child. Let me see…you."

Aven's breath caught as she first scanned the door to the Temple, and then the open windows on the adjacent walls. No faces peered through the massive openings, not even a shadow shifted in the distance. With the day drawing to a close, hopefully no one else would come seeking the Priestess or time with the Maker.

At least they were in the safest place in Yunaii, though. If anyone walked in on what was about to happen, only Dia'veh could save them from the wrath of the other dragons.

Aven waited with her back to the pool, tension keeping her shoulders raised beneath her ears. How she knew when it was done was another mystery. The feeling lived inside, where Kali's intuition reigned. She felt Mist like a growing breeze through the forest. When Aven turned, a girl replaced the feathery dragon that once stood beside the priestess. Her umber skin was warm against a sleeveless, muslin dress that split halfway up her thighs, while a veil of white hair shimmered on her head. Familiar hues of rose, violet, and cerulean danced in their waves. Weaving braids into those long, silky strands always soothed disappointments and frustrations.

This was the dragons' greatest secret. If the other shifters knew their pets were actually the old ones, the first shapeshifters, their way of life in Yunaii would be over. Mist said they would kill to keep their secret and Aven had no intention of ever testing that resolve.

CHAPTER
Three

Mist

Colors dimmed as Mist finished shifting out of her dragonskin. It almost hurt to let go of the pure saturation and hues that most couldn't see. They were her favorite part next to her feathery wings and the freedom they granted.

This form had its perks too, though. Like the way Aven's eyes widened when she turned around, her cheeks growing rosy. Mist couldn't help smoothing the dress Ifera gave her, fiddling her family's delicate, silver armlet on her right bicep, anything to distract from the way Aven stared.

'Admiring' didn't describe it. Nor did 'devouring'. Kali shone through that yellow-eyed gaze, pulling searing heat into Mist's face. She should really break free of it. Thank the Priestess for the clothes and Truthseeker Gaelin for his protection. He still stood by the door, blocking anyone from entering. What would her Papi say if he caught her forgetting all the manners he preached when she was little?

If only Aven would stop looking at her like that. Her gaze had dropped to the slits in the side of Mist's dress, dragging over her bare thighs, then up to the armlet she fiddled with, before finally settling on her face. Then she strode forward like the predator she was, yellow eyes slipping back to their usual warm brown.

"Are you okay?" Aven asked, touching Mist's elbow. "How are you feeling?"

Her concern flamed the heat beneath Mist's skin. Feathers and flight were all well and good, but speaking to Aven would always be better. "I'm just fine."

"Are you sure? Is it safe for you to be shifting?"

"Look," Mist said, sliding away her hair to reveal the wound. The motion caused a twitch of pain, but she hid it behind the veil of white strands. No need for Aven to see that. "You worry too much. It's already scabbing."

Priestess Ifera peered over Aven's head, brows high as her gaze flicked between them. "I will give you two a moment."

Ifera's knowing look had Mist biting her lip as her insides jumped. "No, you don't need—"

"I need to retrieve my salves for you." Ifera winked one golden eye before walking away. "I will not be long."

Curiosity lit in Aven's eyes as her nostrils flared. Sniffing for truths? Mist couldn't be sure. Hopefully, nothing in her own scent gave away the thoughts rolling inside her head.

"Are you alright?" Mist asked, taking stock of Aven's bronze face, her round cheeks, and how much tension clenched in her hands.

"I'm not the one who got bitten."

More heat had Mist twisting a silver band on her pointer finger. "No, but the other riders. And Pryn."

That blew Aven's pupils from round to little slivers of black. "I'll be alright. I wasn't kind to her either."

It wasn't just their words, but Mist kept that to herself. Not long ago, Aven had loved Pryn and today she nearly killed them both. Accidental or intentional, Mist's heart would be a shattered mess on the ground.

They could talk about it more another time, though. Exhaustion made emotional conversations that much harder, and Pryn was a sore subject on good days.

As silence fell between them, Mist's gaze fell on the pool near their feet. White flowers floated on the surface, glowing in the light, smelling painfully sweet. They lit a familiar ache to step into the water, sink into the soothing cold and what awaited there.

"Do you mind if I…?" Mist motioned to the pool.

Aven stiffened, face pulling into some mixture of sadness and anger. Whatever thoughts bounced inside her head had no need to be spoken. Mist already knew where her mind had gone.

She'd once confessed a hope to find something in those waters. As a child Aven had stepped into them, but for whatever reason, Dia'veh offered only silence to her sorrow. It had been years since that day and she hadn't tried again.

"Do you mind waiting here for me?" Mist asked, sliding a hand over Aven's sienna forearm. Freckles dotted her skin, like little constellations begging to be traced, framing the arrowhead tattoo on her bicep.

"Go ahead," Aven said with a shrug. "I'll be here when you're done."

Regret crashed through Mist's chest. They shouldn't have come here. The price was too high. If she'd been more vigilant, Fennicks might not have bitten her. If she'd paid attention they wouldn't be standing here with empty bellies and more reminders of Aven's lonely childhood. They'd be off enjoying a hot meal and a restful night.

"I'll just be a moment."

Aven shrugged softly, staring out one of the open windows in the Temple wall. "Take your time."

Mist had to make this communion quick. Not just for her weary body, but also for Aven's tired soul. A quick twist of her dress lifted the hem as she waded into the pool, going far enough to bring her knees beneath the surface. Cool water enveloped her sun-warmed skin as she sank into the beckoning peace, eyes slipping shut to the rhythm of her deep, even breaths.

Mist.

A smile pulled across her lips, so wide it almost hurt.

Seeking?

No. She turned her face to the ceiling, cringing against the pain as she chased the essence of her Creator. Sunlight danced across her closed eyes as a breeze kissed her cheeks. It was hard to tell if the feelings blossoming in her chest implied words or if someone actually whispered them in her ear, but she didn't care either way. This feeling, this voice, was what had guided her across the sea, bringing her to Yunaii when she hadn't the strength to go on. It whispered Aven's name before Mist ever laid eyes on her. A promise for a purpose awaiting her in this den of shifters.

Today the Creator's voice came as cool as the ocean, soothing the discomfort in her neck, while also warm enough to leave her full and content. She could have stayed there all day, channeling Dia'veh's heart, clinging to every moment the Creator focused upon her.

Need?

Mist touched her chest, fingernails tracing tiny circles against her skin. *Just to thank you. Thank you, Creator, for your servant, Dev. He saved us today. He saved Aven. Thank you for protecting her—us.*

An urge to turn and set eyes on Aven's face welled in Mist's chest, almost breaking the connection. Did she stand at the edge of the pool watching, seeing Mist speak to a power that never answered her? Or had she moved away?

Why don't you answer her, Creator?

The water lapped against her knees, moved by something no eye could see.

Need. It is you she needs now.

Mist dropped her head without thinking and had to smother a hiss of pain. If Aven heard she would wade into the pool, despite the sadness it would bring.

She needs you.

Soon, Mist. Soon. Today she needs you. Warmth blossomed at the base of Mist's neck, as if a hand laid over the source of pain draining her body. *Rest. Heal.*

Mist flattened her palm over her chest. The pulse of her heart beat rapidly beneath it, like a bird's wings against the bars of a cage. One day she would soar with her Creator. One day she would see the wonders awaiting beyond, in places reserved only for those done with their journey in Sholindrea.

But not today. Today, she was here in Yunaii. Today, she was alive, with Aven, and so much living left to do. Today, they were safe.

Safe.

Mist nodded without thinking. *Yes. Safe.*
Safe. Safe!

An icy chill crawled up her fingers, biting and painful. As if she'd buried her hands in snow. She tried flexing them, but the cool burn lanced through her arms, freezing her blood, sending an ache through her chest. Mist doubled over, eyes wide as she gasped, sucking in air. Fingers clawed at her chest, her throat. It took her a moment to realize her own numb hands scratched at her skin. What was happening to her? Black spots burst over her eyes, the edges of her vision growing dark. She swayed as everything spun, blurring what little she could still see.

Safe!

Mist swayed as light crept back into her sight, her limbs twitching and weak. Everything was going topsy turvy. The floor of the Temple tilted. Her head flashed hot. Instinct had her arms flailing about for something to grab. Thankfully, they connected with something soft and warm. A body, maybe. It took focus to flex her hands, working Yunaii's heat back into her frozen fingers. They resisted bending,

"Mist?" Aven asked near her ear. "What's wrong?"

She blinked against the spots in her vision until Aven's face came into focus. She stood so close. Her hands gripped Mist's forearms as if she feared the water might steal her away. The lone freckle near her mouth had no cheerful dimple to hide in. A frown had creased the lines of her round face as her assessing gaze swept over Mist.

"Are you okay? What just happened?"

Mist pressed icy fingers to her forehead, blinking until her vision cleared. "I…I'm not sure."

"Bring her out of the water," Priestess Ifera said from behind them. "Bring her to me."

Aven wrapped an arm around Mist's shoulders and led her from the pool. Strength and warmth radiated from her body, tempting Mist to lean in close. They were together. They were safe. Just as Dia'veh said.

Weren't they?

Ifera led them to a collection of pillows nearby. Mist sank onto the plushiest one she could find while Aven crouched at her side. Concern overtook every piece of her, darkening her eyes, clenching her fists, tightening her shoulders so badly Mist wanted to massage away the fear.

"I'm alright," she whispered, clasping Aven's hand.

"You don't look okay." Aven glanced back at the pool almost accusingly. "What happened? You nearly fell face first into the pool. I thought you might drown."

Priestess Ifera knelt onto the pillow beside Mist. "What did Dia'veh show you, child?"

Aven's eyes widened. "Show?"

"I don't know," Mist said as a shiver slithered down her spine. "It wasn't a vision. It was just—"

The Priestess blinked patiently. "It was what?"

"Cold. So cold." Mist wrapped her arms around herself, shaking despite the warm air. "I thanked the Creator for keeping us safe, but I—I don't think we're safe yet. Something bad is coming."

Aven's shoulders drew even higher as flecks of yellow melded into her eyes. Kali was fighting to come out, to protect against this unknown threat. "What does that mean? Are we in danger here?"

"You are safe within these walls," said the Truthseeker from behind Ifera. Despite his assurances, he gripped the hilt of his sheathed dagger. "Dia'veh protects the Temple from all violence. It is sacred ground."

Aven stared at him, hackles practically raised until Mist touched her hand once more. "He's right. We're safe here."

"Didn't feel safe a moment ago," Aven grumbled.

"It was a warning," Ifera said. "Not an attack."

"But a warning against what?" Mist asked, tightening her fingers around Aven's. Her skin was warm, welcoming, grounding. The Creator said Aven needed her, but right now, Mist was the one needing. This closeness kept her from spiraling into fears she hadn't thought about since arriving here. Fears she thought she'd left in Estellias, dangers that weren't supposed to follow her here.

"You think Fennicks might finish what they started?" Aven asked, looking Mist up and down.

"No. I—I don't think so. What happened was for the race. For the win. Not for sport or malice. Dragons don't like to lose, especially not Fennicks."

"I have never sensed murderous intent within their heart," the Truthseeker said, still hovering behind the Priestess like a ghostly shadow. No concern lined his stoic face, only thoughtful contemplation. "Malice. Perhaps some vengeance, but never a desire to kill."

"Vengeance?" Aven hissed, more yellow seeping into her eyes. "I'll give that spineless lizard a taste of vengeance."

"No," Mist said, squeezing her hand. "That's suicide, Aven. You understand that, don't you? Fennicks will kill you."

A crooked smile slanted Aven's lips. "They can try."

"Your bravery is admirable," said the Truthseeker, folding his hands behind his back. "Despite its misplacement."

Priestess Ifera stifled a chuckle behind her hand. "My dear Gaelin, let's not tease."

Aven's nose curled in a snarl, bitter words and snappy replies no doubt dancing in her mind. Before any could slip free, Mist dragged her fingers over Aven's forearm. Slow. Deliberate. Eliciting another stare that warmed every part of Mist's body.

Unfair, but effective. Poking at the Truthseeker was just as pointless as picking a fight with Dev. Elves were too level-headed for banter, aggressive or otherwise.

"If you don't think the danger is from Fennicks," Mist said, glancing between the Truthseeker and the Priestess. "What do you think we're not safe from?"

The Truthseeker's brows rose. "I cannot know the answer to this. I deal in truths, not speculation."

Ifera's golden bangles jingled as she waved a hand at her counterpart. "No one but the Creator can be certain. Take the warning and keep it close to your heart. Use it to keep you cautious."

Mist nodded, despite her disappointment. Exhaustion, fear, all of it buzzed beneath her skin, tightening her chest, leaving her twitchy and even more uncomfortable. Never had one of her communions felt this way. Not even when she'd grown weary of her flight here and the ocean waves nearly claimed her life. Even then, her attempts to reach the Creator had resulted in encouragement and strength.

Ifera interrupted her thoughts by holding up a jar of salve. "May I?"

With a nod, Mist pulled her long white hair over one shoulder, exposing Fennicks' bite. The Priestess tsk'd a few times, before gently smoothing the salve over the wound. It went on cool, but the longer it was on the warmer it became. It itched too, but Mist held back from scratching. She could almost feel her skin closing faster than her healing ability could manage.

"I know Dia'veh's warnings can be quite intense." Ifera's fingers massaged the nape of Mist's neck. "Do not let fear seize your heart. The Creator shared this with you for a reason, and it was not to frighten you."

"Then what could it be for?" Aven asked. Irritation simmered beneath each word.

Mist couldn't blame her for it. Any number of dangers could be lurking outside the Temple walls. Irritable dragons. Slighted Tribouin. Prideful Qinawe. Hungry lynx. All dangers she expected in a village of shifters. Even more than that lay beyond Yunaii's canyon, things Mist had fled that she had never told Aven about.

"How can I heed it without knowing what to avoid?" she asked.

"It was to prepare you." Ifera glanced at Aven with raised brows. "You are a hunter, no? Like all Qinawe. It is hard to sneak up on a doe when she has heard you step on a twig? She might not know who is there or what they intend, but her senses are alert. She is ready to fight or flee. So must you be."

Aven made a little sound between surprise and disbelief. "Fair point."

"Of course it is." Ifera tapped Mist's head, like a hen pecking at her chicks. "Now, you rest before going on your way and heed the Creator. We will leave you in peace."

CHAPTER Four

Aven

Much of the crowd had dissipated when they left the Temple, and the lack of noise and bustling movement drew a sigh from Aven. Her mind still raced with what happened to Mist in the pool. Not having to dodge scents and limbs and stares was a blessing she hadn't asked for but would gladly take.

A quick trek through the peaceful market brought them to the river cutting the canyon in half. The source of all life in Yunaii, the Lighe river stretched so wide that three bridges had been built for the flightless shifters. Most didn't attempt swimming from one side to another, but occasionally a bold Tribouin or untried Qinawe gave it a try. Lucky for those fools, the currents were fairly easy to master thanks to the Eilawi's dam far up river, a wonderful but invisible protection Aven had never set eyes on. Without that bit of ingenuity, Yunaii would flood with every rainy season.

Aven and Mist made their way over the splintered wood of one of the bridges, before trudging onto the sand and rock at the edge of the Eilawi's sapling forest. The trees across the river were not as mighty as their mother, but their height and width still rivaled what grew outside the canyon. A desert of boulders and rolling mountains ruled up there.

A quick turn right led them towards the Qinawe's patch of forest. Lynx and griffin lived on the lands between her people and the Tribouin, who dwelled on the western side of the woods. While shifters enjoyed the benefits of having their kin races close, most did not mingle much. Tribouin took issue with Qinawe being matriarchal, and Qinawe didn't appreciate Tribouin relying on escorts for their women. Somehow the lynx and griffin tolerated tense bickering over customs, while the Forest elves settled the more tenuous disputes.

Aven picked through the dense underbrush, her senses strung taut, ready to snap at the slightest crack of a twig or rustling of leaves. Mist and the Priestess' voices echoed in her ears. Danger lingered close.

What form would it take?

She scanned their surroundings, tracking Mist's proximity even as she took in the familiar trees and bushes. Nothing amiss. Nothing the matter. If only she could shake the quivering beneath her skin.

With no way to ease her frustration, Aven sank into habits Mama had taught her. Step without leaving footprints. Scent for anyone on their trail. Her nostrils flared as she did so now, sniffing for any hint of elf above, lynx in the shadows, or Qinawe lurking nearby. She found nothing in the rich scent of dirt but the musk of a few deer ghosting between the trees.

The familiar should have soothed her, but Dia'veh's warning lingered in the ringing silence. It seemed so unlikely that the Creator of the world would bother with them. Aven barely believed it at all. The only proof she had was Mist's silence and the tension hardening her body. Soft grace had been replaced by caution and fear.

"Are you okay?" Aven asked, holding aside a low-hanging branch. "Do you need to rest?"

"I'm alright," Mist murmured, offering a weak smile.

Despite the lack of heart in that look, Aven's heart still leapt into her throat. The slightest curve of Mist's lips did things to her not even Pryn's had.

Some people's smiles creased their faces, some gave them a glow. But Mist's? Hers rivaled the plunge in a dragon race or the leap before prey caught Aven's scent. It was better than watching the sun fall and the stars rise.

"Tell me if you need a break," Aven said, touching her elbow.

Mist's gaze dropped to that brief connection, lips parting with a ragged breath. Whatever flitted through her head stayed there, despite Aven's yearning to pluck it like fruit from a tree.

"I will," she finally said, fuchsia eyes staring Aven down. "I promise."

With that, she continued her gliding steps through the forest, her movements too perfect. Unnatural.

Aven stood transfixed, as always. How did anyone look at her slender body and not realize there was more than she pretended? Tribouin and Qinawe were more comfortable in their two-legged forms. Clever, but awkward, prone to clumsiness and short-lived foolishness that didn't plague creatures like dragons. Mist could steal their shape, but nothing else mirrored Aven's kind. Otherness hummed around Mist, no matter what form she took.

Somehow no one else noticed.

They walked until the bushes and saplings died off, giving way to cleared space between the trees where light actually broke through. Anything the golden rays touched cultivated plants. Beans, vegetables, bushes full of ripe fruit. It was hard to grow things in the middle of the forest, but the Qinawe found a way. No one told them what they could and could not do.

Any other day, returning home brought an anxious twist in Aven's gut. The Qinawe never let her forget her life as a nameless amongst their number. Yet, even as her people's eyes found her, a sense of safety beckoned from between the trees.

They had made it to the realm of the Matriarchs, where every member of the bond was trained with blades and claws, and even dragons yielded to the eyes of these fierce women.

She and Mist were safe. For now.

Only in daydreams could a visit to the Temple help Aven ignore the whispers from the women tanning hides or the children gathering crops. The gossiping birds meant nothing when she and Mist had almost died, especially when the threat of worse hovered at their backs. Let them gawk at the Qinawe-Tribouin child. If she held their attention then that meant nothing terrible lingered behind her. Nothing awful waited ahead.

Animals crossed their path as Aven led Mist deeper into Qinawe lands. Each one held the distinct essence of her people. Two wolves padded by, followed by the smell of leather and herbs. Sawdust and fire wafted from a hawk screeching above on a tree branch. Weasels, bobcats, songbirds, foxes; all shifted Qinawe. All at ease. All enjoying the ending of the day and its sweltering heat. Manners and propriety vanished beneath animal instincts, leaving them shamelessly goggling as Aven passed. They undoubtedly scented Papa in her, even if she didn't have his face-changing power.

She lifted her chin as they reached the largest clearing in the trees, the Qinawe's gathering place. Dust danced in beams of light shining on the packed forest floor. Her people's comings and goings kept any weeds from sprouting. A fire crackled at the center of the glade, contained by a ring of reddish rock. The evening's hunt turned on a spit over the flames—a massive ram with curved horns so long they seemed impractical. It must have taken half the hunters to bring it down. It would be well worth the effort. Cooking fat sizzled and popped, its smell wafting with the zing of many spices. Women immersed themselves in meal preparation, while children milled around with anxious energy. Their eyes shone with the same hunger gnawing at Aven's belly. She stepped towards the fire, mouth slipping open as she imagined pulling away a chunk of glistening meat.

"Navya's cub," said a stern, female voice.

Aven froze. Again. The familiar tension coiling in all the usual places. Eyes turned her way, some curious and a few pitying.

A woman approached, her copper brow creased with lines, giving her a permanent frown, even when she smiled. As if she'd spent so much time disapproving of others it etched into her face. A severe beauty, with coal black hair streaked with silver and a series of piercings ringing the shells of her ears. The one in her stretched, right lobe held a spikey, bleached bone.

Matriarch Hanawi. One of their best leaders and an absolute dung heap of a person.

"It's Aven." She flexed her hands against the stiffness creeping up her arms. The musk of the woman's desert cat pulled at Kali's soul, summoning the pride leader she'd once been.

"Not yet." Hanawi's reddish brown eyes narrowed. "You have yet to take your place amongst the bond."

The urge to clench her fists, to narrow her eyes, it took all the resolve Mama harped about to hold herself back. One wrong look could be taken as defiance. Disrespect. Bared claws or fangs could earn exile.

Danger, Dia'veh had warned. Had the Maker meant the Matriarchs were unsafe?

Aven drew in a breath through her nose. She couldn't destroy Mama by getting herself banished. "Allow me to hunt with you, Matriarch. Let me prove my worth to the bond."

"Perhaps that time will be soon." Hanawi lifted her chin, bringing a spattering of sunlight across her high cheekbones. "Then we will feast together."

Liar. Her revulsion stunk like rotting meat. Hanawi would never let that day come and she didn't care that Aven scented her deceit. She only performed this show for the eavesdropping Qinawe.

"I look forward to it." Aven couldn't force a smile, not even when she snuck a peek at Mist. She'd bowed her head, attention locked on the ground, hands clasped before her. The perfect, demure posture for the master of the Matriarch's game, invisible to her ire.

"Word reached us of the attack on your dragon." Hanawi dragged her gaze over Aven's body. Searching. A gleam of hope shining in her reddish eyes. "I am *relieved* to see you are unharmed."

Liar. Aven swallowed hard. "Thankfully an *elven* rider saved us."

"Thank the Maker for elven kindness," Hanawi said, lips pursed in a thin line. "I trust things are settled between you and the rider who attacked you?"

"Are you—" Aven searched for the right words to avoid giving an opening. "Do you worry I plan on taking revenge on Pryn?"

Hanawi's eyes widened. "It was the Tribouin girl's dragon? The one you used to tumble with and challenged you to be her mate?"

Aven's face burned as she scanned the nosey Qinawe nearby. A woman preparing vegetables had forgotten to keep peeling, while a group of adolescents stood oddly quiet with their faces turned away. Aven longed to glare at each of them, but the Matriarch expected to hold her attention.

Behind her, Mist shuffled some fallen leaves in what must have been a deliberate step. Any other time she moved like shadows. Her closeness blossomed warmth up Aven's spine, tempting her to lean back to ease the thumping in her chest. If only people didn't talk enough already. Everyone in Yunaii gossiped about what happened between her and Pryn.

"There's nothing to worry about," Aven said, insides squirming.

"Kali's fire is strong in you." Hanawi folded her hands over her waist, her voice unusually kind. "I see your struggle. She was a Sholi. A shifter. Her soul is not like the rest we guard. It would be...understandable if she brought out an instinct to fight back."

Aven curled her toes, the satisfying pops soothing the urge to unsheathe her claws. Hanawi would love for her to slash and bite her way out of the clearing. She'd finally have an excuse to deny Aven any place in the clan's bond.

"Pryn did nothing wrong. I don't blame her for what happened." *I blame Fennicks.* The filthy lizard hurt Mist. It wasn't Pryn who would catch Aven's teeth.

"No? She almost killed you and your dragon."

After another deep breath, Aven chanced a look at Hanawi's eyes. Just for a moment. Not long enough to offend the Matriarch. "I know the risk I take by choosing to ride. It's not the same as keeping my feet on the ground."

Hanawi tapped the toe of her leather boot, hands still clasped before her. If frustration had a smell, Aven would have caught it sizzling off the Matriarch. She didn't need elven magic to know the truth in Hanawi's heart: she'd failed to box Aven in. Again. She'd failed to disgrace Mama through her nameless cub. She'd failed to prove having a Tribouin for a father made Aven unable to honor the Qinawe's ways.

"Leave the cub be," rasped another familiar voice.

Aven raised her eyes as their eldest Matriarch approached. Despite the curve of her spine and the spots on her skin, she moved with a grace that belied her age. Only her gnarled staff betrayed the tolls her years had taken. The end of it slid through the soft dirt of the glade, heralding her shuffling steps.

"Matriarch Yana." Aven lowered her gaze from the woman's weathered face, where a bone shard pierced the septum of her wide nose.

"You look none the worse for wear." Yana stopped at Hanawi's side and leaned forward on her staff. "A relief. We need not lose any more women to Tribouin nonsense."

Women like Mama.

Aven swallowed a tremor in her lips. While Yana might let a clenched fist or furrowed brow slide, the rest of the bond would not. She'd held the role of Matriarch longer than any in generations.

Yana tapped Aven's foot with her staff. "I am pleased you take no issue with the Tribouin girl. You understand what is best. What is *needed.*"

"Strong bond," Aven said, killing a snicker when Hanawi's mouth pulled down until she resembled a disapproving toad.

"Strong people." Yana smiled approvingly. "Thank you for your time, cub. Hurry on to your mother. I am sure she is concerned for your safety."

Aven bobbed her head as she took a step back. One did not turn away from a Qinawe woman. "Yes, Matriarch."

Hanawi's gaze flicked from Yana to Aven. "Please pass my regards on to Navya. I miss hunting at her side."

Liar!

Aven's throat seared with all the things she could say. All the raging accusations. Her fingers curled one by one, claws itching to dig into Hanawi's treacherous face.

This time, Mist moved like the Truthseeker. Her cool hand slid up Aven's back, melting the anger with soft fingertips. She knew best how Aven felt about the Matriarchs. Especially Hanawi. Their bias against Papa made them deny Mama her rightful place amongst the bond. If she had chosen a Qinawe for a lifemate she would be a Matriarch instead of Hanawi. She had more skills than most of them combined, with a powerful wolf soul to guide her in protecting others.

Of course, she had to be the best of them all since the bond refused to care for her family. The rest of them enjoyed the comforts of shared warmth, safety, and fresh meat.

"Good night, Matriarchs," Mist said, her shoulder bumping Aven's. "We will speak your regards to Navya."

"See that you do." Triumph flashed in Hanawi's eyes, her toadish frown replaced by a catlike sneer. She'd gotten *something*. Even if Aven hadn't spoken a word, fury had seared through her blood. Enough for Hanawi to smell. Enough for Yana to sense. The old woman's sharp gaze locked on Aven's face, one eye narrowed. She lingered a moment longer than the other Matriarch, before they walked off together. No doubt headed to discuss the exchange with the third of their number, Matriarch Revari.

Aven hoped they liked the taste of disappointment. She *wouldn't* fight Pryn. Their one dance of blades had been enough. Even if she'd ordered Fennicks to bite Mist, the black dragon would pay the price. No Qinawe or Tribouin knew they were shifters. They wouldn't care if Aven took a chunk out of one. Or at least she hoped so.

With one last longing gaze at the cookfire, Aven abandoned the clearing and its delectable smells, kicking at rocks along the path home. Hanawi and the other Matriarchs never had to do much to get under her skin. They'd spent a lifetime scratching away at any armor she built for herself, picking at her strength like a scab. That's all she was to them. Something irritating to discard so it wouldn't leave a blemish.

"She's such a nasty little worm," Mist said, wrapping an arm around Aven's shoulder. "I'd love to see her face if she ever threw that attitude at your mother."

Aven snickered. "I'd give up hunting for a year to see that."

"I'd trade all my gems."

"Wow," Aven gasped playfully as she looped an arm around Mist's waist. "That's serious."

"I know it kills you to put up with her. It takes everything in me to keep my mouth shut when she comes at you like that. *I'm so relieved you're unharmed—*" Mist made a disgusted sound. "Does she really think anyone buys her pile of lies?"

"I like when you get angry." Aven dropped her head against Mist's soft, warm shoulder. "Makes me feel less like an awful person for wishing Hanawi and the others would catch a pile of falling dragon crap."

A chuckle shook Mist's body. "I could arrange that."

Aven cast a grateful look before tucking into her embrace. Life and its mess always slipped away when Mist's rosy scent filled her nose. Funny how it even killed her worry about gossip. Let the Qinawe ogle and whisper. Let their envy over not having Mist as a friend devour them.

Not long after leaving the clearing, the trees grew thick and mighty again, some wider than a woman was tall. Family burrows dug into hollow cavities in the largest ones, providing sleeping dens for most of the bond. A few were higher up, nestled into wide openings like giant owl nests, all full of sleep furs, trinkets, weapons, and dishes. Qinawe shared almost everything. Being part of the bond meant being a piece of a whole. Their strength was their ability to bond with animal's souls, to shift and roam, and numbers kept them safe. Had Aven not been born as she was, she would have belonged to them by now. Everyone served the bond in some way.

Except her. They feared her. Feared her bond with Kali. Feared the Tribouin ideas Papa taught her. No doubt they worried she'd teach their sons and daughters that customs should enrich, not worsen, one's life.

Fear kept her family on the outskirts. They didn't get a big burrow or the safety of numbers. She'd find Mama and Papa where they always were, at the edge of the forest, where trees met cliffs, and most of the greenery turned to saplings and bushes.

It couldn't be helped though. Mama and Papa made their choice when they chose each other. Instead of a den cut into one of the humongous trees, Aven's home was a cave, dug deep into the cliff face. She didn't know if Mama and Papa had found it, or if they had carved it out themselves, but it was where she learned to walk, how to whittle and fletch arrows, how to throw a hatchet. The other Qinawe maybe thought they'd win by pushing Aven's family so far away, but she loved the quiet. She loved their place.

As the mouth of it came into sight, the glow of firelight flickered against the rocks, accompanied by the smell of spice and cooking meat.

Aven had almost reached it, when Mama charged out of the cave, all fierce black eyes and copper skin, her hair coiled into a dozen braids, some thick, some thin. Aven knew well how long they took to weave together. She helped tame the sleek black locks, braid each strand, and tie them back. It was too much for one person to do.

Thankfully, Papa took some simple pleasure in undoing all that mess.

Aven and Mist slipped apart as Mama drew near. No matter how kind or welcoming, Mist still handled her like any other Matriarch. Her chin dipped towards her collarbones as her shoulders drew back. It didn't matter Mama only commanded her tiny family. She had the fiercest countenance of any Qinawe Matriarch.

Mama's gaze traveled over Aven, starting at her boots and painstakingly dragging up her legs, over her arms. When her attention finally settled on Aven's face, some of the tension eased from her own.

"Are you hurt?"

"I'm fine, Mama." A smile pulled at Aven's lips, the last coil of fear finally unraveling.

"And your little Feather?" Black eyes searched Aven's, looking for any proof of a fib. "Is she alright?"

Aven fought the urge to glance at Mist, to where her long hair covered the wound on her neck. She'd sworn Aven to secrecy about the dragons being the first shifters. Even Mama and Papa didn't know.

"She's okay. A judge bandaged her up and I sent her off to the dragon roost to rest."

Mama's lips pursed disapprovingly. "You should have brought her home so your Papa could check her over. Those judges are lazy and biased."

"I can fetch her after supper." Out of the corner of Aven's eye, Mist's lips twitched, holding back a smile.

Mama sighed and shook her head. "That Pryn will be the death of you."

"She's harmless, Mama."

Her brows creased, but Mama didn't voice the angry thoughts. "Thanks to Dev. We'll invite him to supper tomorrow night as a thank you."

"Of course, Mama." Aven's cheeks hurt from the grin she couldn't hold back. No one could claim her mama wasn't hard as steel, but inside she burned molten hot.

"Well, since you're not hurt and it's near time for supper," Mama pointed at the cave, her wolf tooth swaying back and forth from one ear. "Get your bow and go bag us a few thumpers to add to the stew. Your papa is cooking up a storm but the ones I caught didn't yield as much meat as I'd hoped."

Aven glanced towards the cookfire by the entrance of the cave, but Papa was nowhere in sight. He must have gone inside for spices or dried herbs.

"Couldn't I hunt without the bow?" That would be much more fun. Of course, Aven didn't say that. Mama didn't care about fun. What was practical was best in her opinion.

"You could try." Mana's eyes narrowed. "But from the looks of you, I think you'd end up devouring whatever you caught with your teeth. So off with you."

"But Mama I—" Aven grasped for a lie, some reason she couldn't go bow hunting right now. Saying she'd rather goof off in the swimming hole with Mist would not be a good excuse.

Mama flashed a wolfish grin. "Well, now that you have sufficiently run through all your possible lies and found yourself wanting, off you get. You had your race, now there's work to be doing. Go."

Aven's head fell back as she dared to groan. Loud. Arguing with Mama never ended well. Snotty retorts like, 'what would you have done if I'd died' stayed in her head where they wouldn't get her into trouble. With a huff, she slipped into the cave, lingering long enough to hear Mama's tone soften as she told Mist not to worry about hunting and go wash up for supper.

CHAPTER
Five

Mist

Mist smiled softly. "Thank you. I won't be long. Once I'm done, I'll help Aven with the hares."

"You'll do no such thing." Navya's brow furrowed with the kind of disapproval only a Qinawe could muster. "You go wash up and come back here. Tomen could use some help chopping greens. No sense in you hunting and skinning thumpers after a bath."

Knowing better than to argue, Mist bowed respectfully. "I will return shortly."

Navya's eyes drooped politely, the rest of her standing tall. A clear dismissal.

Mist learned at a young age that to impersonate other races meant blending in. Qinawe Matriarchs demanded respect from everyone, not just their own people. She'd even seen Elementals avoid looking one in the eye. Never mind they could end a Qinawe with a wave of their hand. So, to play a convincing Tribouin girl, Mist could never demand anything of a Matriarch, even if Tribouin did privately think themselves better.

She backed away as Navya walked back into the cave. Once she was gone, Mist headed for the small swimming hole nearby. Sansia was going down, but the water's warmth would linger a while. The golden light baked everything left out in its harsh rays. If the Elementals hadn't established and grown the forest here, the canyon would be a desolate tundra of rocks and dirt. Just like most of the land around this place was. How the shifters had the fortitude to reach this little oasis spoke to their strength.

She'd barely made it here herself.

Mist admired them for coming to what appeared to be a barren island, crossing over its unnatural mountain range, then traversing its sweeping desert, and not giving up. To keep on pushing until they happened upon this fertile secret. It gave her a new respect for their perseverance. There were Qinawe and Tribouin back home, but they enjoyed living close to humans and their blessing of abundance the Great Mother gave them. It was an easy life back in Estellias.

Growing up near them had given Papi the chance to teach her their ways. He'd unknowingly prepared her for life in Yunaii, where formality and manners were essential to survival. Qinawe rules, Tribouin customs, the different Elven tribes with all their ideas and beliefs. Sometimes it gave her a headache keeping it all straight. She rubbed at her temples as she followed the path Aven and her family had worn into the forest floor.

Yunaii was so different from her home. The races jumbled together there, creating a melting pot of culture. In Estellias no one cared that Papi was human and her *eega* was dragon. Not unless they envied him for charming his way into her heart.

Aven would love it in Estellias. If only Mist could get her there. Between losing races and the problems Mist had left behind, it felt impossible some days. All she wanted was to give Aven her dreams. Even if it meant they would part ways one day.

Mist's chest tightened. She couldn't go back, no matter how much she missed her papi or her childhood friend, Adair. This place wasn't like the village of Tem'bria, with its quiet streets and smiling people, its tiny square smelling like garlic bread and peppered meats sizzling on hot slabs of cooking stones. There were so many rules here. In Tem'bria the only rule was to be a good neighbor. She smiled as she pictured Papi's face. Like the midnight sky; so dark, but calming and welcoming. She needed to write him soon, to let him know she was doing well.

At least here she had Aven. Her smile came easily. Her deep brown eyes never missed a thing, and her gentle voice soothed away everything but joy. She made it worth it to stay a while.

Mist rolled her shoulders, a sound of disgust scratching up her throat. Curse these melancholy feelings. It had to be Dia'veh's warning and Fennicks' bite. Every nerve twitched over little sounds of the forest and pain seared every time she turned her head. Aven was probably right. She should have stayed in her dragonskin. It was just too tempting to speak for herself, to make Aven laugh and bring out that sparkle in her eyes. Mist gritted her teeth and quickened her pace.

The trees grew thick, and the sound of running water cut through the quiet chirping of birds and buzzing bugs. The water hole lay just ahead. She should jump into its calm depths. Wash away the pain and fear. Clear her head.

She broke through the tree line and a wave of cool, mossy air filled her lungs. Mist breathed deep, pretending she was home, where clouds shrouded the sun. Everything was so dry and hard and hot here. But she still found the beauty in it. Gold and pink light glittered on the surface of the water, reflecting Sansia's retreating halo. It'd be like jumping into cold fire.

Her bare feet carried her through grass and moss, before she jogged over the smooth rocks creeping above one side of the pond. From there she launched, eyes on the sky as she leapt off the tallest boulder. The urge to shift itched beneath her skin, to let wings burst from her back and carry her into the color-streaked sky. It would be so easy to be free from everything as wind whipped around her.

Instead, her body arced through the air, a thrill jolting up her spin as she plunged towards the pond. She broke through with a mighty splash, cool water enveloping her in a soothing hug.

Silence. So quiet, calm. Her limbs mutely cut through the water, pushing her into the shadows. It didn't take long to reach the muddy bottom. When her fingers sank into cold slime, she brought her feet down and kicked off, shooting back the way she came. Bubbles escaped her nose and lips, skimming her face, showing her the way. Mist crashed through the surface, sending another splash towards the darkening sky.

It wasn't flying, but it was almost as beautiful. Maybe one day she would return to the ocean she'd crossed to get here. It couldn't be too hard to grow some gills and live amongst her serpent kin dwelling in the deep. The options were limitless. She just had to learn how to change her lungs into something else, how to grow webs between her toes instead of eagle-like claws. Her eega had taught her to never doubt. Only her mind held her back.

Mist kicked around the pond a while, smiling at the fish nibbling her toes. Silver rings adorned almost anywhere she could put them, along with strings of aquamarine gems that hung from her long ears, her navel, and her family's silver armlet around. The light glittering off their surfaces sent bubbles of happiness popping in her chest. All of it attracted the fish like bees to colorful flowers. She didn't mind their attention, as long as they didn't steal her rings.

Then they'd be dinner.

Once she'd sated herself on splashing, diving, and darting around the pond, Mist kicked over to a collection of rocks where she kept a sack of soaps and oils she had made for herself. When she untied the knot, scents of rose, vanilla, and cinnamon burst free. Mist drew in a deep breath before rubbing the soap into her skin, then the folds of her tunic. Bath day, laundry day, why not get it all over with in one fell swoop? Probably best for her ruse if she didn't smell of dragon dung.

Mist the Tribouin was not a dragon rider.

She rolled her eyes as she worked some of the rose oil through her hair. Back home she didn't have to hide. The Estellians hadn't forgotten what dragons could do. That's why Yunaii would never be home. The ability to shift was a blessing from Dia'veh, not some scandalous, shameful thing.

She would never have stayed at all if not for Aven. This life suited dragons like Fennicks, but not her. There had to be places in the world where their kind lived as they were meant to, soaring the skies and walking amongst the other Sholi, being diplomats, protectors, and teachers. Dragons were meant to bring peace to the places they dwelled, not suck away resources to satisfy their laziness.

As if her thought was a summons, the air shifted, carrying scents of hay, leather, and beeswax. Her heart thumped in reply, the Creator's essence echoing in her mind. Dia'veh said she wasn't safe. How could she pretend like she was safe?

Mist ducked under the water, rubbing furiously at her hair and body. Bad enough to have this encounter dripping wet. She didn't need to be half bathed as well.

Once her hair turned to silk between her fingers, she kicked for the surface, only this time there was no dramatic bursting from the water. Instead, she drifted up, stopping just as her nose crested above its surface. Her nostrils flared, scenting the breeze.

Where? Where? She hadn't smelled wrong. Fennicks was here. She scanned the forest, looking for an oddly colored tree, a rock with the eye ridges of a dragon, anything unnatural.

Something plopped behind her so Mist whirled, dipping down until the water skimmed eyes. Ripples caressed her face as her gaze settled on the rock she'd leapt off.

There Fennicks was. Sitting on the very edge, ankles crossed, a mischievous smile pulled across an adorably human face. Another new form. Petite nose, round cheeks, brown hair pulled into two braids, freckled cheeks, a girl's body aged no more than seven. Different, and yet familiar too. Fennicks constantly shifted, playing with different bodies and looks, embracing a shroud of mystery. Mist didn't even know the dragon's true name.

This was different, though. Fennicks had never come to her as a child.

Their scent always remained the same, and their eyes. Always yellow, like a cat's. Each dragon had something they never changed, something to remind them of who they were.

Papi always loved Mist's white hair and pink eyes, so she kept them in whatever shape she took.

"Didn't want to mingle with us today?" Fennicks asked, playfully tossing pebbles.

Mist tilted her head. "You tried to kill me."

"Only a little."

Those yellow eyes held no spark of regret as they rolled, a smile lingering on that strange face. Mist wasn't fooled. Aven's voice screamed 'danger' in her mind. Something deadly gleamed in the tightness of Fennicks' jaw, in the clenched fist skipping rocks along the water.

Mist drifted backwards, clinging to an outward calm as her nerves twisted. Most days Fennicks was a nuisance, reminding her not to mess with the way things were in Yunaii.

Then a day like today came, when she had done something to really offend the flight of dragons living here. She could deal with bullying, but she had no desire to be reprimanded by a bunch of creatures that used the other shifters to make life easy for themselves.

"Why aren't you off celebrating your win?" She scented the air again. Had Fennicks brought others? What had she done this time to make them think she wouldn't keep their secret? Was this the danger Dia'veh had warned her about? "I'm sure you've got better things to do than come talk to me."

"I would prefer it," Fennicks said, still perched on the rock. "But I'm not here because I want to be."

Mist frowned as she reached the edge of the water. Fennicks' childish voice had turned petulant, whiny, and she didn't understand why.

"I made Fennicks come," a male voice said behind her.

Oh no. Questions disappeared as Mist turned, tucking her chin to her chest, catching only a glimpse of the copper-skinned man standing close enough to touch. Rielnor. Flight leader of the dragons. The oldest being she had ever met.

Face him with respect. Don't challenge him with a stare. Much like the Qinawe Matriarchs. Except the flight leader could rip her apart if he wished. *By Dia'veh* she missed living amongst humans. Even when completely enamored with themselves they weren't as bad as shifters and their pride. She could smile in the face of an egotistical human and it didn't matter if they didn't like it.

"Flight leader," she said softly, heart hammering in her chest. She focused on his large, scarred feet planted bare in the grass. Wait. Wait for a sign she could look up. Wait to look upon Topaz's human façade as she wondered once again why he'd saved her from being a pile of broken bones and mangled flesh beneath the Eilawi tree. There was some agenda. Dragons did nothing they did not intend. Especially not their leader.

"Take a breath, Mist," Rielnor commanded with a sigh. "*You* are not the one in trouble today."

A growl drifted from Fennicks, sending ripples across the pond. They lapped against the backs of Mist's calves like some ominous doomsdayer poking at her.

I'm so dead.

When she finally lifted her chin, Rielnor wasn't looking at her. His green eyes, usually so bright, were dark and narrowed as they locked on Fennicks. All of his many scars made for a terrifying appearance. Two stretched from cheek to cheek over the bridge of his nose, one ran down his eye, and a row of gouges on one side of his skull looked distinctly like a dragon had used his head to sharpen its claws. It left him with a long green mohawk that fell past his shoulders. Some days it hurt to look at him. Like this very moment. Mist hoped he never turned such a murderous stare on her.

Rielnor would hold his steely gaze until the other dragon backed down. Most of the flight gave in easily, but Fennicks was the quickest to challenge and the slowest to yield. One day the flight would be under their command and Mist hoped to be long gone when the balance of power shifted.

Right now, she didn't dare turn, didn't dare move. Beneath Fennicks' familiar scent lingered something cold. Like an endless winter's night, full of snow and ice. The same timeless smell shrouded Rielnor, who had walked Sholindrea's lands for well over a millennium. Mist had only just reached her second decade. She was an infant in their eyes.

Rielnor's age made his ruse as Dev's racing dragon quite the oddity. He had watched generations be born and die over and over. He'd probably seen civilizations crumble in his time. Why did he bother with something so trivial as pretending to be Topaz the racing dragon?

After a bit more growling and nostril flaring, Rielnor's lips perked into a satisfied smile. Fennicks must have given in once again. The other dragon hissed at Mist's back, but she continued to stare at her flight leader. Acknowledging dissent in his ranks would embarrass Fennicks and disrespect Rielnor.

When his green eyes turned to Mist, she threw back her shoulders and straightened her spine.

"How is your neck?" Rielnor stroked the thin beard growing from his chin. He'd woven it into a loose braid like he often did, as if he needed something to toy with when he shed his dragonskin.

Mist touched the tender spot and tried not to wince. "Healing."

"Do you want vengeance for what Fennicks did?" His steady voice didn't hold a hint of levity.

"Is that why you're here? To hold Fennicks down or something?"

A crooked smile stretched across Rielnor's face, veiled by his long green hair. "Is that what you would like?"

"No." Mist clutched her sack of soaps as she stepped further out of the pond. "Estellians don't believe in such things. Dia'veh has taught me better."

"We know," Fennicks said from the rock. "Because you're better than us."

Rielnor only smiled wider, tilting his head to shift the hair from his face. "But you are not *in* Estellias. You are only bound by the flight's law. So, I ask again, do you yearn for vengeance?"

Mist hid her recoil by looking to Fennicks. The other dragon stared back from a childlike face, mouth parted slightly. For once their eyes had gone wide and round. Not pleading. Just calm. Innocent. It had to be a ruse. Fennicks wouldn't accept it if she tried to inflict a wound like the one she had received.

Would it be worth it? Just recalling Aven's face pressed into her neck, icy fingers clinging for purchase, left Mist swaying from a dizzy wave of anger. She had been helpless, unable to save her best friend.

Qinawe lived by a code. Watch over their own, protect their own, but violence—they indulged some bad tempers, but never true fighting. Nor the Tribouins. Both would welcome death before raising a hand against another of the Sholi. But what of Aven? They held her outside their customs for so long, would their ways save Fennicks from her raking claws?

More so, why did Rielnor hold to this eye for an eye sort of justice? Humans, Elementals, elves, they held to Dia'veh's laws of love and selflessness. This wasn't how things should be done. Surely a millennium of life had taught him better.

Or not. Maybe all his long years had shown him this was the best way. Swift justice to keep his flight in line.

Mist shifted from foot to foot, running a fingertip over the round pendant of her armlet, where her kin's crest had been pressed into the silver. She traced the circular serpent shape, around and around. A nervous tick she couldn't shake.

In the end, her eega gave the answer with the one question she always asked: What would Papi say? He held to Dia'veh's laws of hospitality and morality. If he knew Mist even considered hurting someone out of anger, a dark scowl would overtake his near black eyes and steal his usual amusement over life's strange turns.

Mist looked back at Rielnor and knew he guessed her answer. One thick, green brow quirked upward, the hint of a pleased expression beneath all those scars. Papi stared back at her in that look, even though he was leagues away.

Before she could speak, a roar shook the forest. Birds screeched, leaves shook, and the smile fell from Rielnor's face.

Mist turned just as cool, cedar fur and massive teeth streaked for Fennicks. Aven, in all her raging, saber-toothed glory. Fennicks had time to jump up, already shifting when they collided. Snarls and snapping jaws echoed with a splash, as both cat and dragon tumbled into the pond.

"Aven, no!" Mist had to stop them. Her body moved on its own, wading into the water, tracking every swipe of claws. She had to get them apart.

The water reached her waist when Rielnor's arms wrapped around her, his grip bruising. He hauled her backwards, completely unfazed when Mist thrashed and kicked against him.

"Foolish kit! They'll kill you!"

"Fennicks will kill her!" Mist clawed at his arms. There was so much splashing. Limbs all over the place. She couldn't tell if Fennicks had fully shifted yet. Aven had the upper hand as a giant, saber-tooth cat, but once the dragonskin came out she'd be done for.

Black wings burst from the water, flapping hard, pulling Fennicks' upward. Aven clung to the shoulder she'd sunk her claws into, but as the dragon spun once, twice, her grip loosened bit by bit. A few more painful twists and both creatures shrieked. Fennicks in pain and Aven in anger. One shot up, one plummeted, and a ravaging scream ripped from Mist's throat as the cat slapped against the roiling water of the pond.

Mist flailed against the arms pinning her tight.

She'd never get anywhere like this. It was time to think. Her body stilled, earning a relieved sigh from Rielnor. Premature on his part. Mist had sparred with Papi, a ridiculously tall human built like a wall of stone. He'd taught her how to knock him down and get free from any hold. Calm rushed like ice water through her veins. She had to be smarter than bigger opponents.

Mist took a deep breath and kicked backwards. The force set them both off balance, Rielnor lurching so far, he lifted her feet off the ground. Time for another deep breath, then she hooked one leg around his, grabbed tight to his arm, and used every shred of strength to curl forward. Whether it was surprise or technique, Mist didn't know, but she hurled him over her shoulder, sending her thousand-year-old flight leader slapping into the pond with a startled grunt.

He'd probably kill her for that. Dia'veh's warning had spared her nothing, but it didn't matter now. She needed to get Aven out of the water.

Mist ran a few steps before diving into the choppy waves, hands held above her head to cut through the water. The idea of webbing stretched between her fingers became reality, helping pull her towards Aven's sinking body. One more thought had her legs sealed together, her toes sprouting into a tailfin for even more speed. In just a few strokes she reached her friend, whose own body shrunk in on itself. Claws retracted into fingernails, forelegs slimmed into muscled arms, teeth grew small enough to fit into a parted human mouth, bubbles escaping with what little air remained in her lungs.

Mist's heart leapt into her throat. She grabbed Aven beneath both arms and shot for the surface, slashing her tail through the water as fast she could. When they burst through, no blessed coughing or sputtering filled the air.

"Aven!" Mist shook her. Still nothing. No, no, no. Mist raced for the shore, muscles burning. The moment she could stand, her legs split apart, shedding the tail in favor of thick calf muscles and biceps. Mist dragged Aven's dead weight into the shallows, before dropping her onto the mushy, muddy bank.

Now what? Mist stared at Aven's still, naked body, willing her to breathe, to move.

"Aven!" She shook her bronze shoulders once, twice. Nothing. Mist thumped her on the chest just above her heart.

That got the desired effect. Aven released a wet cough, water gurgling from her mouth as she rolled over, hacking it out of her lungs.

"Oh, thank you Dia'veh." Mist sank back on her haunches. *Thank you.*

Aven sputtered a few more times before she went still, forehead resting in the mud. She must be exhausted. Shifting fast and giving in to the rush of Kali's soul took a toll *without* adding a wrestling match with a dragon.

Mist cast a glance at the sky, searching for a sign of Fennicks. Light retreated rapidly, pink and gold giving way to blues and twinkling stars. Soon Fennicks would have all the advantage.

"We have to go," Mist whispered, rubbing Aven's bare back. Chill bumps shivered over her freckled skin, tiny tremors twitching through her muscles.

Curses. Mist had nothing to warm her. No extra clothing or even a cloak to spare. Just her own body heat. Hopefully it would be enough. She looped an arm under Aven's face, giving her something solid to rest on, then used her body as a blanket to stave off the cold. They laid there together, both of them sucking in lungfuls of blessed air as the evening cooled their wet skin.

Mist laid there, Aven's scent in her nose, listening to her steady breathing. The rhythmic rise and fall of her chest eased Mist's racing heart. Everything would be fine as long as Aven was okay.

If only Fennicks would let it go. The earth rumbled from the force of one furious dragon careening back to the ground. Trees shook overhead, sending birds screeching into the air as rocks rained from the cliffs. This fight was far from over.

CHAPTER *Six*

Aven

Aven's eyes flew open at Fennicks' earth-shattering roar. The egg-breaker was still looking to fight and Kali's instincts raged in reply. Her heavy arm reached for the lynx's fang, ignoring Papa's voice of reason whispering in her mind. Silly Tribouin ideas wouldn't save her now.

"No," Mist said, taking her hand in a cool grip. "You can't fight a dragon."

Oh, she'd fight, and she'd win. Silky blood still coated her tongue. Like life-giving liquid fire. "Fennicks hurt you."

"That doesn't matter." Mist's arms looped around her shoulders, stopping her from pushing onto her elbows. "You'll regret this once the bloodlust fades."

"They deserve to bleed." Aven strained for Fennicks' snarling face as they reared up, their horns creeping into the canopy. Fire licked between bared teeth, capable of melting flesh and bleaching bones.

"Stop!" a male voice roared. "Both of you stop!"

Mist curled inward, pulling Aven back as if her own skinny frame could block those killing flames. She'd lost her Dia'veh-loving mind. Aven rolled her friend aside, only to find herself tossed away again, leading to a flailing mess of limbs as they tumbled towards the water, matched in strength and terror.

Only when Fennicks bellowed did Mist stop fighting to be the shield. She whipped around, chest heaving. The dragon was back on all fours, growling at a host of blurry figures around them.

Aven rubbed at her eyes, wiping away mud and water clinging to her lashes. Someone stood where she and Mist had once been, tattooed arms held out wide. As they slowly came into focus, fear flashed hot through her skull. She would know those arms anywhere. They'd held her tight on stormy nights, her nose buried in his thickly coiled hair. She'd loved to play with those long locks as a cub.

"Call off your flightmate. Or the Linseen will make you." Papa's tone held its usual steel, and Aven didn't need to see his face to know the set of his stubborn mouth.

A massive black wolf snarled in front of him, her silver-streaked hackles bristling like spikes. To anyone else, the rumbling sound was a heart-stopping threat. For Aven, the growl sapped all tension from her limbs. Only Mama could make her feel safe enough to peel her gaze from dragon fire and focus on the one who held her parents' rage.

A ferocious man stood between Mama and Fennicks, acting a shield to the dragon as if they needed it. Deep scars clawed across half his head, his muscular chest, and one arm in a very familiar pattern.

Where had Aven seen such scars before? Or caught his scent? Just a whiff rose the hairs on the back of her neck. She knew it from somewhere. It stung her nose as if winter's chill lived in his bones.

Old. Dangerous. Take caution. Just like the Maker warned.

The man looked unphased by the snarling wolf before him. Nor by the two saber-tooth cats growling at each of his sides, standing almost as high as his shoulder. Aven blinked a few times to make sure she wasn't seeing things. The lynx avoided the Qinawe, so what brought them here tonight? Had they come for her? Or because she carried their old pride leader's soul?

Despite the chorus of growling and bared teeth begging to sink into him, the scarred man didn't even glance at the beasts surrounding him. His gaze remained locked on Aven and Mist. Unblinking. Calculating.

That's when it hit her. Papa had said *flightmate*. This man was a dragon, like Fennicks. That also meant Mama and Papa *knew* the dragon's best-kept secret.

"Navya, Tomen, no!" Mist pushed to her feet, bitterness streaking through her scent. Something Aven rarely smelled in her. In others, it meant time to hunt, time to win. Fear came just as she was about to sink in with claws and teeth. It was delicious in anyone but Mist.

She put herself between Mama and the shifted dragon, waving back the snarling lynx with frenzied motions. Aven pushed up on trembling arms with every intent to follow, but Papa slammed his foot down in front of her.

"Stay down, my girl." His tone left no room for argument.

"Rielnor, please," Mist said to the scarred man. "They don't know—they don't understand."

"Step. Aside." The man's teeth sounded clenched despite the indifference he wore.

"Flight leader, please."

Aven shuddered. *Oh no*. Those scars. She *had* seen them before. This was Dev's Topaz. The beast who could level trees with the swipe of his tail or burn the whole canyon to ash with as much effort as it took to blink.

"You can kill us," Papa said, spine ramrod straight. "We can't stop you. But, before you do, look to the trees."

The flight leader turned, shifting his mohawk like a silky, green veil, his narrowed eyes looking from branch to branch. Linseen elves hid in the shadows with bows raised and drawn, their arrowheads gleaming. The greens and browns of their leather armor melded them with the forest. Were it not for Kali's powerful eyesight, Aven might not have even seen them.

"The Linseen are prepared to stop you," Papa said. "You disturb the peace they guard."

The flight leader's lips peeled back in a snarl. "*We* did not start this."

Papa's arms lowered as he glanced over his shoulder, blue swirling through his confused brown eyes. His gaze locked on Aven so she pushed into a crouch, muscles burning despite the cold.

"Papa, I—"

Mama growled through her wolf's teeth, and Aven dropped back down, ducking her head. She'd really mucked things up this time.

"Rielnor, they are just defending their kit," Mist said. "They mean no disrespect."

His nostrils flared, so focused on Aven he ignored Fennicks creeping closer to his shoulder.

"Flight leader," Papa warned as flames curled between the dragon's bared teeth.

Rielnor's attention slid to his flightmate. *"Enough."*

The black dragon's jaw lowered, a ball of fire welling over their tongue. Fennicks had slunk close enough there would be no stopping the flames. Linseen arrows would be no better than kindling. Someone Aven loved would take the blast.

The flight leader called out once more, before a roar reverberated from Mist's hunched form, rage replacing the fear in her voice. A clear warning as she crouched in the night, ready to pounce.

If Fennicks attacked, so would she.

The black dragon looked into Aven's eyes; their pupils slitted. Fury simmered beneath, burning them both with a hatred she'd never known before today. Resentment churned every time her people whispered as she passed, but she didn't hate them. Papa taught her that hating small-minded people gave them too much power. But Fennicks. Somehow Fennicks had taken that power all the same. They'd turned her into something she didn't recognize. Before today she had never gone so far, never pushed her people's laws to the breaking point.

Time stretched as she stared into those eyes. Maybe she would have lost today, maybe she might have won. Just a little closer and she could have sunk her teeth into Fennicks' black throat, gotten a true taste of dragon blood. What she'd drawn had seared as she swallowed it down, each drop worth the pain. Every bite and rip of her claws had brought such delightful cries. If Fennicks walked away with nothing but the memory of what she'd done, Aven would sleep better tonight. Next time the black dragon might think a little harder before attacking Mist.

Rielnor glanced between Aven and Fennicks, and then planted himself at the end of the black dragon's snout. "I said *enough.*"

Fennicks' yellow eyes locked onto the flight leader, the inferno between their teeth growing stronger. The dying sunlight faded with every breath they took, leaving the orange gleam of fire shining bright in the clearing. Then, as if they decided this was all a waste of time, Fennicks burped a cool flash before snapping those deadly jaws shut.

Aven nearly choked on a shaky breath as the dragon backed away. Could this really be happening? Had Fennicks actually backed down? It seemed impossible after the day they'd had.

"On your feet, my girl." Papa hauled her up, radiating warmth, and the smell of cooking fires and citrus. In one quick motion, he shed his off-shoulder cloak and wrapped Aven's bare body in his scent and heat. She clutched it gratefully, trembling not only from the cold but the terror of meeting her pacifist father's eyes.

She had broken their highest law. Violence without provocation was barbarism. Violence even with provocation was unnecessary.

His brown face creased with worry as he looked her over, no doubt searching for any wounds. Even in the dark, flecks of red and green swirled bright in his brown eyes, colors reserved for whenever he looked at her or Mama. His show of love in his own Tribouin way.

Mama's soft growl drew both their gazes back to the other dragon. The one who held their fates in his hidden claws.

"Navya," Mist whispered, head bowed, her knees now deep in the grass. She hunched her shoulders in a show of submission, even allowing her long white hair to slide away, baring the back of her neck to Rielnor.

He surveyed her with narrowed eyes, lips pursed in what was not quite a frown. In fact, Aven caught almost a hint of affection in his gaze. It permeated his scent, softening it to something not so frightening.

"Your packmate has shed the blood that was yours," Rielnor said. "Are you satisfied?"

"I—" Mist jolted up. "Yes, flight leader."

"Stand then and speak no more of this." He shifted his gaze to Aven, his pupils so small they nearly disappeared into the yellowy green of his eyes. "Another attack will be taken as an act of unprovoked aggression. We will retaliate swiftly. Is that clear?"

Aven nodded, clutching her father's cloak tighter. "Clear."

Rielnor exhaled slowly, his attention shifting over Mist, Mama, Papa, to the lynx and then the forest where the elves still lurked. A weary look overtook his face before he turned to Fennicks. The other dragon rumbled a deep growl, malice lingering in those yellow eyes. The flight leader's decision did not sit well. Hopefully, Rielnor had enough control of his flight to keep them from coming after Aven's family.

If they did, she would be ready. She'd take Fennicks with her if came to it.

None of them moved until the dragons faded into the night. Mama stood watch, muscles tensed like a coiled viper until Fennicks' rumbling footfalls faded. Their loss yielded the night back to chirping bugs, signaling an end to Aven's few moments of peace. Facing down dragons was nothing compared to what was coming.

Mist stared at the spot her flight leader had once been, her crown of white hair glowing in the rising moonlight. She was so still, her hands fisted over her thighs. What she searched for was a mystery. Eventually, her shoulders dropped and she rose, attention locking with Aven's. In just a few steps, Mist had her caught up in a tight, wet hug, water still dripping from her clothes. Not that Aven minded. She nuzzled into the embrace, breathing deep the smell of rose and vanilla. Maybe she could stay like this and hide from her parents' reproachful looks.

Mama's *whuff* drew all eyes to where she stared at the forest. A Linseen elf had dropped from one of the low branches, his tightly coiled hair pulled into a large knot at the top of his head. His warm brown skin quite darker than Papa's, helping hide his movements through the shadows.

The lynx trotted beside him with perked, fluffy ears. They went straight for Aven, their gleaming eyes pulling her to them with outstretched hands. The larger reached her first. His fuzzy head bumped her face as he purred, then the second chuffed before rubbing against her side. She sank into their feline embraces, breathing deep their woodsy scents. So familiar and safe, like when she passed out between her parents as a child.

Though she'd never met these lynx, their markings stirred something inside her. It had to be Kali's soul. She had been their pride leader for decades. "Thank you for coming. I owe your people. *Again.*"

"You saved our family, Zoli," Papa said, bowing to the Linseen elf. He had lingered behind the lynx, waiting for them to finish their greeting.

Zoli's brow furrowed as he slung his bow over his back, leather armor fitted perfectly to his warrior's body. "I am not so sure we did. Are you unharmed?"

"We are," Papa answered. "Thank you for coming. I might have lost my girl if you hadn't been out patrolling."

The elf pursed his lips as he looked at Aven. "We will always come, even if our weapons would do little against such as that black dragon. I believe our presence made its keeper call it off. I cannot guarantee a similar outcome should another confrontation happen, though. Do you understand?"

Aven peered from behind the lynx as heat flushed her cheeks and nose.

"The dragons live outside of our reproach," Zoli explained. "See to it you do not put yourself in a position to be at odds with them."

"We will make sure this does not happen again," Papa said, putting a hand on Aven's shoulder. The weight of his touch killed her snide retort.

Maybe she was wrong for attacking Fennicks, but she wasn't sorry. She and Mist would be dead if that egg-breaker had their way, and no one would have said a word since the attack happened during a race. Aven was only wrong because she didn't slip in between the rules that allowed violence.

The unmistakable pity creasing Zoli's face made Kali's hackles rise. If only Aven could pull at those lines, smooth them out until his feelings hid beneath an indiscernible mask. She didn't want the sorrow he thrust upon her.

As if sensing her offense, Zoli looked away, running a thumb down the string of his bow. "Shall we escort you home?"

The larger lynx yowled at the elf, its ears pinning back.

"Pardon me." Amusement chasing away the pity in his eyes. "It would appear you already have an escort."

Mama barked at the great cats, who both looked at her before bowing their heads. Aven could only guess at their exchange, but she'd wager Mama had thanked them in her own way. The itch to shift returned, so she could make sense of the chirps and yowls, but she didn't need to earn a swat from those large wolf paws.

"This is where I leave you then." Zoli touched a fist to the center of his chest. "I must take a report to Commander Senwe. He will be concerned by the dragon's behavior."

"Will anything come of it?" Mist asked, her voice soft and trembling.

Zoli tilted his head, eyes narrowing as he looked at her. "Unlikely. We are peacekeepers, not law enforcers. It would take a mighty threat to soul-call my kin and I to face off against anyone. Especially dragons. Unless all of Yunaii seeks banishment for them, there is little we can do. Commander Senwe will simply wish to know there is at least one amongst their number who has shown a proclivity for violence."

Mist pursed her lips, and Aven couldn't ignore the concern twisting her face. It wasn't the dragons' safety she worried about. More likely she feared what would happen if the Linseen confronted Fennicks. Nothing would keep Pryn and her winged cockroach from racing, so it was only a matter of time before the elves identified the dragon.

Only one thing would keep another fight from happening.

"I attacked the dragon," Aven whispered.

A sigh escaped Papa, echoed by a loud whine from Mama. Their disappointment flooded the night air, filling Aven's nose with its stench. She could barely look at Zoli, let alone chance a glance towards her parents. The only thing worse than this would be challenging the Matriarchs in open combat.

Zoli blinked repeatedly, staring as if she'd sprouted horns. "Why in the Great Mother's name would you attack a dragon?"

Why indeed? How could she explain without sounding petty, childish, …temperamental? Hanawi had been right about her. Aven had done exactly what she'd warned against.

"Fennicks—" Aven licked her lips, stubbornly looking only at Zoli's boots. "—Fennicks attacked my dragon today. Nearly killed her, and me. I saw them in the woods and my anger got the best of me."

"I see." Zoli sounded neither angry nor surprised, so Aven chanced a glance at his face. He plucked at the string of his bow with a pensive look. "Perhaps next time find a more constructive outlet for your anger."

Aven nearly choked on a bitter laugh. "Right. Of course."

"I do not jest." He stepped closer, his soldier-like posture so much like Dev's. "I do not wish it to be you that we aim our arrows at one day. I would hate to give certain people that satisfaction. The Linseen believe you are more than what is whispered of you. *Prove it to them.*"

Aven's mouth fell open as the larger lynx rumbled angrily.

Zoli regarded the cat like a fellow warrior. "Kali's pride believes in you. They entrusted you with a powerful gift. Do not waste it on vengeance."

Aven didn't need to shift to understand the smaller lynx's sad yowl. Zoli was right. She had let down more than just her parents, and Kali's instincts weren't to blame.

"Thank you." Aven lowered her eyes politely. She wouldn't bother debating the finer points. Someone had to back Fennicks up a step, but maybe Aven could find a balance between doing what was right and not letting down her loved ones. She didn't expect an elf to understand that.

A sigh slipped from Zoli's lips as he gave a slight headshake. One of the perks of dealing with elves: they were too polite. It didn't matter if she'd disappointed him, Zoli would never speak it aloud.

He cast another look at her, before offering soft goodbyes to Mama and Papa. Then he padded through thickets and discarded leaves to rejoin his people. Or return to where they had been. It was so dark Aven couldn't tell if they had retreated without him.

His departure left an uncomfortable silence. Only the bugs chirping and a soft purr from the lynx kept Aven's ears from ringing.

"Come," Papa said, his soft voice clipped. Without a glance to see if Aven followed, he moved in the cave's direction with Mama trotting at his side.

The time had come, and lynx or no lynx, the lecture her parents brewed would not be pleasant.

CHAPTER *Seven*

Aven

Aven stood near her family's cave, hands outstretched to her lynx escorts. Mama and Papa had gone inside, most likely so she could shift and he could finish dinner. So they could prepare.

Whatever they cooked up was worth putting off a little while longer. Aven broke Qinawe law. There had to be consequences. All she could hope was that those consequences didn't include Mist. Aven couldn't stomach the thought of them sending her away.

The larger lynx purred before rubbing against Aven's chest, drawing her into a round of scratches and petting. She dreaded saying goodbye, but their time together needed to end. Stars twinkled above, their shimmering outdone only by the two moons, Levia and Konia. Both of them were nearly full now, blanketing the forest in silver light.

Aven couldn't wait for the night they ruled the sky. She and Mist always flew to the cliffs, where cook fires and lamplight couldn't hinder their beauty. Last time it happened, they stayed up until near sunrise just looking at the stars and dancing nebulas, counting each time light streaked across the black. Aven could have stayed there forever.

She turned to smile at Mist who had lingered at the entryway instead of going inside. Her head rested against the cave wall, eyes heavy and dull as her lashes fluttered.

By Dia'veh, I'm so selfish. Aven had to stop dawdling, face her parents, and get Mist to bed.

"Thank you so much," she said to the lynx, petting both of their fluffy heads. "Please tell your Pride leader I owe him even more now."

The smaller lynx bared teeth in a catlike smile, while the larger bowed its head. Then they trotted into the darkness, their stripes and speckles blending in with the monochrome of the forest. A shiver trembled through Aven's limbs at the thought of ever being their prey instead of whatever she was to them. Kali's guardian? Their pride leader reborn? Hopefully, their current leader, Kanai, was smarter than that. But then he was Kali's *son*. The ache in Aven's chest over just thinking his name no doubt flared in him when he thought of her.

A soft snore drew Aven's attention back to the cave. Mist's eyes were shut, her head tilted at an uncomfortable angle as she slumped precariously against the rock. Dribble slipped out the corner of her mouth, pulling a smile from Aven.

How did she make drooling in her sleep look adorable?

"Hey, let's get you inside."

Mist jerked upright with a snort. "I'm not sleeping."

"No, of course not." Aven bit her lip to keep from smiling. "Just resting your eyes."

"Right. That. Yes." Mist scratched and rubbed at her face as she blinked rapidly. "Smells like your papa is done with dinner."

Aven longed to loop an arm through Mist's, but she still wore only Papa's cloak. Tomorrow, she would have to retrieve her wrap dress and weapons from where she'd discarded them in the woods.

"Let's go eat." She bumped Mist with her shoulder, earning a half smile as they walked through the entrance of the cave. Hopefully that little curve of her lips meant Mist wasn't angry with her too. She had every right to be.

Soft, yellow light beckoned them down the narrow walkway, which ended abruptly at the open living section of the cave. Aven carefully brushed off her dirty feet before sinking her toes into the layers of animal furs on the floor. They cushioned the aches creeping through her bones and softened the room's echoes.

Patches of moss that Mama cultivated climbed everywhere, bringing some life and moisture to the red and yellow rocks. She'd done it for Mist. Yunaii's dry air gave her nosebleeds, but the plants helped ease her discomfort. As soon as she stepped into the room, her breathing grew deep, as if she'd happened upon a flower instead of soft, musty plants.

Mama and Papa's handwork filled the cave, Aven's current favorite being the raised platform of her bed reaching no higher than her shin. Furs and woven blankets covered a mountain of pillows, beckoning Aven to collapse into the softness instead of sating her gurgling stomach.

From the way Mist stared, she probably had the same thought.

But the need for food won out. The pot of stew rested in the middle of their small table, which stood as high as her bed, and was surrounded by throw pillows. Steam coiled over its rim, illuminated by the mass of glowstones dispersed throughout the room. It took nearly all the extra meat her family caught to trade for the stones. Such simple, beautiful things, in all shapes and sizes, set up on the floor, on little stands, hanging from the walls by intricate knots of soft, woven rope.

Aven hated them.

They were another creation of the Eilawi—gems infused with Sholindrea's energy to capture and hold sunlight. Traders brought them from across the sea. An expensive and rare commodity. Mama said they were worth it though, to make the cave feel like a home.

If her family had the protection of the rest of the blood, they wouldn't *need* to spend everything they had on light. If the Qinawe didn't deny Mama her place, they wouldn't have to live off thumpers and thick stew meant to stretch out their scraps of food. Bitterness tainted the walls of this cave, waiting for the simplest things to pull it out. Especially after today. Hanawi's smug face waited just behind Aven's closed eyes, false smile twisting like a knife as she whispered one day they would hunt together. That this would all come to an end.

Lies. It would never end.

Aven glanced around the large room, but Mama and Papa were nowhere in sight. A small passage in the rock opened up just beyond the dining table, leading to their room. They must have retreated to talk or collect themselves.

Or perhaps to discuss what her punishment would be.

Aven shivered again. Would it be the dragon races she'd have to give up? Or some of her freedoms, maybe? Qinawe usually kept their youths quite busy as they proved themselves useful to the bond. Strong bond, strong people.

Since they didn't want Aven at all, Mama and Papa asked very little of her.

She forced her thoughts from the anger roiling inside of her. Hanawi and those like her didn't deserve a home in her head. There were better things to focus on. Like Mist, who hovered nearby, eyelids drooping as she swayed on her feet.

"Go eat."

"Come with me." Mist fumbled for Aven's shoulder.

"I'll be right there. Just let me get dressed."

Mist nodded once before weaving towards the table. As she began scooping the stew into four bowls, Aven went to the baskets containing clothes, trinkets, and shoes nestled beneath her bed. Even at home, she preferred easily shed clothing, just in case she had to shift. Tonight called for her favorite pair of high-waisted pants that billowed around her calves, and a drapey, thin-strapped top that she tucked in.

Mama and Papa stepped into the room just as she headed for the table. They both stopped at the sight of her, Mama's brow creasing as Papa's mouth thinned. Out of the corner of Aven's eyes, Mist settled into a weary posture on her knees, hands resting together in her lap, chin tucked against her chest.

Neither Mama nor Papa acknowledged her. They were both so focused on Aven. Mama's lips parted, but nothing came out.

Had Aven angered her so much she actually had nothing to say?

She'd barely had the thought when Mama barreled towards her, snatching her up so tightly she squeezed the air from Aven's lungs. She stood in shock, eyes wide as brave, no-nonsense Mama trembled against her, wetness dripping onto her cheek.

"What in Dia'veh's name were you thinking?" Mama choked out. "You could have been killed. *Again.*"

Papa's hand came down on Aven's shoulder, his callouses warm and scratchy against her skin. "You scared the life out of us, my girl."

Aven's lip trembled. "I'm so sorry. I didn't mean—I didn't want to hurt you two."

"Hurt us?" Mama pulled back, her eyes red and puffy. "This isn't about *us*. My poor cub. Have we taught you no pride or love for yourself? Why would you take your life into your hands like that?"

"I wasn't thinking," Aven said. No sense in lying. Mama would see through it, straight to her heart where little regret lingered. Fennicks deserved the claws and the teeth. How could she possibly explain that to her pacifist parents?

Yet, as fear poisoned Mama's scent, tainting her woodsy smell with an acrid bitterness, shame crept through Aven's blood. This was worse than the anger she'd expected. Mama, who had defied the Matriarchs to be with the man she loved, who lived in exile from her family, who had to learn every craft of the Qinawe because none of the bond would help her. Aven had made this fierce, wonderful woman afraid.

"I'm sorry," Aven whispered. "I just wanted to hurt Fennicks. To get revenge."

"Revenge is a moment's satisfaction." Papa motioned the three of them towards the table. "The consequences it brings are rarely worth the feeling."

Aven didn't agree, but there was no sense in fighting with him. A heady rush came at the memories of Fennicks' pained cry and their blood on her tongue. Hopefully, Papa couldn't see the chill bumps rising on her arms. She quickly situated herself on a throw pillow so he wouldn't notice.

Mama and Papa settled themselves at the table, silently accepting the bowls Mist offered them. She didn't speak, and they offered nothing either, feeding the tension growing in the air.

"Things could have gone horribly wrong today." Mama swished her wooden spoon through the stew, black eyes fixed on Aven. "That dragon could have killed you. I'm still baffled we all made it home in one piece."

Papa made a disgusted sound. "And Fennicks will be none the worse in a few days' time. Wouldn't you say, Mist?"

She jumped, shoulders tensing, her eyes staying focused on her bowl. Almost absently, she rubbed the back of her neck. "Most likely."

Papa studied her as he ate a spoonful of stew. "So, it was for nothing."

"Maybe next time Fennicks will think before attacking someone else," Aven said, though it was probably a pointless hope. Next time it would just be her who caught the dragon's anger instead of Mist.

"It's a good thing that overgrown bat has no interest in mating you, cub." Mama waved her spoon through the air. "They're *shifters!*"

Aven and Mist glanced at each other, the question lingering between them. How did she know?

"What you did today could have been taken as a mating challenge by a Tribouin or Qinawe. A lynx or griffin wouldn't have even stopped to wonder about your intent." Mama dropped her spoon, sending a splash of stew across the table. "Is that what you want? To be stuck with some fire-breather because you let anger drive you? I thought you didn't want a mate. That's why you're not with Pryn anymore. Isn't that right?"

Aven would have preferred a slap to her mother bringing up Pryn. "Yes, mama."

Mama looked up at the dark ceiling, brows furrowed, her black eyes catching every reflection of the dozens of glowstones. They reminded Aven of the stars.

"They very well could follow some of the old shifter ways," Papa said as he rested a hand on Mama's forearm. "Maybe not as much as us, but they know what matters most. Strength before love, my girl."

"Strong bond, strong people," Aven spat. She didn't need the lecture. Shifters chose their mates through combat to keep their people strong. It helped them survive during the Time of Sorrow, when war touched every continent, every race, every person. It had become the heart of the shapeshifters' ways. Now, Qinawe and Tribouin no longer engaged in conflict unless it was to propose.

Aven didn't understand why they adhered so strictly to the belief. Dragons fought for power, lynx protected their pride, griffin sought challenges. But they all still lived within the ways of the shifters. Only the Qinawe and Tribouin trained their people to fight and then asked them to never use their skills, save for one fleeting moment.

"It's not a life bond at least." Mist's voice trembled. "W- we don't mate for life."

Mama didn't even look her way. She simply lifted her hand in a silence motion. "Not your turn."

Mist ducked her head and stared at her food. She had never gotten the Matriarch tone before.

"What's going to happen now?" Aven asked, drawing the weight of disappointment back to herself. It wasn't Mist's job to bear their frustration.

Mama glanced at Papa, who tilted his head. "What do you think should happen?"

Aven clamped her mouth shut. *That* was a trap. He wanted to gauge how seriously she took this situation. "I don't know, Papa. I know what I did was wrong."

"*Do* you think it was wrong?" He relaxed back on his pillow with an all too familiar look in his eye. If she lied, he would see through it. He wanted to hear her truth, even if it hurt him.

Aven squared her shoulders and stared into his eyes. "No, actually. I don't."

Bursts of blue streaked through the brown. Disappointment. He knew it was coming, though. He had to. "Violence for the sake of violence is not wrong?"

"It wasn't for the sake of violence." Aven tried to keep from grinding her teeth. He wasn't being purposefully obtuse. Papa had a way of trying to force her to examine herself. To question what she did or thought. "Fennicks deserved to be hurt. They know right from wrong."

Papa nodded. "Of course. As do you."

Mist bit her lip, but Aven still caught the hint of a smile she'd tried to hide. There was no winning with Papa. He had his view of things.

Aven was mama's child. though. Her eyes narrowed as she looked over Papa's muscular arms and broad chest. Tribouin were just as skilled with weapons as Qinawe, but also as staunchly against anything but ceremonial combat. How far would his pacifism would go?

"What if Fennicks had killed us, Papa?"

"Ah, yes." His mouth pulled into a frown. "Let us debate hypotheticals. That will get us far."

Aven blew a sigh through her nose. "I just want to know. What would you have done?"

Her parents exchanged a long look, Papa's brows rising once or twice in some silent language only they understood. Mama's mouth twitched before she shrugged, her attention sliding back to Aven.

"Your father is a better soul than us," Mama said.

Papa rubbed her back, his calloused hands large against Mama's slim, but muscular frame.

"Killing Fennicks would not bring you back, my girl, and that anger would destroy me." He leaned forward without breaking contact with Mama's back. "Some people can live with anger, devastation, hate. They cultivate it, use it to drive them, but not me. I would not seek vengeance if that's what you're asking. I would do what I could to keep from breaking."

Aven turned her gaze to Mama. Those near black eyes locked on her, waiting, anticipating. She knew the question lingering between them.

"*My cub.*" Mama licked her lips, her usually firm voice giving in to a tremble as tears welled over her lashes. "I would kill them all."

"What?" Aven drew in a quick breath. She hadn't heard right. She couldn't have. Sarcasm and attitude, that's what she'd expected. Not something capable of breaking everything she believed of her parents.

Papa's hand moved back and forth over Mama's shoulders, seeming unsurprised by her confession. He watched his *Chosen*—his lifemate—brows furrowed with such a deep sadness. It etched lines into his dark skin with a weariness Aven tried to ignore.

Mama reached across the table, and Aven immediately took her hand. The grip was tight but soft, loving but firm. Everything Mama was. She trembled under the fierce stare fixed on her. Beneath the table she reached for Mist and earned a squeeze that jolted warmth through her chilled fingers.

"Aven." A tear slipped down Mama's cheek. "If the dragons had killed you today, I would have hurt them back. If the Tribouin ever dared sling anything more than spite, I would bring them to their knees. If the Qinawe ever raised a hand against you, I would end them. Because you are mine and I know that I have failed you."

"Mama, no." Aven swiped her thumb over the back of Mama's hand. "What are you talking about?"

Mama glanced at Papa, who nodded.

"We have expected you to live in our ways," Mama said. "We ask you to believe what we believe, even though the people who live that way and believe those things have never made you feel a part of our bond—*our family*."

"That's not your fault." Aven cast a look at Mist, silently begging for help.

"You're not responsible for the Matriarchs' choices," Mist said, her focus on Papa.

"Perhaps." He scratched at his beard with the hand not stroking Mama's back. "But we raised you here."

Mama nodded in agreement. "I knew the risks I took. I knew what it would cost to choose your father. I knew what it meant for us, and we accepted that. Together. *You* did not choose this."

"What else could you have done?" Aven asked. Not once had she blamed her parents for how the other shifters treated her. The Matriarchs made their choices. Their stony hearts, their mindless clinging to rules and culture, that was their burden to bear. What did it matter how strong their people were if they were irredeemably selfish? They chose a pointless saying over a living member of their bond.

"Sometimes I think we should have left Yunaii," Mama sighed.

Mist dared meet her gaze. "Leave safety for uncertainty?"

"Quite the debate that's been. Ever since the day Aven was born." Papa's mouth quirked into a half smile. "Neither of us has ever left Yunaii, so we chose the dangers we knew over the unknown."

"At least here, we could trust the Tribouin and Qinawe would not put a hand on Aven." Mama shook her head, frustration twisting her lips into a frown.

"They still haven't," Aven said.

Mama nearly growled with disgust. "No, they just drive you to desperation. First by frightening the rest of the bond away from ever befriending you, then leaving you to hunt on your own, until your only option left was to turn to dragon racing to escape them. I can only imagine Hanawi's delight when that finally caught up with you."

Aven wrinkled her nose. "She got a good look at me when I came home."

"I'm sure." A spark of red burst in Papa's brown eyes, rare evidence of his temper. Tribouin trained to show no emotion, to be as cool as stone. He never risked the Qinawe seeing since they already thought him weak. "That one thinks herself so important."

"That she does." Mama reserved the disdain in her voice for only the Matriarchs, women she would have been in charge of. Her skills should have earned her the highest regard. "Hanawi is afraid of you, cub. And jealous."

"Jealous?" Aven frowned. "I have nothing. I am nothing in her eyes."

Mama pointed at Kali's fang. "You have power she does not. All she has is the soul of a mountain cat. A fierce hunter, but not a Sholi. She envies Kali's power. She would never again have to prove herself to the other Matriarchs. Her place among them would be secure."

Aven released Mama's hand to grip the fang with shaking fingers. Each icy breath dragged, seizing in her chest, leaving her limbs heavy. "But she couldn't take it, could she? Kali didn't choose her."

"Not rightfully." Mama toyed with the wolf fang dangling from her ear. "But you need to understand, cub. The bond is *responsible* for Kali's soul. She entrusted you with it, but what happens if you cannot keep it safe?"

"Only when I die—"

Mama cut her off with a wave of her hand. "*Think*, cub. It is not just exile the Matriarchs threaten. If they hear about what happened tonight, they will get what they want. Hanawi will get what she wants. It will be the bond's responsibility to ensure Kali's soul is safe. If they find you breaking the Qinawe's laws, they will declare you lacking the ability to protect her gift. They must guarantee she will move on to her place of peace after your death."

Mist squeezed Aven's numb hand beneath the table. Her heart pounded in her ears, chest heaving with each breath. She had never considered, had never even *thought,* she could lose the power and freedom Kali granted her. The great cat had come to her when she was a child. Slipping into her form was second nature.

"Do you understand now?" Papa asked, pushing his bowl aside to make room for his elbows. "If you give the Matriarchs a reason, they will break you, my girl. Kali's soul will be denied you for the rest of your days.

Aven

A boot might as well have been pressed to Aven's chest. Every breath heaved into her lungs, leaving her trembling like a newborn fawn.

"It is your choice to live how you live, my girl." Sorrow filled Papa's eyes. "I hoped you might see the world as I do, but I don't expect it. All I want is for you to be safe, whole, and free."

She nodded weakly, before locking her attention on Mist. They could run from the cave, fly high into the sky, go where they would never have to look back. That was safe. Only far out of Yunaii would she truly be free.

Mist must have seen it in her eyes. Her hands wrapped around Aven's fingers, determination overtaking the exhaustion etched into her face.

"Say the word."

A deep breath whooshed over Aven's parted lips as relief chilled her veins. It wasn't actually possible. They'd never make it across the desert, let alone the ocean. Not on their own. But Mist was willing. If Hanawi came for Kali's fang, they would escape this prison of rock.

Her parents watched them, their eyes shifting from her to Mist. Mama's gaze assessed and Papa's—Aven wasn't sure. Her heart kicked up a notch, but she wouldn't shrink back. Instead, she squared her shoulders and returned their stare, waiting for them to voice whatever they were wondering.

Mist didn't give them the chance. "How long have you known?"

Mama tilted her head, surprise widening her eyes. Her features lacked the softness she usually wore when speaking to Mist. "About you?"

"About me, and the flight." Mist shifted a lock of white hair back from her face. "Did I give them away?"

"Your scent made me suspicious." Mama tapped the bridge of her strong nose. "The same smells clung to you as Aven's Feather. You can lie to people's eyes, you can even trick their minds, but you cannot lie to a wolf's nose. A girl who doesn't ride dragons should not smell exactly like a dragon."

Papa chuckled and waved a hand through the air. "Once we figured you out, we began watching your flight. The absence of some when in the presence of dragons, or the absence of dragons in the presence of people. The strangers who never appeared again, the odd smells. They cleared the situation, this odd enslavement of the dragons."

"Enslavement?" Aven sputtered.

"You think they are the ones enslaved?" Mist scoffed, clearly forgetting herself, even under Mama's severe look. "People in this city don't even realize how manipulated they are."

"Explain," Papa urged, resting a hand on Mama's knee.

Mist cast a sideways glance at Aven as she pushed at the beds of her fingernails. It had been hard for her to share the secrets once. If Rielnor heard her speak of their ways, he would have grounds to banish her or even end her life.

"You don't have to." Aven squeezed her hand.

Mist shook her head, full lips pulling into a familiar stubborn line. "They deserve to see the truth of things."

"What truth?" Worry crept into Papa's tone.

Mist entwined her trembling fingers with Aven's. "The dragons—they pretend to serve. They yield to their riders, but think about it. Their trust must be earned. They cannot be captured and beaten into submission. Someone else pays for their food, their lodging, all the luxuries they enjoy. They don't even bathe themselves. They race, mate one another, and bask in everyone's admiration. By playing at being beasts, they live the life of royals who give nothing in return."

Aven's parents stared at Mist for a long while, blinking fast, each of them mouthing silent words to themselves.

Mama found her voice first, anger turning it guttural and deep. "And to think I felt sorry for them."

"Perhaps they mean it differently," Papa offered.

Mist's lips curved in a loving smile. "I wish that was so, but I know these dragons. I know myself. We're not the most productive creatures when left to our own devices. With full bellies and all the entertainment we could have, we're about as lazy as pampered cats."

Aven snickered, imagining Mist lying about like some overfed pet.

"Is that what you are then, girl?" Papa's eyes narrowed. "Where do you fall in all of this? Have you made my daughter your servant?"

"Of course she hasn't," Aven snapped, anger rising at the hurt twisting Mist's face. "I've known what she was from the first day we met."

"When I arrived here, I didn't understand. I'm still not sure I do." Mist shrugged. "Dragons don't hide in Estellias. When I got here, I didn't get on with the flight and I had no one else to talk to. I was lonely. Then I saw Aven and…"

"You saw some sad little girl in the market and took pity on me."

The look Mist sent her way belonged better to a falling star or brilliant sunset. "No. I saw someone like me."

Aven's fingers itched to trace the curve of Mist's cheek, to linger near those bright eyes. She lived for the moments they crinkled with joy or adoration.

"So where does that leave Aven?" Mama asked. "The flight leader seemed ready to kill us all for knowing the truth."

"He might have." Another tremor shot up Mist's arm. "I don't know how things came to be like this, but Rielnor believes keeping the dragon's abilities a secret is essential. Not just to their way of life, but to their survival."

Mama scowled. "Their survival? What does a dragon fear other than the Maker or the Mother?"

"I don't know." Mist sighed. "The Elementals maybe? I learned of the dragons here from my egg-layer. She told me I could seek refuge among them."

"Refuge from what?" Aven asked, heart leaping in her chest. This was new information. Was something after Mist? Were the dragons in danger? Aven had no illusions of defeating an Eilawi, but she'd try if she had to.

Mist fidgeted more, spinning a ring on her pinkie finger around and around. "Something is brewing back home in Estellias. The Earth and Air Elementals are warring with each other. The Fire and Water Elementals are disappearing. My egg-layer is in the thick of it all, but when my Papi begged her to keep me safe, she couldn't deny him."

"Warring Eilawi," Papa said, scratching his beard. "Not the thing I was expecting to learn this night. You carry heavy burdens, girl."

"So," Aven said, exhaling slowly. "Estellias isn't safe?"

Mist immediately sandwiched her hands between her own. "If my eega has her way, it will be again. Soon. She does not want to see our cousins destroy themselves."

"How is one dragon going to stop living nature from clashing against each other?" A sickened feeling twisted Aven's insides. All this time. All this hoping. And for what? To find out the only guaranteed place that would take her was about to be ripped apart.

Fierceness entered Mist's voice as she leaned closer. "Trust in my eega. She is a force of nature in her own right."

"This egg-layer of yours sounds mighty indeed." Mama took a sip of her evening tea before adding, "I see where you get it."

A grin pulled across Aven's face as tears prickled in Mist's eyes.

Mama took a long draught from her cup. "I saw you trying to protect my cub tonight. You were ready to fight your flight leader. You were ready to take fire for her. Thank you for that."

Mist bowed deeply, her long hair veiling her face. Aven didn't need to scent the salt in the air to know tears slipped down her cheeks. Being accepted by Mama and Papa was something she worried over often, though Aven didn't know why. Her temper was always in check and her words aimed true. Aven sometimes wondered if Mama and Papa wished she was more like Mist. Aven certainly did.

The hollow feeling in her heart bloomed without Mist's gentle hands to distract her. All hope of leaving Yunaii and going to Estellias laid dashed to pieces. She'd focused on getting there for so long. Without that dream, weariness crept into her bones.

She busied herself with gulping down her spicy thumper stew, not even bothering with a spoon. The first few mouthfuls warmed her belly, the next filled it, but she kept slurping until discomfort replaced the sadness inside her.

"So, what happens now?" Aven asked, staring into her empty bowl.

"What do you mean, my girl?" Papa leaned back once more, his arms laying across his knees.

"I failed the bond." Aven's hands shook. Good thing she'd forgone the spoon so there was nothing to rattle around her bowl. "You've always taught me actions have consequences."

Mama rose to her feet, her own bowl held in a white knuckled grip. "Unless the dragons come to the Matriarchs for a complaint, I don't see why they need ever know."

"We do not agree with what you did. It was reckless and dangerous." Papa's voice was soft despite his harsh words. "But it is your life, my girl. We taught you our ways. Strong bond, strong people. Now you must decide what that means to you. Not living by our ideals or finding your own interpretation of it, is your choice to make. Not all shifters hold to the belief that self-defense or defense of a loved one is against our ways. The lynx and griffin do not live thus, and despite the insistence of the Qinawe and Tribouin that their way is the only way, we all still find peace between us."

Mama's lips pulled back in a snarl. "My cub will not be banished because some lying, overgrown lizard thinks they can do whatever they want without consequence."

Tears blurred Aven's vision as she rose and reached out for her mother. No matter how sharp Mama was, no matter how angry, she always watched out for Aven. Always. It was one of the few things she could count on. Her parents would always be right here, defending her, even when she'd made such dangerous decisions.

As soon as Mama's arms wrapped around her, she released the ache tightening her throat, setting free her tears. Some days she begged the Maker to tell her why she'd been born an outcast. Some days the bitterness over the stares and whispers made her want to rail at everyone in her path. Then Mama would hold her tight and Papa would kiss her forehead, and their family became all that mattered.

"Cub," Mama said, stroking her hair. "Our people might have their ways, but they're not the only ways. They weren't for me, and they don't have to be for you."

Aven sniffled and wiped at the tears on her cheeks. "Why doesn't it bother you, Mama? All their fussing and judging."

Mama's gaze drifted to Papa, traveling over his face and lips. Even a stranger could see how she felt about her Chosen. Light sparked in her black eyes, softening the severity of her face. One corner of her mouth curved upward as she cupped Aven's cheeks.

"Your father was what I wanted. *You* are what I wanted. They will not drive me from my home because I chose not to walk their line. You and I both know that isn't easy, but I'll not deny myself happiness so they can live in denial of just how big this world is. Yunaii is only one tiny piece of it."

Papa's fingers slid through Aven's hair, drawing her attention to him. "I know staying here was not the easiest thing for you and I am sorry for that, my girl. I am sorry they have never accepted you."

"And because of that, we cannot fault you for not accepting them," Mama said.

Aven bobbed her head, not trusting her own voice. Any tremble, any softness, and she'd be wailing in her parents' arms again like an injured pup.

"We will have to be careful," Mama said, resting her hands on Aven's and Papa's shoulders. "Avoid Rielnor and the flight. Don't give Fennicks especially any reason to go to the Matriarchs. Don't give the flight leader a reason to think we will betray their secret. He had murder in his eyes today. He won't hesitate to end us to protect his people. Isn't that right Mist?"

Her answer was a soft snore.

Aven peered around Mama to find Mist's cheek resting on her forearms, her body hunched over the table.

Papa's chest rumbled with a soft chuckle. "It would seem today's events have caught up with her."

"Can you help me get her to bed?" Aven asked.

Together they hefted Mist from the table and got her settled beneath Aven's pile of blankets and furs. Once done, they headed back to clean up dinner. Papa collected the dishes while Mama took care of storing the leftover stew in the icebox deep inside the cave.

They worked in silence for a bit, cleaning the bowls and utensils, then drying them off. Aven noticed Papa's gaze lingered on her, an unspoken curiosity in his eyes. Yet, even as they came to the last dish, he didn't voice what was on his mind.

His loss, since Aven had questions of her own. Ones she'd asked often as a child, but hoped for a deeper answer this time. "Papa?"

"Yes?" He said, putting down his damp drying rag.

"You and Mama. How did you end up together? The truth, please." Aven leaned a hip against the cave wall and fixed him with a pleading look. "Don't tell me you saw each other in the forest and it was love at first sight. Tell me how you got past everything that said she wasn't the one for you."

Papa stroked his cropped beard, the lines of his face crinkling in a thoughtful look. "Nothing ever told me she wasn't the one for me."

Aven resisted the urge to glance over at Mist asleep on her bed. "How? You and Mama, the Tribouin and the Qinawe, they're oil and water. Night and day. Strong men. Defiant women."

His teeth flashed in one of his hearty smiles. The kind that brought warmth and comfort swelling in Aven's chest.

"You see, my girl, the Qinawe, they misunderstand my people. I never looked at your Mama and thought there needed to be something different about her. The Tribouin don't believe women are meek and unable to defend themselves. Not most of us, anyway. There's always some hot-headed fools too drunk on themselves to know better, but you'll find those in any walk of life. Our women are what I have taught you to be." Papa tapped Aven's nose. "Respected. Revered. Protected. We don't hold our girls back. You've seen that. For all her failings as your lover, you know the power in Pryn."

Golden eyes flashed in Aven's mind. The day Pryn challenged her, blades whirling, a smirk on her dark lips. Power sang in her veins. It hummed around her like the shroud of a storm.

"Yes," Aven murmured. "I've seen it."

Papa nodded thoughtfully. "We teach our girls to fight, same as we teach our boys. We just don't want them to have to. Where the Qinawe keep their boys soft, subdued, the Tribouin instead use them as shields. It is not much better, my girl. Their freedom is sacrificed until their sisters and cousins have found their own happiness."

"Like Pryn's brother," Aven said. Thinking of him as a warm body that existed to serve Pryn's needs instead of the boy with a forked tongue—it changed him a little. Had all his barbs and attitude been to hide his own loneliness? "But why do that to them? Why do any of us still live like this?"

That brought a great sigh from Papa as he leaned against the wall as well. "All this began when shifters fought over mates to keep from dying out in the Time of Sorrow. Those of us without talons or claws had to make rules to survive. It was raw and heartless, perhaps necessary, but I cannot say.

I have only lived in times of peace. I've never known what it is to be nearly hunted to extinction."

Aven drew in a short breath at the thought. *The Time of Sorrow*. The great world war that ravaged the face of Sholindrea, many millennia ago, even before Rielnor had crawled from his egg. The great enemy of the Eilawi tried to make the world their own and all the Sholi paid for their greed.

"So, you see," Papa said, tilting Aven's head with a fingertip beneath her chin. "Your Mama, she is the embodiment of everything our women are. Everything they *were* when our ways were born. Powerful. Confident. Unbeatable. I wanted my Chosen to be my equal, and your Mama was even more than that."

A smile pulled across Aven's face as she pictured not for the first time, what Mama and Papa's mating challenge must have been like. All fierceness and fire. Neither had ever admitted which of them yielded in the end. She would probably never know.

"I wish things didn't have to be like this," Aven said, staring up into Papa's warm eyes.

"So do I, my girl." He shrugged one shoulder. "Our people are not so different. We have simply drifted apart and forgotten that our ways were all born from the same moments in time. The same needs. And we have forgotten that those ways never existed for the sake of existing. They existed to protect our people. Not ostracize them."

Aven dropped her gaze to the ground. She wasn't the only one. Sometimes it felt that way, but the sad spark of otherness lived too in the eyes of the Qinawe's youth. The girls who struggled with their blades, because their hearts lived amongst the trees and flowers. Or the boys who watched the Matriarchs with envy written across their faces.

"Customs should never come before happiness."

Papa sighed, a wide smile on his face. "Well said, my girl."

"I should probably get to bed," Aven said.

"Agreed," Papa said, glancing back towards the passage to his room where Mama had disappeared. "As should I."

He drew Aven into a tight hug, his chin resting on top of her head. She couldn't help taking a deep inhale, basking in the familiar scent of safety and home.

"Tell me one thing, my girl."

Aven drew back so she could look up at him. Of course, her questions would draw out whatever was on his mind. "Okay, what is it?"

Papa jerked his chin towards Aven's bed, where Mist still laid snuggled beneath the blankets and furs. "Is there something going on here that we should know about?"

Aven blinked. "S-something?"

"Between you and Mist." Papa cupped Aven's cheeks, forcing her not to look away. "Everything that happened today, everything you did—it was for her."

"No."

"Yes, it was." He offered a gentle smile. "Fennicks hurt Mist. Fennicks was speaking *to* Mist. All of this was to protect her."

The air in the cave grew thick and warm. Too warm. Aven squirmed, but didn't break from her papa's hold. "She's my best friend. That's all."

The tilt of his head and the gleam in his eyes told Aven he wasn't convinced, but what more could she say? Even as he left her alone with nothing but her thoughts and Mist's soft snores, the answer to his question evaded her.

Estellias was Aven's dream. War or no war, it was a place Sholi could just be what they were. They were free. If only it beckoned Mist the same way. She wouldn't go home. Couldn't, she said, though explaining why was something she seemed reluctant to do. Was it the Elemental war? Did the dragons expect her to fight?

Either way, Mist's refusal was the final say on the matter. Aven would take what Estellias offered and Mist would one day explore the world as her heart desired. There was no hope. Just like with Pryn. Clinging to scraps of childish desire wouldn't shove life into a pretty little box. Pryn had taught her reality had a bite.

Aven couldn't be so foolish as to let herself fall for someone who wanted different things than her *ever* again.

CHAPTER Nine

Mist

Mist awoke, snuggled beneath a layer of soft furs, with Aven's back pressed against her own. For a moment, she considered burrowing deep into the warm pillows and blocking out the world. What she wouldn't give to hibernate for a day. She'd never heard of dragons doing that, but it worked so well for other creatures. After what happened yesterday, sleeping for a few moons sounded wonderful. Maybe the flight would forget if she disappeared for a while.

But who would watch Aven's back?

Mist groaned as she sat up, hugging her knees to her chest. No disappearing for her. Not with so much to do.

The glowstones around the cave remained covered, and Navya and Tomen were nowhere in sight. Probably still asleep. She must have woken quite early. They had a tendency to rise at an obscene hour, bustling about the cave loud enough to wake half of Yunaii.

For now, silence lingered, save for Aven's occasional snores. Mist gazed down at her round face, admiring the lone freckle above her left eyebrow, then the one on her right cheek, before tracing her angled, bronze cheekbones. Hair tangled around her head and little snorts escaped her perfect pink lips. Mist couldn't help snickering each time one did. Could a person be any cuter without even trying?

She slept so much better here than at the dragon roosts. Serpents snuggled together up there, piling on heated rocks.

Some furry, some feathered, while the smoothest and the scaly nestled in for warmth. A different world, even for Mist. Papi was human, and he'd raised her far from any dragon flights. One of his many deals with her eega.

Sorrow clenched her chest. Leaving Estellias hadn't been too hard, but leaving Papi and his village hurt. Sometimes the ache gnawed worse than any chill.

What would *he* do in this awful situation? Mist snorted as she rested her chin on her knees. She didn't have to wonder. 'Up, my little love!' he would shout. 'We've got work to do.'

Indeed, she did.

Mist slipped out from under the furs and went to the shelves behind the table. Tomen kept all the food and supplies meticulously sorted, stored just so, and in all the proper containers. A few glances were all she needed to take stock of it all. The vegetable baskets and spice jars were full, but the dried meat was almost gone and the salt canister needed to be refilled. She made mental notes of everything, then went over to the washbasin to get ready to leave.

Clean rags hung beside a small barrel of water. She took one from its hook, filled the basin, and washed off her face, neck, and shoulders. Fennicks' bite still pinched, but she could at least turn her head without the sensation of something tearing.

Aven's family had to lie low for a while. Give the dragons time to forget all this nonsense. That meant staying away from the market, so the least Mist could do was make sure their food stores could hold them over. It was safer for her. Rielnor made it clear he didn't tolerate infighting. If the other dragons came for Mist, she'd direct them to Fennicks. They were the one who shifted into dragonskin smack in the middle of the Qinawe's bathing pool. Anyone could have seen.

Sansia hadn't even crested over the tree line when Mist emerged from the cave in a muslin dress the same color as her eyes. She squinted against the light peeking through the leaves and readjusted the Priestess' folded dress draped over her forearm. One more task to complete before an afternoon of lazing around the cave with Aven. Hopefully, she would be back before Sansia's touch left her pouring sweat. By lunch it would be throat razing hot and she had no intention of being outside when that happened. Humid heat, dry heat. All of it left her miserable.

The trek to the market gave her time to think. Racing would be off the table for now, snatching Aven's only way out of Yunaii. Mist doubted her own strength to whisk them from this place. Outside the canyon Sansia ruled unforgivingly. Not much grew, save for fleshy, water hoarding plants, saplings, and prickly bushes. Rocky, red land stretched as far as the eye could see, and it took days of travel to reach the mountain range to the west. Once there, a steep, hazardous climb over sharp rocks awaited, leading to an ocean on the other side.

Aven needed something better than a tiny dragon to get her out of Yunaii. That meant finding other means of travel. Maybe if they brought in more meat for trade, saved every spare coin, they could barter with a Tibri transporter.

That meant no more new gems or rings for a while. A small price to experience Aven's joy over escaping Yunaii.

The burble of the Lighe river drew Mist from her thoughts. She hastened across the wooden planks, ignoring her growling belly when light glinted off darting silver in the water. No time for fishing. She could grab a quick bite while she shopped. Something cheap and small.

Noise from the market rose, its pathways and stands already bustling. She kept her eyes and nose sharp for any other dragons about. Playing at docile, rule-abiding shapeshifters went against their instincts. Like the Elementals, dragon souls were born of nature—a mating of fire and air, trapped within the flesh the Creator had shaped for them.

Mist circled the base of the Eilawi tree, avoiding the busiest section of the market and any chance of making eye contact with anyone. Qinawe sold the morning's catch while Tribouin bartered over their finest weapons and craft; all taking advantage of morning's 'chill'. Some would get her attention soon.

Her path curved along the roots of the tree, until the sand-colored walls of Dia'veh's temple appeared. She would return Priestess Ifera's dress, thank Dia'veh for their warning of danger, and then get her shopping done as quickly as possible. The fight with Fennicks had no doubt been what the Creator had warned her of, but there was no need to tempt fate.

Get in, get out, and get home.

She made her way into the Temple, admiring its splendor as she went. Once inside she drew in a deep breath, reveling in the scents of fresh water and morning flowers. Back home in Tem'bria, Mist's people had only a well and a little creek to take their prayers to. Peaceful, but underwhelming at times. Not like this place. Something about stepping onto lands blessed by Dia'veh themself set a buzzing beneath her skin, like they might appear before her in all their glory.

The Priestess knelt by the prayer pool, running her hand over the surface of the water. "Good morning, young Mist. How can I assist you today? Do you require more salve?"

Mist lifted the hem of her dress and swished a foot through the water. Her rings glistened, and she wiggled her toes to make them glitter more. "No, Priestess. I just came to return your dress."

"Ah, very good then." The woman rose, a mischievous smile pulling across her dark-skinned face, making the golden ball pierced just above her mouth gleam in the light. "And how has Dia'veh's warning sat with you? You are safe? No great sources of conflict, I hope."

Mist spun one of her turquoise rings as her stomach clenched. Ifera's tone implied more than the words she spoke. "You've seen Rielnor."

"I have." Ifera smoothed the lines in her black dress. "He came seeking counsel."

Mist cringed and twisted the ring more. "I hope you encouraged him away from anything violent."

"Of course she did," said a male voice behind them.

"Good morning Truthseeker Gaelin." Mist turned, slipping into an informal bow to the Illieve elf.

"Good morning, dragon." His silver eyes were devoid of the humor the Priestess so easily wore. "Do you seek communion or justice?"

"Neither." Mist hoped he didn't hear her voice tremble. "I have to be on my way, actually."

He dipped his chin politely. "As you will, then."

"Dear one," Ifera said, running her fingertips along his bicep. "Tell young Mist what you sensed of the flight leader during his visit. Perhaps that will ease her concern."

The Truthseeker tilted his head, silver eyes growing hazy and far away, as if he'd returned to the moment Rielnor stepped inside the Temple. "I sensed nothing of great concern. I would have alerted the Linseen had I sensed any implication of violence in his heart. His words were truthful when he spoke of maintaining peace."

Mist hadn't even heard him approach. "Can you be certain?"

His eyes slid to the side as he contemplated, before eventually nodding. "Quite. Rielnor harbors no desire to harm your—*friend*."

Cool relief flooded Mist's chest. "Good. Aven and her family will be staying away for a while. Hopefully that will appease the other dragons."

"I am sure it will," the Priestess said. "A shame that even with Dia'veh's warning such conflict even occurred."

Mist swallowed down the urge to bristle and bow up at the two of them. "I can't blame Aven for being angry. She nearly died yesterday. Maybe if she'd had time to calm her fire before she saw Fennicks again, but it was just too much to ask of her."

Ifera nodded silently, even though her face spoke the thoughts playing in her mind. Thoughts Mist didn't care to ask for. Both the Priestess and Truthseeker were gentle souls who'd lived and served pacifists for many years. Anger did not seem a feeling Ifera entertained or that Gaelin seemed capable of feeling. Mist respected them for it, but it seemed better to not enter a debate about violence with these two.

"Well," she glanced between them. "Thank you for your help and protection yesterday. I know I can always count on you and that means a great deal to me."

"Of course," Ifera said, gently touching Mist's cheek. "You are always welcome here, no matter the need."

***

Mist emerged from the Temple, running her shopping list over and over in her head.

Get food. Get home. Get food. Get home. Maybe if she hurried, she would catch Aven before breakfast.

Her focus centered so wholly on scanning sellers, that she walked right into something massive and soft. A growl rippled through the air as a lynx whipped its head around and locked eyes with Mist. Anger rumbled as its pupils turned to tiny slits, framed by feline gold. Mist swallowed hard, dropping her gaze as she stepped back.

Oh, just one day. One day with no problems. That's all she asked for. The toes of her boots held Mist's attention as she waited. What would the cat do now?

A few deep chuffs ruffled her hair, moving back and forth as the saber-tooth scented her. Then a moment of silence rang before a soft purr grew in the cat's chest. When Mist dared raise her gaze her reward came with a gentle headbutt.

All seemed forgiven.

"I suppose you smell Aven on me?" Mist asked cautiously.

The tawny cat cocked its head to the side and whuffed in her face. Was that a yes or a no? Mist couldn't be sure. The lynx harbored a fondness for Aven that her own people should have given. Too bad bitterness and jealousy kept them from seeing what Kali saw. Aven had the potential to be one of the Qinawe's greatest Matriarchs. If only the old shrews didn't fear Tomen's influence.

"Have you seen any Tibri about today?" Mist asked, resting a hand on the cat's furry shoulders. They were almost level with her own. "I need to inquire about transport."

The lynx glanced towards the Eilawi tree before throwing an expectant look at her. So similar to the way Aven communicated in Kali's form. The familiarity had Mist following the cat into the market, trekking between stands, past Tribouin, Qinawe, and griffin, their path aiming for the hollow beneath the tree.

She couldn't help admiring her guide as they went. Kali had been shadowy brown with silvery stripes, perfect for blending into the rich forest. This one's coat must help with hunting outside the canyon, where its golden fur could hide it amongst the rocks and yellow grass. Even when they stepped into the shadows beneath the tree, the warmth of the cat's coat went undimmed.

Roots tumbled like vines from above, glittering with tiny glowstones shoved into their tangles. Like pixies trapped in knots, alighting the shaded world where vendors made expensive trades. Of course, the Tibri would be here.

A knot of lynx and griffin gathered together in their human-forms, standing out thanks to the tails and cat ears on the lynx and the wings and feathers on the griffin. Mist's guide yowled at its pride-mates, who waved clawed hands at the golden cat before returning to their business. The close-knit pride was more like a family, and Mist envied them for that. The dragons stuck together, but their ways were not gentle. Everything revolved around eating, mating, or fighting. Most of which Mist wanted little to do with. Only their proclivity for snoozing the days away in Sansia's light gave her something to do with her kin. Who didn't love a warm, cozy nap?

The sight of the Tibri drew Mist's thoughts from the dragon roost. The short merchant stood on a wooden counter to speak eye to eye with a Tribouin elder. Heated words flew between them, with the Tibri shaking their head repeatedly while the man pointed a finger at them. Mist hung back respectfully, not wanting to eavesdrop on their debate.

She slid her attention to the lynx before patting the cat's shoulder. "Thank you. I could have spent half the day looking."

It chuffed happily before giving her another gentle headbutt.

"I don't want to be rude, but have we met before?"

What looked like a grin stretched across the cat's mouth, revealing a row of sharp teeth. It shook its head, tail whipping back and forth.

"Well, if you're ever around in your other skin, please let me know. Perhaps I can repay your kindness."

The lynx purred as it rubbed its body against hers, its sheer size and strength nearly knocking Mist over. Something she was quite used to since Aven often forgot just how big she was in Kali's form. There was honesty in their ways. Purity. Mist envied their easy affection. Things were so different within the flight. A twist of sadness pulled at her heart when the cat rumbled a goodbye, before trotting back to its pride-mates they had passed on their way.

Now alone, Mist waited for the Tribouin to conclude his business, shifting from one foot to another as she tried not to rush him. If Qinawe were tricky about manners, Tribouin were even worse. Though they would each say it was the other, that was in fact more difficult. How Navya and Tomen ever managed to fall in love when their people were at such odds was a miracle of only Dia'veh's doing.

The elder dressed in their traditional cream-colored cloth that left his arms and calves bare to the warm air. Tribouin gifts were less obvious than other shifters, with most changing things like eye, hair, or skin color. Face-changers, some called them. Color-changers too. Papi had said their gift was more than that; it was adaptation at its finest.

She admired this elder's style, even as he continued to argue with the Tibri. Beaded earrings hung from ears he'd elongated and curved into crescent shapes. The look had Mist touching her own, which she normally shaped into long points from each side of her head so she could fit more space between earrings. Would a shape like his look better than her long ones?

When the Tribouin finally finished his business, he turned and motioned Mist forward. A soft smile graced his weathered features, proving her ruse as one of his people to be effective. An elf would have gotten a respectful dip of the chin. A Qinawe would have gone unacknowledged.

Mist took a step closer before bowing politely. No need to invite questions or conversation. All of them would lead to why she stood alone in the market when most unpromised Tribouin had an escort. Hopefully, her uncovered brow told him she already had a Chosen and no longer needed protection.

He lingered a moment, no doubt thoroughly analyzing her before he walked into the crowd. Mist held the bow until he was gone, and then turned to the Tibri perched on the counter. Only there could he look her in the eye, since on the ground he wouldn't be higher than her knee. He gave her a once over, round catlike face shrewd in his appraisal. Tibri acted as go-betweens for the animal-like Sholi. This one undoubtedly interpreted lynx and griffin's body language, as well as spoke the tongue of the Tribouin, Qinawe, and elves.

"Hey there, missy. What can I do you for?" His nose twitched and Mist had to remind herself that petting a Sholi was not always a welcome thing. "Looking for some more finery? I have all the shine."

Oh, the temptation! Mist toyed with one of her earrings as she focused on why she'd come. "Maybe in the future. For now, I'd like to know about your mount and how far you can go."

He tapped the goggles wrapped around his head. "I have a *Loyara* that helps me ferry goods on and off the island. She's enjoying the Lighe at the moment. I also have Fantuga willing to help me on three continents."

"That's good." Mist rubbed her chin. The loyara could get Aven off the island. They were feathery, winged creatures similar to the horned narwhals she'd read about in books. The fantuga, an enormous, tortoise-like beast, could finish the journey to Estellias. "How far can your loyara go? Can she make it to the shores of Rodawnlia?"

The Tibri whistled. "That's quite a trek."

"I know," Mist said, trying not to flinch at his tone, or the way his hand rested on the fat purse tied to his belt.

Business was obviously good, which meant he didn't need her. That left him with all the power.

"Tell me you're not looking to stop there." His brow furrowed, concern lighting in his brown eyes. "That land's for humans. No place for shifters to settle."

Mist stroked her armlet. "I'd heard rumors about that. Is it not safe there?"

His nose twitched again as he crossed his arms. "I don't stop there. Those humans guard their blessings like a dragon hoards jewels. From what I hear, they do all sorts of tests to ensure no other Sholi enjoys Sholindrea's favor. Getting in is almost as hard as getting out."

Well, that sounded awful—and frightening. Humans were all over Sholindrea. Papi was one of the many, and she'd seen firsthand the Great Mother's gift to them. Humans couldn't shift like dragons or wield elements, but wherever they went, weather calmed, land produced, and animals were more prolific. They were blessed. Sholindrea's favorites. Estellias welcomed them to live peacefully beside the other Sholi, as the first law decreed. Live and let live. A belief born during the Time of Sorrow, when Estellias' founders had been soldiers and refugees needing somewhere to land after the war.

Rodawnlia was to the west of Estellias, where humans went when they tired of fairies toying with their minds, Elementals shaking the earth, and dragon wings leveling cities. It had once been a refuge. Now, who knew?

"What would it cost to bypass Rodawnlia and go all the way to Estellias?"

The tibri stroked his furry chin as he scrutinized her face, her bag, her waist where she noticeably lacked a purse. It took everything Mist had to resist lifting one eyebrow and possibly offending him. She knew too little about Tibri customs.

He cocked his head to the side. "You smell like a fire-breather."

Mist resisted the urge to sniff herself. "A dear friend is a dragon rider."

The tibri grinned, his fuzzy cheeks scrunching up like a cat's. "Now *that* has value."

"How so?"

"Here's a deal for ya." He rubbed his hands together before pointing one round little finger at her. "Get me a dragon for three—no five transports, some long ones, and you'll be on one."

"You ask a heavy price. Dragons are not easily tamed into such things."

"Don't I know it!" He slapped his knee. "I've sweet-talked loyara, fantuga, even a *galgyran* once."

Mist's eyes widened. "A galgyran? Really? How does one even get close to a lizard that eats lightning?"

"Very carefully. They're prickly buggers. Just don't love themselves as much as dragons. Them fire-breathing bats like them high perches. No time for helping us tiny two-leggers."

"They're quite lazy creatures." Mist couldn't deny it, even of herself. She still wished she were back under those sleep furs with Aven.

"They are that," the tibri said. "But you go a-gossiping. Rope in your rider friend. Perhaps *her* dragon, eh?"

Time to tread carefully. Mentioning Aven too soon could end this transaction completely. Tibri were not shifters, but everyone in Yunaii gossiped. The lynx didn't make a fuss, but even some dragons wrinkled their noses over the human blood they smelled in Mist. Some thought it made her too soft and gentle.

"I will see what I can do." Mist could only hope that if she pulled off the Tibri's request, he wouldn't care if Aven showed up as the passenger instead of herself.

"You do that," he said, holding out a hand.

Mist glanced at the four-fingered appendage and held out her own. With more force than she'd expected of him, he slapped her palm.

"*Shalist*! We have a deal."

Mist repeated the word that meant they'd agreed on a trade. "Thank you for your time."

She ambled away, disappointment hovering like a dreary cloud. That was that. She couldn't fathom taking such a request to any of the dragons. Maybe Rielnor would know of one hoping to travel. Perhaps one of the egg-layers had the itch to lay a clutch. They usually left to find other flights and new dragons when the urge hit them.

She would have to think about it later, after shopping and food. Mist sniffed, nostrils flaring as she scented for something appetizing. A few deep breaths told her meat was cooking somewhere off to her left, and to her right something sugary beckoned to her growling stomach. In the end her sweet tooth could not outdo the urge to devour sizzling meat.

She passed lynx and a few Qinawe along her way, but a Linseen patrol made her pause. The elves marched in perfect formation, one in front, followed by three sets of two, each holding a curved scimitar in one hand and a round shield on the opposite arm. Their calm manner and slow pace didn't make their presence any less unnerving. Linseen patrolled when they were looking for something. They safeguarded peace; they didn't enforce it. The Linseen soldier, Zoli, had said his commander would be concerned about what happened last night, but she didn't expect that to result in soldiers scouring the market. Were they looking for dragons? Or something else?

Mist shivered as she thought of Dia'veh's warning. Surely it had been about the fight between Aven and Fennicks.

Elves served the Creator, and the Linseen could sense when the peace they protected was threatened. Illieve elves, like the Truthseeker, granted protection and justice, Klesian elves, like Dev, guarded warriors when they could no longer protect themselves, and Linseen elves brought peace to Sholindrea by whatever means necessary.

One Linseen meant nothing. They shopped. They socialized. But a patrol of them in the market—that had everyone nearby eyeing the elves nervously. Mist sniffed as they passed. Their scents reminded her of a horse as it prepared to run. Anticipation jittered through them as their eyes skimmed over faces they passed. Despite that, the hands on their scimitars remained loose. Ready, but not worried. Hopefully, they were just being cautious.

Another shiver slid down her spine as they moved away. *Time to finish shopping.* Mist turned her nose back to the sky and sniffed out the meat once more. She could knock out breakfast for herself and Aven's family, as well as procure whatever the trader had cured and ready to sell.

She wove through the ever-growing crowd, led by the strengthening smells wafting through the air. Eventually she found a tent set up away from the rest, its open flap allowing the most delectable scents to drift out. Mist's belly growled in response, earning a laugh from a passerby. Heat seared her cheeks at the sound, so she quickly ducked inside to hide her embarrassment.

Salted and dried game sat on shelves to her left and right, while the back of the tent opened to a large fire pit. Canvas walls enclosed the cooking space, no doubt to keep sneaky fingers from stealing bites of the morning's catch, something Mist's mouth watered at the thought of doing. The smell of pepper and spices accompanied the sight of a fresh boar turning on a spit, while bundles of wide leaves lay near the embers, no doubt wrapped around smaller cuts of meat.

A pair of lynx bustled about, their humanlike appearance thrown off by their large, catlike feet, swishing tails, and triangular ears sticking out from the sides of their heads. A reddish fuzz accented the female's creamy-colored hair, while her male companion had a tousle of black waves, a tangled beard, and gray fur over his arms, chest, and legs.

Mist should have known the smells she'd followed were coming from them. Nodi and Rymia didn't come to the market often, but when they did, Mist always bought something from them. The trick was finding their stand. It popped up all over the place. First come, first serve when it came to space in the market.

Rymia flashed sharp canines in a feline grin when she noticed Mist. "Mornin' there, cub! What can we help you with?"

"Breakfast," Mist mumbled, barely tearing her gaze from the roasting pig.

"Come, come," Nodi chuckled and waved Mist forward. "You look like one of the firebreathers before they pounce."

"Sorry." Mist swallowed hard. Hunger had fought back her manners. This wasn't the roost where she could grab her prey and feast. "It's been a long morning."

"Don't worry, cub, I know the feeling." Nodi crouched by the fire and pulled one bundle of leaves from the embers with the tips of his claws.

"I forget myself in work sometimes," Rymia said. "Then the hunger hits and I have to remember to sniff before I hunt. Scared a good number of Qinawe thinking they were prey."

Mist snickered at the thought of a Qinawe in rabbit form, finding themself hunted by a sabertooth cat as tall as a person. What a sight it would be to see the Matriarchs scurrying about in fear. She'd have to tell Aven when she got back.

"Is this all you'll need?" Nodi offered her the leaf-wrapped bundle.

"No," Mist said. "But—"

Rymia elbowed her pride-mate. "Let her eat. The cub's practically drooling."

They hurried off to help another customer, leaving Mist to unwrap her food with trembling fingers. Inside was a handful of spicy meat patties, triangles of soft flatbread, and warmed fruit the lynx must have picked off the prickly water plants outside the canyon. Juice from the patties coated the bread and fruit, giving each bite a flash of salty sweetness. Mist devoured the meat, then dredged her bread through the juice before enjoying the achingly sweet bites of green fruit.

She'd begun licking dribbles from her fingers when the warmth of another body moved up behind her. The other customer, most likely. Mist immediately drew her tongue back between her lips as heat seared her cheeks. She'd just been caught acting no better than a satisfied house cat. Certainly not the right look for a Tribouin girl. The stranger's stare weighed heavier than a lynx on her chest, and all Mist could hope was that it was a Qinawe studying her and not a Tribouin elder.

Too afraid to look, Mist sidled over to where Rymia chopped meat with a cleaver the size of her head.

"Feel better, cub?"

"Much," Mist answered. "Thank you."

The lynx's yellow eyes sparkled, her pert nose crinkling. "Anytime. What else will you be needing?"

Mist considered the stock on the shelves as she counted on her fingertips. "I could use about four- or five-days' worth of salted pork and maybe a sack of the fruit if you can spare it."

"I think we can." Rymia pulled aside a few sacks laid against the tent's canvas wall, her gaze assessing. "Anything else?"

"I wouldn't turn down a handful of the jerky too."

"You going away for a spell?"

Mist shook her head. "No. Staying in, actually. Just need some time away from all this."

"But it's so lovely here," said a voice behind Mist. "Why ever would you need a break from such a homey place?"

The customer who had caught her licking her fingers stepped beside Mist, his hood still pulled up. It hid all but a thin, pointed nose from sight. That had to be stifling for him. Beads of sweat formed on Mist's brow just from being inside the tent.

"It's just nice to slow down sometimes." Icy chill nipped Mist's fingertips, warning her to step away. The stranger had to be hiding their face for a reason, but his scent revealed nothing. No smell of leather or fire. Just a coppery tang underlaid by a hint of smoke. Not Fennicks, but perhaps another elder dragon had a bone to pick with her. "Are you new to Yunaii?"

"Yes. I've only just arrived," he said, dropping his hood.

His slate gray face matched the crushing mountain stones that tumbled from the cliffs. Cold, sharp, and just as deadly. White triangles were painted across his angular jaw and cheek bones, as if meant to mimic the unpredictable force of nature, and his night black hair was held in a knot by a sliver of sharpened metal.

Time slowed as the urge to swipe the weapon from his hair flashed through Mist. She should cut his throat. End things before they began.

"Soulless!" Mist hissed.

A smile pulled across his face, flashing a bit of fang just before his cool fingers wrapped around her throat. The touch burned, searing her skin and choking off her scream. Panic blanketed her thoughts as he hauled her off her feet. She tried to kick and tear at his arms, willing claws from her fingernails that didn't come.

By the Creator, this couldn't be happening. How? Why? Of all the things Dia'veh's warning could have been about, she never dreamed it would be the Soulless coming to Yunaii. It wasn't possible.

Yet somehow, the monsters from the Time of Sorrow and the enemies of the Elementals had found her.

CHAPTER *Ten*

Mist

*R*ymia launched over the counter with a screech, claws slashing for the Soulless' throat. He didn't even blink. One arm swiped through the air as he stared into Mist's eyes. A blade sung, flesh squelched, and blood splattered across his face.

Mist clawed at the fingers around her throat. She wanted the sweet lynx with the adorably pert nose to still live, but she knew better. Rymia had collapsed at the Soulless' feet with a few gut-wrenching thumps.

An angry yowl made Mist's captor turn, just as another Soulless impaled Nodi. Mist stared at the undulating, black weapon stuck into the lynx's chest. How had everything gone so wrong so fast?

When the Soulless released the blade, it wisped away, leaving a gaping blotch of red and open flesh. Tears blurred Mist's vision as Nodi gurgled, the light going out in his eyes.

Moments ago, he'd been laughing.

"Well done, boys," said a woman. "Let me see our prize."

The Soulless' arm tensed before he tossed Mist like a sack of feathers. She tried bracing. She tried curling into a ball. Anything to save herself, but her temple still slammed against the ground with an awful crack. Darkness crept around the edge of her wobbly vision and warmth pooled beneath her cheek. Wet. Coppery. *Not good.* It took all her strength to push onto all fours, blood dripping from her head, pain lancing through her shoulder and kneecap.

"It's just a hatchling." The woman sounded disappointed. "I'd hoped for a challenge.

"You know how they are about their young, Ukila," said the Soulless who'd thrown Mist. "If we make a good show of it, we might lure the flight leader to us."

"You're—wasting—your time." Mist's raw and ravaged throat barely pushed the words out. "They won't come for me."

The woman's black boots stepped into view before she crouched, her fingers delving into Mist's hair. A gentle stroke slid over her sensitive scalp, eliciting a horrified shiver. She tried jerking away, but the touch immediately turned harsh. Nails scraped into skin and Mist's head wrenched back. A wail of pain caught behind her teeth, contained by biting into her bottom lip. They wouldn't get the satisfaction, not even when the pale face came into focus, the Soulless' black eyes round and slanted.

Summoner—a commander of corpses.

"Poor baby dragon." The Summoner's gaze roamed over Mist. "You'll do nicely. Pretty face like that, once we're done the whole flight won't stomach the sight of you."

Mist gritted her teeth. "They're not that easy to bait."

"I guess we'll find out. Well, I will. You'll be dead."

Fear curdled Mist's breakfast. She needed to fight. To do something. Images swam behind her eyes, claws and feathers, wings to carry her away, but they wouldn't come. Her focus went in and out, fractured by the throbbing in her temple.

As if she'd read her thoughts, the Summoner slammed Mist's head against the ground, once, twice, then let her go. Spots danced behind her eyelids as the metallic tang of blood coated her tongue.

"Do we do it here, Ukila?" The other Soulless asked, the one who'd killed Nodi with shadow.

The Summoner, Ukila, kicked Mist hard, the toe of her boot digging into her ribs. The force sent her flopping onto her back, clutching at the searing pain in her chest.

This was it. Mist was going to die here. After the flight from Estellias, over Rodawnlia and an entire ocean, she would die from one of the dangers she had fled from. At least they'd come for her here, in the market. Better than them tracking her to Aven's cave.

Mist drew in a shallow breath, gasping at the pain it caused. One of her ribs was broken, for sure.

"What do you think, little one?" Ukila asked. "Do you want a quick death?"

All three of them stood over her. The Summoner, with her bone-white face. The Shadow, with skin black as night, and white angular markings. Then what she guessed was their Mimic, with the gray face. Whatever they were doing here, they had come in force. She had never actually seen all three gathered together before.

After another shaky attempt at breathing, Mist imagined Aven's raging face when she'd attacked Fennicks. *She* wouldn't lay down and die. She wouldn't beg.

Mist turned her head and spat blood on Ukila's boot.

One corner of the Summoner's mouth curved as her companions chuckled.

"I love baby dragons," the Mimic said. "They're so spunky."

The Shadow rubbed his hands together. "Let's get her out of here so we can play a while."

"Let's not," someone hissed from behind the Soulless. Her pitch and tone were so familiar Mist could have cried.

A blade slid against its sheath, and blood splattered. Mist instinctively curled into a ball as the Mimic's head fell towards her, followed by his decapitated body.

Horror twisted Ukila's face as she tracked the Mimic's collapse. Beside her, the Shadow summoned his blade of shifting darkness. The way he reached for the Summoner seemed almost too kind. Too protective. It warred with the monsters who had killed Nodi and Rymia in cold blood.

"Let the hatchling go," the newcomer said. "I'm a lot more fun to play with."

Mist ignored the throbbing pain in her chest to push up onto her knees. That voice. It couldn't possibly be—"Em?"

Her sister's blood-red lips pulled into a luscious smirk as she tossed her bright orange hair. "Don't I just have the best timing?"

"How?"

Emriel stepped closer, one dagger aimed at each Soulless. "Not now, bloodkin. On your feet. It's time for you to scoot."

"You're only buying the little one time." Rage simmered in Ukila's voice. "I'm going to eviscerate you for killing him and use your bones to light his pyre."

"Sounds fun." Emriel looked her up and down with lowered eyelids. "Let's make it a date."

Mist chanced a glance at the Soulless as she struggled to rise. The Shadow circled them, trying to block their exit while his companion played the distraction.

"Em."

Emriel's gaze never left Ukila, but her arm slashed through the air and a howl of pain ripped from the Shadow. When Mist looked, her sister's blade was buried hilt-deep in his shoulder.

"Go Mist. Now."

Mist tried, but the best she managed was a shuffle across the dusty floor, towards the sliver of light peeking between the tent flaps. She'd almost made it when the Shadow stepped out of a flicker of black like it was a doorway. His blades arced towards her, sending Mist stumbling back into Emriel.

Her sister didn't miss a beat. One hand wrapped around Mist's midsection, pushing her to the side as the dagger in her left hand whirled to meet the attack. They spun together, bringing Mist face to face with Ukila, whose lips pulled into a freakishly wide grin, baring all her teeth.

"You're going to die," Mist hissed, planting her feet. She couldn't beat the Summoner, but she could shield Emriel long enough for her to finish the Shadow. At least one of them could get out of this alive.

"I'll gladly take you as my dance partner, hatchling."

Ukila lunged, elbow aiming for Mist's chest. Only instinct saved her, the urge to live stronger than the pain in her knee and chest. She sidestepped, though not as smoothly as she'd been taught. The Summoner's hands latched around her arm, wrenching Mist into swinging range. Only memories of Papi's voice kept her will from melting. As Ukila reared back for a skull-crushing punch, Mist grabbed her trapped hand and yanked, popping her elbow up into the Summoner's chin.

"Cute," Ukila said through clenched, bloody teeth.

"Turnabout and all that." Mist edged away from her. "Shouldn't sucker punch people."

"You're right. We should have just slit your throat."

"Good idea!" Emriel shouted, wheeling around with the Shadow's collar gripped in her fist. She'd yanked her dagger from his shoulder, leaving the wound gaping and gushing. Em paused to lock eyes with Ukila as she raised one blade to his throat and sliced.

"NO!" The Summoner rushed forward with tears sliding down her cheeks. As if expecting just that, Em kicked the Shadow, sending him careening into Ukila.

"Go!" Emriel said, shoving Mist towards the exit.

She shuffled beside her sister, knee and hip pulsing with each step. The tent flap stood half a ways away when her leg buckled and she nearly fell. The light from outside felt impossible to reach.

A frustrated sound slid from Emriel's lips just before she wedged beneath Mist's arm. "Move it, bloodkin. She's already working her ritual."

Ritual? Mist looked back, but Emriel hauled them through the tent flap. Sansia blazed, her light scorching. Mist blinked rapidly, stumbling into the market, bumping into bodies half blotted out by black spots. People's frustrated grumbles turned to shrieks of horror as they most likely noticed the blood soaked into her clothes and streaked across her face. Calls for the Linseen rang through the air and soon a wall of bodies blocked Mist's flight.

"You all need to run," Emriel yelled. "Go! Before it's too late."

But it already was. The Summoner sauntered from the tent, hands raised to the sky, both of them coated in blood.

The black of her eyes had overtaken the white as her lips moved silently. Her head lolled back, a look of ecstasy slipping across her face. A moment later, the tent flap lifted again and screams filled the air. The decapitated body of the Mimic wobbled into the market, followed by the Shadow with his cut throat. Nodi and Rymia were next, with his chest sliced open and half her torso missing. They stumbled around like puppets being jerked along on strings.

Mist covered her mouth as her breakfast rose in her throat. It was true. Summoners could actually raise the dead. Part of her hoped it was just a horror story the villagers back home used to scare children.

"Run!" Emriel affixed herself between the dead and the surrounding shifters.

Mist shook her head. "You can't beat that."

"Easier than putting a dragon kit to bed." Emriel raised her daggers, the excitement in her eyes almost as frightening as the corpses staggering around. "As long as all these lookie-loos get their asses out of the way."

Mist took stock of the horrified Qinawe and Tribouin nearby. Nothing like this had ever come to Yunaii. The Soulless hadn't bothered with anyone but the Elementals since they'd been driven back to Perdiohl. Estellias hadn't just been a sanctuary to any Sholi. It was once the closest established city to the Soulless' island home and was now one of the first lines of defense.

Only here and now, there were no Elementals to protect Yunaii's shifters. No armies. Just two daughters of Estellias raised on tales of horror and fear.

Mist had to do something. Save someone. She waved a hand at the nearest Tribouin, letting childhood fears twist her voice. "Go! Run. She'll kill us all."

The Tribouin blinked, a dazed look shadowing his eyes. It took a shove to knock him back to the present. He rubbed the spot Mist had touched and turned to flee, opening the floodgates. A few women shrieked, joined by a chorus of panicked voices and rushing bodies. The market exploded in pushing and shoving towards the three bridges.

Through the chaos came the Linseen patrol, headed up by Zoli the elf who'd spoken with Aven the night before. He led his people with their shields raised and scimitars at the ready. At their sides were two griffins with talons the size of a person's head, along with three lynx. Heart-wrenching yowls rumbled from the cats as Nodi and Rymia stumbled forward with claws extended.

"Release your power and surrender," commanded Zoli. All his warmth and kindness had been replaced by steely eyes and lines of anger on his dark face.

Ukila bared her teeth as her fingers twitched like snakes about to strike. Slowly the Mimic's arms lifted, his dead hands shifting around and around as if a ball hovered in front of his chest. The more they circled, the more the Summoner's fingers jerked, until fire sparked between the Mimic's palms.

"Go, Mist," Emriel hissed. "You're no use in this fight."

"But—" Mist swayed, her vision still unfocused.

Fire lashed at the elves' shields and Emriel cursed before throwing herself into its path. Her body arced like a dancer's on a stage. Elegant, but deadly. The momentum sliced her arms through the flames, cutting it short with the Elemental energy forming her soul. Then she landed on tiptoes, whirling once to draw in the last of the fire, all before she launched straight for the Mimic's headless corpse.

The Linseen sprinted after her. A few shouted a battle cry as they veered for the Shadow's body.

"Cut them to pieces!" Mist screamed. That's what Eega taught her. "Leave nothing for her to use."

The lynx looked between Mist and their dead pride-mates. The pain in their eyes hurt more than the wounds the Soulless had inflicted. Mist shook her head, wishing there was more she could do. "Don't let her use them."

The largest of the lynx growled as he shook his golden mane. With a commanding yowl at the smaller cats, he charged for Nodi, hesitating only a moment before setting upon the corpse. Together, the three of them pulled their pride-mate apart, forcing Mist to look away.

She caught a blast of dust in her face as the griffin launched into the air. Tears leaked from her eyes as she coughed, and by the time her vision cleared, the flying creatures circled like eagles preparing to dive. An urge to join them slithered through her aching bones. She was more dangerous with claws and teeth, but there was nowhere she could shift without being seen.

Helplessness gnawed at her as she looked for a way to help.

The Summoner lingered near the tent, working her fingers back and forth, whispering commands to her dead comrades. Her eyes locked on Mist, malice gleaming in her gaze. A nightmare come to life with blood smeared and spattered like war paint.

She slunk forward, protected by the attacks she pulled from the dead Soulless. A jerk of her wrist had the Shadow drawing weapons from the air. Elves descended on him, but Ukila kept her hands moving, jerking the Shadow into dodging and deflecting their blows. The Linseen slashed at him, but even when their curved weapons cut deep, he didn't stop. With jerky precision, Ukila moved her puppet through the fray, hacking at the elves without mercy. When one of his shadowy blades tore through a Linseen's armor, her scream caused a momentary pause in the madness. Heartbreak etched across Zoli's face as his companion went down, her back sliced open by shadow.

Across the market, the headless Mimic kept Emriel engaged. Icy water whips lashed out, leaving cuts and welts in their wake. She danced between the attacks, her lithe body slipping around, drawing closer and closer with every leap and twirl. The lynx darted back and forth, getting close enough to draw the strikes, only to pull back when one hit its mark.

Ukila smiled as she drew closer. No one stood in her way. No one could get close enough. Mist glanced from market stand to market stand, searching for something, anything, she could use as a weapon. She would not lay down and die for the Soulless. There had to be some way to end this fight before anyone else died.

"Poor hatchling," the Summoner said. "Come, come. Why don't you show me what your claws can do?"

Mist narrowed her eyes. She wouldn't give in to goading.

"Your kin made your death much sweeter." Ukila drew closer, almost within reach of a sword. If only Mist had one. "I'll enjoy dismembering you like she did my brothers."

Mist took a step back and a hiss slid over her clenched teeth. Every move blazed with bone-chilling fire. Her body had never been so spent. She searched for the itch to shift, but the power slipped through her fingers no matter how she grasped at it. Not that it would save her. If she fought as a dragon now, the others would punish her for revealing the secret later. Too many eyes watched this fight. There was nothing left to do but stand her ground and buy Emriel time.

"Mist!" her sister screamed from somewhere to her left, but she didn't take her eyes off the approaching Soulless. Death would follow if she did. Instead, she drew a deep breath, bent her throbbing knees, and forced claws out of her fingernails. Pain thudded through her head, but her body yielded, her nails lengthening to razor sharp points.

"I'm not—I'm not afraid to die."

The Summoner smiled. "Good. Come into my realm."

Mist's arms laid heavy against her sides as her heartbeat pounded in her skull. She strained to raise her hands enough to fend off attacks. It would have to be enough. The distraction could help Emriel end the Mimic a second time. It could allow the griffin room enough to attack.

"I'd heard your kind worshiped death." Mist breathed through the ache in her temple. "Did your brothers know they were better off dead to you?"

"How dare you?" Ukila's face twisted with rage as her fingers twitched.

Air blasted Mist's chest from the direction of the Mimic. She soared backwards, unable to brace as the ground rushed towards her. Breath whooshed from her lungs when she slammed against rocks and tree roots that bit into her skin. She gasped once, twice, clutching at her chest until a weak gulp filled her lungs.

A shadow fell over her face as Ukila raised a triangular blade above Mist's chest, her black eyes simmering. "I'll use your corpse to finish your kin."

Mist wanted to fight, but her body didn't respond. She tried rolling, kicking. *Something.* From somewhere distant, Emriel screamed her name. It took everything she had to seek her sister's eyes. Emriel stood trapped in a cyclone of sharp rocks, bleeding welts sliced across her pale skin. Her eyes were panicked as she pushed through the tiny missiles, taking more damage than even she could handle. Mist smiled weakly, wishing she could reassure her sister. She had to know this wasn't her fault.

Mist's smile dropped as yellow flooded Emriel's blue eyes. She couldn't. She wouldn't! Rielnor's first law: dragons couldn't shift in front of others.

But Emriel didn't know. She was from Estellias, where dragons lived free.

Claws burst from black painted nails. Her clothes and skin melded into feathers as wings exploded from her back. She dropped to her knees, body growing, forcing the lynx to leap away.

"No, Em," Mist whispered. Not in front of them. Not where the shifters could see.

In a few blinks, a dragon's body hurled towards Ukila, ruby plumage flashing in the sun. Her jaw hung open, ready to snatch up the Summoner in a mouth full of fangs.

Ukila was ready for her. Shadows shifted and her brother's corpse stepped through her place. She sent him charging towards Emriel as she vanished into the pathway his power created. Mist could barely understand what she'd seen before her sister slammed into the dead Soulless. With a sickening crunch, she grasped his head and shoulders in her mouth before shaking him back and forth. His legs waved through the air like the wings of a bird trapped in a cat's mouth, before Emriel bit down with a bone-shattering chomp. Mist cringed at the shower of chunky blood and body parts raining down around her.

Emriel veered with a deafening roar and launched at the Mimic. Linseen scattered, lynx yowled. No one came between the ruby dragon and her prey. Emriel's talons came down on his headless body, pinning his arms before her mouth found dead flesh.

All around, the Linseen, lynx, and griffin stared. From across the river, even more eyes watched the dragon lift her blood-covered head to search for the last of the Soulless.

Only, Ukila was long gone.

With a pained groan, Mist rolled over and forced herself up. Everything ached, but she couldn't just lay on the ground. There wasn't time. Soon word would spread and questions would come. Then the flight would descend upon Emriel. Seeking vengeance. Mist had only one chance of saving her sister from Rielnor and Fennicks, from all the elders who would want her blood.

The ground shook as two clawed red feet stepped into view. Mist crawled towards them, but her body wasn't working like it should. Just sliding her knee across the ground was like wading through mud. Her muscles resisted even the tiniest movements. She would not make it. Spots danced in and out of her vision. She would pass out before warning Em.

Mist lifted a trembling hand, desperately fighting to stay awake. She almost sobbed when Emriel's soft snout slid beneath her palm.

It took all Mist's strength to grab her sister's head. Her fingers would barely make a fist anymore. She did it though, clutching every bit of downy feathers she could hold. As if realizing how much she struggled, Emriel nudged her face beneath Mist's torso and brought them eye to eye.

"We need to get to the Temple," Mist whispered. "Now!"

Emriel blinked twice, then nodded in understanding.

CHAPTER *Eleven*

Aven

For the first time in Aven's life, she threw aside manners and politeness. Yunaii's shapeshifters stood between her and Mist. They'd get no scraping and bowing today. Bodies pressed together beneath the Eilawi tree, the stink of sweat and death hanging in the air. She could hardly stand it. Only the thought of Mist lying hurt in the Temple kept her slipping beneath arms and shoving between those huddled together, ducking her head whenever someone complained. Maybe in their panic, they wouldn't remember.

Even worse than the smell was the noise. Not even the dragon races brought about such a shrill, awful commotion. People shouted over each other, demanding answers of the Linseen commander and his squad standing before the Temple entrance. The Truthseeker accompanied them, waving his hands in a request for silence, only for more questions to be slung at him.

"There were Soulless! Soulless! In Yunaii!"

"That girl shifted into a dragon!"

"Has a dragon chosen a Qinawe as a soul guard?"

"Are we safe? One of the Soulless got away!"

Terror fouled the air, clinging to people worse than a hard day's labor. Kali's soul latched onto the tang, bringing out the urge to hunt, but Aven shoved the desire down. These were her people and neighbors. They were not prey… until one of them clamped onto Aven's wrist. She growled deep in her throat, instincts screaming for her to bite and slash. Clawed fingers clamped onto whoever dared such a touch as Aven whirled upon them. Ready to fight.

Only instead of a cranky Elder or disapproving Matriarch, she found Pryn's wide, terrified eyes. With a silent tug, the other girl pulled Aven away from the elves, pushing past everyone until they broke free of the shoving bodies.

Aven followed, breathing hard as she went through all the things Pryn would want to talk about. The dragon in the market? Mist? Had she heard about her fight with Fennicks? Aven could at least trust Pryn wouldn't tattle about that last one. Probably. Things were awkward between them, but Pryn couldn't want her exiled. Could she? Things had ended badly between them because Pryn tried to make Aven *stay* in Yunaii.

They veered toward a side wall of the Temple, where Pryn spun around to fix Aven with a scowl. No gold shimmered in her eyes today. They were dark as tarnished copper, her pupils round as saucers.

"Did you know?"

Aven blinked. "Know what?"

Pryn pursed her lips, brows drawing into an even deeper frown. "Don't, Aven. Don't play the fool. Not today. Not with me."

"I don't know what you're asking, Pryn. Maybe if you wouldn't dance around everything you have to say—"

Hurt flashed through Pryn's eyes as her bottom lip trembled. "Did you know the dragons were shifters?"

Aven cursed in her head. *Of course. She just wants the gossip.*

No. Aven shook away the thought. Pryn had her own stake in it. Being a rider put her in danger. What would happen if Rielnor found out Aven ran her mouth? Would he come for her? For her parents? Would Fennicks just dump Pryn one day in mid-flight? She wasn't sure what they were capable of or how they wanted to handle this mess.

"Don't lie." Pryn crossed her arms. "I know you well enough to know when you're lying."

"You never knew me 'well enough'," Aven muttered.

"This is no time for petulance!" Gone was the confident rider. In her place was a girl Aven didn't recognize. "Honestly, don't you know what this could bring? My people are scared, angry, confused. I'm sure yours are too."

"Why are you assuming it wasn't just a Qinawe guarding a dragon's soul?"

Pryn rolled her eyes. "Because I'm smarter than that. I was there when Kali chose you to guard her soul."

"I don't th—"

Pryn waved a hand, looking angrier with every word Aven spoke. "I know what it means for a Sholi to give their soul instead of moving on to their peace. And I remember the fit the Matriarchs threw when Kali chose you instead of one of them or their cubs."

Aven sighed. Pryn was right. The day the lynx pride leader had come, weak and listless, her kin hovering nearby, all eyes had been on Aven. Kali had pressed her soft, wet nose to her little forehead and just breathed, her soft inhales and exhales so calming. Welcoming. Even as a child, Aven hadn't been afraid.

When Kali's faded yellow eyes had slipped shut, the other lynx roared their grief. Then, with the help of a shifted lynx and Mama's strong hands, they took a fang from Kali's mouth, drew blood from both her and Aven, and painstakingly carved the base of the tooth into a likeness of Kali sitting on her hindquarters. When the tooth had been laid in Aven's hand, Kali's soul called out to her.

Sholi rarely chose a soul guard. It meant lingering instead of moving on to the place of peace Dia'veh made for them. It was a responsibility rarely entrusted to a child.

A nameless outcast was *never* the recipient of such a gift.

"If a Qinawe had been gifted the soul of a dragon, *everyone* in Yunaii would have heard about it," Pryn said. "The Matriarchs would have shouted it from the cliffs."

"Maybe this Qinawe isn't from Yunaii."

"Maybe." Pryn looked at her like she'd just said the sky was green. "And maybe if I wasn't a dragon rider I would buy the lie, but I spend enough time around them to have noticed things."

"Things?"

"Just details probably even Fennicks doesn't notice. Scales are different sometimes, saddle straps won't fit even though they did that very same morning. As if Fennicks had shrunk or grown in the span of a day. It never made sense. Plus, I never see Feather when you're with that Mist, and they both have the same eye color."

"That's it?" Aven laughed. "That's not evidence, just proof that a jealous little girl can't keep up with her gear."

Splotches of red flared in Pryn's cheeks and eyes. "At least now I know you didn't dump me for a different Tribouin."

Aven's breath caught in her throat as heat flashed up her neck. "I didn't."

"It must have been thrilling, trading up from a boring shifter like me for a *dragon*."

"Mist has *nothing* to do with why we're not together anymore. *You* know that."

Pryn's eyes narrowed, but she didn't argue. Instead, she ran a hand through her long, black hair, her eyes fixing on the Temple. "I suppose you'll say next that there's nothing going on between you two."

"Now you're just prying." Aven turned away. This conversation was over. There were more important things to worry about than her ex's wounded pride.

"I think I have a little right," Pryn muttered.

Aven spun back around. "No, you don't. I might have ended things, but *you* gave me no choice."

Pryn blinked rapidly, and Aven's shoulders dropped at the sight of tears pooling in her eyes.

"I was trying to help you."

"Your help was a cage, Pryn." Aven took a step closer, her skin burning hotter with every word. "If you still don't see that then there's nothing left to talk about."

Aven hurried away from whatever look crossed her once best friend's face. She walked along the walls, searching for an open window or door into the Temple, trying not to think about Pryn. The pain and anger between them got worse any time they spoke. It didn't help when Aven always said all the wrong things. She didn't want to hurt Pryn, no matter how badly she'd betrayed her, but that's always what she ended up doing. Her temper would flare and the next thing she knew, Pryn was crying and Aven was ready to fly off on another rant about all the things wrong with her life. It got neither of them anywhere and kept all the hurt alive.

She needed to stop thinking about it. There was no way to undo Pryn's mating challenge. It would have given Aven an unwelcome place amongst the Tribouin, and no escape from Yunaii. The future was all she could affect, and that future included Mist. Aven just had to get to her. Rumor was, she'd been carried into the Temple because of some horrible injuries. Hopefully, the Priestess tended to her, but she wouldn't know until she got inside.

"Ho! Stop there!"

Aven froze, muscles tensing as she turned towards the voice. She had no patience for any more surprises; her every nerve felt on the edge of snapping.

Two Linseen jogged towards her, their weapons sheathed and shield arms relaxed. Despite that, Aven stayed tense, her knees bent and arms held out to her sides. She'd pounce if she had to. Perhaps leaving her hatchet at home had been a mistake. She hadn't wanted to send the wrong message to the Matriarchs, but now she wasn't sure it mattered.

"Is something wrong?" Aven asked.

The first elf looked at her like he thought she might shift into a Soulless. "Where are you sneaking off to?"

"The Priestess has asked for privacy," the second elf explained. "The injured need tending, not gawking eyes and an interrogation."

"The injured are why I'm here." Aven held up her hands at the sour look she received. "It's not like that! I know someone hurt in the battle with the Soulless. I need to know if she's okay."

The first elf gave her a suspicious glance. "A likely story."

"Please. I can wait here. I just need to know if Mist is alive." Aven clasped her hands together, not above begging if it would get her inside. "She's the girl with the white hair. The Soulless attacked her. Please. I heard she was badly hurt."

The two Linseen looked at each other, and eventually the second one nodded. "Come with us. We'll see if your story checks out."

They led Aven back towards the Temple's entrance, where the crowd still lingered. Their shouts had died down, allowing the Truthseeker to speak. He pointed at one shifter at a time, letting them take a turn asking a question. Aven considered staying to hear how much the Truth elf revealed with direct questions being asked. He danced a fine line of knowing most shifter's secrets, keeping those secrets, while also not lying when specifically asked about something. It was an art Aven had never learned, that's for sure.

"Wait here." One of the Linseen jogged over to the commander at the Truthseeker's side, who Zoli had said was named Senwe. He was an interesting man. Tall, bald, with skin so dark and cool it reflected the sun's light in blues and purples. Where Zoli and Dev had a soldier's build, Senwe's shoulders were thinner, and he stood a head shorter than the Truthseeker. Despite his stature, his soldiers regarded him with respect, their posture perfect, with eyes downcast.

Senwe listened to his subordinates' whispers, then looked at Aven with piercing eyes. She stared back, willing him to remember whatever report Zoli had given. Had he been told her name? Did they catch Mist's at all? Aven held her breath, hoping he would help her. When Senwe gave a curt nod, she expelled it with a loud, relieved sigh.

The Linseen guard bowed his head before returning to Aven and his comrade.

"Come. Mist is inside."

Relief's cold splash washed through Aven. She didn't know what she would have done if they turned her away. Break in? Fight through the elves? She couldn't imagine how that would go.

They slipped through the archway of the Temple, their retreat bringing on another wave of shouting. Aven was certain at least a few people screamed about the nameless getting to go inside. The urge to throw an obscene gesture had her nearly turning around, but the scent of Mist's blood stopped her. Aven broke into a run, dashing through the short stone corridor leading into the main chamber of the Temple.

Once inside, her nose faced an assault of rancid copper. Mist's blood. Elven blood. And at least one other dragon. Death lingered in the air, its rot so strong Aven nearly gagged.

Please don't be Mist, Aven prayed. *Not Mist. Dia'veh, I'll do anything.*

A squad of weary looking elves sat around the pool at the center of the room. Aven approached as quietly as she could, afraid to draw even one eye to her. All of their attention locked on three mats laid on the floor, occupied by Linseen. One had a gaping slash through her arm. Another's thigh was split almost down to the bone, and a horrid burn seared the forearm on his other side. The final was the source of death's stench.

A woman lay unmoving on her stomach, her back split wide open. Muscle and bone had been sheared straight through, stretching from shoulder to hip. Black liquid pooled everywhere, and it took Aven a moment to realize it was blood. She'd seen it that dark from prey on her hunts, but never from a Sholi. Never an elf or shifter. Priestess Ifera knelt at the dying elf's side, whispering prayers as she cleaned the wound, while Zoli knelt on the other side, his face contorted with pain. Piles of linens littered the stone floor, all stained with gore. Neither spared Aven a glance. Zoli watched his dying comrade like one blink would bring her end, while the Priestess locked solely on her task. As if prayer and salve could heal such a thing.

Aven glanced around, her throat tightening when she didn't find Mist amongst the elves.

Where—?

Just as panic muddled her head, a pile of cushions near the back of the Temple caught her attention. A young woman with bright orange hair knelt beside them, dabbing a wet cloth across Mist's snowy crown.

Aven dashed towards them, desperately sniffing out the severity of Mist's injuries. Before she could get close, though, the orange-haired woman stood, eyes shifting to amber, her blood-red lips peeling back in a silent snarl. Her fists curled at her sides, claws ready to come out, even though she had two daggers sheathed at her waist.

Aven skidded to a halt and scented the air. Smoke clung to the stranger, along with an odd saltiness she'd never encountered before.

This had to be the dragon. The one who shifted in the market.

"Who let you in here?" the woman asked. She was lean for a fighter, but muscle curved around her bare forearms and beneath her tight, leather pants. An interesting clothing choice for a shifter. Most in Yunaii wore loose, flowing garments that were easily removed.

"The Linseen." Aven eyed Mist, straining for a glimpse of her wounds. "Please. I'm her friend."

The woman arched a perfectly curved brow. "She'll have no friends once this is over."

"She'll have me," Aven snapped, welcoming the familiar buzz of anger. "Who in the torment are you?"

Tension eased from the woman's posture as she brushed shoulder length hair from her face. "I'm her sister. Who in the Creator's name are you?"

"Stop it, Em," Mist croaked, pulling a trembling arm over her face. "Aven is my friend."

The dragon's gaze dragged over Aven as if she were food, her predatory eyes a wash of yellow with slitted black pupils.

"Em!"

With a flare of her nostrils, Mist's sister flopped onto an empty cushion with a childish huff. If that was the best Aven would get, then she'd take it. She donned pettiness like armor, indulging a triumphant smirk as she went to Mist's side.

Dried blood matted her hair and the skin of her forehead, while scrapes and tears left Mist's arms, legs, and clothes a tattered mess, as if she'd been tossed around like a toy.

Aven wove their fingers together, reveling in the cool touch of Mist's rings against her skin. "How are you?"

Mist shifted her arm enough to peek beneath it. "Alive."

"Thank Dia'veh."

"And me," Em said.

"You'll need to do more than thank Dia'veh before the day is through," Aven said. "It's a matter of time before the dragons come. Everyone is talking. Pryn seems to know, which means the Tribouin leaders do too."

Mist dropped her arm to glare at her sister. "You shouldn't have done it."

"It was either shift or let the Soulless kill you. I made the right choice."

Aven's lips twitched. "I would have made the same call."

The satisfied smile on Em's face made Mist groan. "Don't vindicate her."

"No, please. Vindicate away." She shifted closer, the yellow in her eyes melding into a sky blue. "I'm Emriel."

Aven failed to stifle a chuckle. "Aven. Is that all it takes to buy your good will?"

"We dragons love praise." Emriel stretched her long legs and leaned back on the cushions. "Please, continue telling me how right I am."

"Please don't." An unusual edge crept into Mist's voice. "She already thinks she's right about anything and everything else."

"You never told me you had a sister," Aven said, sliding her thumb along the smooth surface of Mist's rings.

A wicked gleam shone in Emriel's striking blue eyes. "She's ashamed of us."

"*Us?*"

Mist sighed. "Our egg-layer has quite a few children. I haven't even met all my bloodkin."

"That's on you," Emriel said, brow furrowing. "*I've* met them all."

Mist covered her face again, her hand falling away from Aven's. Silence fell, stretching on and on, Aven fidgeting beneath Emriel's unflinching stare. It seemed only boredom deterred her from letting things stay so awkward. Eventually, the dragon huffed dramatically and rose to her feet.

"I'm going to check on the elves."

She walked towards the Priestess without a look back, moving like Mist. Her gait was a little too smooth and her steps perfectly silent. Aven wouldn't want that dragon sneaking up on her in the dark. Where Mist smelled of vanilla and wild roses, Emriel's predatory musk railed against Aven's instincts.

She looked back down at Mist, only to find her staring back. Her full lips pulled into a deep frown, fuchsia eyes troubled. When she spoke her voice barely rose above a whisper.

"Be careful. Em—she's—she's like the tide. She'll pull you under if you're not careful."

Aven laid down on the cushions, propping her head up with one hand. "She's not pulling me anywhere. I'm staying right here."

Mist chewed on her lip instead of responding, her gaze fixated on the glass ceiling. Each breath came uneven, ragged, and occasionally a quiet sniffle slipped out. Tears welled in the corners of her eyes, but she continued to stare up above.

It was more than Aven could take. "What happened in the market?"

Mist closed her eyes, and a single tear escaped from beneath her lashes. "It was awful. I was helpless. Useless. I'm always useless."

Aven frowned. "No, you're not. You're many things, but useless isn't one of them."

"What happened in the market is why I left home."

That wasn't what Aven expected her to say. Facing Soulless had to have been terrifying, but to think Mist came from such violence was not something she'd imagined. The way she spoke of Estellias always left the impression it was peaceful. A place to simply *be*.

Aven rested her chin on Mist's shoulder, stroking her arm with a feathery touch. "Tell me."

Mist released a shuddering breath, blinking rapidly until the tears dried. "Home with Papi was quiet. Tem'bria is a bit off the beaten path. Very close to the border, so few paid us any mind. I think people come to Tem'bria because it's so far from the Elemental cities. You can escape there, avoid the kingdom's drama. Me and my best friend growing up didn't know things were going sour up north until merchants started talking."

"The Elementals?"

Mist nodded. "It still doesn't affect most of us. The Elementals expect little of anyone who can't conjure tornadoes or drown armies in a tidal wave. Humans, elves, shifters—they just keep their heads down and stay out of the way. But not the dragons. Em says we owe it to the Elementals to fight. We were their greatest allies in the Time of Sorrow. Papi and I weren't surprised when Emriel came calling, expecting me to stand with our bloodkin. What I didn't expect was for her to entreat the entire village."

Aven sucked in a breath. "Isn't your Papi human?"

"He is." Mist spun the ring on her middle finger. "My best friend—his name's Adair—he and his family are, too. Most of Tem'bria are humans or shifters, with some Fae or Dryads who come and go."

"Emriel expected them to get between warring Elementals?"

"That's what I said," Mist spat. "I begged her to not get them involved. Dragons have some advantages. Our souls are made of the same stuff Elementals' are. Many of their attacks ripple right off us. There was a Mimic Soulless in the market today. He must have faced an Elemental last, because he had their power. His fire and water attacks did nothing to Emriel."

"The elves weren't so lucky."

A cringe twisted Mist's face. "No, of course they weren't. Adair's father wasn't either."

"Oh, no."

More tears pooled in Mist's as her lower lip trembled. "He was one of the many who agreed the fighting affected us all. That it was the Estellian people's duty to get involved. But how can flesh stand up against rockslides and infernos? We never saw Adair's father again."

"That's not your fault." Aven rubbed Mist's arm, wishing to touch her face instead, to stare into her eyes and make her believe that truth. "You're not responsible for Emriel. And you're not responsible for the choices other people make."

Mist finally looked at her, sorrow in her eyes. "That's what Papi said. And I know it. I do. But my heart doesn't believe it, especially when Adair got the news his father would never come home. It felt like it was my fault. Em never would have come to Tem'bria if it weren't for me. So, he might never have left."

She looked back up at the ceiling, breathing hard. "And today the Soulless killed Nodi and Rymia just so they could get me alone. Maybe if I hadn't been there, maybe if I had just stayed in bed, those lynx would still be alive."

Aven ground her teeth, fighting to keep her claws sheathed. She should have been there. If she hadn't been such a fool and attacked Fennicks, she might have been. Mist wasn't trained to fight like she was. Qinawe might not believe in violence for the sake of violence, but fighting was a dance they all learned. Their customs demanded the only reason one should raise arms, or claws and teeth, was to defend against or secure an unrivaled match. For some shifters, it was especially serious, since a Chosen one was for life.

Not that matchmaking mattered when Soulless were here, toying with shifter lives as if they were dolls. Aven stroked Kali's fang, already certain what the great lynx would have done. She didn't have to think about it. To the torment with customs. If fighting Soulless kept Mist or other shifters safe, Aven would face the Matriarchs' wrath without hesitation.

"I know that look." Mist shimmied onto her side, wincing as she settled her battered body into a comfortable position. "I haven't dissuaded you at all."

The look of sadness on Mist's face was all that kept Aven from smiling. Her thoughts might as well be words over her head. She could hide nothing from the girl beside her.

"I know I've been reckless. I promise I'll do better." Aven chose each word as carefully as she could. "I won't just stand by if I can help, though. Not after spending a lifetime wishing someone would step in for me."

"I do!" Mist tried pushing up on her elbow, but a flash of pain crossed her face. "I have your back."

"I know," Aven said. "And I've got yours."

They smiled at each other, sorrow still marring Mist's gaze. It was the best Aven could offer her. She would get her temper under control, and face what was coming with a clear-headedness Mama would be proud of.

"Oh barf," came Emriel's voice from behind them.

Aven sat up so she could glare at Mist's sister. "Don't be jealous. I can watch your back too if you like."

Emriel spun around and put a hand on her hip. "Admire away. But come along while you do. If Mist is all done talking about how awful I am, we should probably help her to her feet. We're about to have company in the form of a pissy, fire breathing lizard.

CHAPTER Twelve

Aven

"**Y**ou don't know these dragons, Em," Mist said, struggling onto shaking arms. "They're going to be more than *pissy*."

Emriel tilted her head, watching Mist strain to rise before sighing dramatically. With unnerving grace, she slipped beneath one of her arms before fixing Aven with a judgy look.

"Are you going to help, or will you just continue to admire us in all our perfect glory?"

The apologetic smile on Mist's face killed Aven's sarcastic reply. She would not get into a sass-off with this— *woman.*

"Can you blame the girl?" a deep voice asked.

"We are lovely to behold," a higher voice chuckled.

As they helped Mist to her feet, Aven got her first look at what a dragon could be when they weren't in hiding. Hopefully, she didn't look as astonished as she felt.

Neither had bothered with imitating humans, shifters, or any Sholi Aven knew of. They embraced unique forms, possibly even to them. Yesterday, Rielnor himself could have been mistaken for any race in Yunaii. The most striking thing about him had been the horrid scars raked across his body.

These dragons could no more be compared to other shifters than butterflies could be to even the most beautiful of moths. One had chosen the color of charcoal for his skin, with smoldering embers for eyes. Horns protruded from his forehead and curved over his skull to extend far past his red, spiky hair, while plated scales covered his forearms like bracers. The other beside him had tanned skin, rippling with a rainbow of color thanks to its snakeskin texture. Even the whites of her eyes had given way to violet, surrounding vibrant, glowing green irises. Her fawnlike ears extended far out from her head and a pair of horns stretched above them, coming to sharp points. Her hair reached past her bottom, shimmering like a purplish-black veil of oil flowing from her head.

Emriel moved one foot in front of Mist and Aven as she crossed her arms.

"Thudan," she nodded to the one with fiery eyes, then looked at the snake skinned dragoness. "Anyvath. I see the flight leader sent the muscle and the sweet talker."

Mist looked sharply at her sister, brows raised in surprise.

"You're lucky it's us, Emriel." Thudan said. "Some of the others weren't feeling as generous."

"Meaning you'll *ask* her to come instead of dragging her to face the flight," Mist said, her tone making Aven's hackles rise.

If they tried, she would be ready.

"You know how things are, darling," said Anyvath.

"But Emriel isn't a part of the flight." Mist took a shaking step towards them. "She didn't know the laws."

"She can make her case to the flight leader," Thudan said, giving Emriel an earnest look. "Everything about our lives here is about to change."

Aven snorted. "And someone has to answer for that?"

Thudan's nostrils flared. "I'm afraid this matter is not your concern, Qinawe."

"It became my concern when your flight leader threatened my family over the same nonsense just yesterday."

The two dragons exchanged looks, the smallest bit of surprise in their eyes. Perhaps Rielnor had kept the details to himself after all.

"No matter, darlings." Anyvath stepped closer, hands held out passively at her sides. "We are here to guide Emriel to the flight."

"Gotta get your revenge *before* you make things right with the other shifters."

Thudan bared his short fangs at Aven. "You test my patience, little cat. Didn't your Matriarch teach you manners?"

"She did," Aven snarled, moving forward despite Mist's death grip on her arm. "But Yunaii has taught me not everyone deserves my manners."

"Aven." Mist tugged on her arm. "Please."

It would have been easy to rake her claws across the snarling dragon's face. Aven's skin already itched with the desire to let fur overtake it, to let fangs replace teeth. Only her promise held her back. When Mist gripped both of her shoulders, squeezing so tight it hurt, Aven focused on the rings of pink circling her best friend's eyes. They pleaded with her to calm down, even as Mist spoke her name, telling her to breathe.

After a few deep inhales, Aven relaxed. "I'm sorry."

Mist pulled her into a tight hug, blood and fire still lingering on her skin. The dragons were a problem, one that needed solving, but at the moment they were not the enemy. There was still a Soulless out there.

"Aven, I need you to stay here," Mist said, lips almost touching her ear. "I have to go with Em."

"You should not shift, kitling," Anyvath said, her severe features softening with a mothering gaze.

Mist withdrew enough to fix the other dragon with a glare. "Maybe not, but I'm not leaving my bloodkin to face you lot alone."

Aven grabbed hold of Mist's forearms. "Let me come. Don't make me sit here waiting, wondering."

"Absolutely not," Thudan snapped. "The roost is not for you. Or any of the other shifters for that matter."

"Stay here, Mist," Emriel said, all sarcasm and wit replaced with a commanding tone. "Rest. You need to reserve your strength so you can heal faster."

"No, Em." Mist's voice was firm, her mouth set in its stubborn line. "We're not debating this. I don't care if I have to ride up there like a hatchling new to its wings. I'm going."

Emriel's nostrils flared, but after giving her a once over, she eventually nodded. "Fine."

Mist looked back at Aven and nervously smoothed hair off her shoulders. "I wish you could come. I do. But it's not safe. Em shouldn't even be going."

"But my bloodkin knows better than to even argue that with me."

A growl rumbled from Thudan. "That is not an option anyway. Emriel will face the flight."

"Or what?" Mist waved a hand, motioning towards the Temple. "You cannot do violence here. Dia'veh demands it. If you tried to take her, the Creator's power would stop you."

"That is why she insisted I come here, of course." Emriel grinned at the sour looks on Thudan and Anyvath's faces. "My bloodkin is nothing if not a devout little dragon."

"If you do not come with us, darling, eventually the flight would come to you." Anyvath raised a dark brow, her mouth curving into a challenging smirk. "And with the current state of things, I cannot imagine that would go well. The Tribouin and Qinawe might think themselves above violence, but perhaps we could test what happens when the entire flight descends upon Yunaii."

"No need for threats." Emriel waved a placating hand like a weary mother sick of her child's tantrum. "They're boring and hollow."

"Now I almost want you to refuse," Thudan growled.

"Stop it." Mist stepped between the dragons and Emriel.

Aven shadowed her, slipping against her back while keeping one eye on Anyvath. She'd heard the claim about Dia'veh protecting the Temple against violence, but she didn't have the strength of faith her friend did. Sometimes the Creator expected you to trust in the wits they gave you instead of energy you couldn't see.

"Emriel and I are coming," Mist said, looking between the three other dragons. "Just give me one moment to speak with Aven. *Alone.*"

Emriel raised a brow before shrugging one shoulder. "Fine. I'll be at the entrance waiting for you."

Mist nodded. "And don't even think about leaving without me. If you do, I *will* shift and fly myself up there. Even if that means I have to listen to you channel Eega and lecture me once I arrive."

Irritation flashed in Emriel's eyes, a look so similar to Mama's that Aven wasn't sure if they should ever meet. It could end up very entertaining. Or it could be like kindling on a fire.

Emriel marched off with a huff, tailed silently by Thudan and Anyvath. Once they were on the other side of the pool, Mist turned back to Aven.

"I need you to do something."

Aven grinned. "Anything."

"Talk with the Linseen while I'm gone. Talk to Dev too. Maybe even the lynx and griffin."

"About what?" Aven asked, stomach knotting at the thought of reaching out to so many. A life of otherness hadn't yielded great people skills.

"Make sure they understand there is at least one more Soulless out there. There very well could be dozens. They don't just run away, and these were on a mission. What they'd planned, what they said."

She paused as a shudder rippled through her limbs.

Aven glanced at the injured elves nearby, focusing on their scents, the moans of pain. The Soulless inflicted such hurt with no hesitation, but it was their words reducing Mist to a trembling, hunted fawn.

"What did they talk about?"

Mist rubbed the injured spot on her temple. "They wanted to provoke the flight by killing me. They're here to hurt the dragons. We need to know why, and the Linseen need to prepare for another attack. The Soulless are not done yet."

Now Aven understood the tremors plaguing her friend's hands. "You're certain?"

Silence met her question as Mist turned towards the elves. She studied them, her brows pinched. "Very certain. Soulless don't just walk away. The Summoner is coming back, and most likely not alone. We need to be ready when that happens."

"The Qinawe and Tribouin won't fight if they do," Aven said, biting back her rising fear. If the Soulless came *en masse*, what would happen to her people? To her parents? Could she get them to run before death descended on them?

"I know." Mist laid her hands on Aven's shoulders, this time her thumbs coming to rest at the base of her throat. "That's why we have to be ready. We have to protect them."

Warmth filled Aven's chest as she imagined pressing her lips to Mist's, sharing the gratitude rolling through her. The thought stole her smile as a wash of shock trembled through her bones. She couldn't be having these kinds of thoughts. Not about Mist. Maybe if things were different, if they wanted the same things, but they just weren't meant to be. She wouldn't trap Mist the way Pryn had tried to trap her.

"Thank you," Aven said, laying a hand atop Mist's. "Thank you for always being here. For always caring, even when I make a mess of things."

Mist slid her hand to Aven's cheek. "Friends help clean up each other's messes. I know you'd be right here if it was my family in danger."

"Yours is," Aven said grimly.

The rekindled spark in Mist's eyes shuttered out. "Maybe so, but Emriel is up to something. She's far too pleased with herself and apparently, she knows the flight. I think I've missed something somewhere, which doesn't surprise me. Rielnor loves his secrets as much as the next dragon. That he might know my bloodkin is absolutely something he would keep from me until it was convenient."

"Be careful up there." Aven squeezed her hand. "Fennicks will be there too."

"I will." Mist pursed her lips, but still nodded. "You be careful too. Watch your back and don't go wandering alone. I don't think that Soulless went far."

Aven's heart pinched. "I promise I won't be so—"

"Reckless?"

"Sure," Aven said, grinning. "We'll go with that."

"I'll see you soon," Mist promised, her pupil's as wide as a frightened cat's.

As she stepped away, cold rushed where her hands had been. If only Aven could cling to Mist's warmth, keeping it bottled with a whiff of her rosy scent. Sadly, it faded away, replaced with the muggy heat of Yunaii's afternoon air.

Aven watched the four dragons leave the temple, wondering about the scene they were about to make upon their exit. If she didn't have a job to do, she would sneak behind them, just for a chance to see the crowd lose their wits at the sight of the dragons flying off.

There was no time for that, though. Aven had to protect her parents, and her people, especially if they would not protect themselves. If only she knew where to start. The Qinawe and Tribouin would not listen to her. They might not even listen to Mama and Papa. She needed to find someone that most shifters respected. Someone Yunaii would listen to.

Her best bet was the elves. Neutral, loyal, selfless—and currently broken.

Aven glanced at the three injured Linseen, and a tremor jolted up her spine. Zoli was gone. The Priestess was gone. In their wake, a veil of lacy, black cloth now laid over the elf with the gash across her back. While she and the dragons were exchanging useless words, the Elven warrior had been granted her hard-earned peace.

Aven's feet dragged like stone as she made her way over to the body. This was her first time seeing one void of its soul. Had the elf rejoiced in returning to the Maker, or did she cling to every moment, unable to let go? Regrets had eaten up every moment of Aven's plummet from the sky yesterday. She wasn't done. She wasn't ready to stop her journey in Sholindrea. Even if the Priestess claimed peace and joy awaited beyond the moment of death, she still had dreams to live and work to do. Tomorrow had been out of reach for so long. If she passed on from this life, how would she find joy knowing she'd left so much undone?

With a deep inhale, Aven knelt beside the fallen elf, searching for the warrior's chest rising or falling. For any twitch of limbs or shift in attention. She was so still beneath her veil. An acrid, but familiar copper smell hung in the air. Aven had been hunting since she could hold a bow, but there was something different about this. Bitterness lingered, as if the elf's soul had left a mark with her death.

"I'm sorry." Aven's fists tightened against her thighs as her knees touched the stone floor. "Maker, watch over you, grant you more for your service and sacrifice. May you find triumph and blessings in eternity."

"A good prayer," Priestess Ifera's deep voice said as she crouched beside Aven.

"Is it?" She blinked a few times, clearing her vision of the blur creeping over her eyes.

"Yes," the Priestess said, her cool hand resting on Aven's shoulder. "She has earned her place and many blessings."

"How do you know that?"

Ifera motioned to the pool nearby. "Dia'veh is in the water. Dia'veh is in the air. You may speak, you may ask. The Creator will answer."

Aven glanced at the pool and snorted. "Dia'veh never answers me."

"Perhaps you do not hear."

"Convenient." If only it were that simple. If only the Maker really just lingered around, waiting for her to pray. Waiting to give simple answers.

"Hardly. Nothing about existence is convenient." Ifera waved her hand, the turquoise paint circling her wrists bright against her umber skin. "Dia'veh is here because we need them here. That is design. Perhaps you do not hear because you do not wish it."

"I have wished for Dia'veh to answer me since I was a child," Aven snapped. Heat burned behind her eyes as blood roared in her ears. "I have waited. I have listened."

Ifera fingered the choker around her neck. Long white beads made up the central layer, strung between a row of round black ones. It reminded Aven of the style the Tribouin wore, but as far as she knew, the Priestess hailed from no shifter blood.

"I know this pain, child. The anger is an old friend." Ifera tilted her head, staring at the pool of water with a faraway look. "I have found it hard to hear anything when anger comes yelling in my ear, let alone the whisper of the Creator."

"Are you saying the Maker cannot be louder?" Aven asked with a smirk.

Ifera's golden eyes crinkled from her smile. She tapped her nose with a finger adorned by many rings. "Ah, but why bother shouting over someone? I've achieved nothing that way, except for making myself angry too. Have you had better results than I?"

Aven hesitated, even though the answer was obvious. She was wise to this sort of logic. "You sound like my papa."

"I shall take that as a compliment," Ifera said, rising to her feet. "Perhaps he can make sense of what you seek better than I."

A chuckle bubbled out of Aven despite her lingering irritation. She hadn't been seeking chastisement over her struggles with the Maker. Paying her respects was all she'd wanted to do before tackling Mist's request.

Perhaps there was help to be found with that, though. "Priestess."

"Yes?"

"If you had to rally shifters for battle, who would you go to first?"

"After my dear companion, the Truthseeker?" A feral amusement twinkled in the woman's eyes as she stroked her choker. "The griffin flock leader. Yliva is a patient diplomat. Her favor will earn you pride leader Kanai's time. With them secured, seek Commander Senwe. If the peace the Linseen foster is disturbed enough, they will be drawn to you long before you seek them out.

CHAPTER *Thirteen*

Mist

Wind whistled in Mist's ears as she clung to Emriel's mane of sunset-colored hair. For the first time she understood why Aven endured the flying leathers. Icy chill plastered Mist's legs to Emriel's sides and bit into her skin. If only there'd been time to change her clothes. The sheer fabric of her ripped and bloody dress whipped through the air, strengthening the urge to push a layer of downy feathers over her skin. Maybe it wouldn't hurt too much if her shape didn't change.

The thought vanished as they crested over the highest branches of the Eilawi tree. Thudan and Anyvath soared nearby, hovering at the tips of Emriel's wings, no doubt ready to stop Mist's sister if she veered from their flight path.

Not that Emriel would. She eagerly pulled ahead, aiming for the island of floating rock hovering high above Yunaii.

It spanned nearly the same width as the tree's foliage, the lowest point of its craggy bottom far from the highest peaks of the canyon's cliffs. Boulders drifted around it like moons, caught in the power the Elementals imbued it with who knows how long ago. Mist wondered what possessed an Air Elemental to put so much into a rock that it remained trapped like this. She suspected the answer would be vague and a little condescending. Papi often said Elementals did things just for the sake of seeing if they could. She didn't know if that was true. The only Elementals she'd met had been curious, but they were also too young for such feats.

Emriel banked sideways, her wingspan aligning with the sheer rock face. Her muscles strained, each flap bringing them closer and closer. Mist's belly warmed at the sight of leafy vines dangling over the edge of the island. They were almost there. This was her favorite part of coming to the roost. Another two strong beats of Emriel's red and gold wings, and Mist's eyeline crested over the edge.

She smiled despite the light stinging her eyes. The dragon roost was a world apart. Down below, warm-colored rock framed everything, the cliff walls a fortress surrounding the shifters' wooded home. An echo always lingered in the air. A sense of stifling closeness.

Up here was freedom. Nothing closed her in or kept her trapped. She didn't have to fight against currents of air to escape rock walls. Up here, they carried her into Dia'veh's blanket of cold blue.

The floating island was an abhorrently bright oasis in a desert. The rock was bleached almost white, and despite its rough and lifeless bottom, the surface of the island teemed with all sorts of green growing things. Bugs, brightly colored birds—and dragons. So many dragons.

They lounged on moss-covered rocks with their bellies exposed to the sun. They slept coiled like massive snakes in the shade beneath the Eilawi tree's saplings. A few gorged on the carcass of a ton beast, one of the large, bull-like creatures living outside the canyon. None paid any mind to Mist's arrival with members of their flight. They were oblivious to the panic settling down below.

With a growl, Thudan shot ahead, his leathery wings crossing into Emriel's span. She shrieked as a gust shoved her sideways, wrenching a scream from Mist's throat. Pain seared through her aching hips as she tightened her thighs to keep from being tossed. Her sister veered back towards him, but Thudan had already committed to a dive, his thick, spike-covered neck dipping towards a clearing in the trees. Mist took a deep breath as Emriel followed, curving down to the rock at a terrifying speed. Wind whipped at Mist's face.

Tears pulled from her eyes. Then Emriel flapped her wings once, twice, slowing their descent.

Mist would have to remember how her lungs closed as they dove. How her stomach flip-flopped. Sometimes she forgot what it was like to be the passenger. How often had she subjected Aven to such feelings?

Emriel's feet connected with the ground and she bounced, leaping around and around like an excited puppy, jamming Mist's teeth together over and over.

By the Creator, did she even remember someone was on her back?

Anyvath landed with much more grace. Her back feet touched down as her feathery wings brought her peacefully to all fours. A haughty look crossed her snake-like face as Emriel jostled Mist through two more excited circles before they finally halted in the middle of the clearing.

As if finally remembering Mist was there, Emriel's head swiveled around to stare with sky-blue eyes. Her tiny, feathered ears perked up before she shifted, nearly dumping Mist as she lowered one leg to the ground.

That was probably the best she would get. With a deep breath, Mist lifted her leg over Emriel's back. Her muscles were so stiff and sore. She had to grab her ankle and pull it over. How did Aven endure this position for so long? Once Mist managed to get both feet on one side, she slid down Emriel's cascade of feathers, knees jarring when her feet contacted mossy rock.

If this was what being a dragon rider felt like, Mist was glad to be the dragon. Her legs spasmed, and it took some weak stretches to pop the crick out of her back.

How was Aven not constantly walking bow-legged?

"Thudan, you useless sack of ash!"

Mist sighed at the animosity in Emriel's voice. She had shifted back to two legs, with her shoulder-length orange hair, leather pants, and a tight blue top that exposed her midriff. A golden chain wrapped around her middle, attaching to a piercing through her navel, matching the strings of thin gold dangling from her long ears. Mist just barely caught sight of scars carved up her sister's back before she realized Em stomped towards Thudan—who was still in dragonskin.

"You nearly knocked my bloodkin right off my back!"

Mist grabbed at Emriel's bicep, but it wasn't enough. She poked the dragon's nose over and over. Even Thudan drawing himself up on his haunches didn't deter her. Nor did the fire licking between his teeth. A deep growl sent pebbles vibrating over the ground and Mist instinctively slipped between him and her sister.

Hot breath fanned across her face, but Mist stared him down. She'd done nothing wrong. He couldn't hurt her. Rielnor had made it clear that was not allowed.

"Oh, he's not going to do anything," Emriel said, shouldering forward. "Are you, Thudan? Not without permission. So why don't you be a good lapdog and go find your master."

Sweet Blessed Mother, Em had lost her mind.

Mist hadn't even grown up around dragons and she knew mouthing off to one of egg-rearing age was more dangerous than climbing an erupting volcano. Even if his fire wouldn't kill them, his claws and teeth could.

Thudan growled as Emriel sauntered away, nostrils flaring, his tail whipping back and forth. The air grew thick and Mist wondered if this was how she would go, paying the price for Em's runaway mouth. It wouldn't be surprising.

It must have been Dia'veh's will she not die, because Thudan eventually furled his wings and stomped away with a hiss.

Mist released a slow breath. If it had been *her* poking Thudan's nose, she would have gotten a tail whip at the very least. Emriel must have some connection to these dragons. Perhaps her egg-warden—her father—lived among them. Mist had never met him, but it would explain how Eega knew of them. The elders would be reluctant to harm a kit they'd raised. The young belonged to the flight, not just the ones who made their egg.

"Breathe, bloodkin," Emriel whispered, her chin coming to rest on Mist's shoulder. "You're tenser than a mouse in a hawk's shadow."

Mist pressed on her nail beds one at a time, counting to the beating of her heart. "Why aren't you?"

"Because these dragons have forgotten the way of things," Emriel said. "They're no more frightening than a freshly gelded horse. And about as useless too."

Mist shook Emriel off and fixed her with a glare. "How do you know that? How do you know anything about this flight?"

Emriel's red lips curved, but she didn't answer. Of course. Why answer questions when Em could leave her feeling like a foolish hatchling? Mist would give anything to make her sister understand this was one of the many reasons she had left Estellias.

"It is time," Rielnor's voice rumbled nearby.

Emriel's gaze shifted over Mist's shoulder, her pupils narrowing to pinpricks as a hint of fear tinted her scent.

Good. Maybe Em wasn't as mad as Mist feared. A healthy respect for Rielnor meant she hadn't fallen too in love with herself.

Mist turned slowly, attention falling to the flight leader's bare feet once again. Two times in two days. It was more than she'd ever seen of him in his human form. He stood far enough away she couldn't make out the details on his reddened skin, but she still smelled the age in his blood. Air shifted in his presence, turning colder despite Sansia shining above.

"Always so tense, Mist." Rielnor sighed. "Try to relax. You are not facing the flight. Despite great danger to your life, *you* did not break our laws."

Mist jerked her head up and tried not to stare at his bare chest—at the scars stretching from his shoulder, across his torso, and almost to his navel. Dragons proudly displayed their mating scars, but she'd never seen any so ravaged by battle.

"But Em didn't—"

Rielnor lifted a large hand. "Not yet. Wait for the flight. They all have a right to bear witness. What she did affects their way of life."

A shudder reverberated through Mist's limbs. Not good. An audience meant Rielnor wasn't granting favors today. No matter what Mist argued, the older dragons would uphold his laws.

Em also did herself no favors as she groaned. Loud. Ever the petulant child. Her attitude would be the death of her.

They waited awkwardly as more and more dragons gathered around the mossy circle. Some came on two legs, some on four. Scales, fur, feathers, horns, spikes; the range of colors and appearance left Mist wishing she could draw. The human forms were nearly as impressive as the dragonskins. They were works of art, molded in flesh by creatures who held mastery over their own bodies. A female nearby had feathers erupting from her scalp that lay in layers far past her shoulders. A male had framed the angles of his face with sharp spikes, reminding her of a beard, with horns protruding from his bald head like a range of craggy mountains. Nearby, a dragon coiled its long, snakelike body around itself, its smooth scales shimmering like glass. The one at its side was a stark contrast, with armored scales as thick and hard as rocks.

Mist didn't know who to look at first, or what features she'd attempt to emulate. So rarely did the flight gather together. One of the few similarities was the twinkling of jewels, gold, and silver all over their bodies. They adorned dragon and non-dragon ears alike. Dangling from chains, set in long rows of circlets along shells of ears, studding through nostrils or around lips, decorating their features perfectly. She envied the collection of gemstones. Especially those who had procured larger, hard to come by beauties. Mist dreamed of one day finding a sapphire the size of her fist. What a treasure that would be.

All the dragons' eyes fixed on Emriel, whose teeth flashed in a widening smile as more of them approached. Recognition lit in some of their faces, causing equal looks of curiosity and anger.

Rielnor stood a stone's throw away, his arms crossed over his bare chest, fingers of one hand stroking the scars wrapping from his wrist to elbow. Perhaps Em had given them to him. Challenging Rielnor was just her kind of reckless. The intensity of his gaze curdled Mist's stomach until she had to look away. Was it revenge lingering in his green eyes?

As Thudan and Anyvath gathered around Rielnor, so too did other shifted dragons. These were the oldest of the flight, their human forms each as strange as the next. Thankfully, dragon snouts and tongues were not as effective at forming words. The simplicity of language versus snarls and growls made convergences like this go much smoother. Which meant Mist was not about to be surrounded by a bunch of raging dragons when she couldn't shift.

Not exactly her idea of fun.

Rielnor raised both hands, silencing all the whispers and growls. He looked left and right over the flight, before settling his gaze on Mist and her sister.

"Emriel."

"Hello, old man."

Rielnor's nostrils flared. "Are we expecting your egg-layer as well? Or has she entrusted you with spreading her madness?"

Oh, merciful mother. Mist should have guessed this had something to do with Eega. Heat seared up her spine as she glanced at Emriel, whose eyes were dilated and narrow.

"Just so we're clear," Emriel said, casting a scathing look at the flight. "She trusts me with all her affairs. Coming here was my idea. She thought it was a waste of time. In her opinion, this flight is a lost cause."

"She is not wrong," Rielnor rumbled. "We will not be sucked into the Elementals' conflict."

"We are the Elementals' oldest allies," Emriel snapped. An argument Mist had heard far too many times. "We are kin. We should stand beside them."

Rielnor took a step forward, his scarred face twisting with anger. "It is not our job to end their civil war!"

"No." Emriel indulged an undignified snort. "Better to lounge in the sun all day, gorging on meat you didn't catch, and collecting jewels you didn't earn. Perhaps Eega was right. This flight is too indulgent to be any use on the battlefield."

"Enough!" A guttural roar raged from Rielnor, yellow pooling in the green of his eyes. Fangs descended in a feral snarl that shook Mist to the core. "You and your egg-layer have no sway here. You are summoned to answer for the law you have broken. Not to insult those who know better than you."

Mist sucked in a breath. She'd never seen Em back down from a fight. She took no as permission, and insulting her—it never ended well. How far could Rielnor push before she snapped?

"What do you say to the charge?" Anyvath asked, gaze shifting back and forth between Em and her flight leader.

Emriel waved dismissively. "Oh well? I got what I wanted."

"Yes." Rielnor's voice trembled. "And thank the Creator your bloodkin and those in the market are alive."

Emriel cast a sideways look at Mist, the gleam in her eye mischievous. "Of course. But that's not all I wanted."

Thudan stepped out to Rielnor's other side. "And what did you want, kit? Songs? Praise? To be the savior of Yunaii? You always were one to crow."

Emriel threw her head back and laughed, evoking a shudder from Mist.

Oh, not good. Hunter's excitement flooded her sister's scent. She smelled like a lynx right before it pounced, hovering in that moment before the killing blow.

"I don't care about heroics, dung sniffer." Emriel's lips pulled into a vicious smirk. "What I *wanted* was all of you gathered together. The perfect, enthralled audience."

"Em," Mist murmured, stepping back at the deep rumble thrumming in the air. A collective growl from the flight.

"To what end?" Rielnor asked, moving closer. His arms reached out to his sides to stop the other elders from following. "What have you done, Emriel?"

"I've done nothing." She picked dirt from beneath her fingernails. "I just wanted all of them here to bear witness."

Rielnor glanced at the flight. "To what?"

Mist drew in a fearful breath, looking from her bloodkin to the ancient dragon who had taken her in.

"To *me*," Emriel said, hands falling to the hilts of the twin blades on her belt, "challenging *you* for the position of flight leader."

The clearing erupted in a fit of snarls and shouts. Some dragons unfurled their wings, some rose on two legs to howl at the sky. The chorus of anger melded into a confusing symphony that shook the floating island.

Across the clearing, Rielnor stood with his arms hanging limp at his side. The black of his pupils blotted out the green in his eyes.

"Have you lost your mind?" Mist yelled over the rising storm of dragon rage. "He'll kill you."

Emriel raised an eyebrow. "Have some faith in me, kitling."

Mist grabbed her sister's arm, itching to shake her senseless. "I do, but it isn't blind. Rielnor is older than Eega. He will slaughter you."

"No." Emriel laid her hand over Mist's. "He won't."

She turned back to Rielnor, who stood still as stone. It was Anyvath who called for quiet, arms high in the air as she walked along the edge of the moss circle. Some dragons settled under her fiery gaze. Some snarled in her face. She waved them all off like hyper dogs.

"Silence!" Thudan roared, causing a high-pitched ringing in Mist's ears. She furtively rubbed at them as the dragons settled once more.

"A challenge has been issued," Anyvath said from within the circle. She regarded Rielnor, her brows furrowed in what looked like pity. "Flight leader?"

Rielnor's attention shifted from Emriel to Mist, then back, his mouth pulled into a thin line. With an odd shake of his head, he looked at the ground as his shoulders fell. "I will not kill my own kit."

"Your kit?" Mist's eyes widened as she looked at Emriel. "He's your—"

"Father?" Em asked, eyebrows raising with an amused smile. "As you human-raised say."

Mist rounded on the flight leader, all manners forgotten. "Did you know? Did you know Emriel and I are bloodkin?"

"Of course." His tone screamed she was a fool for asking. "I can scent your egg-layer in you."

"You never said *anything.*"

Thudan drew near, eyes ablaze with excitement. "Not recognizing your bloodkin's scent in the flight leader is your own failing. Reconcile it on your own time. An answer must be given to the challenge."

"I have answered," Rielnor said with a steely glare. "I will not bring harm to a life I created."

"That is not an answer."

Anyvath stepped closer, touching Rielnor's shoulder with a rainbow hand. "You know we cannot accept that. Emriel has challenged you. You must choose the time and place."

Rielnor whirled away with a disgusted sound. It broke Mist's heart. His very scent instilled a heart-pounding fear she might never get over, but he was also fair. She might even say kind. He accepted her into the flight without hesitation and showed great patience with her clinging to Estellian ways. Even now, he separated himself from the dragon customs, all to protect his bloodkin.

And Emriel had thoroughly trapped him.

Anger bubbled in Mist's chest as turned on her sister. "Why are you doing this?"

"Because your egg-layer failed to," Rielnor said, his back still turned to them.

"She made sure you remembered, though." Emriel dragged a hand over her shoulder, indicating the scars etched into Rielnor's body.

He chuckled as he touched his arm. "If you think this angers me, you have spent too long away from the flight, kitling. I kept every scar from your egg-layer. She was a fierce opponent and an even fiercer mate. I will mourn her fall to madness until the sky goes black and the land turns to ash."

"She is not mad," Emriel snarled. "She's just not weak like you."

"Emriel, stop!" Mist squeezed her arm. "If you have such a poor opinion of these dragons, why do you even *want* to lead them?"

"She needs fodder for the Elementals' war," Rielnor said, turning to face them. His eyes sparkled in Sansia's light, but if anyone acknowledged the track of wetness on his cheek, none dared acknowledge it. "I will not allow it. We will not die for *them*."

"So, you will fight?" Emriel asked with a smile.

"No, flight leader." Mist stepped between them and caught a whiff of sorrow curled in his icy scent. "Please. It doesn't have to be this way."

"Perhaps she is right," said a deep voice. "There is another option."

Mist's breath hitched as a tall, muscular dragon sauntered from the crowd. Long black hair had been pulled into a collection of braids, revealing strong cheekbones and familiar yellow eyes. When beeswax, leather, and smoke filled Mist's nose, she knew she looked at another form of Fennicks.

"What other way?" Anyvath asked, her eyes narrow and suspicious.

Fennicks stared Emriel down, stroking two small horns protruding from the strong chin they'd chosen for themself. "The flight leader may choose someone to fight in his place."

"Who? You?" Mist nearly choked on the hysterical giggle erupting from her throat. "How is that any better?"

Fennicks' lips peeled back to reveal two fangs. "You survived my bite, didn't you? Your bloodkin is made of far tougher stuff."

Emriel's warm hand skimmed Mist's shoulder, her fingertips brushing the almost healed wound on the back of her neck. "This was you?"

Fennicks' eyes glimmered as a proud smile stretched across their thin lips. "What's wrong, red? Not jealous I took a taste of your sister, are you?"

Em's brows furrowed in a scowl that matched Rielnor's. "I accept your offer."

CHAPTER *Fourteen*

Mist

Rielnor put a hand on Fennicks' scarred chest, fingers brushing jagged red streaks peeking from beneath their open vest. "I did not choose you."

"No," Fennicks said. "But I *am* the only one who has beaten her before. I'm your best shot at not losing your command."

"No, just their respect."

Had Mist not been standing so close, she might not have heard Rielnor's hissed words.

"These are circumstances many of us understand," Anyvath said. "I, too, would be reluctant to face my kit in a challenge, flight leader."

Mist dared to step closer, darting her gaze from Rielnor's eyes to over his shoulder. "This is a mistake! Fennicks will kill her. No hesitation. Choosing this path will be no better than you facing her."

He stared without blinking until Mist risked meeting his gaze. "I am aware you were raised amongst humans, but this *is* our way. What is a leader if they flee such challenges? If I cannot keep them safe, then what good am I?"

"Letting Fennicks fight for you will not answer either of those questions."

"Perhaps," he said, looking beyond them all towards the sky, as if the future stretched out before him. "At least it will be the next strongest of us who holds their faith."

"But not the kindest of us." Mist laid a trembling hand on Rielnor's forearm. "I think that matters even more."

Emriel groaned once more. "Can we get on with this? Please?"

Mist shot a glare at her sister. A sister she thought she'd somewhat understood. If Papi stood between her and what she wanted, there would be no question. She could never harm him. He'd held her, rocked her, raised her, loved her. Just as Rielnor must have done for Em. Female dragons did not raise their kits.

"I see you have not improved your patience," Fennicks chuckled.

"What can I say?" Emriel batted her eyelashes. "I'm ready for another taste of *your* blood."

Mist searched for anyone with the sense to stop this, but found only eager faces. Their whispers held excitement as the prospect of bloodshed. They didn't care this could end in death.

"Maybe I don't belong with dragons."

Emriel wrapped an arm around her shoulders. "Stop thinking like your humans. You're not as soft as them. Their rules don't apply to us, no matter what Eega's bedmate taught you." She led Mist to the edge of the clearing and deposited her by Anyvath like a stubborn child. "Have faith in me. I didn't come all this way to die."

Mist searched Em's face, desperate for some hint she'd change her mind. "No one ever plans on dying. Adair's father didn't. The Elementals fighting in their civil war don't either. That doesn't stop the massacres from happening."

"Trust me." Emriel laid her hands on Mist's shoulders and squeezed. "I've got this."

Determination glowed in her eyes, but Mist still doubted. Fennicks stood at Rielnor's side in full, muscular glory. Em was not short, but Fennicks stood over a head taller than her, with arms twice as wide and thighs capable of snapping a femur with one harsh kick. She would not walk out of this circle if Fennicks had anything to say about it.

"Em." Mist grasped her sister's forearm. "If it comes to it, please yield. This isn't worth dying for. *They're* not worth dying for."

A quizzical look stretched across Emriel's face. "The dragons or the Elementals?"

"Either." Mist wrapped both arms around Emriel's lithe, yet muscular body. All she got in response was an awkward pat on the back. Not unexpected. She understood her bloodkin a little more knowing Eega and Rielnor had created her. Neither seemed like the most affectionate creatures. Not like Papi.

If only she had someone like Papi.

Emriel winked at Mist before turning, both hands resting on the hilts of her daggers. "Do not let her get involved.

Anyvath touched Mist's elbow. "I won't, darling."

Mist glared at the older dragon, but said nothing. Unless Anyvath sat on her, she was not going to stand by if Fennicks went for a killing blow. She'd never be able to live with herself. Aven should have come to the roost after all. She would charge in with claws and teeth if it came to it.

Across the clearing, Fennicks stared blankly as Rielnor whispered in their ear. The two of them stood so close their shoulders bumped with each furtive gesture the flight leader made. Anger glittered in Rielnor's eyes, but eventually, he stalked away, face hidden behind his long green hair. Even when he settled at Thudan's side, his gaze lingered on the ground.

"I thought he would never leave," Emriel said, facing Fennicks with her shoulders thrown back. "How do you want to do this?"

Fennicks lifted an arm and stretched to one side, then the other. "Well, I've beaten you once with claws. Perhaps you'll have a better chance with steel."

"I let you win," Emriel said, leaning on one leg, her attitude that of a bored teen. "You were interesting back then."

"Pity. So were you."

"We're not here for your banter," Thudan said. "Sort out your bedroom issues some other time. Fennicks fights for the flight leader. Emriel challenges for that right. Take it seriously."

"Okay, so get out of the way." Emriel drew her daggers one at a time, dragging the metal against the scabbards. The twin blades curved slightly at the point with serrated edges designed to bite deep.

Fennicks dropped both hands down and flexed. Within a blink of an eye, each finger stretched into long, deadly claws with thick scales covering up to Fennicks' elbows. They were pitch black and gleamed in the light, thick as any armor ever crafted.

"This need not be a fight to the death," Rielnor said, looking from Fennicks to Emriel. "Life is precious. Let blood be spilt, but yield when the time comes."

Mist sighed as Rielnor gave Emriel a subtle escape. The flight might not like it, but if he deemed a yield was enough, then it would be enough. Hopefully, Emriel cared more about her life than her pride. Fennicks was not one to be trifled with. Mist had seen it time and time again, but there was no better lesson than what had happened yesterday. Fennicks had been willing to let her *and* Aven die.

After sizing each other up, Fennicks took one step to the right. Emriel slowly did the same. This led to them circling one another, blades and claws raised just enough to thwart a surprise attack. They each looked the other up and down, gazes calculating, but still amused.

Mist's heart pounded in her chest. She whispered prayer after prayer, begging Dia'veh and Sholindrea to please protect her sister. Emriel was a lot of things, but Mist couldn't swallow watching her die.

Fennicks made the first real move, dashing in for a swipe of claws much faster than Mist expected. Emriel was ready, though. She leapt with a dancer's grace, twisting through the air to land well out of reach. A smile pulled across her red lips as she twirled both daggers.

"You can do better than that."

Fennicks tried again, using their powerful legs to propel them forward, leading into what Aven would call a dance. Fennicks slashed, Emriel leapt. Emriel charged, Fennicks rolled. They slid back and forth, testing each other's speed and reactions, reading each other. Reacquainting. Mist didn't have to be a fighter to see what they were doing. They'd known each other once. Now they wanted to see what they'd learned since their last match.

Mist could only guess what they'd fought over before. A mating challenge or a fight of passion? She didn't know of other reasons dragons would face one another. Neither of them had anything to be challenged for.

To think Fennicks might have been her sister's mate twisted Mist's stomach. Was that why Fennicks always looked at her with anger and animosity? Had they smelled Em in her blood? It was hard to fathom. Dragons did not mate for life. She'd always assumed it was the tension between Aven and Pryn that earned Fennicks' ire.

The violent dance drew closer and closer. Fennicks was learning Emriel's moves, blocking her leaps now, keeping her from escaping by following close on her heels. Those deadly claws eventually caught Em's arm, slicing three cuts dripping purple down to her fingers. Emriel returned in kind, ducking beneath the next swipe and dragging her dagger across Fennicks' exposed torso. She didn't get close enough to end it, but the wound poured blood.

They spun away from each other, each taking stock of their wounds. Fennicks pressed a hand against the cut, nostrils flaring, a low growl rumbling through bared teeth. Emriel wiped at her own and then flung the blood across the clearing with a wet slap.

"Not bad," she said. "You're faster."

Fennicks smirked. "Where'd you learn that little leap? It was positively human."

Emriel circled again, one corner of her mouth curving up. "Took a spell to play with some up-and-coming warriors. There was a dancer who moved like a viper."

Fennicks marched towards Em, all pretense of circling each other forgotten. "Did she wake up one morning to find you gone, too?"

"She wasn't as foolish as you," Emriel said, flipping one dagger so its blade curved along her forearm.

In two more strides, they slammed together, claws clanging against steel. Fennicks tore one arm free for a deadly slash, forcing Em to scuttle her lower half backwards to keep from being gutted. Then she twisted her dagger, trapping Fennicks' claws, so when she brought her arm down she took theirs along with it. She followed with a swipe at Fennicks' face, forcing them to abandon the upper hand in lieu of keeping their throat. Together they rolled sideways, both grunting as they hit the ground. Emriel was the first to break free, rolling herself over and over before kicking her legs up, using the momentum to haul her body back onto her feet. She landed gracefully and raised her daggers, giving Fennicks a moment to rise.

Mist stared, her mouth hanging open. They seemed evenly matched. At least for now. She'd expected Fennicks to be more ruthless. Was this a ploy? Or had dragon races and an unending supply of decadent food softened the Yunaii dragons more than she'd thought?

Rielnor still looked worried. He stood unnervingly still, save for the thumbnail he ran back and forth over his lip as he tracked every move. Would he intervene if Fennicks landed a deadly blow? Would the flight allow it? Mist knew what Papi would do. He never would have even let Mist step into this clearing. Over his stiff corpse.

Fennicks and Emriel danced through another series of attacks, each of them avoiding near death repeatedly with speed or strength. Blood dotted their bodies, a cut on Emriel's thigh and a deep gash below Fennicks' collarbone, the worst of their wounds so far.

Then Fennicks landed an awful punch to Emriel's cheek, sending her reeling backwards. Mist gasped and stepped forward, only to be jerked away.

"No, darling." Anyvath whispered furiously. "You cannot get involved."

"But—"

"I will put you down if you do."

Mist glared into the dragon's emerald eyes, hating her more than she'd ever hated anything. She turned back, relieved to find Em had not only kept her feet, but had gotten some distance from Fennicks while recovering her wits.

Blood trickled down her cheek where the blow split the skin, but a smile still played on her lips.

"How'd that feel?" Emriel asked.

"Not as satisfying as I thought," Fennicks said. "Don't make this too easy. I was expecting a challenge."

"Don't worry." Em dragged her gaze over Fennicks' body. "I'm not done pounding on you yet."

Fennicks chuckled. Then they ran at each other. Blade met claws, and this time everything changed. Punches hit harder, steel clanged and sparked in a flurry of blows impossible to follow. They kicked and jumped like Sholindrea's pull no longer weighed them down. Wounds gathered faster this time: another gash on Fennicks' torso, a rake of claws over Emriel's shoulder, a blow to Fennicks' knee, followed by a backhand to Em's face. The last one sent her slamming to the ground.

Mist pulled against Anyvath's grip as Fennicks leapt for Em. She'd pushed onto all fours when a well-placed kick sent her sprawling. With a satisfied growl, Fennicks straddled her waist and brought claws towards Em's face. All that saved her was the dagger she raised between them, catching Fennicks' hand just in time. Claws curled around the blade, but she didn't waver, pushing back enough to keep them from raking her cheek. With Fennicks focused on the battle of strength, Em raised her free dagger, aiming for a killing blow. The blade's tip nearly sank into Fennicks' side, but their massive hand caught Em's before she drove it home.

"Cute," Fennicks growled before slamming Em's wrist against the rock once, twice, and over again until something cracked. She muffled a gasp between sealed lips, but Mist heard it.

With the second dagger no longer a threat, Fennicks dragged their claws along the ground, closer and closer until they skimmed Emriel's throat.

Their deadly tips leaving a trail of purple was all Mist could take. Her knuckles tightened as she wheeled around, remembering what Adair once told her: swing with her whole body. Aiming for Anyvath's face. The other dragon never saw it coming. Pain lanced through Mist's hand as it smashed Anyvath's jaw with a sickening crack, buying her freedom.

Mist didn't stop to think. She didn't care what it would mean. That clawed hand now wrapped around Emriel's throat. Despite the pain in her hip and the shouts filling her ears, Mist dashed for her sister. The discarded dagger lay forgotten on the ground. Its curved blade gleamed like a beacon. Mist slowed enough to snatch it up before grabbing the braids coiled tight against Fennicks' skull. She yanked hard, baring throat for her blade to kiss.

"Move even one claw and I'll take that vengeance Rielnor offered me."

Fennicks froze, yellow eyes moving to Mist's face. "Didn't think you had it in you."

"Emriel is my bloodkin," Mist hissed, tugging on the braids.

"Mist," Emriel gasped. "Don't."

"Why not?" Mist didn't dare look away from Fennicks' eyes. One twitch of muscle, one swipe of those claws, and there would be more blood. "Fennicks almost killed me. They were about to kill you."

"This isn't how things go," Emriel said as she freed her dagger from Fennicks' claws. "This match is—"

"It is now forfeit," Rielnor declared in a loud voice. "There is no victor here."

"I was about to end her!" Fennicks' eyes shifted, searching for the flight leader without moving against Mist's blade. "I obviously won."

"Emriel still breathes, and she did not yield." Rielnor's voice was closer now. His shadow fell across Fennicks' face, before his scarred hands grabbed their wrist and pulled the claws away from Emriel. "There. Is. No. Victor."

Emriel made a sound of disgust as Fennicks trembled. Every muscle tensed, making Mist tighten her hold on their braids. She didn't dare let go. Fear coiled inside her as she imagined that anger turning on her. Or Em, who laid close enough for a killing blow.

"The fight is over. Release Fennicks," Rielnor commanded.

Mist finally dared to look at him. His face hovered so close, his winter smell chilling her nose as she stared at the ring of amber around his pupils.

"She's safe now," he whispered.

Mist released a weak breath before letting go of the braids. Her knuckles ached from how tightly she'd clung to them. Like they were the line keeping her sister alive. Fennicks' eyes locked with hers as she moved Emriel's dagger away. The unfamiliar face twitched with an anger and shock Mist couldn't blame them for. She had surprised even herself.

Emriel wore a similar look as Mist grabbed beneath her sister's arms and hauled her out from under Fennicks' legs.

Em rose slowly, her shoulders stiff. When she turned, her words came out deadly quiet. "What in the torments were you doing?"

"Saving your life," Mist said, holding up the dagger. "You're welcome."

Emriel snatched the blade and slammed it into its scabbard. "I told you to have faith in me."

"I have plenty of faith you were about to lose your throat," Mist said. "You can die, just like anyone else."

Em wheeled away with an angry curse. "I see now why Eega let you run away."

"Excuse you?" Heat crept up Mist's neck and into her cheeks.

Rielnor glanced between them. "That is enough. Both of you. There are greater things at stake here."

"No," Mist said, waving him off. "Let her speak."

Emriel spun around, her eyes gleaming. "What good are you in a tight spot? You're either nearly dying or incapable of following orders."

"Because I'm not a soldier!" Mist stomped close enough to give Em a weak shove. "And there's nothing wrong with that! I don't have to be fine with blood on my hands! I don't have to live like that. There's no shame in just being happy with something simple, with someone beautiful. But you wouldn't know anything about that. Apparently, no matter where you go you just leave people so angry with you they want to kill you."

Em stood blinking, cradling her wrist, not saying anything. Beside her Rielnor hauled Fennicks up, keeping a distance between them and Emriel. At least someone had some modicum of sense. If only it was enough. All around, the dragons stared at the four of them, growling and whispering, anger sizzling in the air. Things were close to imploding.

Yet, Mist no longer cared.

She pulled at her hair, fingers dragging against her skull. There was no reasoning with them. They didn't understand how she saw things and maybe she wasn't capable of understanding them. She was raised amongst humans. *By* humans. Dia'veh and Papi taught her that souls were precious. To help, not to hurt. Serve. But how could she serve and take lives at the same time? How could she stand by in the face of such pointless violence?

"If being a dragon means having no regard for each other's lives—I'm not sure I want to be one of you."

Emriel recoiled, but Mist didn't linger for a retort. She couldn't, so she gave in to the itch skittering beneath her skin. Feathers burst free as wings extended from her back. Her vision shifted from the human spectrum to a rainbow of colors she couldn't even describe. Pain pinched in her neck and seared through her head, but she still let her bones stretch and lighten until she was in the form these dragons would gleefully corrupt.

She hissed in her sister's face before shooting up, ignoring Emriel's shout. Let her suffer the flight alone. Mist couldn't save her from herself.

CHAPTER Fifteen

Aven

Aven didn't know silence could be so uncomfortable. Yet here she was; heart in her throat, sweat dripping down her temple, as she jogged to keep up with the Truthseeker's loping stride. He'd woven his long hair into braids, leaving the shaved sides of his head uncovered. She watched those braids bounce between his shoulder blades, racking her brain for any conversation starter. When she'd asked for his help, he'd simply nodded, retrieved an absurd number of knives that seemed impossible to hide on his body, and strode out of the Temple without a word. Now, for all she knew, he plotted her death for bothering him with this.

As they made their way towards the Lighe River and its bridges, Aven considered all the questions she could ask him. All the questions she wanted to ask him. He was the only Steel elf she knew of in Yunaii. How he got here and what had called him was a mystery. Elves and their magic were strange.

"Please wait!"

Aven tensed as she and the Truthseeker turned. Getting out of the market was a tricky feat. Even with the elf at her side, no one had wanted her to leave. People knew she was a dragon rider, so they thought she might have more answers than the Linseen.

Thankfully, it wasn't an angry or confused shifter sprinting after them.

"Dev?"

He caught up to them at the edge of the middle bridge, his brown curls bouncing. Sweat beaded his brow as he came to a stop, dropping into a casual bow before them. "Truthseeker."

"Guardian," the Steel elf replied, dipping his chin. "We do not have time for your questions."

"I do not come seeking answers," Dev said. "I am soul-called."

Aven frowned. "What does that mean?"

"For this one?" The Truthseeker motioned a hand at Aven.

Dev shook his head. "No. I feel it pulling me to follow you. I believe I am called to protect someone close to her."

"I don't understand," Aven said, scratching her head.

The Truthseeker regarded Dev a moment before looking at her. "They call me Truth elf because the Illieve are called to protect the truth. We feel the tug in our souls. For Klesian elves, the call is to guard weary warriors. Young Dev seeks his first ward."

Aven pushed hair behind her ears as she considered her short list of acquaintances. None were *weary* warriors. "I have no idea who you're looking for, Dev. But you're welcome to stay with us until we find them. Maybe your protection will help me convince them to fight."

Dev bowed, gripping the pommel of two short swords she hadn't noticed he'd donned. "Thank you. I hope my presence can be of service."

Aven wrinkled her nose. The awkwardness of this day was getting worse by the companion.

"Do you not wish him to come?" the Truthseeker whispered.

"What?" Aven recoiled. "No, I'm fine with it. Why do you ask?"

He blinked his silver eyes and gave her a once-over. "This is truth, but your soul is unsure."

That was weird. Aven didn't know how she felt about him *reading* her soul. Could he hear her thoughts? Her feelings? She hadn't spent nearly enough time learning about the elves. Their magic was intangible.

"I'm fine with it. I trust Dev."

"As you should," the Truthseeker said in a louder voice. "Klesian elves are devout and reliable."

"Aren't you all?" Aven asked, raising a brow. "From what I've seen, you're the only ones more concerned with addressing the actual problems instead of panicking about dragon secrets."

His thin lips twitched. "Today has held no revelations for me. I have nothing to process. Your people are not in the same place as I."

Apparently, all it took to get anything out of him was for another elf to show. Who knew? She should have asked Zoli to come along, too.

"And the Linseen elves? Did they know?" Aven glanced at Dev.

"About the dragons?" he asked.

She nodded.

"I believe their leaders were aware." He glanced back towards the market. "I have never heard Zoli speak of it, but Commander Senwe seemed unaffected by what transpired today. I was among the soldiers he addressed after the Soulless attack and the impression I got was not one of surprise."

"You know," Aven said, tapping her chin. "If I'd known the dragons getting outed would put everyone in a sharing mood, I might have done it myself ages ago."

As the two elves stared at her with what could only be dismay, it struck Aven how different they were. The Steel elf, with his braided white hair, gray eyes, pale skin, and pristine armor. Then Dev, with his untamed brown curls, leather breeches, and plain white tunic with laces up his chest. The only thing they had in common were their long ears, and apparently utter horror over any kind of sarcasm.

"You would reveal truths for the sake of conversation?" the Truthseeker asked.

"I believe she is not being literal," Dev said, but his voice wavered.

"I wasn't. Sorry. Bad joke. Let's get going." Maybe silence was better after all. Aven's cheeks burned as she scurried across the bridge, heading for the section of forest belonging to the lynx and griffin. The elves' boots pounded behind her, but she didn't wait for them. Their lack of humor would get her in trouble. Hopefully, the griffins were easier to talk to.

Aven grew cautious once surrounded by trees. Despite their size, the lynx left only an occasional footprint in the mud or tuft of fur snagged on a branch. Their musk flitted through the breeze, only to flutter away before she could track it. She had only Kali's instincts as a guide, the lynx's soul brightening as they ventured into her kingdom.

A twig snapped to Aven's left and she froze, nostrils flaring. Was it prey, or was she? She held out a hand to the two elves behind her. Their trek had been quiet for two beings who did not dwell in the woods, but anything with ears could still hear them shifting branches and shuffling underbrush.

"Well, well. Kali's guardian," a voice said, making Aven whirl to her right.

A slender, shifted lynx emerged from a thicket, stepping like a prowling hunter, crouched and cautious. Furry, pointed ears stuck out through shaggy golden hair, and their nose had a cat-like appearance. A leather vest hung open across toned shoulders, held together by a single knot, while the breeches below cut off at the knee, revealing feline hind legs.

"This is a welcome surprise," the lynx said, yellow eyes and tawny fuzz glowing amongst all the green.

"Have we met?"

That earned a painfully familiar smile. "We have not, but you smell of Kali. Her scent weaves through you like the Tribouin's fancy perfumes."

Kali's soul reached out for the lynx, tempting Aven to fall to all fours and step closer. Instead, she touched the fang dangling around her neck, tracing the tiny ridges from years of biting into hide and bone. "I feel her. She remembers you. I can't find your name though."

"This is young Dinon," said the Truthseeker, bowing politely to the lynx. "*They* are quite the tribute to Yunaii. Pride leader Kanai sings only praise of their hunting prowess and standing amongst the lynx."

One corner of Dinon's mouth perked up as humor sparked in their yellow eyes. "Thank you, Truthseeker. You're very kind. May I ask if there's something I can help you three with? We don't get many elves or Qinawe under our trees."

"Did you hear what happened in the market?" Aven asked, silently noting the Truthseeker's subtle guidance.

Dinon's brows pulled into a scowl. "Yes. We lost two of our own. The girl the creatures attacked, the one with white hair—"

Aven's heart leapt. "*Mist.*"

"Yes," Dinon said, a knowing smirk creasing their young face. "She smelled of you."

Aven drew in a few deep breaths, focusing on how it felt to fill her chest with air. Last thing she needed was to give in to the embarrassment rising up. She wouldn't give the cheeky little furball the satisfaction. Not even when two powerful, elven stares bore into her neck.

"Mist visits my family home often."

"Yes," Dinon said again, one eye narrowing. "Well, I was with her right before the attack. Wish I'd known what was lurking, I could have protected her. Is she alright?"

Mist's tears still lingered in Aven's memories. No matter what Mama, Papa, or Hanawi had to say, the Soulless would taste her claws if she got the chance. "She's not well, but she's alive."

"What happened in the market was horrific," Dinon said. "I can't imagine what would've happened had that dragon not involved herself."

"That's why I'm here," Aven said. "The dragons believe the Soulless that escaped is still nearby. They fear more could be on their way."

"That is concerning." Dinon stroked their chin with claw-like fingernails. "What do you need of the lynx?"

Aven opened her mouth, but choked on the answer. Nothing sounded right in her head. *We need you to fight? We need you to defend the Qinawe and Tribouin because they won't defend themselves? Are you willing to die for people who spurn your friendship?* Aven's people made no effort to endear themselves to the other shifters. Not out of malice, but in hopes of protecting their different customs from getting muddied.

The Truthseeker saved Aven, stepping up to put a hand on her shoulder. "We seek counsel, and possibly aid. This will affect all of Yunaii, so we must prepare."

Dinon considered this, gaze staring off at the forest. Eventually they looked back to Aven and the fang around her neck. "I can take you to the pride leader. I dunno what he'll say."

"We also need to speak to the flock," Aven said, pointing at the canopy. "How can I find them?"

A grin split Dinon's face, revealing small fangs. "They are aloft, but I can lead you to the easiest way up. We share these woods, but they have their ways and we have ours."

Aven pursed her lips. Just like the rest of the shifters. What a force they could be if they all just worked together. If only someone could break their focus on each other's differences and unite them.

"Can you take us there now?"

Dinon motioned for them to follow, and they began trekking through the woods, Aven falling into the lynx's steps as easily as she did Mama's. Were it not for the elves snapping twigs behind her, she might have imagined being on a hunt. So often, she and Mama melded into the forest like creatures born of it. Its shadows and twisting limbs called to her. Lessons in stepping just right so prey wouldn't hear, staying downwind to hide her scent. Such simple days she would happily go back to. The darkness stole away her worries. Beneath the trees she only had to think about birds cheeping above as a breeze whispered through the foliage. If she wanted, she could slip into the brush and never come out. Leave all this behind.

If only that didn't mean leaving Mist, and Mama and Papa. They would have only Emriel to fight for them. What would her help cost? Mist's freedom? Mist's life? Aven wasn't sure. Emriel cared for her sister, but she believed in her cause, too. Would her love for Mist win out?

No. Escaping into Kali's world was not an option. No matter how tempting.

After a bit of walking, Dinon led them to the base of a mighty tree. Not as wide as its mother, but undoubtedly one of the older seedlings. Aven couldn't reach all the way around its base, not even if her entire family joined hands. Steps hewn from rough wood wrapped around its trunk, spiraling up, up, up, until they reached the lowest of the tree's branches.

"When we have need of the griffins, we use these." Dinon rested a hand on one of the steps. "They'll take you high enough to request a meeting with flock leader Yliva."

Aven looked at the Truthseeker. "We should be quick. Dev and I will go speak with the griffins. Priestess Ifera said to go to the flock leader first. While we do, can you go to the pride leader to ask for his help?"

The pale elf frowned. "Do you not hold a bond with the lynx? I might presume it would be more fruitful for you to go to the pride leader and I go to the griffin."

Disappointment welled in Aven's chest. Of all the shifters, the griffins were the most mysterious. She'd never seen their nests or had the chance to speak with one outside of simple pleasantries.

Not that things like that mattered right now. She had to do what was best. What was right.

Aven gripped Kali's fang in her fist, running the pad of her thumb over the still sharp point. Dinon's gaze followed the motion, their eyes moving so slightly she almost missed it.

Shame forced her gaze to the ground. That fleeting glance spoke volumes. The right thing was not using Kali's soul to manipulate the lynx. The little bone she carried meant a great deal to them. Possibly more than it should. The old cat was dead and gone.

"Truthseeker, you should go to the pride leader," Aven said, waving a shaking hand when he protested. "The lynx are kind to me because of Kali."

"That's not the only reason," Dinon argued.

"Maybe. But it is the heart of it. I carry your pride leader's soul. You loved her. Respected her."

Dinon's shoulders dropped. "She was a wonderful leader."

"But I'm *not* Kali."

The lynx blinked slowly, staring as if they had not fully seen her before.

"She is here." Aven touched her chest. "I can feel her. She lends me her strength, her power, her form. Every day. But you take this fang away and I'm just me. I don't have her wisdom and knowledge about leadership. Her soul will draw the lynx into a fight that guarantees more death. I can't do that. They have to decide this on their own."

The memory of the Linseen warrior with her back split open drew bile up Aven's throat. "The Soulless kill without hesitation. Someone impartial needs to go to the lynx. At least at first. Someone they respect, but feel no obligation to listen to."

Dinon's brows rose with a sideways look directed at the Truthseeker. "She's got a point."

The elf folded his arms behind his back. "She does. I shall go speak with pride leader Kanai. What intent shall I present?"

"Perhaps," Dev said, stepping in. "We should get the leaders to meet at the Temple. It is safe, neutral ground and Commander Senwe is already there. If we can bring the Tribouin Elders and Qinawe Matriarchs, they might accomplish creating an actionable plan."

Aven clapped Dev on the shoulder, earning a startled look. "Good thinking. Let's propose tomorrow morning. That should give us enough time to speak with everyone."

"Agreed," the Truthseeker said, dipping his chin. "I will take this to Kanai."

"Great," Aven said. "Thank you for your help, Truthseeker."

The Steel elf bowed at the waist. "You may call me Gaelin."

Aven smiled at the realization she'd never asked his name., a habit she needed to break. Something about his scowling face kept her from crossing into familiarity.

As she turned for the stairs, claws tickled the inside of her wrist, drawing her back to Dinon's warm, wide eyes.

"You." The lynx drew in a shuddering breath. "You have more of Kali's wisdom than you know. She lives on in you."

Aven ducked her head, wishing to disappear up the stairway. "I don't know about that."

"You put my people first," Dinon said, bringing her hand between their own. "Thank you."

"I just really wanted to see the griffins."

A purred chuckle rumbled from Dinon's chest. "I am sure. Kali enjoyed them, too. She envied their freedom and how they could fly away from their troubles."

Aven's eyes widened at her own desires spoken aloud. If Kali, the mighty sabertooth cat, wished to flee her problems too, maybe there was more of the lynx in her than she realized.

"I wish I had gotten to know her before she came to me."

"Come to us in the night, when the moons are both full and shining." Dinon's eyes shimmered with unspoken sadness. "We dance and sing of our elders. We'll tell you of Kali."

Aven nodded. "Thank you for your help today. For me and for Mist."

"Of course. Give her my name, please. Tell her I'll be near if she needs."

Aven eyed Dinon suspiciously. Was this genuine or more cheek? Not that Mist didn't deserve friends or— anything else. She was smart and loyal and beautiful, anyone would of course be drawn to her.

As if they could read her thoughts, Dinon flashed one fang in a feline smirk and winked. "Enjoy the griffins."

Without a look back, the lynx waved at the Truthseeker before walking deep into the forest. Aven's last glimpse of them was Gaelin's stiff, proper stride trailing behind Dinon's silent, smooth steps.

Once they were alone, she turned to Dev. "You ready to climb?"

He tilted his head, eyeing the spiral staircase. "It is good that dragon riders are cured of any fear of heights."

"No kidding."

The first few steps wobbled beneath Aven's feet, but she forced herself to keep going. She skimmed her left hand along the tree trunk, tracing its rough bark as she ignored the forest floor slipping away. Two times around the spiral and she started missing any separation between her and open air. No railing protected her from plummeting to the ground. Occasionally, the rough wood dipped beneath her weight, sending a panicked wave of dizziness through her skull. The sensation was an old friend, but she didn't miss it. When Mist would fall into a dive or barrel roll through the air, Aven had to ride out the wave to keep from being paralyzed.

If only Mist were with her. Aven wouldn't need these blasted stairs. She wouldn't need to play at being a diplomat, either. Mist could sweet talk Mama and make Rielnor protective of her. If she didn't have to deal with dragon nonsense, they'd probably already be half done with gathering up the shifter leaders.

Aven glanced upward, worry stabbing through her chest. It hurt not knowing where Mist was and how things were going up there. Hopefully Emriel at least had the sense not to drag Mist into danger. She had such a horrifying sense of duty and need to help others.

"You are uncharacteristically quiet," Dev said from behind her.

Aven chanced a glance back. "Just have a lot on my mind."

"Like the dragons' great ruse?"

She cringed and turned away, focusing again on the steps. This was bound to come up. Dev was one of the few riders she spoke to. Of course he would want to talk about it.

"Did you know the dragons could shift?" Suspicion tainted Dev's voice, and she imagined his eyes boring into her back.

Aven touched Kali's fang. Tell the truth or lie? It had been hard enough to keep the secret, but now that Dev knew, it was completely different. Especially for him and Pryn.

She'd lied to Pryn. But Pryn would run her mouth if Aven told the truth. Then it'd be a matter of time before Rielnor returned to punish Aven's family.

"Before you lie to me," Dev said. "I knew."

Shock tripped Aven up, making her miss a step. She teetered, and the stairs rushed towards her face. Only her claws digging into the tree trunk saved her from a busted chin at best or a deadly fall at worst. Her hands trembled as she hung to the tree like a frightened cat, gasping lungfuls of air. It took forever for her head to clear. The dizzying fear dug in like a tick.

Dev's hands on her shoulders drew Aven back. "That was almost bad."

She snorted and finally retracted the claws buried deep in the tree. A faint burning lingered in her fingertips, but it would fade. The wobbling in her knees though, she didn't know.

"Are you alright?"

"Yeah," Aven said, glancing at Dev's hand on her shoulder. "Thanks."

He drew himself up, fingers wrapping back around the pommel of his sword. "No thanks needed. You saved yourself."

She rounded on him, planting her fists on her hips. The look always served Mama well. "You knew about the dragons and you never said anything?"

Dev put one booted foot on the step above his and leaned back against the tree. "You still have not answered *my* question."

Aven huffed and continued her climb up the winding stairs. "First tell me what you know, and then I'll tell you what I know."

"That hardly seems fair."

She tossed her hair over one shoulder to better showcase a shrug. "Maybe not, but I said it first."

The elf fell quiet just long enough for worry to bloom. Yes, he'd saved her life, and Aven wanted to one day be friends, but maybe he wasn't there yet.

"As you know, I am the only Klesian elf in Yunaii," he said.

She paused her climb long enough to throw a look of disdain at him. "Dev."

"Of course you are aware." He shifted his attention to the expanse of open air. "I was drawn here. I did not know why until yesterday. I feared my intuition had led me astray, but I am certain there is someone here in need of my aid."

Aven drew in a deep breath, clamping down the urge to rush him. "What does that have to do with the dragons?"

"Is it not clear?" He sounded genuinely confused, but Aven wasn't going to look back again. "I am not from Yunaii."

"So?"

A heavy sigh escaped him and Aven choked back a laugh. That was probably the rudest thing he had ever done. Dev never dared to so much as roll his eyes at someone, even behind their back.

"Dragons exist outside of Yunaii, Aven."

She cringed at the way he said her name. It might as well have been Mama or Papa scolding her with how well he'd captured a disappointed tone.

"Dev." Two could play the condescending parent game, though. "I've never been outside of this canyon. I don't know what's normal out there."

"I assumed your friend Mist had provided sufficient stories for your daydreams of leaving Yunaii."

They had almost reached the lowest of the tree branches. Two more turns and they could begin climbing. That would take more focus than this conversation allowed, so Aven plopped down on a step. "She's told me a little. Have you been eavesdropping?"

Dev straightened, thrusting his shoulders back. The image of a perfect soldier. "Of course not. Everyone simply knows of your dream to leave Yunaii. That is why you race, is it not?"

Why she raced. He wasn't wrong. Races were the fastest way to earn coins or trades. The Tibri would barter for short rides, but a long one to Estellias needed something better than whatever meat she could hunt or hides she could tan.

"Mist is from Estellias. I believe here and there are the only places she's ever been."

"I see." Dev looked out at the forest once more. "I apologize for my frustration."

Aven braced her elbows on her knees. "You don't have to be that formal with me. You're not going to offend me."

He searched her face before bobbing his head. "That is appreciated. Understand, my people spend our youth preparing to serve the world. The wrong tone or attitude can hinder our ability to help others. It can even hurt. The Linseen are peacekeepers. Could you imagine the harm a sarcastic remark might yield during a peace summit? Or the betrayal someone might feel should an Illieve appear to mock their truths when confessed?"

"I get it, Dev." Aven fought back a smile so *he* wouldn't be offended. "I'm just saying, you don't need to worry about that with me. Especially since you're not here for me, right? I'm no soldier. I'm just a girl with an axe. Some other weary soul has called to you."

He pushed at his tumble of brown curls, his brow glistening with sweat. "They're connected to you. I can feel that much."

Aven rolled the fang back and forth as she thought. What warriors might be in need of help? Rielnor and Fennicks were dangerous enough, but they could take care of themselves. Emriel maybe, but nothing about her attitude said she needed a guardian. "Hopefully you'll find them soon."

"The wait has been uncomfortable, but not hard. I will find the one who needs me."

Aven rested her chin on her palm. "And until then you'll ride around on dragons killing time?"

Dev's lips slid into what might have been a smile. One he struggled to hold back. "When I found out people rode dragons here, I cannot deny I was excited."

"You? Excited?" Aven gasped. "Are elves allowed to feel excited?"

The glare Dev threw could have struck down a Soulless. "My people are not without our joys. Serving is simply our calling. There is so much suffering in the world. It is better to dedicate oneself to serving the hurting instead of ridiculing, or worse, pretending the hurt does not exist."

"Wow. I—I suddenly feel like I've done nothing with my life."

Dev went down to one knee, bringing them to the same eye level. "You have spent your life straining to rise above the ire of people whose very culture demands they protect you. *You* are in need of love, friendship, and patience. You need lifting up first. Only then Dia'veh will show you how you can serve Sholindrea."

Aven took a shaky breath and stood. Dev didn't need to see the tears welling in her eyes. Had he just looked into her soul? Could elves do that? A lump rose in her throat she struggled to swallow down.

"I have upset you." Concern laced his voice.

"No," Aven said, forcing a smile to her lips. "You and the Priestess are determined to lay me bare today."

"She cuts to the quick. I imagine especially for you since serving in the Temple has spared her the negligence you endure."

Aven whirled around, grabbing hold of Kali's fang. "Are you saying she's not an elf?"

Dev rose to his feet. "She *is* an elf, though my understanding is her bloodline hails from shifter as well."

It couldn't be possible. All this time? "She's never said anything."

He arched a brow. "Perhaps you should frequent the Temple more before expecting confessions of her family and culture."

"I suppose that's fair."

"I would say so," a female voice chuckled above their heads.

Aven jumped and Dev unsheathed his sword, the ring of metal echoing through the forest.

"Oh, my," gasped a shifted griffin perched on a branch far above. "Such a violent little elf."

Dev lowered the blade, but didn't put it away. "On the contrary."

The pale girl dropped, wings tucked against her back as she landed gracefully on the steps. Gray feathers burst from her head where hair would normally be, reaching just past her ears to frame a heart-shaped face. Her yellow tunic dress split above her thighs, its color perfectly matching her honey-colored eyes.

The griffin tapped the point of his sword with sharpened fingernails. "And yet you've still got out that pig sticker."

Once more, Dev's shoulders went back as he slipped the blade into its sheath. "Apologies."

She smiled crookedly and turned to Aven. "What brings a Qinawe and an angry elf to the griffin nests?"

It couldn't be possible for Dev's spine to go any straighter, but the tightness in his jaw made Aven's ache. "The Soulless attack in the market. If it's possible, I need to speak with your flock leader."

The girl cocked her head, reminding Aven of a curious bird. "Our flock mates brought us the news. I didn't quite believe it."

"I wish it wasn't true, but it is," Aven said. "And, unfortunately, one got away."

"What do you want of us?" Her gray colored wings flexed nervously. "If you're here to ask us to hunt it down, I'd say take that to the dragons. I hear the one in the market walked away without a scratch. Our flock mates who fought have burns all over. One might not fly again."

Aven cringed, wishing again she had been at the market during the attack. "I'm so sorry."

"We seek no hunting party," Dev said, his stoic mask once more in place. "The Truthseeker has gone to the lynx to request the presence of their pride leader. We are here to ask for your flock leader's aid in preparing a course of action to protect Yunaii's shifters."

The girl pursed her lips. "But the Soulless is gone."

Aven drew in a deep breath. Some pushback was only natural. "The dragons are worried the Soulless will return. Possibly in greater numbers."

"Sounds like lots of assumptions."

"Perhaps," Dev said, staring hard at the girl. "The wisdom of Yunaii's leaders will hopefully lead to more clarity. I imagine your flock leader may wish to be a part of such proceedings."

"I do love a clever boy." Amusement lit up the griffin's eyes. "Alright then. Follow me."

"That's it?" Aven jumped two steps to stay on the girl's heels.

"Sure. I was just pulling your tail, lynx girl. My flock leader sent me down to get you."

Aven peered over her shoulder at Dev, eyebrows raised as he worked his jaw back and forth. With a choked laugh, she jumped two more steps to draw alongside the griffin.

"I think I like you."

The girl laughed, wings buffeting her leaps up the staircase. "Of course you do. I'm hilarious!"

"I'm Aven."

They'd reached the top of the stairs so the girl braced a hand on the branch, head cocked like an owl, gaze traveling over Dev as if he were a mouse. "And your scowling friend?"

Aven glanced at the elf when he didn't answer. His mouth set in a stubborn line, brow twitching. Maybe it was a good thing Aven held back all the times she'd wanted to tease him. "That's Dev."

The girl peered around Aven, mischief in every line of her body. "What kind of a name is Dev?"

His eyes narrowed almost imperceptibly. If Aven hadn't spent over a year trying to crack his shell, she might not have seen the irritation bubbling beneath the surface.

"I am Dev o'Din'Arin," he said with a disdainful sniff. "Is yours so wonderful that it pales mine in comparison?"

"It's Wilella." She smiled widely and glanced at Aven. "*You* can call me Willa."

CHAPTER Sixteen

Aven

"Y ou'll have to climb from here," Willa said, hopping onto the lowest branch, gaze darting between their faces. "It won't be easy."

Dev hauled himself up without hesitation. "We are quite capable."

"My, my, so strong." Willa whistled as she eyed his flexing muscles. "Elf maidens must love being wrapped in your arms."

Aven coughed to hide her laughter, but Dev's searing glare told her she'd failed.

"I am a servant of the Creator. I have no time for dalliances."

"No, just lots of dragon races," Aven said, claws extending to help her climb from branch to branch.

"Your friend doesn't have your back," Willa cackled.

"I have noticed." Dev's focus stayed on the climb, but his loud words had claws of their own. "I do hope she remembers this in the future."

Aven snapped her mouth shut, her smile falling away. What would revenge from Dev be like? Fun amusement or horrifying embarrassment? Neither sounded all that great, so she focused on the climb.

Leaves the size of her face sprouted everywhere, blocking out the forest floor. With the trees shifting and swaying, she hovered weightlessly in a secret world between earth and sky. What if she fell now? Her heart fluttered at the thought.

This would be so much easier with Mist. Her silent wonder at learning or experiencing new things made every task exciting. They should have tackled all the shifters together. Aven knew who to fight, but Mist always knew what to say. She'd have already finished with the griffins, convinced the lynx, and would probably be working on the Matriarchs by now.

"Almost there!" Wilella called, leaping from branch to branch, fearless in her ascent. A little clueless too, because she drew farther from Aven and Dev as they climbed.

Just when Aven worried they'd lost her, branches grew sparse, revealing roughly built platforms balanced atop larger tree limbs. Not unlike the little houses Qinawe built above their burrows for food storage and extra space.

Aven angled her climb to avoid the braces, then followed them until she reached the edge of the largest platform. Wilella awaited them, perched on all fours, head cocked sideways with wings tucked in close. When Aven tried scrambling up, Willa offered a slender hand that looked like it might break if squeezed too hard. Only when she wiggled her fingers did Aven take it.

Aven's concern died with a gasp when Willa hauled her up without so much as a grunt. Then she did the same for Dev. Good thing Willa had been sent to guide them instead of stop them.

With her feet planted on something solid, Aven took stock of her surroundings. Nests dotted the branches, filled with both bird and shifted forms. The half-eagle, half-lion creatures rivaled the lynx in size, colors ranging from light grays to dark browns, with some even sporting bright crests or chests. Like the small birds that stole seeds from Qinawe crops.

Their two-legged flockmates peered from around tree branches, sharp claws extended on their hands and feet. Surprise coiled through their scents, tickling Aven's nose until she sneezed. Thankfully, no tang of fear choked the air.

Convincing already frightened creatures to consider fighting Soulless would be next to impossible.

"That was quite the exercise," Dev said, turning to take it all in.

"And look at you," Willa said, sidling up to his side. "Barely sweating. Are you sure you don't have time for *dalliances*?"

Dev blinked slowly, red blossoming across his cheeks and creeping into his long, pointed ears. He held Willa's gaze, but his trembling hands made Aven think he'd rather leap from the platform than answer.

Merciless Willa stepped closer, her fluttering wings sending his curls bouncing. "Has anyone told you, you're adorable when you blush?"

A shift in Dev's scent called for Aven's intervention. The bitterness she'd searched for in the griffin soured his nervous odor. Jokes were one thing, but fear was a line no one should cross.

Aven laid a hand on his shoulder and angled her body in between him and the griffin. "Where is your flock leader?"

Willa's eyes sharpened as she zeroed in on Aven. Hunter versus hunter. Like the times she'd interrupted another Qinawe and their prey. The urge to shift slithered beneath her skin as Kali's soul rose to the challenge. If Willa wanted a tumble through the leaves, Aven would oblige her. What would claws versus talons be like? Easier than dealing with a dragon, she guessed.

Tense moments dragged on until Willa flashed a smirk. "Look at that. She has your back after all."

Dev cast Aven a sideways look before lowering his eyes. He didn't need to speak his thanks. She acknowledged the silent look with a squeeze of his shoulder before she turned her attention to the surrounding griffins.

"Your flock leader?"

Willa lifted both hands. "She is aloft."

Aven swallowed an exasperated sigh. "Do we need to keep going?"

"She is coming to us!" Willa beat her wings, hovering just above the platform as she pointed to a break in the trees.

A creature soared their way, light gleaming across white and gray plumage. A few powerful flaps brought the griffin between the branches, her expert navigation of the space enough to make even a dragon envious. By the time Aven could make out the slender shape of her beak and crest of white feathers, she'd already begun shifting. Clawed feet gave way to fingers and toes. The crest lengthened until it cascaded down her back. Her wings flapped a few more times, bringing her gracefully onto the platform, with every inch of her tan skin unashamedly bare.

Aven respectfully lowered her gaze, fingers itching to slap over Dev's eyes. Elves seemed the type to fuss over nudity. Thankfully, the moment passed quickly as Willa reverently laid a cloak of feathers over her flock leader's tall frame.

The woman slid each arm through openings in the sides, then waited as Willa tied the cloak shut. It fell past her toes, pooling around her feet like the most divine of dresses. Only her thin shoulders and arms were left bare, which she held perfectly poised before her, bent at the elbow with her hands interlocked.

An array of colors wove through the cloak. Each feather must have been plucked from a different griffin, maybe even from other birds. They ranged from bright yellows to deep, navy blues, with even some as black as a raven's wing. Aven could have studied it for far longer than she had time for, just to see if any two feathers were actually alike.

Mist would have *loved* to see it.

The flock leader herself was an exquisite work of art. Her birdlike face, hollow cheeks, and long nose came together as if shaped by a master sculptor. Beautiful in the same vein as a freshly made dagger. Sharp and pristine. Dark gray eyes studied Aven thoroughly before giving Dev the same treatment.

"You are Kali's protector," she said, drawing out her syllables as if creating art with her deep, sultry words.

"I'm Aven. Daughter of Navya and Tomen." A bite crept into Aven's voice, one she didn't mean to let out. How many more times would it be Kali others mentioned before even asking who she was?

"I am Yliva," the flock leader said, a knowing gleam in her eyes. "Daughter of Aylolon and Bivali."

Aven gripped the lynx's fang, searching for any feelings or instincts. "Did you know Kali?"

Yliva nodded. "Not only were we neighbors, but I cherished her grandcub dearly."

Aven frowned. "I—I have never met her grandcub. I didn't know she had one."

"Nya left Yunaii not long after Kali's death," Yliva said. "Her mate faced similar treatment as you, so they left to find a better life."

The revelation sent Aven's world spinning. Was that why Kali had chosen her? Sholi rarely lingered when the Creator called them free of their bodies. Kali putting off going to her place of peace always seemed like an act of pity. Perhaps she'd decided after seeing her grandcub's mate be treated like an outsider as well. Had they been Qinawe? Tribouin? An elf that didn't fit in?

The flock leader's eyes crinkled. "You have many questions."

Aven snapped her mouth shut. "I do. But that's—"

"Not why you are here." Yliva began walking a slow circle around the platform, adjusting her cloak so the colorful feathers dragged over the wood in her wake. Aven ached to lift the hem, to protect it from any nicks and grooves. It was such a beautiful thing, finer than anything she'd ever owned.

"I understand the Soulless are what have called you to climb so high."

"Yes." Aven pulled her attention back to Yliva's thin face. "And I'm so sorry for the harm your flockmates endured. They were brave to face down a Soulless."

"Thank you." The flock leader spared a loving glance for her watching people, admiration radiating like Sansia. "They will live, and we are grateful for that. I am proud of their lack of hesitation. They have strength of mind, not just blood."

"Strength of mind?" Aven asked. It wasn't time for distracting questions, but she'd never heard that shifter saying.

"Strong mind, strong people. When blood is being spilt, is not the mind the greatest weapon? A strong flock, a powerful shift, these cannot be all. Especially when they go untested. What is a strength if it is never used? Do the Qinawe have an answer for this?"

Aven glanced over the staring faces around them, noting the way Yliva said *Qinawe*. As if she spoke of an unpleasant bug. She imagined how Mama's brow would furrow and her eyes would darken. The claws wouldn't unsheathe, but Mama always had just the right barb to throw at questions against the Qinawe's path.

"I'm not a very good Qinawe," Aven admitted. "But Mama would say it's better to retreat than bear the blood of another."

"And if one cannot run?" Yliva tilted her head like a hawk sighting its prey.

A grin spread across Aven's face. "That's when I would be a really bad Qinawe."

Willa giggled from her perch. "You would make a wonderful griffin, though."

"Perhaps that is the lynx in you," Yliva said, touching a clawed fingertip to her chin.

Aven recalled Dinon's shining admiration as they'd spoken. "I'm starting to realize Kali has more influence over me than I thought."

"There could be worse souls to have such sway." The flock leader stroked her cloak of feathers, sharp features pinching sadly. "Kali was not only brave but wise. It is why she ruled so long without opposition. It is a shame she is not here now with Soulless prowling about."

Dev shot Aven a pointed look, his mouth pursed in a thin line. The topic had strayed long enough and the Tribouin and Qinawe still had to be convinced after this.

Aven had to move this along before the moons claimed the sky. "The dragons believe the Soulless will return. Possibly with more of their kind."

"I supposed they would know better about such things." Yliva glanced at the sky. "If history is correct, the dragons stood with the Elementals when the Soulless made their bloody march across Sholindrea."

"That is what they say," Dev whispered.

Yliva stalked along her invisible circle, her predatory energy forcing Aven to turn. "Who says?"

Dev frowned. "Pardon?"

Willa snickered, still crouched like she might attack at any moment. "Who says dragons stood with the Elementals in the Time of Sorrow?"

"Besides your flock leader?" Dev asked, staring Willa down. "*My* elders taught us of such things. Dragon souls are made of the same forces of nature as Elementals'. They may not appear so, but dragons are their closest kin."

"I wonder," Yliva said, eyes narrowing. "Which of those *forces* helps them shift?"

Aven inhaled sharply, glancing at the sky as if Rielnor would descend on them for even discussing the dragon's secrets.

Dev clearly harbored no such fear as corner of his mouth almost twitched into a smile. "I do not know the lore of what gives shifters their power. What parts of *your* souls aid griffins in shifting?"

The flock leader's stare chilled Aven to the bone. It wasn't a disrespectful question, but many Sholi races guarded the secrets of their souls. They all had a bit of Dia'veh and something of Sholindrea. Qinawe claimed a part of the Maker's connection to all and a piece of what bound nature to the Great Mother. It bonded the Qinawe to the souls they guarded, giving their flesh the ability to slip between the bodies of each. Tribouin believed they had a touch of Dia'veh's love of creation and Sholindrea's power to mold flesh, making them capable of shifting hair color, eye color, even muscle and skin texture. Whatever it took to survive.

If Aven had to guess, she'd say air and some connection to birds of the world came together inside the griffin.

Yliva's eyes bored through Dev as she continued walking. Her hands remained clasped before her, but the white flush over her knuckles gave her away. She met Willa's gaze for a moment, before looking Dev up and down.

"You have a sharp mind. Are you as worthy an opponent with your blade?"

Dev straightened, one hand gripping his sword while the other fisted by his belt. "My people's way is the sword and the shield. We serve without fear."

Unease settled in Aven's stomach at this exchange. Had they begun a new game or did Willa harbor a genuine interest in Dev? Griffins followed the shifter ways: Strength before love. Aven wouldn't see him go through what she did. The thought of her own unwanted mating challenge still sent tremors through her. She could only hope griffins found unsolicited challenges as horrific as the Qinawe did.

As subtle as she could, Aven tracked the flight leader's path and used it as an excuse to step between Willa and Dev. He immediately stiffened behind her, but dealing with his pride would be a lot easier than his discomfort over being mated to someone he just met. Papa's people demanded a clear line of sight and direct eye contact. Keep the challenge obvious about who it is for. That's why Tribouin always went everywhere in pairs until Promised.

"We didn't come to discuss blessings and power," Aven said, hoping to change the subject.

Yliva didn't break her staring match with Dev. "So what did you come here for?"

"We request your presence and your aid," he said, tracking her as she circled behind them again.

"I am sure you do, Stone elf. My presence where?"

"Tomorrow at Dia'veh's Temple," Aven said. "The Truthseeker has gone to the lynx, to request the pride leader come as well."

Yliva tilted her head. "Why did you not go instead? Kanai would not deny you anything."

"That's why I didn't. Each and every one of us needs to make informed, rational decisions about the days ahead."

Yliva dragged her gaze from Aven's feet all the way to her face, slow and calculating. "Very noble, but that does not make me inclined to do your bidding."

If she hoped to knock Aven off-kilter, she had the wrong impression. "Understandable. I wouldn't want you to do me any favors."

"No?" Yliva mused. "You don't intend to rally us to fight?"

Aven bit back a laugh. "No, no matter how amazing that would be. I just want you to come to the Temple so we can figure out what to do next. Yunaii is a free land, but right now there are Soulless here and we need a course of action before more innocents die."

"So, your plan is to have the elves get us to fight and then keep your own conscience clear?" Willa asked, the mischief gone from her face.

"An elf is here," Dev said, stepping around Aven. "We bleed for Yunaii, for nothing but love. A Linseen paid the gravest of prices for that devotion. We have no need for the unwilling to stand beside us. The fearful will not be a shield at our backs, but a hole in our armor."

Willa stiffened, her wings flaring out at her sides. "I am not afraid, blood-seeker."

Hush fell over the canopy as Dev's hand tightened on the pommel of his sword. The insult lingered like the stench of death, punctuated by ringing silence. Aven wasn't sure whether to interfere once more or let him have a crack at the griffin. The sour anger roiling around him left Aven worried for Willa. Until this moment, she had never wondered what he was capable of, never feared him.

Yliva broke the tension, stepping between them with hands clasped over her heart. Sunlight danced across her tanned skin and feathers as she bowed. "Forgive young Wilella. The loss and suffering inflicted by the Soulless still hangs heavy."

Dev didn't move at first. His eyes stayed fixed on Willa, who still crouched on a branch. Only when Aven touched his arm did the tension ease. Color returned to his knuckles as he loosened the grip on his sword. To strangers, it wasn't much, but he'd taken control once more.

"My people do not *seek* blood. We guard against it." His voice strained, the hazel of his eyes stormy beneath his heavy frown.

"Wilella spoke out of turn." The faint tremble in Yliva's bony fingers spoke true of what Klesian elves could do. "The griffins know what the elves give to the Sholi."

Dev stared a moment longer before turning on his heel, heading for the edge of the platform. "Aven, I will await you on the stairs."

"O-okay."

Silence reigned as he leapt to a lower branch, grabbed hold of another, then swung beneath a swath of foliage. Nothing lingered in his wake but the screeching songbirds he disturbed. Aven kicked herself for worrying about him now, and for thinking racings tips were all he could offer. Dev obviously knew how to handle himself and when to call it quits in a tense situation.

"The Soulless bring out the worst in us," Yliva whispered.

Hot irritation blossomed in Aven's chest. "Or the best. It brought out bravery and selflessness in your flockmates."

"This is true." Yliva glanced at her brethren, arched brows drawing into a mothering look. "I *am* proud of them. But hear this, Aven, daughter of Navya and Tomen. I will grant your request and come speak with the other leaders. Just know that I will not send my flock to suffer such painful deaths as the Soulless deliver. I will order them on a flight to distant lands before I allow more griffin blood to be spilled.

CHAPTER Seventeen

Aven

Even after Aven rejoined Dev on the stairs, the somber trek down was silent. Tension still showed in his raised shoulders and the pursed line of his mouth. He seemed intent on keeping his own counsel for now. Unfortunately, that left Aven trapped with hers, and her thoughts were not good company. She'd take an awkward exchange with the Truthseeker over the roiling confusion inside her.

Yliva had chosen to come to the Temple, so Aven shouldn't feel so defeated. The lynx and griffins had no reason to fight for her people. Maker knows, the Qinawe were pricklier than a dragon who hadn't eaten in days. The other shifters had every right to not care what happened to them or the Tribouin. *Aven* had every right to not care, but she didn't want to see them slaughtered. Not to mention Mama and Papa. Could they be convinced to fight? To hide? To at least keep to themselves until the Soulless moved on? Would the Soulless even move on? They'd once aspired to conquer all of Sholindrea. How many corpses would be enough to sate them?

Aven would drown in what-ifs by the time she made it to the ground, and the more that came, the more her chest tightened. Fear threatened to crash over her and drag her screaming beneath its depths.

She glanced back at Dev, missing the crack in his mask she'd glimpsed on the way up.

"You need not worry about me," he said, startling Aven enough to pause her steps.

"I wasn't."

Dev tilted his head, brows rising in obvious disbelief. "You attempted to step between me and Wilella."

"Oh." Aven sucked her teeth as her cheeks grew hot. "It's not what you think."

"Do you think me a blood-seeker?"

Aven stopped in her tracks. "What? Of course not."

He blinked a few times, as if he didn't understand. His eyes shifted back and forth before settling on her again. "Then why step between us if not for her protection?"

Heat seared up the back of Aven's neck. He was going to make her explain, as always. There was no dancing around things with Dev. She continued walking down the steps, considering each word before she spoke.

"I was worried about you."

"Me?" Dev touched her shoulder. "Why worry for me? Surely you do not think me so inept that a single griffin could fell me."

Aven picked some bark off the tree, trembling as soon as her eyes left the rickety steps. Surely, he realized they had only shared sadness over losing races. Maybe an occasional drink. Then they went their separate ways. "Before today, I had never even seen you hold a weapon. You've always just been an obsessed dragon rider like me."

"But you are aware I am a Klesian elf."

"So?" Aven ran a hand through her hair, wishing she were better with words. Mist would easily diffuse this conversation. She would have handled everything about today so much better than Aven. "Not every Linseen is a weapon master. Not every Qinawe is a legendary fighter. We're more than our blood, aren't we?"

Dev fell silent so long, Aven thought the conversation over.

"So, you feared for my safety?" His voice was a confused whisper.

"I was afraid she would claim you as a mate." The words tumbled out of her mouth before she could rethink them.

Thank goodness for the lack of railing and slim stairs. They gave her a reason to keep her attention on her feet. "I wasn't sure of her intentions."

"I think her intention was to be as annoying as a squawking bird," Dev said, bitterness creeping into his tone. "You thought I would lose in a fight with her?"

The question came out calmer than she expected, leaving Aven afraid to turn around. Was his jaw clenched or were his eyes curious? Did such an assumption insult him or endear him? Kali's soul clawed at her desire to avoid this conflict like Papa taught, urging her to turn and stare him down. It took a few deep breaths to fight back the itch.

"I didn't know what you were capable of," Aven admitted, steeling herself as her truths came out. Being honest ripped her apart, but laying herself bare might help him understand. "I didn't want you going through what I did, no matter if you could handle it."

Silence fell, leaving only the roaring of her heart pounding in her ears. She imagined slipping into Kali's fur and bounding away from this embarrassment. He could mull over her whispered secret and take what he would of it. If it wasn't enough to make him understand, then he probably never would.

After they'd made almost a full circle around the tree, Dev's voice cut through the deafening quiet. "Pryn?"

"Were you there when she—?" The familiar ache twisted in Aven's chest. Would it ever *stop* hurting? One of her most horrible moments had been an embarrassing, terrifying, public affair.

"Challenged to be your Chosen right in the middle of the crowded market?"

Aven swallowed hard as she nodded. She didn't like to think of that day, let alone speak of it. The day her best friend had betrayed her.

"I was not." Dev's steps quickened behind her. "Everyone knows, though. My understanding is that unreciprocated challenges are strongly discouraged."

A snort of disdain escaped Aven. "'*Discouraged*' is not the right word. Losing changes everything for the challenger. They might as well steal from Dia'veh's Temple. They won't lose as much face as trying to force someone to be their mate."

"That is why Pryn holds such animosity for you."

Aven shrugged, hoping he couldn't see the flush blossoming over her skin. Pryn's animosity. Pryn's pain. That's all anyone talked about since her childhood friendship imploded. As if Pryn had a right to be angry at *her*.

"She brought it on herself. She knew I didn't want to stay in Yunaii, and she never wanted to leave. Moving from the Qinawe's lands to the Tribouin's would change nothing for me. They resent me more than Mama."

"You truly did not know she saw you as her Chosen?"

Claws ached to slide from Aven's nails. "I was *perfectly* clear with her. No matter what the gossip is or the lies her family spreads. We might have been romantic at one point, but as soon as I realized she would never leave Yunaii, I knew we could never be Promised."

Aven's heart nearly stopped when Dev scurried along the edge of the steps to get around her. She grasped his shirt in shaking hands, only for him to plant himself in her path, brows furrowed as he stared up at her. No signs of disbelief shone on his face, but she searched anyway. She knew what many said about her and Pryn. The Tribouin whispered about how Tomen's forest cub tricked Pryn into hurling herself at the lowest caste of their people. The rumors they sparked spread like a weed until even some Qinawe gave her the same looks of disgust.

"To be Promised is to know you will one day battle and be mated, correct?"

Aven straightened. He'd accepted, without questions or arguments. What she would have given for that consideration after beating Pryn in the challenge fight.

He stood there, waiting patiently for an answer, demanding no proof or assurances she hadn't led Pryn on. So Aven considered his question. How could she describe shifter promises so they made sense? Settling a lifelong coupling through muscle and a mastery of weapons was not the way of humans, elves, and many other folk.

The answer came from the forest. Her eyes lit on the leaves rustling in the breeze, brushing against one another like two shifters in battle. She imagined it like she'd done so many times. She'd listened to Mama and Papa talk of their Promised day, when they'd faced each other in battle, knowing if the challenger won they would be together forever. As a child Aven had wondered if there'd ever be someone for her. She'd once thought it would be Pryn. Until the day they spoke of leaving Yunaii, resulting in a fight that left them angry for days. Family was everything for Tribouin, and leaving hers was too much to ask of Pryn.

"Mama says the challenge is more of a dance than a real fight." Aven pictured Mama with her axe, and Papa with his curved, short sword. To this day, she sometimes found them sparring in the clearing by their cave. They both always had such determination on their faces, but the brightest joy shining from their eyes.

"When both are Chosen, they know how it'll end." Aven looked back at Dev, willing him to understand. "Tribouin and Qinawe teach everyone their own style and grace that suits them, to make them strong for their Promised. It's like this flirtatious game when it comes, thwarting each other until the challenged yields or feigns a loss. Mama and Papa still joke about not knowing which of them lost their challenge. I'm pretty sure it was Mama. The Tribouin say awful things about her stealing him away, but I think he made the challenge. I wish I saw it. Their dance must have been beautiful. My people say the more passionate the couple, the more magnificent the challenge."

Dev glanced in the market's direction as if he could see through the trees. "I have seen a few in passing. It has been an interesting thing to witness. For my people, combat is a grim duty. Yours make it lovely to behold."

Aven stroked Kali's fang as the idea of facing down Mist snuck into her thoughts. Would her full lips set in a determined line or would a smile stretch across her face? Would they fight with weapons or claws? She imagined their blows bringing them closer and closer in the kind of dance she'd hoped for as a child. How long would it take to pin Mist to the ground and win her hand? Aven shivered, but quickly squashed it all down. Indulging in this fantasy was too dangerous. Dreaming left room for disappointment.

"Do your people do ceremonies like humans?" Aven cast a sideways look at Dev. Elven customs were a mystery to her, though they shouldn't be since the Linseen protected Yunaii. "Humans do vows or something, right? Rings and parties and stuff?"

"I *believe* so?" Dev scrunched up his nose. "I am loath to admit it, but I have interacted quite little with humans. My people's settlement is deep in a mountain range. Quite isolated, save for a Linseen encampment and some very shy fairies."

"So, what do elves do?"

Dev stared glassy-eyed into the distance, seeing something she couldn't.

"As all things, we are called to our intended. It is difficult sometimes to make a connection, since many of our clans are made of large families. My parents did not meet until their time of serving. They were soul-called to the same battlefield. Father says he saw my mother across the chaos of defending a human city under siege, and he knew he was meant for her. Of course, Mother claims it took her time to feel the same, but when one is soul-called to a charge, that takes hold of us. It becomes hard to see or feel beyond the need to aid. In the end, the pull brought them toward each other. When that happens, there is a joining ceremony. For Klesian elves it must be held on a field of stone, under the eyes of Dia'veh."

"The eyes of Dia'veh?"

"The stars, Aven." A near smile almost crept across Dev's lip, his eyes brightening. "Elves must join only under the stars. When one of Dia'veh's eyes streaks across the sky, the joining is blessed by the Creator."

"What if it takes days for a shooting star to come?" Aven pictured two elves staring at the sky, night after night, waiting for a tiny streak of light.

"We are a patient people. And we seek the Creator's approval in all things."

Aven almost whistled at such confidence in Dia'veh. "Do your people ever join with others? Humans, shifters, fairies?"

Dev raised a brow, giving her the most incredulous look she had ever seen. "A soul is a soul, Aven. The body means nothing. The one intended for us need not be our reflection. Dia'veh created a vast, diverse, beautiful world. What would be the point of it all if like only stayed with like?"

Aven would have thrown her arms around Dev if she wasn't certain he would hate it. Why, oh, why could she not have been born an elf? She didn't understand how shifters lived alongside them for this long when they saw things so differently.

"I have made you happy," Dev said, his hands moving to their usual spot on his sword pommel. "You look as if you just won a dragon race."

"I've done something better." Aven indulged an affectionate punch on his arm as she stepped past him. "I've decided we are officially friends, whether you like it or not."

He tilted his head quizzically before following her down the stairs. "I was unaware we were not already."

"Well, now you're stuck with me."

CHAPTER *Eighteen*

As the forest floor came into sight, so did the Truthseeker sitting with his back to the tree. His head rested against it, eyes closed, legs folded beneath him as if he were meditating. When he didn't acknowledge their descent, a hunter's desire welled in Aven's chest. She cast a look at Dev, holding one finger over her lips. Not that he needed shushing. Silence was his default, but Aven didn't want him ruining her fun.

She crept lower, stepping on tip-toe until coming low enough to leap safely from the stairs. Her stomach coiled, nerves vibrating as she shifted from foot to foot. Out of the corner of her eye, Dev shook his head, but foo on him. Her knees bent, then she launched, arching and turning as the ground drew near. Upon landing, she sank into a crouch amongst the leaves and shrieked in the Truthseeker's face.

The Steel elf didn't so much as flinch. He sat still as his namesake, hands resting on his knees. Were his shining white hair not a stark contrast to the forest's deep greens and browns, he might have disappeared into the shadows. His chest barely rose with breath. Aven frowned as she inched closer, staying on all fours, careful not to shift the underbrush. She sniffed at him, searching for any hint of injury or pain, but only found cold steel and mint.

"That seemed unnecessary," the Truthseeker said, his eyes opening lazily.

Aven froze, horror seizing her limbs. He blinked slowly, his mouth curving into a disapproving line. How did she look to him on all fours, her neck stretched out as she smelled him like a nervous dog? She'd come close enough he could wave a hand and accidentally slap her. Lucky for her, she guessed Gaelin the Truthseeker frowned on such behavior. Mama would have already whacked her head and called her a foolish cub.

The Truthseeker raised one white brow and sighed. "If your intention was to startle me, I could potentially fake such emotion should your ego require it."

A chuckle echoed above Aven's head, lilting and completely unfamiliar. It took her a moment to realize it came from Dev. It had to. His genuine smile all but confirmed it.

"I do not know which would be more amusing," Dev said, striding down the stairs. "Aven attempting that again or the Truthseeker feigning surprise."

"Oh, shut it." Aven sidled backwards, but didn't rise from her crouched position. "My ego doesn't need any stroking."

"Very well." The Truthseeker nodded before rising to his feet.

Aven watched him brush leaves from his breeches, never letting her attention stray. A Qinawe would look for a chance to thump her, but the elf didn't seem inclined to do the same.

"Any luck with the lynx?" Aven asked as she rose.

He shook his head, braids stiff against his neck. "I fear not as much luck as you."

The smile slipped from Aven's lips. He was hard to read, but she caught an unpleasant scent weaving through him. Not sorrow. Maybe disappointment. He was clearly unhappy, and she didn't need Kali's nose to be certain of that.

"What happened?" Dev asked, stepping beside Aven.

The Truthseeker gave him a quizzical look before clasping both hands behind his back. "Young Dinon took me to pride leader Kanai. A gracious host, but one unwilling to make any decision until he spoke with you."

His pale finger pointed at Aven.

"Me? Why? Did Dinon not tell him what I said?"

The Truthseeker nodded. "Despite that, Kanai insisted he speak with you and only you."

Aven rubbed her palms over her dry, weary eyes. So much for selflessness. Now she would waste more time going to the lynx before tackling the real battle: convincing the Tribouin and Qinawe to hear her out.

She glanced at the sky, tracking where Sansia hung. "How am I going to find time to speak with everyone today?"

The Truthseeker glanced at Dev before pursing his lips. "If I may, this task is not yours alone."

"I know." Aven fiddled with Kali's fang, fighting back the hopeless feeling devouring her. "It just feels like everyone is so concerned with only their piece of Yunaii. Why am I fighting to get them to care about our home?"

"Fear can bring out many things," Dev said, pushing curls from his face. "It is not always a willingness to fight that people find in themselves."

Aven knew he was right, even if she couldn't relate. The urge to slash and bite, to scream and rail, had always been inside her, ever since she was a cub. Even before Kali took pity on her.

"What do I do? I need to see the Tribouin and Qinawe, and those will not be easy conversations."

The Truthseeker thrust out his chin and a spackle of golden light fell across his pale cheeks. "I will speak with the Tribouin on behalf of Yunaii."

"Are you sure?"

"I am aware of their feelings for you." His silver eyes bored into her. "It might be prudent for someone else to go to them. I do not believe they will hear anything you have to say."

Aven's shoulders fell. "You're probably right. Thank you."

"Maybe the Priestess could accompany Aven to speak with the Qinawe Matriarchs?" Dev said, stroking his chin. "She holds a great deal of respect from all the shifters."

The corners of the Truthseeker's lips perked up in the oddest smile Aven had ever seen. It didn't fit his stoic face, nor did the softness in his silver eyes. "She would be quite willing to aid Aven in this. I will send her to the Qinawe as soon as we finish with the lynx."

Aven's face twitched over his assertions. The Priestess and the Truthseeker lived together in the Temple. Just the two of them. Until now, she'd thought of Gaelin as an immovable, impassive rock that glared at people and picked their thoughts. The idea of him and the wickedly amusing Priestess tumbling around the Temple made her close her eyes and swear.

"Oh gross." *Not* an image she needed in her head.

When she opened her eyes, Dev and the Truthseeker were staring with raised brows and confused expressions.

Searing heat washed through her cheeks. "Sorry. Um, Truthseeker—"

"Gaelin."

She drew a breath, ignoring the way Dev judged her with his gaze. "Gaelin. Please take me to pride leader Kanai."

"Of course," he said with a dip of his head. "Follow me."

Aven followed in the direction he and Dinon had gone earlier, kicking herself for being such a childish fool. When Dev slipped beside her with a curious look, she resolved to never meet his eyes again.

"What was gross?"

She sighed as loud as she could. "I've changed my mind. I don't want to be your friend anymore."

Dev blinked a few times as his brow furrowed. "I am unaware of whatever misstep I took to cause this."

By the Maker, Aven just couldn't this time. She'd embarrassed herself enough today. She would not say out loud that she'd imagined the Truthseeker and the Priestess in any kind of intimate way.

"I'm joking, Dev." She gave his arm an affectionate punch. "Let it go."

She pulled ahead, slipping between bushes and saplings with a skill he couldn't mimic. He mumbled his confusion, but she'd reassure him later that all was fine between them.

Right now, the comfort of moving through the forest beckoned. She dipped beneath low hanging tree limbs, skirting thorny bushes, stepping so she didn't rustle fallen leaves. This was peace. It was a place she couldn't slip up and make stupid mistakes. Where she could focus.

What did Kanai *need* to speak with her about? She had never met him. He couldn't have much interest in her outside of his mother's soul. Was that all it was? Maybe knowing Aven had stepped into his woods left him missing his kin. She couldn't blame him if that was it, she just wished it could be at a better time. Dancing through Willa and Yliva's word games had already taken longer than she liked. Aven needed as much time set aside as possible to go to the Qinawe Matriarchs.

The forest announced their arrival, larger trees falling away, leaving saplings to populate a large clearing. Dirt yielded to smooth, red rock, and water splashed from the cliff high above. The waterfall poured out of a large groove over their heads, crashing into a massive pool much like the bathing pond near Aven's home. It fed into a small stream rushing into the forest, most likely pouring into the Lighe River.

All around the water lounged the lynx. Their colors ranged from light grays to dark browns, some with stripes or spots and others with splashes of color that were more like Kali's. Most of them were on four legs, but she recognized Dinon amongst a small group of shifted lynx gathered near the pond's edge.

When their eyes met, she received a bright smile on the lynx's sunny face. They quickly leapt from their perch on a boulder, landing gracefully amongst the sparse patches of grass before running her way.

"Aven!"

"Hello."

"I'm glad you came." Dinon glanced back towards the water. "The pride leader wishes to see you."

"So I heard."

Their smile faltered before they beckoned her forward. "Don't worry. Kanai wants to set eyes on you. To hear you speak."

Aven trailed behind him, unable to hold back her mountain of questions. "That couldn't wait for a less stressful day?"

"Aven," Dev whispered at her back. "Perhaps save such impertinent questions for when we are not surrounded by mouths full of flesh tearing teeth."

She threw a teasing grin at his scowling face. "What's wrong? Griffins that want to mate you are child's play, but lynx are too much?"

Dev's shoulders thrust back. "Hardly. I am only thinking of your safety."

"Don't worry." Her claws extended against the scars on her palms, "I've got fangs of my own."

Dinon led them to where a large male basked in Sansia's warmth, spread out across a flat rock like a lazy cat. Scars raked into his shoulder, and his hair fanned around his head and from the corners of his jaw like a lynx's mane. He'd thrown one arm over his eyes, and as time ticked by, Aven wondered if he was actually sleeping.

"Kanai?" Dinon whispered, stopping just out of arm's reach. "I brought Aven to you."

"I know," the pride leader's deep voice rumbled. "I smell my mother. I could almost pretend she was here."

Aven's heart clenched. What could it be like? To scent and sense someone long dead? If one day someone possessed Mama's soul, she didn't know what she would do. The thought of her parents eventually leaving her was hard enough. To know one of them lingered on with someone else—she couldn't imagine it.

"I've—" Aven glanced around, unsure if she should come closer. "I've wanted to speak with you for a long time."

Kanai exhaled slowly before sitting up, his knee bending for him to lean an elbow on. As his temple rested against one curled fist, he studied her face, Kali's fang, taking in every detail all the way down to her feet. When their eyes finally met, Aven mustered an uncomfortable smile.

"It's a strange thing," Kanai said. "My eyes don't believe she's not standing before me."

Aven skimmed her claws over the soft flesh of her hands, searching for the right words to say. "You must miss her a lot."

"We all do." Kanai tilted his head against his hand. "I lost my mother and not long after, my cub decided to leave Yunaii. It has been a lonely time in my life."

Yliva had mentioned Kali's granddaughter. Nya. She'd left with her mate because they didn't fit in. Aven ached to ask about Nya's mate and where had they gone. To Estellias? Somewhere to the north? Were there other places where someone's family and background didn't matter?

"You have her curiosity." A half smile stretched across Kanai's face. "You are bursting with questions."

Heat crept through Aven's cheeks. "You have no idea."

"I'm sure I do."

"I told her to come when the moons are full," Dinon said. "I told her we dance and we remember."

"Yes." Kanai ran a clawed hand through his mane of burgundy hair. "You are always welcome. You can tell me of her soul. How she fares. What you discern from her. I would be grateful."

Aven lowered her eyes and for once didn't hate it. "I'd be honored."

"You could bring Mist," Dinon said almost too softly for her to hear. "She would be welcome too."

Aven ducked her head, hiding from their smile. Dinon had too much feline mischief. What would they do when Mist stood before them?

"A conversation for another time." Kanai stretched in the sun, fingers flexing, his bare chest a mix of brown fuzz like Kali's, with a streak of silver down the middle like the soft underbelly of a cat's.

"The Truthseeker said you had to speak with me."

Kanai glanced at the elf. "Yes. He informed me you went to the griffins. Tell me, what did Yliva say to your request?"

Aven ran her thumb down Kali's fang. Was Kanai looking to follow the flock leader's direction? "She will come tomorrow to the Temple, but—"

"But she will not fight the Soulless. As I expected."

"I can't blame her," Aven said, wrapping her arms around herself. "I saw what the Soulless did to the Linseen that fought them. It was awful."

Kanai scratched at the hair framing his strong jaw, his gaze lingering on the waterfall. "We have all lived quite sheltered here, hidden away from the Soulless. From the world. Sometimes it feels like the rest of the Sholi have forgotten us."

"I doubt anyone who doesn't know Yunaii is here would ever stumble upon us," Aven mused.

He raised one clawed finger. "Yet here we are, with not one but three Soulless stumbling upon us. How has this come to pass?"

Aven straightened as her confusion cleared. So that's what he wanted. Not just a whiff of his mother. He wanted information. Did he hope to get something different from her than the Truthseeker? Or had the elf simply denied him on the grounds of protecting the secrets of others? Aven cast a sideways glance at Gaelin, but he didn't so much as blink at Kanai's question. Would he stop her from being honest with the lynx? She'd danced with Pryn and Yliva, but looking into Kanai's bright yellow eyes brought answers bubbling to her lips.

"I have been made aware of the Linseen's losses." Something simmered in his voice. Maybe anger. Maybe sorrow. Aven wasn't quite sure. "But no one has acknowledged how my pride lost two members today."

Everything slowed and sped up all at once. Aven's heartbeat roared, watching lynx perk their ears forward. Her stomach felt like it dropped out of her, leaving a hollowness inside.

Kanai rose to his full height, his long tail swishing back and forth. "Two lynx who were selling their daily catch in the market. My understanding is a girl with white hair went into their tent, but she was the only one who made it out alive."

Mist. She'd told Aven about Nodi and Rymia, and yet somehow their loss and their faces had slipped beneath fretting over griffins and fearing the Qinawe and Tribouin would not listen. Is that what bloodshed did? Force politicking to the forefront, while something precious and irreplaceable got pushed to the wayside? She glanced around the clearing, seeing the lynx with fresh eyes. Few smiles lightened their faces and the great cats watched with lowered ears and tucked tails.

"Pride leader I—"

"The Soulless killed my pride members." His calm voice made Aven's heart quicken. "No one will tell me why or what became of them, or the girl who witnessed their deaths. But I have a right to know. Their families have a right to know."

"You're right," Aven whispered, blinking fast against hot tears. Which of these lynx would never see their loved ones again? Who had lost a daughter or son? A sibling or a cousin? All for what? Aven still didn't understand why the Soulless were here. Mist said to hurt dragons, but why?

"I'm sorry, Pride leader Kanai. I should have given my condolences as soon as I arrived."

Kanai rumbled low in his chest. "I prefer explanations. How did they die? What became of the girl? Why has she not come to explain what happened?"

Aven took a step forward. "She had to attend to her own kin. She meant no disrespect."

Kanai's catlike ears flicked back as his lips pulled into a frown. "Did her kin die today?"

Aven opened her mouth, but found the lies too bitter to spew. "N-no."

"Did she feel no duty to come before me and explain?"

"I'm sure she would have once she could. She was hurt in the fight." Aven glanced first at Dev, then at the Truthseeker, pleading silently for help.

"These are truths I could not speak," Gaelin said, his arms folded behind his back.

Aven could have clawed his face off for not even hinting at what she was walking into. "You could have warned me."

"So you might prepare a believable lie?" Kanai asked. "I hoped you, the guardian of Kali, would spare me the half-truths and nonsense being spewed throughout Yunaii. No one knows what to think or believe, but all I know is that two lives under *my* charge are dead. Have you nothing to offer me?"

Aven gripped Kali's fang in a fist, wishing not for the first time to ask the great cat for help. She would know how to handle this; what truths to share and how to diffuse the situation without putting her family in danger. The dragon's secrets would come out, eventually. Could Rielnor really punish her now? Could he blame her for Emriel's choice?

"Why do I scent fear in you, cub?" Kanai asked. He'd stepped closer as she wrestled with herself. Close enough to see his nostrils flare as his familiar scent filled her nose. Spicy. Woodsy. She didn't understand how she knew that scent so well.

Aven tightened her grip on Kali's fang, breathing deep as she made her choice. "The truths you seek could put my family in danger."

Kanai glanced towards the members of his pride, his gaze searching. Aven caught his half of a silent exchange—his eyes widening, lips pursing. When he looked back at her, a hint of understanding crossed his face.

"Would this have to do with the dragon you attacked yesterday?"

Aven searched the surrounding lynx for the markings of the two who had protected her from Fennicks. They must have told Kanai what they knew, but how much had they gleaned from her parent's brief exchange with Rielnor?

Kanai rested a hand on her shoulder. "We can protect you. You have no need of fear."

Aven should have felt relief. He was trying to reassure her, comfort her, but all that came was anger. Hot, searing anger. Her eyes snapped to his face, and she knew he knew it because he immediately withdrew his touch.

"Your pride couldn't protect my family yesterday in the clearing." Aven stepped towards him, claws distending from fingers that were no longer clenched. "Even the Linseen were helpless. My Papa almost took dragon fire for a choice *I* made."

The Truthseeker said her name, but Aven ignored him. She stalked towards Kanai, sinking into the burning lighting in her chest. Fangs brushed the tender flesh inside her mouth, but even that didn't stop her.

"Only the dragons' self-preservation spared my family yesterday. Not mercy. Not intimidation. They just didn't want to bring more trouble on themselves."

Kanai stood his ground, his chest heaving as she drew closer. Claws extended from his hands, but she was too sick of being bullied and manipulated to care.

"I understand your fear, cub."

"You don't!" Her words echoed through the clearing. "All day I have been hounded for answers, threatened and cajoled. Everyone wants to know what I know, and then they rage at me for not saying. Yet no one asks me why. No one thinks maybe I can't speak."

A hand touched her shoulder. Aven whirled, claws ready to slash at whatever lynx had dared. But it was just Dev. He watched her with wide eyes, his lips parted in surprise.

"Take a breath," he urged, voice barely a whisper as a surprising tang wafted off of him. Dev was nervous, maybe even afraid.

She glanced around and found all the lynx watching intently. Some had stood with hackles raised and tails puffed out in anger. Most of their ears were pinned back and their teeth bared. She had threatened their pride leader. They were ready to act.

Aven drew in a deep breath through her nose and held it. When her exhale came, she imagined blowing the anger away. Then she did it again. Even as she calmed, she held onto her claws, willing them to stay despite the shift melting away.

When Aven looked back to Kanai, she couldn't interpret what she saw. His brow furrowed like a snarling cat, his pupils so thin they were almost entirely yellow, but he didn't threaten back. He could have. His people would support if he lashed out with teeth and claws to remind her who ruled this place. Yet even his scent lacked the anger she expected.

They stared at each other as Kanai seemed to consider what to do with her. His head tilted to one side as he looked her over in that same scrutinizing way he had upon her arrival. As if he saw things others didn't.

"You have my mother's fire, little sister." One corner of his mouth lifted in a fanged smile. "I see you now. I understand."

"Do you?" Aven asked, not ready to yield. She'd spent too much of the day being treated like a cub that needed to sniff the ground and show her belly. "I understand you want answers. Believe me, I *want* to give them to you. You deserve them. Everyone does. But I've spent since last night having to scrape and beg mercy from everyone only to be threatened and talked down to. All the while, people I love bleed."

Kanai blinked once, a look of resignation overtaking his face. "Very well. We are at an impasse."

Aven hated herself for the defeat in his voice. The death of his people needed to be answered for and the pride deserved the whole story. But with Rielnor's mercy standing between her family and the flight's wrath, she was helpless.

She was. What about Emriel? If she survived whatever the flight planned for her, of course.

"I'll make you a deal, Kanai," Aven said, hoping the Truthseeker wouldn't take issue with her plan. "Come to the Temple tomorrow. If the answers are not given to you at the meeting, I will introduce you to the ones who have less to fear than me."

The pride leader tugged at his mane as he considered her proposal. She couldn't blame him for his hesitation. The lynx weren't bound to protecting others like the elves. They'd given enough blood, and like the griffins, leaving would be easier for them. As Kanai's gaze slid over his pride, his mouth a thin line, Aven grew certain that was exactly what he intended. Perhaps he would seek his cub instead of bothering with troubles that weren't his.

When Kanai extended his clawed hand, Aven fought to keep her face blank.

"Tomorrow it is," he said, flashing his sharp canines in a feral smile.

Aven bit back an excited whoop as she grasped his forearm in a tight grip. The urge to hug him nearly got the best of her, but she swallowed down the childish desire. "Thank you, pride leader."

"Until then, little sister."

CHAPTER
Nineteen

Mist

ist didn't know where to go, or even where she was. She'd finally picked up Aven's hint of desert flowers over the strong traces of lynx musk. It led her deeper than she'd ever gone into the cats' territory. Hopefully, that was a good sign. They needed all the shifters to take the Soulless seriously. If Aven was here, it meant she was doing what Mist had asked.

Her chest tightened as she searched. Every rustle of green or shadow made her jump.

Where are you, Aven?

The space beside her was a gaping hole Aven filled every day. It didn't feel right being apart. The life Mist had before Yunaii was a living dream that faded with each passing day. Chasing Dia'veh's voice in search of a purpose ended when she looked into the blend of bronze, emerald, and gold in Aven's eyes. Maybe a smile stretching across her pink lips could pull Mist from the hollowness dragging her down. Or one of her deep, enveloping hugs. Perhaps that might purge the pieces of her that Emriel had shattered.

"Mist?"

A sob rattled through her as exactly who she needed appeared from a dense thicket of saplings.

"Aven."

The smile she craved crinkled Aven's eyes. Mist was so enraptured she didn't quite realize when Aven had broken into a run, or when she'd done the same. They dashed towards each other, dipping beneath branches and wheeling around rocks. She barely noticed they had an audience following Aven's path. Whoever it was didn't matter.

After leaping over a fallen tree, they collided, Mist returning the fierce hug wrapping around her. Sweet desert flowers filled her nose as she pressed her face to Aven's neck, losing control of the tears running hot down her cheeks. She didn't care, though. This was home.

Aven was *home*.

The thought shuddered through her. When did she fall so hard?

"Are you okay?" Aven's arms trapped their bodies together.

"A little better now." She would tackle those questions another day. She wouldn't let them ruin this moment.

Aven smiled against her neck, so Mist pulled back just enough to catch another glimpse. Joy shone like Sansia, warming her heart. She yearned to do more than stare at Aven's perfect lips. The urge to brush a peck over their softness nearly got the best of her. It was so tempting. But until Aven knew what she wanted, Mist wouldn't add to her woes. She'd never betray her the way Pryn had.

"What happened with the dragons?" Aven asked, hands settling against Mist's back. "Is Emriel okay?"

Mist hated how bitterness poisoned their moment. "She was alive when I left. Despite her best efforts not to be."

Worry stole the light in Aven's eyes, bringing everything crashing back to reality. Sounds of the forest pressed around them. Twigs snapping. Footsteps shuffling. Reminders they were not alone.

"I'll tell you later," Mist said, untangling from Aven's body. Cold rushed over her, summoning that hollow feeling again. She mustered a false smile as Aven's companions drew near: Dev and Truthseeker Gaelin.

"Ah, young Mist." The Steel elf dipped his chin politely.

"Truthseeker," she said before turning her attention to Dev. "How did Aven wrangle you into this?"

He scrutinized her face, staring so long she fidgeted. His eyes darted back and forth, as if he'd never seen her before, like he took in every detail. Whatever he searched for, though, he didn't find it. A disappointed sound rasped out of him as he straightened his shirt.

"I needed no wrangling," he said, giving Aven a sideways look. "I am soul-called."

"Really?" Mist tried to hide her disbelief—and concern. "Do you know to who?"

"I do not." His disheartened tone pulled at her heart. "For a moment, I thought it might be you. But it is not."

Mist stifled a weary laugh. "I'm no warrior."

Dev cocked his head to the side, sending a tumble of curls flopping over his forehead. "You have a fighter's soul."

"I definitely do not." She tried not to picture Emriel's infuriated face as her angry words ricocheted in her head. "I know my way around a pike or spear, but as my sister so kindly informed me today, I am useless in a fight."

Aven's head jerked up, her brow furrowed. She didn't need to speak for Mist to know her thoughts. If their hands were intertwined, she was certain the prick of claws would brush against her palm. Itching to cut and slash. Em was lucky her face wasn't there to catch a ripping swipe, even if she deserved it. She'd come in true form to Yunaii, with all the headaches and frustration Mist had fled from.

"I was unaware you had family here in Yunaii," Dev said.

"She only just arrived." And she would hopefully be leaving soon, before Mist had to watch her, or someone else she loved, get hurt. *Again.*

Dev cast another sideways look at Aven, leaving Mist wondering what she missed. They seemed comfortable with each other. If that was the right word. What had happened while she was dealing with the dragons' drama? She hadn't been gone *that* long.

"So, was the red dragon in the market your sister?"

Aven's eyes went wide while Mist's jaw dropped.

"How did you—"

"Well, that answers two of my questions." Dev brushed a thumb over the pommel of his sword, with an almost satisfied smile. "Aven, is there not more we must accomplish today?"

"Wait, wait, wait," Mist said, intercepting him when he tried stepping away. "How long have you known about us? Did Rielnor tell you?"

Dev arched a brow. "I know no Rielnor. I have simply encountered dragons outside of Yunaii."

"I'm going to need more information." He'd known all this time? How many flights did he know of? Where were they?

"Welcome to my day," Aven said with an exaggerated eye roll. "But Dev is right. We need to get moving."

Mist glanced at the forest they had emerged from. "The lynx and the griffins?"

"They're reluctantly coming to the Temple tomorrow," Aven said. "I think Yliva of the griffins is considering leaving Yunaii."

"I wouldn't blame her if she does," Mist said, glancing up at the trees. If only she'd been the one to go up there with Aven. Seeing the flock must have been thrilling. "This isn't their problem."

"The Soulless made themselves a problem for us all," Dev said. "If they return, it must be all who handle this."

Aven stared towards her people's lands, a pinch of worry creasing her brow. "We'll need the Tribouin and the Qinawe to do that, and I've got no idea on how to get them to listen."

"Let me worry about the Tribouin," the Truthseeker said. "They will not hear you out."

Aven's nostrils flared, but he was right. They would be the hardest to convince. Between their resentment of Navya and disgust over Aven's raising, it would be pointless for her to go before them.

"Would it help if I went with you?" Mist asked reluctantly. "I—" she glanced at Dev. It was strange that he knew her secret. "I have been impersonating a nomad Tribouin."

The Truthseeker's brows drew up. "It is unlikely your presence would be of assistance. In matters of leadership, they will not care for the advice of a girl, especially not one of their own. I will inform the Tribouin Elders that Pride Leader Kanai intends to come. His presence may yet sway them. That is their way."

Aven crossed her arms. "It's nonsense."

"It is not," he said, waving his finger at her. "The Qinawe way is not so different. Matriarchs are awarded more respect than others. Your people do what they believe is best for their people. This is the Tribouin way as well."

Mist rested a hand on Aven's arm. The Truthseeker meant well. Seeing the truth of things and in others was a part of him, even if it biased him to the Tribouin and Qinawe clinging to customs more than the people the customs were made for.

"Use the flock leader agreeing to come to your advantage," the Truthseeker said, pinning Aven with a hard stare. "The Matriarchs may respect her decision. Even if it seems unimportant to you."

Aven's lips parted, but before she could speak, Mist gave her arm a gentle squeeze. "We'll take that into consideration."

"Very good. I will send Ifera to you as soon as I get to the Temple." He looked at each of them before lowering his eyes. "I will see you all tomorrow."

Aven visibly stiffened. "We can come to the meeting?"

The look in his silver eyes turned calculating. "You have made this happen. Tomorrow, we meet with those who will put Yunaii's people and their safety first. You have earned the right to be there."

"Even though we're not leaders?" Derision dripped from Aven's lips like something bitter she wished to spit on the ground.

"Yunaii has never had need of a ruling body," the Truthseeker said. "We all have our own ways and respect each other's right to exist. We must come together to maintain our safety. If the other leaders have issues with your presence, I will remind them no leader has looked out for yours."

Aven smothered a snort of laughter, and as the Truthseeker gazed with a deadpan stare, Mist found herself unable to stifle the giggle bubbling out of her chest.

"That was not intended as a joke." Gaelin glanced at Dev. "I will inform the leaders of this truth should they disparage your presence."

"Oh, I hope you do," Aven said. "Just please wait until I'm there to see their faces. The only thing better than that would be dragon dung plopping on their heads."

This time Mist snorted as she pictured the shifters' horror and disrespect. It would be worth whatever haughty snobbery they cooked up later.

"Well," the Truthseeker said, appearing perplexed. "Until tomorrow. Good luck with the Matriarchs. I am certain Dia'veh will guide you. You have achieved much this day already."

"I'd almost prefer facing a dragon over them," Aven muttered, but the Truthseeker must not have heard. He bowed to Dev before making his way west, towards the Tribouin's lands in the canyon. Once he had disappeared between the trees, Dev looked at Mist and Aven with uncertainty.

"I am unsure I would be of any help with the Qinawe. I doubt they will care for anything I have to say."

"Most likely," Mist said, trying not to wince. The Matriarchs had little use for the opinions of boys.

"You can walk with us though." Aven offered a friendly smile, but Dev only sighed.

"Thank you, but I think I will go to my cousins and speak with Zoli and Commander Senwe." Weariness lingered in the lines of his face and the depth of his hazel eyes. "They will undoubtedly need to be at the meeting tomorrow. Plus, there should be a platoon to guard the Temple should the Soulless to strike when all of Yunaii's leaders are gathered together."

Mist shivered at the thought. It would be a massacre. The Temple's lands were guarded against acts of violence, but once the leaders stepped outside, they would be at Ukila's mercy.

"Will the dragon's flight leader be in attendance at the meeting?" Dev asked.

"I don't know." Aven smiled as she picked dirt from beneath her fingernail. "If you see Topaz before us, you should ask him. I'm sure he'd like to be there."

"Aven!" Mist gasped in horror. What had compelled her to say that?

"Topaz is—" Dev's lips parted as his breathing slowed. A confused look crossed his face, one Mist had never seen on an elf before. "I have been riding the leader of the dragons—in *dragon races*?"

"There it is," Aven said, grinning like a lynx about to feast on its morning kill.

"How? Why?" Dev shook his head, his shoulders drawn so tight he looked almost in pain. "Why would he?"

Aven clapped him on the shoulder. "Mist and I have been wondering that for *ages*. Now you can suffer with us, my friend."

He blinked a few times, eyes unfocused, then waved weakly before wobbling off into the woods, looking like he'd just gotten proof Dia'veh wasn't real.

"That was mean!" Mist gasped once he was gone.

"He deserved it," Aven said, tapping the tip of Mist's nose. "He's been dropping surprises like that all day. I'm pretty sure he'd have been cackling every time if he knew how."

Mist snickered despite herself as Aven headed east, towards the Qinawe's lands. She followed without question, trusting her sense of direction. Mist easily got turned around without Sansia or stars to guide her. Tracking was not one of Papi's skills, so he had little to pass on to her. He was a blacksmith by trade, and only an average hunter. They'd relied much on Tem'bria's market when she was growing up.

Her body ached as she trudged through the forest, remembering to follow Aven's steps even though each of her own dragged. Dealing with grumpy old Matriarchs was not how she imagined ending this day, but of course she hadn't planned on starting it with a Soulless attack either. At least she was heading in the direction of clean clothes. The scraps of her bloodstained dress kept snagging on branches and thorns.

"You're quiet," Aven said with a curious look over her shoulder. "Are you okay?"

Mist shrugged. "I'm tired. Thinking about home, Papi, Adair."

Aven sidestepped a thick bramble, then held it back for Mist to follow. "I know you miss them."

"I do," she replied, lifting a branch in turn so Aven could pass. "I wish they were here. I wish Papi could help."

"I get that," Aven replied, leading them onto a barely noticeable hunter's trail. She stepped through twigs and leaves so perfectly, barely a mound of dirt shifted under her feet. "Do you want to talk about what happened at the roost?"

Mist worked her jaw back and forth, grinding her teeth together. There was so much to tell. Where should she begin? The revelation that Rielnor was Emriel's egg-warden, or that Fennicks was once her mate? Or that Em used the Soulless attack for her own gain? Mist's head spun every time her mind wandered to the dragons. Things had always been complicated with them, but now—now how could she ever go back? Did she even want to?

Without even meaning to, she let all her thoughts and worries pour out, one thing after another. The way the challenge went between Em and Fennicks. How she'd saved Emriel's life only to be chastised. Then the implication that Eega thought Mist was useless.

She didn't mean to thrust it all on Aven. There was nothing anyone could do about any of it, but screaming at Em would get her nowhere. She *never* listened. So, Mist ranted on and on, her chest burning like fire. Even when tears blurred her vision and slowed their trek, she kept going, leeching the poison with every word, dispelling her fear that she was nothing more than a failure—that she would never be dragon enough. This was a thought she'd never voiced aloud, but had worried her from time to time.

When she'd run out of things to say, Mist fell silent, every cut on her body stinging. She hadn't meant to stop walking, but at some point, she had. The sky pressed down on her, trying to force her to her knees. If she sank to the soft, cool dirt, Mist wasn't sure she'd be able to rise again. Fennicks' bite pinched, her knees throbbed, her shoulder was stiff each time she moved. It was so tempting to lie down right there.

She stared at her feet when Aven stepped close. Heat radiated, and when her fingers slid over Mist's cheeks, they blazed with warmth that sent her skin tingling.

Mist lifted her chin and gazed into Aven's eyes. She couldn't help noticing how long her lashes were or how her plump lips puckered before she spoke. They looked incredibly soft.

"I'm sorry," Aven murmured, the movement of her mouth ensnaring Mist's focus. "I wish I'd been in the market today. I wish I could have gone to the roost with you. I wish we could restart this day."

Her palms cupped Mist's cheeks, bringing her thumbs to brush against the corner of Mist's eyes. The touch almost had her sinking into Aven's body, collapsing against her shoulder, where she could bury her face and hide from the world. Aven would let her if she did.

"I'm so tired." Mist's head fell forward until their foreheads touched.

"I know," Aven whispered, caressing her cheekbones. "I promise I've got this. I've got you."

Mist exhaled slowly. "It's not your job."

"It is." Aven bumped her nose against Mist's, prompting her to look up. "It's my job to help you. You're my best friend. If I need to carry you instead of you carrying me, that's what I'll do."

A smile pulled at Mist's lips. There was no arguing with Aven, and honestly, she didn't want to. She wanted this, craved it. To be close to her, be weak with her. She always had to be the strong one, the calm one, the person holding

Aven back or pushing her forward, depending on what fight they faced. After the last two days, Mist didn't know if she could be anything but a sobbing pile of tired old bones.

"Aven," Mist whispered. She could stare into Aven's eyes all day, mapping each streak of color or the little spot of black amongst the brown. She'd memorized them all long ago, but still loved losing herself in their depths.

She lifted her chin enough to bring their noses together, heart beating loud in her ears, thumping against her chest like it wanted to escape. Aven's breath fanned against her lips, that's how close they'd drawn together. For just a moment, she wanted to cross that last bit of distance, to touch the warm flesh of Aven's mouth with her own. Would she soften and yield, or would she recoil in fear? Mist wished with all her heart to not be plagued with these what-ifs. If only Aven would do it. If only she'd cross the divide keeping them apart.

A shaky breath slipped from Aven, her eyes darting back and forth, searching for something. Mist didn't know what. Whatever answer Aven wanted, she would give it to her. If it closed the gap between them, she'd say whatever Aven needed to hear, no matter the price.

The fingers holding her cheeks pulled so gently, Mist almost didn't feel it. Only when she saw Aven moving closer, felt the heat of her breath against her face, did Mist realize what was happening. Her lips parted in a gasp that was almost a sob as she leaned in too.

But before she could explore Aven's sweet mouth with her own, an angry shout ripped through the forest. Birds screeched; leaves rustled. Aven whipped around, muscles tensing against Mist's body as she searched for the source of the sound.

Mist glanced from tree to tree, scanning the shadows, her attention jumping to anywhere the foliage moved. Another shout echoed, coming from the direction of the Qinawe's encampment. Mist's stomach dropped, and she guessed Aven realized at the same time she did that something was wrong with her people.

Without a word, they dashed towards the noise, exhaustion beaten back by fear. Mist tried not to let the pain in her knees slow them down, but Aven still pulled ahead. The voices grew louder, a cacophony of anger and frustration belting out. But at who? Mist couldn't make out what they were yelling.

Signs of the Qinawe popped up around them: spatterings of crops, cooling cook fires, abandoned hides ready for tanning. Yet not a single Qinawe in sight, on two legs or four.

They followed the rising noise, nearing the clearing where the Qinawe held meetings for the bond, the same place Hanawi had confronted Aven only yesterday. Smoke wafted from the giant fire meant for larger kills, the smell mingling with the scent of cooking meat.

As they drew closer, Mist grabbed at Aven's elbow and tugged. It sounded like a large crowd had gathered, all shouting over one another. They heard voices of young and old, all laced with anger and confusion, the topic a mystery without making out their words.

Until a single sentence rose over the din and sent ice through Mist's blood.

"Where is your cub, Navya?"

Aven clamped a hand over Mist's forearm and darted behind a tree. They were almost there. Mist scented the Qinawe now, their musky smells woven through with bitterness that crinkled her nose. With their hands clasped together, Aven and Mist darted from tree to tree, sneaking closer to the clearing, ducking out of sight as members of the bond moved around its edge. Their backs were to the forest, giving them the chance to get close enough to a tree with a terrace built around its trunk.

Aven's claws unsheathed as she leapt, ripping through bark as she hauled herself up to where she could see over everyone's heads. Mist followed as best she could, but with the mad dash over, her body moved like sap dripping down the tree. Everything hurt, and her back felt so tight she could barely turn or tense without a bolt of pain.

Thankfully, as soon as Aven scrambled over the edge of the terrace, she threw a hand out for Mist to grab. With only a strained grunt, she pulled, bringing them both onto the wooden planks. Once they settled, Aven touched a finger to her lips before crawling towards the side overlooking the clearing. Bodies shifted and flailed beneath them as the Qinawe crowded around, their attention and shouts directed beyond the low burning fire in the cooking pit.

The Matriarchs all gathered at the base of one of the larger trees, two sitting on its massive roots, while Hanawi stood before them. Her sour face scowled at the person standing alone beside the fire pit.

Mist didn't have to see her face to recognize who had drawn the Matriarch's rage. The rows of braids over her head, the old and beautiful axe on her belt, and the straight-backed posture were nearly as familiar as her own Papi's face. Navya stood with her shoulders thrust back and arms relaxed at her sides, seeming almost oblivious of the people shouting around her. Even when Hanawi marched towards her with head lowered and her fists balled, Navya didn't so much as twitch a finger.

"Answer the question," the Matriarch snapped. "Where is your cub? Present her now, or face exile from the Qinawe and our lands."

CHAPTER

Twenty

Aven

Aven was off her belly and leaping from the platform before Mist could blink. Sometimes she forgot how fast she was, how deadly. Mist stared where Aven had been, trapped in a heat-induced stupor. Only when claws raked through bark did she realize what was about to happen.

Her body protested, but Mist pushed to her feet and jumped. Wings weren't an option, so she imagined the muscles of her legs bulging, her bones fortifying for the impact. It took all her control to hold the shift and keep her shins from snapping when her feet hit the ground. Her teeth slammed together as tremors shot through her legs, but her bones held. Mist had just enough time to catch Aven around her waist and shove her back against the tree with enough force to stun.

"Wait!" Mist pleaded. "Think."

Aven drew in a deep breath, her chest heaving against Mist's in a way she didn't want to notice. They didn't have time for distractions.

"Your mama can handle herself," Mist said before looking to the crowd. So far, only one or two Qinawe had noticed them. That wouldn't last long. "Follow her lead."

Aven nodded over and over, as if struggling to understand Mist's words. "Okay, but we need to get to her."

"Absolutely." Mist indulged an angry smirk. "We're not letting Hanawi talk to her like that."

Aven grinned, showing off Kali's fangs, the amber in her eyes melding back to brown. She gripped the hand Mist had planted over her heart and pushed off the tree. With their fingers wrapped together, they walked towards the crowd with heads held high. The few Qinawe who saw them coming nudged those nearby, their whispers chasing Aven and Mist long after they passed. A pathway parted, creating a straight line for Navya, whose black eyes flicked their way without so much as a smile.

Hanawi was another matter. Her lips thinned, gaze darting over their joined hands, and Mist's blood splattered dress. Aven's murderous glare made her eyes widen.

"Where have you been?" Hanawi drew herself up, as if that gave her a haughty edge.

Mist almost laughed in her face. The Matriarch was taller than Aven, but not her. Their gazes were level, and today Mist wasn't lowering her eyes. Especially not when Aven's fingers tightened around hers. The Matriarchs' derision and condescension were hard for Mist to swallow. She couldn't imagine how it made Aven feel. Or Navya. She was still as the Eilawi tree, her attention focused on the Matriarchs. Only when Aven stopped at her side did she drag an assessing look over every part of her.

"Are you hurt?" Navya asked, looking from Aven to Mist.

"I'm fine, Mama."

Mist plucked at her stained dress. "This isn't all mine."

Navya frowned, but didn't comment. Her piercing gaze looked over the rips in Mist's clothing, to the blotches of purple bruises all over her body. Anger simmered in her black eyes, her brows furrowing in a look Mist never wanted aimed at her.

After a resigned sigh, Navya faced the Matriarchs and motioned to Aven. "My cub. As requested."

Three women stared them down, their varying looks of scrutiny moving over Navya, then Aven, then Mist, taking in every detail. Mist tried not to fidget when she caught one of them staring at her and Aven's joined hands or her injuries from fighting the Soulless. These women were like Navya.

Shrewd, skilled, and deserving of their roles as leaders if they didn't put customs before people. It took a great deal to become a Matriarch of the Qinawe. Mist could only guess what these women were capable of when compared to Navya.

The oldest of the Matriarchs sat on a large root of the tree at their backs, her coppery hands grasping the end of a gnarled staff. Yana, the dangerous one. Being a Matriarch required serving the people. With her body falling victim to time, she needed a calculating, clever mind to keep her position.

"You were asked a question, cub," Yana said in a raspy voice. The bone of the soul she guarded curved through the cartilage between her nostrils, in a piercing Mist guessed had been torturous.

The bodies pressing around them with different levels of curiosity and unease reminded Mist of standing in the circle of dragons. This would be another game of words and manipulation. Hopefully, she could match Emriel's cunning.

"I was assisting the Truthseeker, Matriarch Yana," Aven said.

Mist's lips twitched. Not an outright lie, but a clever tale. No one that followed Dia'veh would argue against helping the Steel elf. Or any elf, for that matter. They served the will of the Creator.

"Assisting him with what?" The sour look plaguing Hanawi's face seemed even harsher today. "Our people have been pleading for answers that neither elf nor Matriarch can give them."

"Why do you think I can?" The tightness in Aven's voice earned her a severe look from Navya, the warning in her eyes clear. *Watch your tone.*

"You are a dragon rider," said Matriarch Yana, tapping the end of her staff on the ground. "You know more about them than us."

Aven glanced at the gathered Qinawe, her attention lighting on the other riders in the crowd. "I'm not the only one."

"We have already spoken with them," the third Matriarch said. This one was closer to Hanawi and Navya's age, her ebony hair cropped short, and a bone thrust from the front of her ear to the outer shell. Like Navya, she wore an axe at her belt, and a knife peeked out of her boot. "They answered our questions willingly. Now it is your turn. Tell us what you know of the market, the Soulless—all of it. Our understanding is that your companion was there. It would seem the two of you have more answers than anyone else."

"What does this have to do with dragon riders?" Aven's question earned her an elbow in the side from Navya. "Apologies, Matriarch Revari. I just don't follow."

"You all have been keeping secrets for them," Hanawi said, her ire not only directed at Aven. This time she cast suspicious looks at all the riders amongst the Qinawe.

Navya snorted disdainfully. "That makes little sense, Matriarch Hanawi. What secrets are being kept?"

Hanawi matched her glare for glare, and had the two women been dragons, the tension between them would be a precursor to a challenge. "You're telling me none of the riders knew the dragons were shapeshifters?"

Aven swallowed a sharp inhale, her hand tightening around Mist's.

"We did not know," one of Pryn's snickering toads called from the crowd.

Aven bit her lip, seeming to consider her words after being elbowed once already. "Matriarch, is there proof the dragons are shapeshifters? How do we know those aren't rumors?"

Hanawi lifted one brow. "That's why we required your mother to hand you over, cub. I knew your shadow would appear, as she always does. She has the answers we seek. No one has disputed that a dragon shifted in the market, not even the elves. Now, we want to know what she saw."

All the Matriarchs' attention shifted to Mist.

"Well?" Yana's eyes narrowed, as if she were a Steel elf who could pierce the cloud of truth and lies. "Tell us what you know."

Anger lit from Mist's fingertips to her toes. For all their posturing and crowing, the shifters were all the same. They demanded answers of her, just as the dragons demanded Emriel to speak for her actions. Actions that saved lives. Even if the Matriarchs deserved answers, this was the first time any of them had ever spared a moment to look her way. They didn't even know her name. She was just someone they thought to push around if they didn't get their way. Just like the dragons. They had surrounded Emriel with wings and fire, and expected her to break.

That's what Hanawi and the Matriarchs wanted now. Navya would not speak back for Tomen and Aven's sake. Aven would not, for the sake of her parents. These tactics of fear and loss kept a family under their thumb long after they should have rebelled.

But there was nothing the Qinawe could take from Mist.

She tilted her head as she sank into whirling chaos. "Why do you expect me to tell you anything?"

She didn't know who the words surprised more. Aven drew in a sharp breath. Navya's head turned almost imperceptibly, her lips parting silently. The whites of the Matriarchs' eyes were bold in the shadows of the trees.

"How dare you?" Hanawi's nostrils flared with an anger she'd never shown. "You come onto our lands, you hunt our game, you court one of our cubs—"

"One of your cubs?" Mist pulled her hand from Aven's and laid it on her shoulder. "You mean this cub? The one who, in all the time I have been here, has never been permitted at your fires or included in your hunts? The one who has no name, because you won't let her earn her place? The one you whisper about and treat as an outsider, even though she and her mother are more accomplished than some within the bond?"

"You do not understand our ways," Hanawi said, her breathing coming fast and deep. "You have no right to judge us."

"Maybe so." Mist took a step forward. "But I can judge your hospitality. Not once have *I* ever been invited to share your meals or enjoy your harvests. Only one Matriarch has given to me without a thought to what it cost. Only one has invited me to her cook fire every night and shared with me even though she had nothing to spare. If I owe answers to any Matriarch here, it is to Navya."

"Navya is not a Matriarch." Hanawi pointedly did not look at Aven's mother, as if ignoring her would make the words true.

"Navya is the Matriarch of those you refuse to protect and care for." Mist looked at the woman in question, who wore the barest hint of a smile. "She is Aven's Matriarch. *My* Matriarch. If I am to be berated for answers, those answers will be to her first and foremost, because she is the one who accepted *me* into her family without complaint."

The Matriarchs all murmured to each other as whispers swept through the crowd. Mist couldn't insult these women like Emriel, but she'd learned enough from her sister to trap them. If they would play this game of threatening Aven's home, Mist would establish that Navya held more power than they wanted to admit.

"You make a fair point," Matriarch Yana said, who rose with a weary sigh. "Our hospitality has been lacking, and that is a failure my sisters and I will bear. We have not shared with you, so perhaps we should not demand you share with us."

Hanawi's mouth curved in a repugnant scowl, but maintained the appearance of unity between them. She would not risk her place with the Matriarchs by arguing against Yana.

"Perhaps." Mist drew out the word. Had they backed down because no one ever spoke to them as she just had, or was this another move in the game? She chanced a glance at Navya, hoping for a sign of what to do next. Hanawi had been silenced, but the Matriarchs were still in control. How hard could Mist push before things turned ugly?

Navya stood with her head cocked to the side, blinking slowly. She didn't acknowledge Mist's look, but thoughts practically buzzed over her head. Her hands dangled at her sides and she cracked her knuckles, one finger at a time.

"If it isn't too painful," she said with a mask of neutrality in place. "Please tell us what happened in the market."

Mist swallowed hard as memories rose like bile. Warm blood slapping across her cheeks. Nodi gurgling before he died. Lifeless bodies shambling through the market. A shudder trembled through her chest as she drowned beneath the horror.

It was Aven's warm hand that drew Mist out of the darkness. She stepped close, the heat of her body a beacon to focus on. Their eyes met. Aven's were soft and familiar. Safe. Light crept back into Mist's vision. She hadn't noticed it bleeding away in her panic.

It took a few deep breaths before she felt in control of her thoughts, or her tongue, before she could relay what she'd seen. She thought about Emriel, her cold calculation, how she'd smiled in the faces of the Soulless. Mist tried channeling that strength. Staying strong in the face of their brutality was an act of defiance.

"Keep it simple," Aven whispered, her chin almost brushing Mist's shoulder.

She gave a weak nod before glancing at Matriarch Yana. Her eyes were a point of focus, their reflective pits real and tangible, tempting Mist to stare, even as she looked away.

Mist pretended it was just a tale she'd heard, instead of moments she'd lived. "Three Soulless came into the market. They killed two lynx. Attacked me. They intended to kill me too, before a warrior stopped them. She led the Linseen in defense of Yunaii so people in the market could flee."

Yana's clever eyes narrowed as she looked at the other Matriarchs. A few moments of whispering went on between them. Hanawi looked like she was bursting with questions, but she stood silently at Yana's side. Waiting for permission to speak? For a moment to interrogate and berate?

The older Matriarch never gave her an opening. Yana held up a hand, silencing the whispers drifting through the Qinawe.

"What of this warrior?" Yana asked, coming a little closer. "Rumors spread of a red-haired woman who was impervious to the powers of the Soulless. *No* shifter has such a gift."

Mist tried not to look at Navya or Aven. It might give away any lie that passed from her lips. "She was skilled. The best I've ever seen."

"What do you know of warriors and killing, cub?" The question came from the Matriarch with the axe and the knife in her boot. The one Aven called Revari. Her gaze moved over Mist, to the few places she might hide a blade.

Mist lifted her chin defiantly. "Your people are not the only ones that come from a long line of combat."

"And who are your people?" Hanawi asked, shifting her weight from one foot to the other. "You are no Tribouin. You fake their manners, but that is all. You do not dress like them, talk like them. You travel alone, with no family to intercede a challenge like their men insist upon."

Mist was sure these were questions that had plagued Hanawi for ages. How often had they been on the tip of her tongue, held back by propriety? If she thought she had trapped Mist, though, she would see how mistaken she was. The thought of Emriel's face as she'd challenged Rielnor popped into her head. The triumph that had gleamed in her eyes. Mist tried to mimic that as she stared at the Matriarch.

She gave a half-hearted shrug. "I am what I am."

It was Yana who took the bait. "And what is that, cub?"

Mist grasped Aven's hand on her shoulder and squeezed.

"I'm like Aven." She mustered the brightest smile she could, despite the pain and terror of the day. "I am my father's daughter and my mother's kind, but I walk my own path."

Hanawi's lips parted in clear frustration, while Yana narrowed one eye. Qinawe muttered to one another, repeating snippets of Mist's words as they puzzled them out.

"Yes, child," said a familiar female voice.

Mist and Aven turned as the Qinawe stepped aside, allowing Priestess Ifera to approach. Light gleamed on the turquoise paint she'd decorated her night dark skin with, the circles and patterns so bright, and applied with expert precision. They complimented her array of golden rings, necklaces, and bracelets that jingled as she walked. The very sight of her brought a wave of relief crashing through Mist's battered body. Ifera served Dia'veh. The Creator's eye was on her wherever she went. Dia'veh might as well have stridden into the clearing as well.

The Priestess stopped beside Mist, facing the Matriarchs without giving them her attention.

"You are more than what anyone tells you to be, because you–" Ifera put a hand on Mist's shoulder. "*Aven*—" she put a hand on Aven's shoulder too. "—and I are Lecarians."

CHAPTER
Twenty-One

Aven

Aven searched Priestess Ifera's face, from her golden eyes, to her cool, brown skin, to the coiled hair hanging to her waist. None of it revealed what power lived inside her. Maybe she was Tribouin by her tattoos. Maybe Qinawe by the bone-like beads in her choker. Dev said Ifera was like her—more than just an elf and caught between lines she didn't draw—but when the Truthseeker offered the Priestess' help, this wasn't what Aven expected.

"Lecarian." Yana worked her lips around the sounds like a child. "I have not heard this word before."

Ifera raised her chin defiantly, though her eyes remained soft. "Lecarian is the name some shapeshifters, like myself, have chosen to use."

Silence rolled over the clearing. The kind Aven had never experienced before. No whispers. No shuffling bodies. Nothing. The Matriarchs stared as if Ifera had shifted into a Soulless.

"Shapeshifter," Yana said, her eyes growing wide. "Not elf."

Ifera dipped her chin politely. "Both, Matriarch, and so, I am Lecarian."

"What need do you have for a new name?" Hanawi asked. "What need does Navya's cub, for that matter? Is elf so insulting? Is *Qinawe*?"

"Of course, neither are insulting," Ifera said with a casual shrug.

"Then why not choose?" Hanawi's lips barely moved. "Live as an elf or live with us? Why set yourself apart?"

A slew of whispers were released through the Qinawe. Some pointed. Some stared. Many watched Aven, their eyes boring into her. She and the Priestess had been walking the same lonely path. Did they see Aven differently now, knowing their beloved Temple leader was one of the few who didn't fit the perfect mold of shapeshifter customs?

Ifera clasped her hands over her waist. "My mother is Qinawe and my father is Linseen."

"Qinawe." Yana's eyes flicked to Mama suspiciously. "Was your mother of our bond?"

A rare anger flared in Ifera's eyes, sharpening her round face and high cheekbones, revealing the Qinawe within her. "No. I was called *to* Yunaii by Dia'veh."

The Matriarchs looked between each other, mistrust and confusion bittering their faces and twitching through their limbs.

"Why would the Maker choose someone for us that spurns her Qinawe blood?" Hanawi asked in a hushed voice.

Ifera's brows rose. "I spurn no part of myself. I have served you dutifully. Is that not enough?"

"She has led us in communing with Dia'veh many times," Revari said, hovering a hand over her heart.

"She lied to us," Hanawi said in a clipped tone. "She is Qinawe and she never joined our bond."

"I learned long ago," Ifera said, "that while the ways of my Linseen father were not all that different from my mother's bond, it was still enough to keep him at a distance." Ifera shifted her gaze from the Matriarchs to Aven, her smile soft as a breeze. "My father is *part* of my bond, and so I cannot be in a bond that would not have him."

Aven inhaled sharply as those words pierced deep into her heart.

"You could not know if our bond would have accepted him, or you," said Matriarch Yana.

"Yes, I could know," said Ifera, now looking directly at Mama. "I know because you have never welcomed Tomen into your bond."

"That is different," Hanawi snapped, the stench of her anger so strong that Aven wrinkled her nose. "Navya's chosen is Tribouin. They infantilize their daughters and make them weak."

"That isn't true," Aven said, surprising herself, the Matriarchs, and even the Qinawe. Eyes went wide all around her as more whispers rushed through the crowd. "The Tribouin are many things, but their sons and daughters are both strong and competent. They devote their youth to protecting each other. They love their families, just like us."

Matriarch Yana tilted her head as steely calculation overtook her face. "If you truly believed that, would you not have accepted the Tribouin girl's challenge? Isn't it true that *you* found her unworthy?"

Aven drew in a sharp breath. Pryn. It always came back to Pryn. Every mistake. Every moment of weakness. She was a weapon to silence or shame Aven into submission. Even after a day of her nerves being stretched far beyond their breaking, the sorrow still dug in its claws.

Only this time, Mist pulled her back. She took a menacing step towards the Matriarchs, her scent and unnerving motion setting off warning bells in Aven's head. She couldn't help reaching for Mist's arm, even as Ifera stroked the other.

"All who listen know the truth of that matter, Matriarch," said the Priestess. "Young Pryn showed her worth in her friendship with Aven. Her failure in understanding the nature of Aven's desires has nothing to do with her value as a woman or someone's Promised."

Despite the sadness fighting to drown her, Aven still nodded in agreement. "Pryn *is* strong. She could rival any Qinawe woman. So could my Papa. He raised me to be even greater than him. He's never once held me back."

Mama cast a proud look at Aven before her dark gaze settled back on the Matriarchs. For the first time in Aven's life, Mama met them glare for glare, challenging with a defiant smirk. She knew, maybe she had always known, the strength of Papa's people. It simply remained hidden beneath posturing Elders and loud-mouthed boys.

Not unlike the Qinawe's strength, which remained hidden from the griffins and the lynx through distance and mistrust.

If only the Matriarchs could see these truths. Silence had taken over Hanawi and Revari, but defeat had not claimed Yana. Her attention shifted around the clearing, the wrinkles on her brow growing deeper with each passing moment.

"This is our way," she finally said, her voice raspy and cold. "This is how we protect ourselves. Protect our bonds. Our children. What future do we have if we weaken our ways?"

"A wealth of possibilities," Mama said softly. "With even greater strength."

"You cannot be certain of that," the old Matriarch said, locking eyes with Mama. "This is why you cannot be a Matriarch. This is why you cannot be within the bond once more. You would gamble on hopes and daydreams and pay for it with our people's blood."

Aven's hand tightened around Mist's arm, clinging to the connection to remain upright. Yana had always shown such kindness and patience. Her clever mind always seemed to be working, and Aven had wondered if she'd harbored some softness she didn't dare share. For her to dig in her heels in direct opposition to Mama's very way of life was a slap in the face.

"Do you know the history of our ways?" Ifera asked, sliding a finger along the bottom of her chin. "Do you remember how these rules and lines became what kept the shifters strong?"

Yana's curved frame straightened, knuckles blanching over the top of her cane. "Of course. How could I lead without knowing our history?"

Ifera pursed her lips, mischief shining in her eyes. "And yet I am wondering how one could cling to such ways while knowing our history."

Revari took a step towards Ifera as she gripped the top of her axe with a tight fist. "We know. We remember. The Time of Sorrow nearly ended all shifters. We did what we had to do survive, especially after the Soulless tempted some of our kind to their side. We had no other choice when the wolves turned on us and even the lynx could not stop them."

Yana nodded approvingly to the younger Matriarch. "We did not start what they began, but we did survive it. We survived when shifters like the griffins and lynx began using combat to choose mates. They wanted to keep their prides and flocks strong, but they didn't consider what Qinawe and Tribouin would do against claws and fangs. I do not doubt the dragons never considered it either."

"We protected our children," Mama said, grounding Aven with a touch to her shoulder. "The Qinawe made even their weakest more powerful than most and the Tribouin taught their young to travel in packs."

"Those were desperate times," Priestess Ifera said, moving Mist behind her as drew closer to the Matriarchs. "We protected our people. We protected our blood and power to shift. It was a way to ensure our survival in the face of extinction. Now, these ways of battle have been put aside, could not these lines of division between shapeshifters also be put aside?"

Revari bristled. "The ways of the Qinawe have helped us survive for thousands of years."

"We are not fighting against extinction anymore," Ifera pointed out.

"No, we're not," Hanawi finally chimed in, looking far too pleased. "We very well could be soon, though. A Soulless walked into our market today and began killing without hesitation. We face the same threat our people did when our ways took root. Why do we debate these things today of all days?"

Ifera's lips stretched in a wide grin. One of her fingers crooked in a summoning motion towards Aven, tempting her to finally step away from the warmth of Mist's body.

"A very good question," the Priestess said. "The answer is why I currently stand before you."

The three Matriarchs glanced between Ifera and Aven, their confusion as palpable as a breeze. They had been drawn so perfectly into the Priestess' web. Even Aven wasn't quite sure how they had gotten to this point.

"Tell your Matriarchs what you were doing today, young Aven."

Yana's eyes narrowed. "She said she was assisting the Truthseeker."

"I was," Aven said slowly. So many words whirled through her head. So many sentences and points to make. They slammed through her like a river's current, all of them bubbling up at once and leaving her with nothing coherent to say. "I—"

"Speak, cub," Hanawi said, lips pulling into her usual sneer. "Where's that strength you claim your father taught you?"

The anger that immediately soiled the air wasn't Aven's or the Matriarch's. It radiated through the clearing, rolling so powerfully from Mama's direction that Hanawi took a step back. Such a tiny movement and it screamed of power to all who watched. The surrounding Qinawe fell into a terrifying silence as the two women stared each other down. Wolf and cat. Outcast and Matriarch.

Aven glanced between the two, unsure if she should interrupt. Kali's soul vibrated inside her, aching to unsheathe claws and assert her dominance.

Mama's nostrils wrinkled in a snarl, but when her lips parted her voice came out smooth as cream. "Answer her, Aven."

Hearing her name snapped Aven out of her own coiling rage. She drew in a deep breath and turned to the Matriarchs, chin held high, meeting their eyes as she had never done before. "I went with the Truthseeker to speak with flock leader Yliva and pride leader Kanai."

Yana and Revari shared a look, but Hanawi refused to break her staring match with Mama.

"To what end, cub?" Revari asked.

"To break the division between the shifters for the good of Yunaii," Ifera answered, throwing a discreet wink at

Aven. Her game sharpened into focus, a gamble that hopefully paid off.

Judging by the icy look in Yana's eyes though, chances were slim. "Halt there, Priestess. I see you."

"I should hope so. I am standing right here."

Yana put both hands on her staff and leaned forward. "Our people are not as they were in the Time of Sorrow. They took up sword and axe, they bared claws and fangs, and they fought the Soulless. That was a time of war, though. I will not be manipulated into fighting in hopes of proving you wrong."

Aven wilted. That was that. Yana's 'no' was the blood's answer. Hanawi and Revari held sway over their people, but everyone respected the oldest Matriarch. Until today, even Mama had spoken softly of her.

"I did not ask you to fight the Soulless," Ifera said as she sorted the golden bangles around her wrists. "I would not ask you to go against your ways of nonviolence. That is a choice only for yourselves."

Revari tilted her head, concerned lines wrinkling her brow. "Then why are you here?"

"The Truthseeker and I are holding a summit of Yunaii's leaders." Her delivery of the invitation came smoothly, without a hint of eagerness or excitement. She sounded almost bored.

"A summit?" Revari cast an incredulous look at the other Matriarchs. "This is not the way of Yunaii."

"It is not," Ifera said. "We ask nothing of you but your presence to help prepare for the next attack from the Soulless."

Revari threw her shoulders back with an obstinate look. "What makes you so certain there will be another attack?"

Mama snorted as the same look Aven got for being reckless overtook her face. "Because they are Soulless. You said you know our history. The Soulless tried to conquer the world."

Revari stared her down. "None could forget what they did. There are still ripples to this day, and scars that will never be healed."

"So why do you think a Soulless would pick one fight and then flee?" A growl slipped into Mama's voice. "You three have a responsibility to make sure that does not happen. Even if that means dealing with the Tribouin and the lynx and the griffins."

"Yliva intends to be there," Aven said softly, keeping her gaze on Yana. She was the one they needed to convince.

Revari made a show of rolling her eyes. "Yliva is a manipulative woman that has no respect for boundaries. Her presence is not the bait you think it is."

"Yliva, Kanai, and Commander Senwe intend on coming to the Temple to address this problem." Ifera's voice maintained its cool tone. "The Truthseeker has gone to secure the presence of the Tribouin Elders. Will you be the only leaders who care more for your pride than your people?"

Yana straightened as yellow flooded the dark pools of her eyes. "That is not the issue. You speak words I have not heard from you before. Where has your respect gone?"

Ifera bowed her head. "I have the greatest respect for you, Matriarch Yana. Your wisdom is invaluable. I simply implore you to see past the shifters' differences. We live here together, and benefit from one another. Now, we must ensure we survive this together. Division is our greatest enemy."

"We can protect our own," Revari said.

"Will you?" Mama touched the hilt of her weapon. "Will you draw that axe if the time comes? Will you put aside your pacifism and face the Soulless? They will not hesitate to put it aside for you."

"Look at young Mist." Ifera motioned to her. "The Soulless would have cut her down without hesitation. They killed three today with no remorse. Our people need a plan for what happens when they return. We cannot count on the dragons to protect us again."

"And what of the dragons?" Hanawi finally looked away from Mama, shifting her ire to Mist. She obviously remembered her earlier questions being dodged. "What is their role in all of this?"

"Does it matter?" Mama asked through clenched teeth. "If they will not help us, then they do not matter. We cannot force or coerce them. It would be a waste of our time."

"Why not?" Revari's long face pinched as red splotches spread across her cheeks. "Our people have fed them, sheltered them. Why can we not count on the dragons to protect us against this threat? Did they not once stand against the Soulless?"

Aven pressed claws into her palms to hide her agreement. The thrill of a ride was no compensation for the time and effort spent on the dragons. How could they justify not helping with the Soulless? Thankfully, the set of Mist's mouth and the flare of her nostrils screamed her agreement.

Of course, Aven already knew she would fight to protect the Qinawe, no matter how she felt about violence.

Ifera caressed her beaded choker, fierceness melding into a look of exhaustion. "The dragons are a matter for another day, when the Soulless is gone and lives are not in danger."

Yana nodded. "You are not wrong about this."

Aven almost dared to smile, if not for the gleam in the old woman's eyes. A scheme was hatching in that mind of hers. She was sure of it. Yana was the cleverest of them all and gave nothing without taking much more.

"Will you come and speak to the leaders then?" Ifera lowered her head as if sensing the danger too.

"I will speak with them," Yana said with another nod. "But I will not come to them. If they want my time and attention, they will come to me."

Aven swallowed a gasp. "But they have already agreed to meet at the Temple."

"I care not. They will come to me or they will get no aid from the Qinawe."

"This is folly." Bitter resignation crept into Ifera's voice. "These lands are not protected like the Temple's. Thanks to Dia'veh, violence cannot be done there."

Revari drew her axe and spun it once. "If the Soulless dare step onto Qinawe lands, they will regret it."

Mama snorted again. "Oh, will they? Tell me, Revari, when have you drawn your axe for battle? Dancing with a partner is not the same as fighting for your life."

"What do you know of it, Navya?" Revari took a step forward, axe held at her side. "Your experience is the same as mine. Check that pride before it costs you."

Aven glanced at Mama as the burn of claws distending seared her fingertips. Anger in any Qinawe was new and frightening. Where would Revari draw the line?

"I am not the one trusting in unblooded warriors instead of the Creator."

"You forget yourself, Navya," Yana said, slamming her staff on the ground.

Mama bared her teeth. "No, Yana. That would be your *Matriarch*. It is not my weapon that is drawn."

All looked at Revari, who didn't feign the slightest bit of shame.

"Put it away," Yana hissed, her voice barely above a whisper. "You disgrace yourself."

Aven glanced between the fierce, angry woman. Never had Mama defied the Matriarchs, let alone threaten and insult. A triumphant smile curved her lips, twisting her face into a stranger's.

Ifera's hands drew over her waist in a penitent pose, much like the kind Mist used. "None of this gets us anywhere. Matriarch Yana, I implore you to reconsider. I do not believe this is a wise course of action."

"I do not quite care what you think." Yana's disdain was almost as harsh as a slap to the Priestess' face. It might have been gentler. "I will not be summoned to the Temple like a child. I am a Matriarch of the Qinawe and you have sullied the Temple with your lies."

"Did she lie?" Mist demanded, taking a protective step towards Ifera. "Or did you assume she was an elf?"

"A secret kept is still a lie. She has served our people in communion with the Maker, all while looking down on us and our ways. How can we trust she properly served us as a Priestess when she spits in the face of who we are or who she is?"

Nausea crept up Aven's throat, her empty belly rolling. The truth of Yana's anger was not a revelation. The judgement and fear always hid behind polite masks. Protect their customs. Protect their power. The Matriarchs never tried hiding their priorities. They never offered a chance for Aven to prove she was more than her father's daughter, more than a potential corruption of their children. They didn't want things to change.

Seeing all it directed at someone else, though? To hear the hatred spoken aloud. They didn't care that Ifera was loving to everyone she met. They didn't care she had been raised by a Qinawe mother. They didn't care that Aven stood there, seeing their judgement of her. All that mattered was their customs and rituals and nonsense. Couldn't let in Tribouin thinking. Couldn't let in elven ways. No amount of wisdom or talent could negate the cruelty in their blind eyes.

Aven was almost too afraid to look at Ifera. She knew what she would find, no matter how hard the Priestess tried hiding it. The pain. The rejection. The air reeked with it.

Aven's heart wrenched when she finally dared. Tears slid over Ifera's cheeks. Her jaw tightened. She'd clasped her trembling hands so tight her knuckles blanched. That one look was nearly Aven's undoing. This battlefield was one she trudged through every day of her life. She wished for no one to face it with her.

"What's more," Yana said. "Tomorrow we will all have to address this problem. How can we count on a Priestess that has no respect for us? The other leaders and I must reconsider your service here, Priestess Ifera. Perhaps someone new should take your place."

Mist gasped. "So you're fine with an elf serving you, but a Qinawe woman who chooses her own path cannot?"

Yana lifted a hand. "There are no words I wish to hear from you, either. You have deceived us as well. There is no place for you here or in the bond. You may leave our lands."

The urge to attack slammed through Aven like a kick to the chest. Yana would die for that. Her blood would run until she was nothing but a bag of lifeless bones.

As if sensing her growing rage, Ifera grabbed Aven's shoulder in a painful grip. "I will attempt to convince the other leaders to come here. I cannot guarantee they will."

"I will not step foot inside the Temple again as long as you are Priestess there." The coldness in Yana's voice told Aven all she needed to know. This woman was why she would never have a place in the bond. Not Hanawi. Not Revari. Not the Qinawe who whispered about her. They were all pawns.

Yana cared more about their customs than Aven had ever guessed. For all the kindness the woman showed every child striving to earn their place, this fear she harbored revealed her true face. A cold, malicious monster had replaced wisdom and warmth.

"You may leave now," Yana said, tapping her staff on the ground. "I have much to speak about with the other Matriarchs and there is a great deal to do if we are hosting Tribouin, griffins, and lynx on our lands tomorrow."

Aven shook her head. Could this moment be real? Her mind hovered outside of her body, observing but not understanding. She'd hoped Ifera would make them see their follies. How had she been so wrong?

"I have things to discuss with Aven and Mist," Ifera said.

"Then discuss it on your own lands." Satisfaction shone in Hanawi's eyes. "Matriarch Yana has asked you to leave."

"Very well." Ifera's jaw clenched, but that was the only sign the words hurt her. She clasped her hands over her waist and bowed before turning to Aven. "Come to me tomorrow. We have much to discuss."

"May I come with you now?" Mist asked with a hopeful look. "I want to know more about Lecarians."

"I think you both should go," Mama said, her eyes locked on the Matriarchs.

"Are you sure?" Aven's head dizzied from the angry stench rolling off her. "I haven't been able to tell you anything about what happened today."

"You'll tell me tomorrow, cub." Still, she stared at Yana, Revari, and Hanawi as if she could gut them with just a glare. "Go. Speak with Ifera. Learn what she has to tell you.

Perhaps there are more in Sholindrea that will welcome you. I have a feeling your time in Yunaii is coming to an end."

"We always knew they would never accept me." Aven's heart raced, making it even harder to stay upright. Why was she so afraid of losing this place? She'd never intended to stay. Still, it felt as if she'd been shoved away from a fire on a cold night.

"I had hoped—" Mama's mouth drew into a thin line. "It doesn't matter what I hoped. Yana has lost her way. She clings to power she has little right left to. Customs are the only thing keeping her where she is and she will sacrifice anyone to keep her place. Even one of our own cubs, and I'm sorry for that."

"You have nothing to be sorry for, Mama."

She shook her head, sorrow in her eyes. "We will speak tomorrow. I need to get back and tell Tomen what has happened."

Aven reached for her with trembling hands, desperately needing something she couldn't put into words. Everything about this meeting had a finality to it. Nothing would be the same after today.

Mama's arms wrapped around her shoulders, bringing Aven's face into her chest like she was a child again. A few deep breaths filled her nose with Mama's musky, wood-smoke scent, taking her back to the days of scraped knees and learning to hunt. No matter how the Qinawe beat her like water against rock, it never worked. Every time they tried, Mama showed them how unbreakable she was. Aven only hoped she had enough of that fight in her.

When they drew apart, Mama held Aven's face in her calloused hands. "Stay at the Temple tonight. I will see you in the morning."

"Are you sure?" Aven followed her mistrustful gaze back to the retreating Matriarchs.

"Yes. At least I will know you are safe there."

Aven nodded weakly before Mama planted a fluttery kiss over her brow. Then she slipped amongst the Qinawe milling about, before disappearing into the forest. Her quiet departure left dread in her wake. Had Aven slept in the bed her parents made for the last time? Would she ever see the cave again? Her eyes burned with tears she refused to shed.

Time to go. Before something tipped her over the edge. Mist and Ifera waited nearby, and when the Priestess noticed Aven's gaze, she motioned for them to follow her.

The sea of Qinawe stepped aside, whispers and sneers following like shadows. Those Aven expected. What made her pause were the looks of misery on some of their faces, especially among the younger generations. Ifera had shown every one of them kindness at some point, and now they might live to see her lose her home in the Temple.

"Come," Ifera said, touching Aven's back. "There is much to do and discuss before this day comes to an end."

CHAPTER

Twenty-Two

Aven

Questions buzzed in Aven's head on the quiet walk back to the Temple. Only fear kept them locked inside. Ifera walked ahead in the fading light, shoulders thrust back while her head bowed more and more with each step, as if her own thoughts were too heavy to carry.

Thankfully, it didn't take long to reach the Lighe, trudge across the bridge, and make for the market. Cool, blue sky had given way to fiery colors, making an end to Sansia's reign. How had so much happened since the moons had risen last?

The market was frighteningly quiet, stands and carts abandoned, the roots of the Eilawi tree spattered with burns. Usually, food, drink, and places to converse took over after dark. Its shadowed emptiness chilled Aven's bones.

Upon reaching the Temple, she dragged herself up the few steps, her feet aching. Mist's shoulders dropped within the stone entryway, redness rimming her eyes. She'd begun favoring one leg, and a mottled bruise on her thigh peeked through the fabric of her dress. The fact that she still stood was proof of her strength.

Too bad Emriel wasn't there to see it.

"Come," Ifera said. "I can help Mist with her wounds as we speak more about the Lecarians."

Mist mustered a weak smile. "Thank you for everything. I'm sorry for what today cost you."

"It has cost me nothing I was not meant to move on from one day." Ifera's ever-present certainty wobbled as they entered the main room of the Temple. With a weary tug, she freed her long hair, releasing the coiled ropes of curls to fall around her shoulders. "If Dia'veh's will is for me to travel to a new place, then that is what I will do. In the end, it is the Creator that decides who serves. Not the shapeshifters."

As true as that was, Aven didn't imagine Ifera remaining if all the leaders asked her to go. She was too good a person to force her presence on them.

The Truthseeker rose upon their entrance, snapping shut the book he held as he made a beeline for them. His braids were undone, and he'd traded armor for a pair of black breeches and a loose white shirt, with sleeves rolled up to his elbows. Aven blinked, almost mistaking him for someone else. Something about his cascade of white hair, bare feet, and tattooed forearms softened him.

"I was not expecting you to bring back company, dear one." He gazed at Ifera with a curious look before regarding Aven and Mist. "Is all well? Do either of you require my assistance?"

"No," Mist croaked. "Thank you. We're here to speak with the Priestess."

His silver eyes narrowed as he turned back to Ifera. "Something is wrong. What happened with the Qinawe?"

Ifera feathered a touch over his skin, and when she spoke, all her strength and humor were gone. "Can you light the candles, Gaelin? I need to speak to the Creator before conversing with the girls."

"Ifera, what can I do?" he asked, lips barely moving with his soft whisper.

She forced a trembling smile. "Light the candles for now, dearest. Also, perhaps fetch something to eat for the girls, if you do not mind."

"Of course," he said with a nod. Worry etched into the lines of his face as he cast a questioning look at Aven before doing as requested.

She wished some helpful words would come. Something soft and uplifting for the Priestess, something concise and emotionless for the Truthseeker. Yet, not matter how she tried, it all escaped her. Sadness had sucked away the vitality Ifera normally wore like a cloak of contagious joy. Without it, the Temple air hung heavy, stealing away any comfort Aven could offer.

All she had was her strength. If words failed, she could at least lend a body to lean on and an arm to cling to.

"C-can we come with you?" Aven asked, surprising herself. It had been ages since she last spoke with Dia'veh, but she would do anything to stem the flow of tears welling at the corners of Ifera's eyes.

"Of course," the Priestess said with a wobbly smile. "I would appreciate that very much."

Aven and Mist looped their arms through Ifera's as they walked towards the small pool in the center of the room. The Truthseeker rushed around them, lighting candles to summon the Maker—all four elements for communion with Dia'veh. Ifera threw him a grateful look before leading Aven and Mist into the cold water, wading a little past their ankles before her knees bent. She took all three of them down, kneeling respectfully.

It had been so long since Aven had done this. What came next? She glanced at Mist, whose eyes had slipped shut. Ifera's did as well, and as her chin dipped, the tears finally flowed freely. Her lips shook from the sobs she bit back, and her grip on Aven's arm tightened. Whatever she prayed stayed between her and the Maker, but the words still rang in Aven's head. All the years of praying in the night, all the times the hurt spilled from her heart. She knew what Ifera whispered now.

Aven slid her gaze from the flowers and lily pads to the flickering firelight too the Truthseeker hovering across the pool. Sadness shone in his eyes as he watched Ifera cry, tension bulging the muscles of his crossed arms. A storm played across his face. More emotion than he'd shown throughout the day.

When it hurt too much to watch Gaelin watch Ifera, Aven lowered her chin and shut her eyes. What was she supposed to do now? How did she speak to the Maker? What could she say? Did Dia'veh feel everything simmering in her heart? Was she dooming herself by letting the festering wound inside her grow raw as she knelt in this place of communion?

The more Aven fought back angry thoughts, the more they reverberated like an echo bouncing off cave walls.

Why? Where are you? Why haven't you helped me? What did Ifera do to deserve this pain? How can you let the Qinawe continue on this way?

Before Aven knew it, she was railing at Dia'veh, her face and chest painfully hot as tears she hadn't shed in years dribbled down her chin.

Why haven't you helped us, Dia'veh?

Warmth swirled through the water around Aven's knees, heating her skin, traveling through her until it bloomed inside her chest. Sadness evaporated like dew as a sense of hope she thought long dead rekindled.

I am here.

Aven choked on a gasp. The words were spoken as clearly as any whimper or mutter from those around her. A glance across the Temple revealed no one new. Just the same quiet, darkening space beneath a glass roof, lit with splashes of moonlight.

Her eyes slipped shut as she pondered over the voice. Not male or female, strong and yet soft, comforting and warm like Mama's hugs and Papa's love.

Was it really Dia'veh?

Yes.

Icy shock washed through Aven's body. Was this really happening? After all these years? After all the times she'd screamed and cried?

I am always here.

Where were you when I needed you?

The thought formed without her meaning it to. After an entire day of scraping and bowing and begging, it would figure she'd mess up talking to the Creator of the world.

I was here.

Aven's nostrils flared. *No.*

Always. The word rooted into her heart like a twisting vine. The memory of Kali laying her massive head in Aven's lap flashed behind her eyes. Its weight pressed against her thighs, warm breath fanning her skin as soft fur tickled. She'd been dropped back into the moment all those years ago, her childish confusion replaced by sadness and abiding love.

Despite never speaking with, or even meeting Aven, Kali harbored a deep-rooted affection for her.

Love is true. Love is pure. Love is mine. Do all things in love.

Aven ground her teeth. *That was Kali. That was her choice.*

Yes. And she was mine, too. Her heart was mine to teach. To guide.

Aven touched the fang hanging around her neck. Kali was wise. Everyone said so. That she'd followed Dia'veh so closely wasn't a surprise. All of Yunaii used this Temple. But how did all this work? Had the Maker willed Kali to help her or had she come to care from watching Aven? Had her heart been open because she was a student of Dia'veh or did she sacrifice against her will?

Never, my child. Love is not forced. Love cannot be faked. It is mine, and it is yours, and it should guide you in all you do.

That made more sense than she wanted it to. That's how Mama and Papa lived. That's what they'd taught her. Wasn't that what Yliva was doing when she bent even as she feared for her people? Wasn't that what Kanai did when he put aside his pain to understand Aven's? She could even reluctantly see it in Yana, Hanawi, and Revari. They wanted what was best for the Qinawe, in a messed-up sort of way.

No. Fear destroys love. It destroys what one is meant to do.

Aven's lips parted, but she swallowed the gasp before it escaped.

Why not step in? Guide them to do better? To not fear.

Warmth blossomed over her shoulders before running down her arms, filling Aven to the tips of her aching fingers.

You. I gave them you. You are perfect. You are strong. You are my love. In time, they will see.

After everything that happened today, all the pain and fear, the frustration and heartbreak, it seemed impossible to feel what crept into her heart. Aven had teetered on the edge of collapsing into numbness. But now? This was more than Mama's hugs. This was more than Papa protecting her from a dragon. More than Ifera sacrificing a peaceful life to save others. Something clicked into place, as if her whole life was a puzzle box she'd been shifting and moving and manipulating, only to never find the right button or latch to make it open. Comfort poured into her, washing away every whisper and jibe, every cringe and judging look. None of it mattered as much as it had.

But—why? All these years. Even after Kali. Why didn't you answer me? Why didn't you speak to me? Didn't you hear all my prayers?

Of course.

Another memory formed behind her eyes, only this couldn't be hers. Mist soared through a lightning storm, her feathery wings straining through the wind and rain, her body tossed about like a ship in the sea. She flapped and flapped, but nothing saved her from a powerful gust that threw her towards the water. Her awful, slapping splash almost drew a cry from Aven's lips. Then the memory shifted, and Mist was pulling herself onto a sandy beach, her chest heaving for air, wings sodden and trembling. Despite the wind and thunder, Aven heard her cry out for the Maker, begging for help, for strength.

Keep going. Dia'veh said. *She is waiting for you.*

The words had Mist rising to her feet, straining one slow step at a time up the beach, through the stormy night, fading into shadow. The memory slipped away as Aven opened her eyes, blinking against the shimmering moonlight.

I don't understand.

Water rippled around her knees, drawing her gaze to the pool. She hadn't moved, and yet the surface shifted as if she'd swished her hand through its cool depths. The curving lines of movement drifted past Ifera to lap against Mist, who still knelt with her head bowed and eyes closed.

I heard your prayers, my child. So, I sent her to you.

CHAPTER
Twenty-Three

Aven

ven's exchange with Dia'veh replayed in her head long after everyone retreated to the piles of cushions in one corner of the room. A set of wooden trays sat between the four of them, laden with flatbreads, glazed fruit, salted pork, and bits of smoked, prickly vegetables. None of them fussed over Ifera's red, swollen eyes or the dried streaks of tears on her cheeks. The Truthseeker just kept sliding more food onto her plate each time she took a bite of something, while Mist allowed the Priestess to apply salves to her wounds and bruises.

After listening to Ifera relay what the Qinawe decided, the Truthseeker made a rare sound of disgust. "Yana is a soul-cursed fool."

Aven choked on her bite of sticky sweet fruit. "I think that's the harshest thing I've ever heard you say, Truthseeker."

"Gae-lin." He said the sounds slowly, his stern look leaving no room for argument. "And it is truth. She endangers not only herself. Should this summit be discovered, Yunaii will be left leaderless."

"Will the Linseen still come?" Mist asked, shifting her hair over one shoulder for Ifera to inspect her neck.

"I am certain they will." Gaelin took a bite of pork as he watched them. "Commander Senwe is devout in his duties. He will not risk loss of life in the name of pride."

"Well, that's something." Aven pulled her knees to her chest, insides pattering like a pixie's wings. The Maker's words ran over and over in her head. "Hopefully Yliva and Kanai won't mind. How did it go with the Tribouin Elders?"

Ifera paused her ministrations to regard Gaelin. "I forgot to ask how your endeavors went, dear one."

His lips almost curved into a smile. "The two Elders will attend. I shall do my best to convince them to accompany me to the Qinawe lands upon their arrival."

"That will be interesting. They're not going to appreciate Yana's ultimatum." Aven pictured the two Tribouin men with their dark skin and golden tattoos marking them as leaders. It had been ages since she'd set eyes on them. Her presence wasn't especially welcome on their lands since she and Pryn had fallen out.

"I shall attend to that concern," Gaelin said. "You set your mind to Yliva and Kanai."

She nodded gratefully before resting her chin on her knees. Divide and conquer. It was all Aven could hope for. At least she wasn't in this alone. Or left on the outskirts, fearing her family might fall through the cracks.

"All done." Ifera set down her bowl of salve and admired her handiwork. She'd given Mist one of her white, gauzy dresses to replace the tunic the Soulless had destroyed, coated her bruises in a thick, green cream, and cleaned the cut on Mist's temple that still oozed purple.

"Thank you," Mist said, leaning back against an especially large cushion. "They already feel better."

"I am glad." Ifera settled on the cushion beside Gaelin, who immediately dropped a pale hand onto her knee. "So, you girls had questions for me."

Aven blinked a few times before looking to Mist. She'd almost forgotten. So much was happening without a pause to process. How would she stop herself from collapsing into an emotional, blubbering mess as soon as she stopped moving?

Mist studied Ifera, even she rubbed at all the sore spots in Aven's back. "You called yourself Lecarian. I've never heard that word, even in Estellias."

"I assume you have heard of others like us," Ifera said, resting her own hand on top of Gaelin's. "Anyone with bloodlines from more than one race."

"I suppose I technically am one," Mist said. "My Papi was human."

Ifera nodded. "Exactly. Dragon souls are strong. Like dragon blood. Many yield hatchlings almost as strong as those begat by two dragons."

"I suppose." Sadness flooded Mist's eyes. "They still call me runt."

Aven stiffened. "The dragons don't. Just the people who don't know better."

"I suppose."

"You are as much a dragon as I am a Qinawe," Aven said, taking Mist's hand in her own. "It's not like I can change my body to anything but Kali's form."

"Can't you?" Ifera asked.

Aven shook her head. "Papa tried to teach me, but I've never been able to."

Ifera glanced at Gaelin, who looked surprised. "Perhaps in time."

Their curious looks piqued her interest. "You think I could learn?"

"It took me time," Ifera said, sliding her fingers over the choker around her throat. The center row of beads was bleached white like bone. "I lived as a Qinawe for much of my youth. Then one day a pull in my heart beckoned me out into the world. It drew me to Yunaii. Only when I met Gaelin did I come to understand that I was soul-called here."

Aven shook her head. "I—I wish I'd known, Ifera."

"I wanted to tell you so many times, but so much animosity lived in you, understandably, of course, so I did not want to force my presence, and therefore force Dia'veh, upon you."

Aven smiled as the Maker's warmth flared inside her chest. Every time she thought about their exchange, she couldn't fight the urge to grin or wriggle or even whoop from atop the canyon's cliffs.

You are perfect. You are strong.

She'd heard the words so many times. From Mist, from Mama, from Papa, but the Qinawe's disdain chipped away at her confidence, hollowing out their assertions.

But this gift, they could not touch. What were hurled words from small shifters when compared to those spoken by the Maker of all things? Aven dared to believe she was more than what everyone said. Just like Zoli had told her.

She cleared her throat as she swallowed it all down, hoping to process once the time for rest came. "So what exactly is a Lecarian?"

"It is simply the name shifters from multiple bloodlines have chosen for themselves," Ifera said. "Me, you, Mist, it is a name you can claim if it suits you. Those who resent you have no right to give you a name. Nor the power. Others have done the same. Elementals or elves who share bloodlines with humans, Anlis who share bloodlines with dragons. New Sholi are coming into the world and taking names for themselves, as is their right."

"Where did Lecarian come from?" Mist asked, taking a bite of the smoked vegetables.

Ifera toyed with the gold bands around her fingers. "I am unsure. Dia'veh told it to me, but I do not know how it originated."

"But you've met other Lecarians?"

"Yes. Before I came to Yunaii. I have met some who call this the Second Age of Creation."

Aven glanced at Mist. The Time of Creating was something she'd been told about as a child. When Dia'veh and Sholindrea shaped the world and the Sholi. "What does that mean? You think Dia'veh is creating again?"

Gaelin touched his chest with the hand Ifera wasn't holding. "The Creator is done giving power to this world, but their power still lingers. As our bloodlines mingle and the lines between us grow dim, something new is coming to life."

Mist squeezed Aven's hand as childlike wonder shone in her eyes. "*We're* creating now."

Ifera nodded, some of the familiar joy returning to her face. "Places like Yunaii might one day become hard to find."

"Not soon enough," Gaelin said, his brows furrowing as he took another bite of pork.

"That is unkind, dear heart." Ifera patted his hand. "I wish things were different, but if my time serving in Yunaii is meant to end, then that is what Dia'veh intends."

"It's not fair though," Mist said as she chose a piece of glazed, sticky fruit that gleamed red in the candlelight.

The Priestess shrugged, but her aching sadness mingled with the scents of pork and burning wicks. Yana had cut her deep. "It is what it is."

Gaelin leaned close so she would look into his eyes. "If the time has come for you to leave, then I shall go with you."

Ifera's breathing slowed as her free hand slid over his. "Do not say that Gaelin. You are called to this place. It is where you are meant to serve."

He lifted a hand to her cheek and trailed one finger along her jawline. That touch summoned an energy, one Aven only felt when Mama and Papa thought she wasn't looking. If only she could sink into the floor or merge into the walls. Anything to escape the uncomfortable feeling creeping through her gut. Had they forgotten they weren't alone? The way they stared at each other was more intimate than anything she'd ever witnessed.

"I'll not serve those that spurn you, Ifera." Gaelin's voice cracked from its usual deep rumble. "And I will follow you to wherever Dia'veh leads next."

Ifera swallowed hard before tearing her gaze away. Her eyes lit on Aven and Mist, and an odd smile pulled at her lips.

"Sorry girls." Her voice was breathy and higher than usual. "I believe Gaelin and I have private things to discuss. We must bid you goodnight."

Aven nodded gratefully, hoping they couldn't see the panic in her eyes. Them staring at each other like meals to devour was enough for her. She didn't want to imagine the Priestess of Dia'veh's Temple and the stuffy Steel elf with no sense of humor doing anything else. The way their chests heaved and their hands clasped tight made her wish she could take soap to her brain.

"Goodnight," Mist said, shifting at Aven's side. "We can talk more in the morning."

"Yes," Ifera said, even as Gaelin walked towards the doors against the back wall. She followed quick on his heels, disappearing behind the double doors without so much as a backward glance.

Aven stared long after they were gone, her stomach somersaulting and her cheeks on fire. Even when she'd been with Pryn, the air had never crackled when they looked at one another. Desperation had never lingered in their touches. Things had been comfortable. Safe. For a while, anyway.

That power sparking between Ifera and Gaelin hit too close to Aven's heart. She was painfully aware of her sweaty hand clasped around Mist's, how their knuckles aligned just right. That need to touch and hold. The wish to do more rose from where she always shoved it down.

I sent her to you.

That's what Dia'veh had said. But what for? To be a friend? A guide? A means to an end? Did Aven want to know? She had spent so long being angry at Pryn. The hurt still twisted her up, even as Mist made it bearable. That kept her from indulging even a momentary daydream, though. She couldn't lose another friend. Mist was the greatest friend she had ever had. If Aven let herself hope, she could end up alone again.

What if Mist didn't feel the same way? She would trade all her shapeshifting ability to know what her best friend felt.

"Well," Mist said in a soft voice. "That was—"

"Yeah." Aven licked her lips, focusing on the plates of food. "I always imagined the Truthseeker as this boring old rock that just meditated and listened to people talk."

A giggle escaped Mist, and it broke Aven's fear. She couldn't help looking up, searching for the smile that brightened her days. Mist stared right at her, eyes crinkling with laughter, as her fingers tightened around Aven's.

How could one look make her heart race or her cheeks get so hot? By the Maker, Aven was such a fool. "C-can I ask you a question?"

Mist's lopsided grin shone with curiosity. "Of course."

Aven ran a finger over the sharp tip of Kali's fang. Why did she say that? Now she had to ask what had burned in her thoughts since Dia'veh stopped speaking.

"Your flight to Yunaii." She looked at their joined hands, Mist's fingers so much thinner than hers. Delicate and long. Rings decorated more of them than not, shiny distractions they both fell prey to toying with.

"What about it?"

"You've mentioned it was a hard trip." Aven kicked herself. She shouldn't have said anything. "W-what got you through it?"

Mist tilted her head, long white hair shifting over her shoulder. "What's got you thinking about that?"

Aven fidgeted, her stomach knotting even as she reminded herself that this was Mist. Not only had she never judged Aven's moments of utter foolishness, but she was devoted to Dia'veh. The Temple was her haven, like the cave was Aven's. There'd be no scoffing or disbelief.

Aven glanced at the pool where they'd prayed. Most of the candles had gone out, except for a few near the cushions. Speckles of moonlight broke through the Eilawi tree's canopy, shining through the glass ceiling to alight on the water. The serene picture brought another rush of warmth.

"Aven?"

She dragged her gaze back to Mist, who had begun anxiously stroking her armlet.

"Are you okay?"

Aven released a deep breath and took the plunge. "In the pool, I heard—"

Mist's eyes widened, the corners of her mouth kicking up. "Dia'veh?"

"Yes." Aven stroked Mist's thumb with her own, trying to not let her fingers shake. With another deep breath, she shared everything from her strange exchange. Her anger. The way she'd railed at the Creator. The fear that she had gone too far. Even now, she quaked inside when she thought about the rage she unleashed. They'd been only thoughts, but the Maker knew.

"Aven." Mist scooted closer until their knees pressed together. "Don't worry. This might have been the first time you heard Dia'veh, but it wasn't the first time they heard you. Their first teaching is love. Nothing you could do or say would offend the Creator."

Of course, she knew. Mist always knew. Aven leaned in slowly until their foreheads touched, glimpsing a smile before her eyes closed. This moment was all she wanted. Love. Acceptance. Being understood in a way she never knew she could. If only this could stretch out forever.

"What did Dia'veh tell you?" Mist asked, her breath warm and smelling of fruit.

Aven's heart skipped.

I sent her to you.

"In the storm." She looked up through her lashes. "What did you hear?"

"Dia'veh showed you the storm?" Mist pulled back as a bitter tang wove through her scent.

Why was she afraid? Had Aven given her a reason to fear being honest? Whatever it was, Mist fought it back with a nervous smile and a hopeful glance towards the pool.

"I got so tired, but I heard Dia'veh calling me, telling me to keep going. To get to you. I-I heard your name."

"Why does that scare you?"

Mist shook her head, but they were in too deep to stop now. Aven slid a knuckle down her cheek, tracing the smooth brown skin, until reaching her chin.

"Talk to me."

Mist's sad frown turned piercing and sharp. "You first. What did Dia'veh tell you?"

With that one question, Aven's awareness narrowed to how little space was between them. Their knees overlapped, fingers entwined, and their noses nearly touched. Blood began pounding in her ears, the rhythm of her heartbeat melodic and painful.

Mist's fuchsia eyes bored into her, silently begging for an answer. Could she already know? Had Dia'veh told her more than what Aven had been allowed to hear?

"I asked why my prayers were never answered."

"And?" Mist's voice was soft and clipped, like she feared even breathing.

Aven searched her face, wishing again for the power to pluck thoughts from her head. What did Mist hope to hear? It didn't seem possible, but Aven's heart raced even faster, Dia'veh's words echoing in her ears. Would repeating them ruin their friendship? The Creator of the world had to know how this spark of hope would grow into a roaring fire.

"It was you." Aven's voice shook, despite how she clenched her teeth. "Dia'veh answered my prayers by sending me you."

There. The words were spoken. Now Mist would remind her how they wanted different things. That their paths had converged but would one day split. Aven waited to hear everything she already knew, but wished wasn't true.

Instead, silence stretched between them, aching and empty like a starless sky. Aven's body trembled. She couldn't stop it. It was as if she was searing cold and burning hot all at once. She locked her eyes on their fingers as she tried to breathe. Every moment Mist didn't speak felt like a knife in her heart.

"Do," Mist drew in a shaky breath. "Do you want me to– to be that? To be an answer to your prayers?"

Aven recoiled at the tears she found welling in Mist's eyes.

"I want," she croaked before swallowing the lump in her throat. "I just want you. I want you with me. Being away from you feels wrong. When I see something, I want to share it with you. When I do something, I wonder how much better it would be to do it with you. I want to share every moment with you." Aven's vision blurred as she stifled a sniffle. "And I am so scared that one day you won't be there. That I won't get to share anything with you ag–"

Mist's warm mouth swallowed her sob. So soft and smooth, touched with desperation as she pressed into the kiss. Her lips parted in a soft, inviting gasp, tantalizing Aven to take a deeper taste. But a chill swept over her face as Mist retreated, terror shining through the rings of pink and purple in her eyes.

"I'm sorry. I shouldn't have—I don't expect. I know this isn't how your people do things."

Aven cupped her cheeks, stopping her from fleeing the room like she seemed ready to do. "I don't care how they do things."

Mist's lips trembled as her gaze slid between Aven's eyes and her mouth. "I don't want to be like a Pryn."

"You couldn't be like her if you tried." Aven pulled her in, and this time their mouths collided without fear. Teasing at first. Until tenderness turned bold as she parted her lips, coaxing Mist's to do the same. Her reward was the taste of sugar and fruit on her tongue.

Maker, she was perfect.

Mist's fingers slid through Aven's hair, gliding over her neck, caressing her skin, leaving tremors in her wake. Aven didn't think as she leaned in, pushing Mist against the cushions. Their bodies pressed together, rocking against one another in a rhythm that was familiar and new all at once. Aven drowned in it. The sounds of Mist's sighs, the taste of her mouth, the thrill of every new touch. She could forget about everything that went wrong today. Mist was in her arms, their tears of joy mingling on her cheeks, becoming one, just like them. This moment could span the rest of her life.

Everything ground to a halt when someone cleared their throat, rough and loud. Mist froze as Aven rocked back on her heels, head whipping around. Whoever it was needed a full set of claws to the face.

"You know, the Temple of Dia'veh *might* not be the place for that kind of carrying on." Emriel stood by the pool with one hand on her hip. "I know the Creator of everything probably sees everything, but come on. I want to keep my eyeballs in my head, not have to pluck them out so this isn't seared into my brain."

Mist flopped against the cushions with a loud sigh. "Em, you're the absolute worst."

CHAPTER
Twenty-Four

Mist

Emriel settled on the cushions, offering no proper hello. No apology for how things ended at the roost. She simply helped herself to the last of the food on the wooden trays, oblivious to Mist's internal crisis.

Could Em hear her heart pounding? Did Aven smell how badly Mist wanted to kiss her again? A shiver swept up her spine as she licked her tingling lips. Aven's teasing nibbles left them sensitive and swollen. She needed to stop thinking about their bodies pressed together, before her sister noticed her skin practically quivering.

"What are you doing here?"

Em dropped a bit of salted pork into her upturned mouth before licking the juice from her fingers. "Well, when you challenge the flight leader and lose, you're generally not welcome to stay at the roost after that."

Mist rolled her eyes. "You have nowhere else to go."

"If that's how you want to phrase it." Em shoved the last piece of flatbread in her mouth.

When she reached for the last bits of leftover fruit, Aven blocked her with a clawed hand. "You've got some nerve. You're just going to come in and not even apologize?"

Emriel rose one brow before snatching the fruit. "For what?"

"For how you spoke to Mist after she *saved* your life."

Mist cast a sideways glance at Aven and imagined kissing her breathless. She was so perceptive and selfless.

Perfect. Why did Emriel have to be here right now?

Mist cast a sideways glance at Aven and imagined kissing her breathless. She was so perceptive and selfless. Perfect. Why did Emriel have to be here right now?

With a disgusted sound, Em waved a hand between their faces.

"Hi. Still here. Still don't want to watch you two undress each other. Even if it is just with your eyes."

"Well, fair's fair," Mist said, heat searing through her cheeks. "Imagine how it felt to find out the dragon who almost killed me was once your mate."

Emriel snickered as she swiped her fingers through the juice on the trays. "Oh, they're all talk."

"Fennicks tried to choke the life out of you." Mist couldn't believe her sister's arrogance had gotten this bad. Just because she thought something didn't make it true. "Whoever they were when you knew them, isn't who they are now."

"If Fennicks had changed, they'd be in charge of the flight." Emriel flopped back onto a pile of cushions. "My life was no more in danger than yours. That nip yesterday was nothing compared to what it could have been, bloodkin."

"Nip?" Aven hissed, leaning forward with a snarl. True to form, Emriel sat back up, amber creeping into the crystalline of her eyes. They stared one another down, even as an uncomfortable truth grew blatantly obvious.

So much certainty lived in Emriel's voice, as if she'd seen the attack herself.

"How long have you been in Yunaii, Em?" Mist asked, curling fingers around Aven's wrist. Her claws had distended, fingers twitching for Emriel's throat. "How long did you know the Soulless were coming?"

Em gave a blasé shrug. "I've been tracking them since they snuck off of their dung hole of an island. That's what we do in Estellias, remember? We watch the bastards so the rest of you can live happy, peaceful lives. That's what everyone expects."

"That's not true." Aven's voice shook. "No one expects anything of Estellias anymore. Before I met Mist, it was just a dot on a travelers' maps."

"That does not make the point you think it does," Emriel said, pointedly glancing at Mist. "Your peaceful lives were earned by my ancestors and maintained by our armies. The descendants of Sorrow's soldiers bleed so the rest of the world doesn't have to."

Aven's arm went limp under Mist's hand, sorrow twisting her face. "I guess that's true."

"Even if it is true," Mist said, squeezing Aven's hand. "That doesn't answer my question. Did you know the Soulless were going to attack the market?"

Emriel tilted her head, but her hesitation was just as much of an answer.

"People died in the market," Mist hissed.

"I was there, remember?" Emriel pushed up off the cushions, her mask of amusement cracking. "I did what I could to stop it."

"You could have warned them!"

"Warned who?" Emriel asked, looking at Aven. "You saw today what it's like here. No one works together. No one cares about each other. Everyone looks to their own. So, I put myself in the market and did my duty. I fought, I bled, and I was ready to die, if that's what it took. That's not enough for you, bloodkin? Would it be better if I had died?"

Mist's shoulders dropped. Behind the stubborn set of Emriel's mouth and the furrow of her brow, something shone beneath. Sorrow. Exhaustion. She was doing the best she could, with no one to help her. In Estellias, she had Eega to watch her back. Here she had Mist.

"I don't want you to die, Emriel."

Mist stared into her light eyes and their egg-layer stared back, from the roundness of Em's cheeks and the line of her clenched jaw. Hopefully their eega was proud of Emriel's devotion to her cause, to Estellias. She should be proud of at least one of them.

Emriel pursed her lips with a half-hearted nod. "It was gutsy of you to pick up that knife today, even if I didn't need you to. I'm sorry I didn't say thanks or—that I'm proud of you."

Aven grinned out of the corner of Mist's eye, prompting an exasperated sigh. How did she end up surrounded by stab-happy people?

"So." Emriel cleared her throat once more. "Was a time decided for the meeting tomorrow?"

Aven sat up straighter, brows arched in surprise. "How did you know about that?"

Emriel threw her an incredulous look. "You think there's anything going on down here that Rielnor doesn't know? His spies followed you, the elves, everyone."

"But how?" Aven looked between them, obviously searching for answers.

Mist couldn't squash a soft guffaw. She wasn't surprised, but how had she not seen it sooner? "They impersonated other shifters. The older dragons can make themselves look like anyone or anything."

Emriel nodded. "He's probably always had spies amongst the different groups. Information is power. I'm sure they've all reported back everything that was said and decided. I left before I heard how it went with the Tribouin and the Qinawe."

Blood drained from Aven's face as she looked at Mist.

"Does that mean he knows Yana insisted on the meeting taking place on Qinawe lands?"

"You have got to be joking," Emriel said with a disbelieving laugh. "Prideful old crone."

Mist grew dizzy as realization hit. Rielnor wasn't the Soulless, but he was still dangerous. All the dragons were. If the leaders turned their attention to the flight and what to do with them, Mist couldn't imagine how that would go.

Emriel rubbed her eyes as she sighed. "If we have to deal with dragons on top of a bunch of petty, bickering shapeshifters then we should probably get some sleep."

"We?" Mist repeated.

"I didn't come here just to kill a few Soulless." A wicked grin spread across Em's face. "I came to protect people. I'm not done until they're *all* dead."

Mist shouldn't have felt better knowing there would be more bloodshed, but a weight still lifted from her chest. If Emriel was going to stay, fight, and debate with the shifter leaders, maybe they'd save Yunaii's people after all.

***

Morning came quickly thanks to the glass ceiling of the Temple. Sansia's glaring light was more annoying than a crotchety old rooster announcing the day. For the second time, Mist rose much earlier than she would have liked. Only this time, she woke Aven too. Neither of them could sleep the morning away.

Ifera and Gaelin were up just as early, and neither said a word about Em's presence. They simply brought an extra tray of food, and together the five of them rushed through a breakfast of fresh fruit, nuts, and sweetbread. Once everyone was done, Ifera offered her bathing room to Aven and Mist, with a pointed curling of her nose.

Throughout all their morning preparation, Mist kept staring at Aven, wondering if she was thinking about what happened between them. Did she regret their kiss? Did she want to do it again? Did it even matter right now? Lives were in danger. Guilt ate at her for caring about such silly things, but those feelings refused to be shoved back in their box. Being able to touch Aven without fear was all she'd wanted for so long.

By the time they each finished bathing, Commander Senwe had arrived with a squadron of elves that included Zoli, as had the pride leader, with a younger lynx on his heels. Kanai wore nothing but a tattered pair of breeches ripped just below his knee. He needed little else. A mane of smoky brown hair framed his face, and his fuzzy chest was bare and scarred, reminding Mist of Rielnor. What would it be like to see them in a room together? She imagined lots of growling and glaring.

The elfin leader was a stark contrast to the lynx. He'd come in his finest leather armor, dyed in a green and yellow pattern that made Mist think of sunlight on a forest floor. No doubt it was the perfect camouflage for the Forest elf. Not only had he strapped a pair of scimitars to his back, but she noted at least two, maybe three knives hidden on his body. He was ready for a fight, as were the rest of his stony-eyed people.

Ifera and Gaelin quickly pulled the two leaders aside to inform them of yesterday's developments. Hopefully, the Qinawe's demands would not be taken as a slight.

As they waited for the whispering between the leaders to end, Dev appeared from the among the Linseen's ranks. When he noticed them, he whispered something to Zoli before making a beeline for Aven and Mist.

He'd traded riding leathers for the green and brown armor of the Peace elves, with a sword on either hip. Even with his tousle of curls, he easily slid back into the mold of a warrior.

"Good morning," Dev said, halting before them like a soldier falling in line; shoulders straight, hands behind his back, chin raised. Mist knew Aven hated when he was all business, but she couldn't help admiring him for it. Elves had a discipline she'd never seen from any other Sholi.

"Hey there," Aven said, clapping his stiff shoulder. "You ready for this?"

"I am well prepared." His gaze flicked for a moment to the hilts of his swords before settling on Mist. "I trust the Priestess has cared for your wounds."

"She did. I'll be right as rain in a few days."

"Very good." He almost seemed like he wanted to smile, but didn't give in to the urge.

"It looks like Mister Whiskers and Commander Pointy Ears are taking the news well," Emriel said, appearing at Mist's side. "That's a good sign. Maybe this day won't be a pile of dragon dung after all."

A soft gasp came from Dev's direction, making Mist and Aven look his way. His wide-eyed stare locked on Emriel.

"Dev?" Aven asked, moving closer. "You okay?"

"It is you," he whispered, arms going slack.

Emriel glanced behind her before touching her chest. "Um—do I know you? If I killed someone you love, all I can say is they probably had it coming."

He threw back his shoulders and returned to his tense pose. "I am of the Klesian elves and I am soul-called. To you."

Aven's mouth fell open. "Emriel? You're soul-called to Emriel?"

"Oh, for Dia'veh's sake!" Em raised both hands as if she could wave off the devoted look taking over Dev's face. "I don't need some humorless, duty-bound elf daydreaming of martyring themselves in the name of protecting me."

"The Creator knows better." Dev didn't so much as a blink an eye. "Truly, Dia'veh knows you are in need of someone to watch your back."

Mist's breath caught as he spoke her thoughts from the previous night. She hadn't let the concern build into fear, yet Dia'veh had still handled a prayer that had taken root.

A Klesian elf was the greatest protection Mist could ask for, short of Dia'veh themself.

Emriel sized him up with a frustrated sigh. "Just stay out of my way, elf. Creator knows I've got enough people to worry about without you throwing yourself in the fire."

"Is it my duty," Dev said.

Em made a disgusted sound as she stomped towards Gaelin. If she thought the Truthseeker would talk Dev out of protecting her, then she was in for a surprise. Mist had never known the Steel elf to yield anything, especially what he believed as an order from the Creator.

Aven still gaped at Dev. "Does this mean Emriel is in danger?"

"It could, potentially." He cocked his head like a curious puppy, curls bouncing from the motion. "Or Dia'veh knows that what is coming will be more than she is able to handle."

"Well, that's ominous," Aven muttered.

All of this had to be hard. Just yesterday, she'd grappled with whether the Creator even cared at all. Now she'd not only heard Dia'veh's voice, but seen their power in action. Mist only hoped Dev's call was merely a precaution for a devoted servant.

They waited around until flock leader Yliva arrived. Mist had only heard about her, but there was no mistaking the commanding look in her gaze or the posture of someone used to being in charge. She entered the Temple with her head high, wearing a strip of gauzy fabric that wrapped and crisscrossed her thin body, covering just enough, while leaving her navel and spine exposed. Gray wings extended from her back, matching the plumage bursting from her scalp and cascading past her shoulders like the crest of a bird. She was absolutely magnificent, and when she turned her piercing eyes Mist's way, it took all she had to keep from dropping into a bow.

A younger griffin glided beside Yliva, her coloring similar to the flock leader's, while the feathers on her head barely reached her shoulders. When her amber eyes lit on Dev and Aven, a look of delight swept her heart-shaped face. Without a glance at Yliva, the girl half flew, half skipped to them, dressed in a yellow dress that left little to the imagination.

"I was hoping you two would be here." She slowed only when she was close enough to brush against Dev. "I had to beat two of my brothers in riddle games to earn the right to attend the flock leader." She lowered her eyelids as she gazed at Dev. "You should be flattered."

"I am not," he said in the most unforgiving tone Mist had ever heard from him. "I am soul-called now, Wilella. I cannot allow you to distract me from my duty."

With that, Dev walked back to Zoli, his shoulders so tense Mist could have broken a chair against his back and not gotten a reaction. She glanced at Aven, searching for answers, but found her staring down the griffin girl.

"Elves aren't like us," Aven said in a flat tone. "You can't treat him like a shifter."

"Oh, come now." The griffin fluttered her wings, lifting herself off the floor. "You liked my games yesterday."

A scowl stretched across Aven's face. "It was funny at first. but Dev has made it clear he's not interested in being chased. So, unless you're going to court him his way, you should probably just leave him alone."

The girl rolled amber eyes before her attention settled on Mist. Her tiny nose sniffed at the air, wiggling like a bunny's. "And who is this? You smell like fire and roses. I like it."

Aven laid a hand on Mist's shoulder as she introduced them, every line in her body exuding possessiveness. From anyone else, it would have set Mist's teeth on edge, but with Aven it resulted in warmth flooding her body. She wanted to lean in, tuck herself against Aven's curves, but now wasn't the time. Especially not when the Tribouin Elders entered the Temple, followed closely by Pryn.

CHAPTER
Twenty-Five

Aven

Aven blinked repeatedly as she stared at Pryn. Tribouin didn't give leadership roles to their women any more than Qinawe did to their men, yet, there she stood. Had being the best dragon rider won her privilege or did she manipulate her way here?

The two Tribouin Elders stopped short of the other shifters, their faces familiar. Elder Dasoln had reddish curls and olive skin, with a heavy dusting of freckles, while Elder Jywe's deep brown skin was so dark it captured every flare of candle and sunlight like the surface of a pond. Neither had ever looked at Aven. Neither had even spoken her name. No change now, as their attention locked on Yliva's feathered crown and Kanai's clawed hands. Both dressed in loose pantaloons and buttoned vests that left their arms and calves bare. All in undyed, draped cloth and golden tattoos.

Those markings told what made these men worthy of leading. The shimmering ink identified them as Elders, while wavy lines were for gifts of mind, straight lines for weapons prowess, and circles for communal abilities like hunting, tanning, and cooking. The twitchy windbags wore nothing that Papa didn't wear as well, only he was denied the flashy ink. Just as he was denied a place amongst his people.

It was a shame they didn't see Papa's value, but Aven was grateful she'd grown up on Qinawe lands. Lowering her eyes to the Matriarchs hurt enough. Needing an escort until she had a Chosen would have driven her absolutely mad.

Pryn hovered behind her Elders, tracking everyone and everything. Perhaps she'd come as a servant. Her unsolicited mating challenge might have cost her more than Aven realized.

"Do you think she is here of her own volition?" Mist asked. The concern lacing her voice made Aven want to kiss her right there. Everyone had a place in her heart.

"If I know Pryn, she's exactly where she wants to be."

The Elders waited for Gaelin to come to them. Not surprising. Of all the shifters, the Tribouin walked the strictest line. Keeping their people strong was just the beginning of their ways. They controlled everything, from who joined with who, to what skills were cultivated, and which were abandoned. Papa and Pryn made it sound like their existence was still predicated on pure survival. There was not much reserved for joy or pleasure.

Once Ifera finished speaking with Yliva, she waved Aven and Mist over.

"It is agreed. We leave for the Qinawe lands."

Aven breathed slowly, torn between relief and worry. The game board was set. Time to play. Hopefully, this day didn't end in disappointment or bloodshed.

***

The walk to the Qinawe lands was quiet. Ifera led the way with her chin raised stubbornly, returning to the lands she'd been kicked off of with a glint in her eye that said she was ready to fight. Gaelin stayed with the Tribouin, whispering all the while, as if he had to convince them to take each reluctant step.

The smell of cookfires and leather welcomed Aven home. Would it be for the last time? She wasn't expecting a welcome after how things ended yesterday. With a sad sigh, she drew alongside Ifera to help lead everyone to the clearing they'd met in the day before.

With each step, a weight pressed down on her. She caught herself first hoping the Maker would help them, before outright praying. Matriarch Yana held the power to sway people with only her words. What would happen if she convinced the Yunaii leaders to ignore the threat? She imagined the griffins and lynx simply moving on, migrating as they once had before settling in Yunaii, leaving only the Tribouin and Qinawe when the Soulless returned.

As the clearing came into view, Kali's instincts rose like a cat's hackles. The space was empty around the dying fire. No one peered around trees or snuck through the shadows. She barely scented even a hint of sweat or musk. Just ash and fire.

Something was wrong.

Aven held out a hand in front of Ifera, but her approach had already slowed. The Priestess glanced around the trees with narrowed eyes as Mist came up on Aven's other side.

They entered the clearing together, Aven eyeing the large tree the Matriarchs had gathered around yesterday. A single figure lingered in the shadow of its canopy, lounging on the massive roots, one bare foot perched high for his arm to rest idly upon his bent knee. A sharp breath caught in Aven's throat as she recognized the scarred face and veil of green hair.

Rielnor's mouth curved in a welcoming smile as gasps whispered from the other shifters. With one jerk of his fingers, Anyvath appeared from behind the tree, leading not only Matriarch Yana, Revari, and Hanawi—but Mama as well. Aven started forward, only to get a look that had saved her time and again from being scored by a boar or trampled by a buck.

Danger, cub.

Another dragon rounded the other side of the tree. Their feminine face was framed by black hair falling in waves around pale shoulders, with yellow eyes that were heavy-lidded and tilted up. The newcomer and Anyvath flanked Rielnor on either side, both of their mouths set in grim lines.

Nothing about their presence felt friendly. Even though the Matriarchs stood calmly beside Anyvath, they stunk of angry fear. Aven could only guess the kind of entrance the dragons made. That none of the Qinawe lingered nearby meant the Matriarchs had sent them scattering through the woods.

Emriel slipped between the leaders and the dragons, a bored expression on her face even as her hands rested on the hilts of her daggers. Would being Rielnor's kit buy them mercy? Aven could only hope.

"What's going on there, old man?"

"It seemed the dragons were long overdue for a real conversation," Rielnor's deep voice rumbled. He remained perched on the roots as if he were reading a book, not facing the most dangerous shifters in Yunaii. "And with current events, we decided it was time for decisive action."

"We?" Kanai's face twisted into a snarl as he drew closer.

Gaelin moved between the shifter leaders, all the softness from last night replaced once more by steel and leather.

"Pride leader Kanai, Flock leader Yliva, Elders Dasoln and Jywe," Gaelin glanced at Rielnor as if asking for permission, which he received in the barest of nods. "This is Rielnor. Flight leader of the dragons."

Aven sealed her eyes shut at the flurry of gasps and exclamations. Her heart pounded in her chest, but at least it was done. She was free of the secret's weight.

"Eyes up, cub," Mama whispered in her ear. "Time to fight for our place."

Aven's eyes flew open, and she almost choked on a relieved sob. Mama was at her side, unharmed and ferocious, with her hair pulled back in rows of braids, her wolf's tooth dangling from one ear. Something hard pressed into Aven's palm, and a look revealed the hatchet she'd painstakingly carved and crafted with her own two hands. Qinawe fashioned their weapon of choice as they approached adulthood, giving them enough time to hone their skills for when they danced with their Chosen. The handle had some wear from all her practice, but it still didn't have the look of age that Mama's axe did, which was strapped to her hip once more.

The leaders had fallen quiet, Matriarchs standing off to Rielnor's right, the Elders off to his left, leaving Yliva and Kanai with Aven and the elves. Ifera and Gaelin stood near the fire at the center of it all, their body language pleading for peace.

Kanai matched the flight leader's ferocity. "So, the dragons really are shapeshifters."

Rielnor rested his temple against the back of his hand, a bored look on his face. "Have you all had ample time to process?"

"You show great nerve coming here," Matriarch Revari said. "Especially after everything you have taken from our people."

Anyvath and the other dragon threw looks at her that would have quelled anyone lesser, while Rielnor merely arched one scarred brow.

"We took nothing you did not offer." He shifted his knee and leaned forward, bracing both arms on his thighs. "The nerve your people have shown for generations by relegating us to history and legend, forgetting an entire race of shifters even existed. Be grateful the insult your ancestors slung by downgrading my people to nothing but beasts of burden did not result in a massacre like many of my kind wanted."

Revari swallowed hard and thankfully had the sense to say nothing more. Aven glanced at Kanai and Yliva, hoping one of them would have a clever response, but both looked successfully chastised.

Ifera was not so easily silenced. She took a step closer, pointedly ignoring how Rielnor's companions glared. "Flight leader. There are many concerns brought forth by the leaders in Yunaii. The lies and secrets are only some. I hope your intention today is to address the most severe of issues."

Rielnor tilted his head as he considered her. "You always cut to the heart of things, Priestess. I appreciate that. The Soulless *are* why I am here. I have no interest in debating the semantics of hurt feelings. My flight has allowed themselves to be treated like animals. If anyone takes issue with us, I'll fetch a saddle for them and we shall see how long their ego lasts."

Aven bit back a smile as Mist did the same. None of this should have been amusing, but the befuddled looks on the Elders' and Matriarchs' faces were delicious. If only this feeling could be bottled.

"Now that everyone has seen where I get my dramatic flair from," Emriel said, sauntering towards Rielnor. "Tell me, my egg-warden, what are you planning for the Soulless?"

Rielnor pushed to his feet. "As I said, Yunaii needs decisiveness."

"And you can give that to them?" Em's derisive tone made Aven's eyes widen. "Nothing like the threat of death to gather more power for yourself."

"On the contrary." Rielnor stepped over roots as he approached her with the same unusual grace all the dragons had. On such a large man, it was even more unnerving. "I thought my dear kit could be the one to take the lead. After all, you were ready to kill me yesterday to earn the name of flight leader. Had you succeeded, it would be you facing the judgment now staring me down. I propose *you* gather a small retinue to scout beyond Yunaii and find out if we are even still in danger."

Yliva moved into the clearing with a predator's elegance. Her quivering wings tucked against her back, as if she was prepared to spring into the air if needed.

"I was under the impression that your flight believed the Soulless would return." She glanced back at Aven, her thin brows arched curiously. "Is that not what you said to me?"

A sick feeling twisted Aven's gut, but Emriel answered for her with a glare to match Rielnor's. "The flight leader has forgotten what the Soulless are like. I have been tracking them. I can assure you, they will be back. They came here with purpose."

"And what was that purpose?" Kanai asked in a low tone Aven recognized. The hunt for answers opened before him. He would not miss his chance.

"They came to kill dragons. To stop them from preventing the Elementals' civil war."

"So my pride mates that died yesterday were just senseless casualties?"

Sorrow lit in Emriel's eyes. "Perhaps. Though, knowing the Soulless, when they found a canyon full of highly trained shifters who have remained devout to the old ways, they resolved to end you all. Your corpses are too useful to the Summoner."

"You cannot know that," Rielnor said over another wave of gasps.

Emriel rounded on him, anger tensing her limbs. "You *abandoned* Estellias. You don't get to argue about what the Soulless are capable of."

Rielnor stomped towards her, fury twisting across his scarred face. Just the sight of that rage had Aven reaching for her hatchet. The helplessness when he'd directed it at her and her family clawed at her resolve.

"I did not run from the Soulless. I protected the flight from the politics of Estellias."

"Please stop!" Ifera said, putting her body between them. "You debate things that have no meaning here."

The two dragons glared at each other before Emriel stepped back.

"Thank you." Ifera dropped her hand from Rielnor's chest. "The flight leader's suggestion of a scouting party is good. We must know if the Soulless have moved on or if more are on the way. Can we at least agree on that?"

Kanai and Yliva glanced at one another before nodding. The Tribouin Elders muttered their concession, while the Qinawe Matriarchs begrudgingly did as well. The shock of seeing all of them acquiesce to anything nearly laid Aven out better than a punch to the jaw.

Commander Senwe put a fist over his heart and bowed. "I can prepare a squadron of Linseen to accomplish this task."

"A selfless offer," Gaelin said slowly, as if considering each word. "I believe, though, that flight and speed will better serve this purpose. It would take too long for your squadron to march all the way to Shard's Port. Dragons could be there and back in half the time. While also scouting great distances along the way."

As Senwe gave a resigned nod, Aven sent a pleading look to Mist. It wouldn't be easy, but this was a chance. A chance to prove themselves to the Matriarchs, to earn her place amongst the Qinawe. If she helped her people, maybe she would finally prove Yana wrong.

Whatever Mist saw in her face earned Aven a soft smile. Of course. Mist always had her back, no matter the request.

"Sending scouts is probably the only thing the flight leader and I agree on," Emriel said, gaze sweeping over the shifters. "I can fly to the port and back in five or six days if weather permits."

Dev stepped out of the Linseen's ranks and bowed. "Then I offer my company on this endeavor."

Rielnor stared at him with widening eyes. Before today, they had only met as dragon and rider. Now, Dev regarded him with calm calculation, of course presuming nothing about their previous relationship.

Rielnor seemed to hold no such reservations. Affection crept across his face, softening its severe, scarred appearance. "Your company is unnecessary, my friend. My bloodkin can handle this mission."

Dev's gaze shifted between him and Emriel. "Flight leader, I am soul-called to protect her. I shall not leave her side until Dia'veh wills it."

Emriel groaned as Rielnor's icy scent gave way to nose-tickling shock, the whites of his eyes stark against his copper skin.

"You are soul-called to Emriel?" When Dev nodded, Rielnor turned to the other two dragons standing by the tree. "Then Anyvath and–*Fennicks* shall accompany you as well."

A chill swept over Aven as she looked from Anyvath to the yellow-eyed dragon, whose feminine face had broken into a wide smile. *Fennicks*. How had she not realized the dragon with the beetle-black hair and sun-colored eyes was Fennicks? The face was different, lean muscles replacing the childlike body from two days ago, but there was no denying that smile. Or the scent. She caught a hint as they approached. Beeswax and leather.

"Just like the old days," Fennicks said, looking Emriel up and down.

"Doubtful." A smirk slipped across her blood-red lips. "You used to be fun."

"Flock leader, if I may," Willa said, glancing at Dev with a dimpled smile. "I would like to go as well."

A vein popped in Dev's clenched jaw. "Your assistance is appreciated, but unnecessary."

"Wilella's keen mind and cleverness could serve you well," Yliva said, looking Willa over before giving a slight nod. "I would like it if one of my own set eyes on any potential danger."

This drew the Elders further into the clearing, though their attention remained on Truthseeker Gaelin. "If the dragons and griffins are to have representatives in this party, we must insist on a Tribouin as well."

"Are you so distrusting of one another?" Rielnor asked, his nostrils wrinkling like he'd caught a whiff of something long dead. "Does the word of your neighbor hold no merit?"

Elder Jywe drew himself up, his bearded chin rising so he could look down his nose. "We have no relationship with Flock leader Yliva. As for the dragons, what have you or your flight done to earn the trust of the Tribouin? Would you take our word if roles were reversed?"

"If that is how it's going to be, then I choose who comes," said Fennicks with a mischievous grin. "I already have a rider I can trust to not topple off my back."

Elder Dasoln followed Fennicks' yellow-eyed stare to where Pryn stood at the edge of the clearing.

"No." The Elder's eyes shifted from warm honey to icy blue. "We have young men who are capable riders. Summon their dragons if you will not allow one of them to accompany you."

The look that twisted Fennicks' feminine features reminded Aven of a snarling lynx. Their head lowered, slender fingers flexing as they stepped uncomfortably close to Elder Dasoln.

"No."

"N-no?" The man looked at Rielnor. "You. Control your flight mate."

"I am. You are still alive."

The smile on Emriel's lips was anything but friendly. "It is decided, old man. We take the girl or no Tribouin comes."

Aven glanced at Pryn, who remained rooted to where she stood. Gold shimmered in her eyes as she pressed her lips together, fighting back the smile pulling up the corners of her mouth. She'd won Fennicks' loyalty without them ever exchanging a word.

Elder Dasoln sputtered while Jywe summoned Pryn closer. She dutifully lowered her chin as she entered the circle, the boastful dragon rider hidden beneath propriety. As the Elder began whispering in her ear, Aven turned back to the dragons, not wanting to hear whatever orders were being doled out.

Her attention settled on Emriel, who eyed the unusually quiet Matriarchs. "No demands of your own?"

"I will not bother," Matriarch Yana said, leaning on her staff. "It has been made clear who is in control. You only wish us to speak so you can turn your threats our way."

"It doesn't feel good, does it?" Em asked, stalking towards the Matriarchs.

The old woman lifted her chin, eyes cold as night. "What?"

"Having your power stripped away." Emriel pointedly looked at Aven. "To have no control over your lives, your fate. Say what you will of dragons, but at least we take care of our own."

"Emriel, enough," Rielnor sighed, pinching the bridge of his nose. "Debate customs on your own time. The matter of the Soulless is why I've bothered with this, and things are getting complicated."

"Will we be permitted to send a Qinawe along as well?" Bitterness crept into Yana's voice.

Aven hated the joy she took in the Matriarch's helplessness. Her nails bit into her palms, killing the rising song in her heart when Rielnor looked her way.

"I believe Aven and Mist would be the best choice. I am aware of her standing amongst your people, but Mist is bloodkin to my kit and will serve best alongside her."

Aven didn't need to see the frustration in the Matriarchs' eyes or smell the anger in their scents. Their rage crackled in the air. Between Hanawi's sour face and Revari gripping the handle of her axe, Rielnor's hovering presence was possibly the only thing keeping Aven on Qinawe lands.

"There are other riders," Hanawi said, the scent of her anger so sickeningly bitter it should have summoned claws or teeth.

Rielnor crossed his arms over the scars on his chest. "There are. But their dragons are not ones I would trust with such an endeavor."

"It would seem we are at an impasse," Yana said. "We do not trust the cub on it either."

"I guess the Qinawe will go without," Mist snapped, lunging into the conversation so suddenly Aven grabbed her arm.

A ghost of a smile played on Rielnor's lips. "You heard my flight mate. She will carry no one but Aven."

"If that is our only option, then I will require a moment alone with the cub," Yana said.

He nodded before placing a hand on Mist's back to lead her away, even as she stared at Aven reluctantly. It was for the best. Better to get whatever was coming over with. But then Mama slipped past Rielnor, filling the spot he'd been standing in, summoning a smile to Aven's lips. Yana cast a disapproving look, but that didn't stop her from planting her feet and refusing to lower her eyes.

The Matriarch stood silently, gaze moving over every bit of Aven, analyzing like she was something to be bought. It was hard not to fidget beneath her stare. What did Yana see when she looked at her? A threat to her power? A thorn she could not extract? Her scent remained steady, her face impassive. Aven fixed her attention on the bone from the Matriarch's owl, studying how it looped through her nose.

She just needed a chance. Just one chance.

"Do not allow yourself to misrepresent us," Yana finally said. "I see the war in your heart, the bloodlust you struggle to fight back. You think me unkind, but the Tribouin lessons *have* weakened your will."

"Aven's will is strong," Mama said. "It is Kali's soul that brings struggle. Guarding a Sholi is not the same as an animal."

Yana tapped her staff on the ground. "Others have guarded the soul of a Sholi. None gave in to their urges as often and as recklessly as your cub."

Aven's chest burned, but she refused to release the anger. They had no idea how often she held back the urge to bite and slash. They didn't see the scars on her palms from hiding her claws. They didn't want to. Kali's soul was an excuse they latched on to.

"My cub has always strived to serve the Qinawe," Mama said, resting a hand on Aven's shoulder. "She will continue to do so."

"Doubtful," Yana sniffed. "But it is our only option."

Mama's fingers curled in the fabric of Aven's shirt, biting into her shoulder. She didn't mean for the pinch of pain. Aven knew it. The struggle to remain impassive and polite was hard in the face of such as these. They demanded respect but gave none in return.

"Instigate no fights," Yana commanded, tapping Aven's foot with her staff. "Still your warring heart and put the bond first, cub. Strong bond—"

"Strong people," Aven finished as a hollowness bore into her heart. This should have been it, her chance to earn her place. A dangerous mission, a chance to serve her people. Yet instead of offering her what any other young Qinawe would get, they gave her warnings and insults.

She would never be a part of the bond. Her time amongst the Qinawe really was over.

CHAPTER
Twenty-Six

Mist

The Matriarchs dismissed them all as they had the day before, though this time Mist couldn't blame them. After the scare Rielnor, Anyvath, and Fennicks gave them, the Qinawe wanted the dragons gone.

That left preparations to be made at the Temple. Ifera rushed about, gathering food and supplies from stores she kept in one of the back rooms, while Gaelin packed saddlebags for the dragons to carry. Mist helped them prepare, but her heart wasn't in it.

She couldn't stop watching Aven, whose eyes remained downcast, her shoulders slumped from an invisible weight. That wretched old woman had beaten her down with whispered poison. Poison Mist would dispel by any means, if they could just get a moment alone, an impossible thing with all the bustling chaos around them.

Yliva, Kanai, and Rielnor conversed near the entrance of the Temple, their collection of scars, wings, and fur a strange sight to behold. All three held themselves like humorless predators, regarding one another with the respect they deserved. They were in stark contrast to Emriel and Fennicks, who had not stopped sniping at each other since leaving the Qinawe lands.

"Anyvath, Fennicks," Rielnor called, drawing everyone's attention from their work.

Fennicks paused their packing with a loud dramatic sigh, while Anyvath peered over her bags, attention focused on her flight leader.

Rielnor led the other leaders closer with his hands behind his back. "Kanai has requested to come as well."

"The kitty cat has even less to offer us than the elf," Fennicks said.

"That is a fair assessment," Kanai admitted impressively. The Tribouin and Qinawe had bristled over every slight. "I admit, I make the offer not for the sake of the mission."

"Don't trust us either?" Emriel asked, tilting her head.

Kanai glanced at Yliva, hovering like a wraith at his side. The space between her arched brows pinched, but that was all she allowed herself to show.

"Flock leader Yliva and I trust the flight shall put the safety of Yunaii first," Kanai said. "But for Yliva's peace of mind, I offered my protection to her fledgling."

As attention fell on Willa, a petulant frown crossed her face. "Flock leader, I can protect myself."

Yliva lifted her chin. "You have my trust, Wilella. It is your right to go where you will and do what you must. Simply put, I cannot entrust the dragons with your life, and the flock has suffered enough already."

Fennicks cast a sideways look at Willa. "That's fair. I don't care if the little bird gets barbecued. No offense."

Willa met Fennicks' gaze with a predatory glare. "The feeling is mutual."

Anyvath rolled her eyes before raising her brows at the flight leader. "What does this matter have to do with us?"

"One of you will have to carry the lynx," Rielnor said. "Kanai has explained that their kind does not travel alone. Not even the pride leader. So, there will be two more riders."

"I've already got a package to carry," Fennicks said, jerking a thumb at Pryn. She'd been silent since the leader's meeting, but the gears turned behind her dark eyes.

Rielnor's gaze swept to Mist as his scarred face pulled into a cringed look of apology.

She knew his thoughts without hearing the words. "I can only carry Aven. A second rider on a long trip would be too much."

"It would seem my option is you." Kanai drifted towards Anyvath. "I humbly ask if you would carry myself and a member of my pride."

Emriel threw her hands in the air. "Not that I want to haul you around, Mister Whiskers, but I'm no delicate dove."

"Yes, but I believe the Stone elf has no intention of being parted from you." Kanai arched a brow at Dev, who hovered in Em's shadow, his bag packed and face stoic.

Emriel's frustrated glare almost made Mist snicker. Every interaction between them was better than gooey chocolate after an irritating day. Finally, someone she couldn't bully or manipulate.

Kanai turned back to Anyvath and gave a humble bow. "I pose my question again."

She slid to her feet, oil slick hair and rainbow snakeskin shining in the light. "I am an elder. I've lived long enough to remember when Yunaii was a forgotten oasis."

"I see." Kanai stroked the hair framing his face. "Then your kindness would be a great service."

An approving smile slipped across her lips. "Very well. I suppose it was time you and I got to know each other better. After all, it was your cub that whisked my kit away with nothing but a smile and flick of her tail."

Mist guessed her face looked as astonished as Kanai's. His mouth dropped open, shock widening his eyes. Aven had mentioned something about his cub leaving Yunaii with her mate, but she never would have guessed it was a dragon kit. Let alone *Anyvath's* kit.

"Rourke," Kanai said, licking his lips. "Rourke was a dragon."

Anyvath nodded while Rielnor and Fennicks looked on.

"Did Nya know?" Kanai asked.

"Not at first," Anyvath said, glancing at Rielnor through shimmering lashes. "But truth always wins in the end."

"Well," Kanai said. "I suppose we'll have a lot to talk about on this trip."

Anyvath nodded her agreement. "And who shall be my other rider?"

Kanai motioned to the Temple's entrance, where a shaggy-haired lynx stood, dressed in a buttoned vest and torn breeches. They were younger, softer, and smiled comfortably despite the group's stares.

"Dinon!" A bright smile stretched across Aven's face as she went to greet the newcomer. Mist couldn't help following, curious about their familiarity.

"Aven," the lynx said, before looking at Mist like they were old friends. "Mist."

She searched their gentle features for something familiar, before looking to the strip of cream down their thin chest to the golden fuzz over their skin. Nothing rang a bell. "Have we met?"

The smile dropped from Dinon's face. "I was the one who led you to the Tibri yesterday. I am sorry I did not stay with you. I could have helped when the Soulless attacked."

"Of course. My golden-haired guide." She should have known. The yellow-eyed kindness was the same. "I'm glad you didn't stay. You'd be dead now if you had."

"You all can chit chat on your own time," Emriel said, shoving the last of her things into a satchel. "We have a lot of ground to cover and this trip is getting heavier with every rider."

"Agreed." Rielnor pursed his lips. "You must achieve a good bit of travel before midday. Flying in the direct sun will be draining."

Em raised a finger. "I at least have a plan for that."

***

As they soared through the shade of the canyon, Mist had to praise Emriel's clever idea. Following the winding curves as far as they could would add time to their trip, but provided fresh water and breaks from Sansia's unforgiving light.

For once, Mist relished being so much smaller than the others. She skimmed along the river, occasionally dipping in her toes or sending a splash over Aven when a curve put them in the path of Sansia. Even Anyvath and Fennicks' shadows served her well. They had to fly high where the canyon walls stood farther apart and nothing blocked the light.

Emriel flew ahead, diving into the shade when she could. Willa stuck close to her, abandoning comfortable travel in lieu of hovering over Dev. Sometimes she veered away, alighting on the rocky cliffs, only to scurry back and toss whatever she'd found at the elf. No matter what she pelted him with, Dev refrained from retaliating or complaining.

Aven remained quiet, the lack of her joyful voice an awful void. Most times she chattered on when they flew together. Mist tried playfully banking around sharp curves or riding bumpy air currents, but didn't get so much as a pat on the shoulder. The Matriarch's venom had stolen Aven's love of flying.

It was time to purge it.

Mist tucked one wing in, her body twisting until she splashed through the water, dunking Aven's leg. A screech ripped from her throat as her fingers dug for purchase in Mist's feathers. Once she had a grip, Mist spun into a roll, dragging the tips of her wings through the crystalline river. That earned an excited laugh. With a whip of her tail and another flap of her wings, they righted before slipping over the surface of the water like the ice skaters back home in Estellias.

Aven's hand glided through feathers, stroking until she touched skin. "I'm okay. I promise."

A growl reverberated through Mist's chest. She wasn't acting like she was okay.

Aven sighed as she lowered onto her elbows, shifting her weight to lay down in the saddle. "I was hoping this would show Yana that I could be useful to the Qinawe."

Mist hissed. That old windbag really needed a good swipe from dragon claws. No matter how hard Aven tried, it was never enough.

"I really thought they'd finally let me earn my place." Aven stroked Mist's neck. "But I should have known better. They'll never want me."

I want you. Mist wished she could say it, but she hadn't practiced enough at making her dragon lips mold around words. All she could muster was a sad croon.

"Oh well, right?" Aven pushed upright once more, moving with care like she always did. She'd never carried someone when shifted, but she listened when Mist told her how it felt for someone to flop around on her back.

"Who knows, maybe we'll find a Tibri at Shard's Port that I can convince to get me out of here."

Mist rumbled a reply as she thought of the Tibri merchant. He wanted dragons to help with transports. Maybe she could convince Emriel or Anyvath? No, probably not Anyvath. That she carried Kanai at all was an act of Dia'veh. Mist would have to try bartering again once they arrived at the Port.

"How much farther is the dam?" Aven asked, leaning left as they rounded a bend in the canyon.

The answer hovered above, so Mist climbed out of the gorge with strained flaps of her wings. The goal was to reach the Eilawi dam by nightfall. Emriel was confident they could make it, but Mist couldn't remember. She hadn't left Yunaii since her arrival.

It took a bit of strain to pull ahead of the other dragons before dropping back onto Anyvath's wing. Kanai clung to the saddle, gritting his teeth against wind whipping his face. Behind him, Dinon's head swiveled back and forth, watching everything they passed, be it a bird, a rock, or tree. A goofy smile lingered on the younger lynx's face while their arms fell around Kanai's waist. When Dinon noticed Mist and Aven drawing closer, they waved.

"Be careful!" Kanai yelped, snatching their hand down. "You could fall."

A delightful chuckle sounded from Aven. "Don't worry. Anyvath won't drop you."

The pride leader said nothing, but the sour tilt of his mouth and the tension in his arms showed his disbelief.

"Do either of you know how long it will take to get to the dam?" Aven shouted.

Kanai jerked his chin towards the canyon's winding turns. "It takes my hunters two days to get there, but at this pace we should be there before Konia and Levia claim the sky."

Sundown. Mist's body ached at the thought of flying all day. It was for Aven, though. She needed this. Thankfully, currents from Anyvath's flight helped carry them along, relieving Mist's battered body.

As they cruised, Willa dove into the canyon before shooting back up with something clutched in her claws. Mist couldn't make out her prize, but she was easy enough to track. Her gray and white wings gleamed against the landscape of red rock and sparkling blue water. With the grace cultivated by a lifetime of flight, Willa rose above Emriel and dropped whatever she had right onto Dev's head. His shoulders tensed, but that was the only reaction. No shouting for her to stop. No complaints to the scarlet dragon beneath him. He simply gathered whatever Willa had dropped and continued his silent staring ahead.

"What is Willa doing to Dev?" Aven asked.

"She's courting him," Dinon laughed. "Though I don't know why she's not challenging him first."

"Aven told her to do things his way," Kanai grumbled, shaking his head. "I don't think the fledgling knows how elves court so she's probably doing what comes after a challenge is won."

Mist warbled, cocking her head so the pride leader could see her confusion. It earned her the first chuckle from Kanai since they'd begun the flight.

"She's giving him things to make a nest."

***

Things carried on that way for much of the day. Mist alternated between hiding in the shade and flying with the others. Fennicks and Pryn kept to themselves, occasionally diving into the canyon to splash through a deep part of the Lighe, before climbing back into open air. Anyvath attempted it once, but Kanai's fearful roar as they fell from the sky kept her from doing it again.

Dev and Emriel remained steady as they led the group. No matter what Willa dropped on him or how Sansia shone on his windswept curls, Dev remained upright and stiff in the saddle. His soul-calling had sucked the love of flight from him. In races, he and Rielnor wound through branches, making reckless dives and spirals. Mist didn't understand what left Dev more emotionless than usual. Fear for Emriel? Did he sense danger? She hoped for a chance to talk with him. Serving Dia'veh's will didn't seem like something to be approached without joy.

They all took turns scanning the canyon, riverbank, and desolate rock formations for any signs of the Soulless. Boar milled about in the scrub of bushes. Mountain goats ambled down the cliffs as if laws of nature didn't apply to them. All while massive ton beasts migrated across the rocky hills, eating whatever they could find.

But no sign of the Soulless Summoner.

Sansia had touched the horizon when the dam came into view. Aven gasped, her weight shifting as she leaned in the saddle. The Elemental's creation was as magnificent as the Eilawi tree they'd grown.

Layers of red and orange rock stretched smooth across the canyon, broken only by four spillways allowing water to cascade into the river. A perfect canvas for the art hewn into the expanse of the dam.

The Earth Elementals had shaped a woman as tall as the shear wall, her soft face lit with a loving smile, head tilted as if she watched for those who might approach from below. A wave of curls reached across the dam in a gust of imaginary wind, pulling her draping dress along as well. One of her hands extended outward, beckoning travelers to come to her, no doubt guiding them to the embankment of sand leading to a shaded glen at her feet. The perfect place to eat and rest.

"Great Mother," Aven whispered as they hovered before the magnificent sculpture.

"It is Sholindrea," Dev called from Emriel's back. "The Mother of all Sholi."

Fennicks veered for the glen, guiding them down in a series of circles. The three larger dragons landed in the water, sending waves lapping against the soft sand Mist settled upon. She wriggled her toes as Aven dismounted, delighting in how deep she could get.

"Make camp," Kanai ordered, splashing his way onto the bank. She hadn't heard him dismount, but the look of relief as his feet met rock almost had Mist rolling with laughter. The pride leader was certainly not a fan of flying.

CHAPTER
Twenty-Seven

Mist

Konia and Levia shone in the night sky by the time they'd made a fire. Everyone had shifted and laid out their bedrolls, shuffling around each other in an awkward dance. Cool relief washed over Mist when she found Aven had set theirs up side by side, far from Emriel, Fennicks, and Pryn's. Maybe they would finally have time to talk. So much hung between them. Her heart fluttered every time they passed each other.

Em had boxed Dev out by setting up between Fennicks and Pryn, leaving the elf hovering at the edge of camp, clutching his bed roll. Mist didn't understand what he waited for until she noticed Willa crouched by the fire, watching him with her own things in hand.

"Where are you sleeping, little bird?" Emriel had left him at the mercy of the griffin and didn't even look ashamed about it.

Willa gazed at Dev as she hugged blankets to her chest. "Where should I sleep?"

"Over here with us, fledgling," Kanai called from the other side of the fire. "You're under my charge, not the elf's."

A pout pulled across Willa's face as she obeyed, casting one look back before letting Dinon help her settle in. How had this poor girl fallen for a stone-faced boy whose thoughts revolved only around duty?

With one last glance at Emriel, Dev dropped his things between Pryn and Dinon's bed rolls.

"Don't worry," Mist said, patting his shoulder. "The only danger to Em tonight is Fennicks."

"And I'm currently too tired to kill anyone," the dragon in question said, flopping down by the fire. Their face was the same as the day they'd fought Emriel; long, sharp, with horns protruding from their chin, and high cheekbones. Only this time, the straight black hair hung loose, softening the severe features.

Mist knelt beside them, pretending to warm her hands. "I've never seen you wear the same face before."

"Not in the mood to play today." Firelight danced in Fennicks' yellow eyes.

She wanted to ask if this was their first face or just one they'd practiced a lot? Mist was born in her human-form, but she'd learned to shift at a young age, much to Papi's chagrin. Controlling a baby dragon on his own had been even more challenging than chasing a bull-headed toddler. Mist didn't quite know how it was for those like Fennicks and Emriel. Rielnor chose the same form every time. Em's was often similar, but she played with her hair and eyes. Then there was Fennicks.

"Don't bother with questions," Emriel said from the other side of the fire. "You won't get any answers, especially not without food in front of us."

Kanai's ears perked up. "Allow us to hunt for you. The dragons carried us all this way. Permit me to bring you a meal to show my gratitude."

A smile stretched across Anyvath's face. "Do you think yourselves capable of bringing enough for all of us?"

Kanai's hands moved to the waistband of his pants, undoing the lacings. "Let Dinon and I worry about that. There's a reason I brought them along. They're one of the pride's best hunters."

The younger lynx brightened. "Thank you, pride leader."

"Not to mention, we have my little sister to help us as well." Kanai threw a look at Aven, who'd gone still as stone. "What say you? Will you hunt with us?"

Mist wished she could capture the joy spreading across Aven's face. Her eyes lit up as a smile curved her lips.

"I would love to. It's been so long since I've gotten to hunt."

"Really?" Fennicks asked, lounging back as if enjoying a lazy day on the beach. "Because I remember your claws digging nice and deep into me two days ago."

Aven's attention locked on the fading marks she'd gouged into Fennicks' shoulder. "I'll have another taste if you're offering. From what I remember, dragon meat was a treat."

"Sounds like fun to me," Emriel said, licking her lips as she eyed her old mate.

Mist shivered at the way Fennicks stared at Em's mouth. "Spare me the imagery, please."

"All's fair, bloodkin." Emriel stretched out by the fire, arching her back provocatively. No doubt intending to further agitate Fennicks. "If you're going to hunt, Mister Whiskers, please hustle up. I'm hungry enough to eat someone here."

"Between the three of us, I believe we can bring down a ton beast."

Em waved a hand at him before closing her eyes. "Great. Just hurry."

Kanai and Dinon took to the shadows to shift, while Aven went in the opposite direction. Mist longed to follow her, to catch even a moment alone. To say something—*anything*—whether it was about their kiss or what Yana said or how Aven was doing. Only Emriel's snarky mouth kept her standing by the fire.

When a golden cat with a light-colored belly trotted back into the light, Mist went to them with hands outstretched. Dinon's familiar coat and bright eyes took her back to the day in the market, before everything went wrong and dreams of hunkering in the cave with Aven almost came true. A wet nose pressed into her palm, the cat's chest rumbling.

Kanai stood at the edge of the firelight, looking the part of Kali's regal cub. They shared the same cool, brown coat, with cream-colored stripes over their faces and shoulders.

Only black slashes shadowing the lighter helped Mist know it was him.

When Aven reappeared in Kali's form, the pride leader's majesty crumpled with a sad yowl. He approached slowly, chittering like a lost cub searching for its mother. Aven purred deep and loud in response, rubbing her face against his shoulder.

Hopefully the moment soothed his aching heart. Mist couldn't imagine Papi standing before her without being able to hold him or hear his voice. Just the thought made her stomach drop. Aven's arms around her could have kept her from spiraling, but she had to settle for a gentle headbutt instead.

"Be careful," Mist said, nuzzling into her soft fur. "The Soulless is out there and ton beasts can be dangerous. Their hooves are strong and—"

Aven licked her face, silencing Mist's ramble of worries.

"Okay, okay. Sorry." She threw her arms around Aven's neck, drawing in deep breaths of her musky smell. "I'll see you soon."

As they drew apart, Kanai licked at his paw, before bounding into the darkness. They'd seen goats scaling the wall. If they could get up, so could the cats. Aven and Dinon followed, their eyes gleaming and mouths parted in excited, feral smiles. Mist couldn't begrudge Aven this moment. She'd never been invited to hunt with anyone but her mother.

If only Mist had the strength to help. She thrived on night hunts, when the sister moons' light blanched her white feathers in monochrome shades, helping her hide and sneak without blazing heat pulling sweat down her back. For a moment she itched to slip back into dragonskin, but exhaustion kept her wings at bay. She needed to drink and rest, not chase after goats or boar.

After the night swallowed Aven's form, Mist returned to the fire. Emriel still lounged like a sleepy cat. Fennicks stared up at the stars. Pryn sat watching the flames, while Willa looked as if she'd fallen asleep with her head on her knees. Anyvath had not joined them yet. Her attention lingered on the dam.

"Do you see something?" Mist asked.

The old dragon looked a moment more before sitting by the fire. "No. I caught a hint of death in the air, but it was gone just as fast."

"Could be the Soulless," Emriel said, sitting up.

"Or could be some critter that got caught in the dam's current," Fennicks said without looking away from the stars. "If the Soulless were here, they'd probably attack. Or who knows, maybe they'll slit our throats in our sleep. Then the elf can feel justified in clucking over Emriel like a mother hen."

Dev turned cold eyes on Fennicks. "One can only hope they start with you. The scent of blood will wake the rest of us."

The dragon's yellow eyes widened while Emriel whistled low. "Well, well, hanging out with Mist's kitty cat has sharpened your claws, eh elf?"

"Aven has that effect on people," Pryn muttered.

"Is this how things will be?" Anyvath asked before Mist could round on the Tribouin. "A bunch of kits sniping at each other each time they see an opening?"

Dev dropped his gaze like a chastised child and sat cross-legged beside Mist. "You are right. I should not give in to such childishness."

"Please do, elf." Fennicks finally tore their attention from the sky. "It makes you slightly more tolerable."

Dev sighed as he unwrapped a small satchel in his lap, not much larger than the space between his knees. Mist sniffed at it hopefully, her stomach gurgling as she imagined the provisions Ifera gave them. She found nothing to sate her hunger as the scraps of fabric fell aside. Instead, an odd collection of sticks, feathers, and rocks laid in the flickering firelight. Each one Dev handled with care as he peered at them with furrowed brows and his lips pulled to one side.

"What is all that?" Mist asked as Dev lifted a piece of downy fluff.

"These are items Willa gave to me today."

Em peered around the fire. "That's the junk she pelted us with the entire flight here? What in Sholindrea's name is all that?"

Mist snuck a glance at Willa, whose forehead still rested on her knees. Her breathing came slow and no tension tightened her arms. Either she really had fallen asleep or she'd mastered the art of eavesdropping. "Kanai says it's to make a nest with."

Dev's brows rose a little, but he didn't comment. Instead, he put the fluff back and examined a small white rock that shimmered as if made with flecks of starlight.

"Griffins are so odd," Fennicks said.

Mist pointed at the scar creeping from Fennicks' hairline to their eyebrow. "No odder than dragons. We tear each other up and act like it's some declaration of love."

Em's eyes slid sideways as she admired the angry streaks across Fennicks' skin. "It's flattering when a mate keeps the marks you gave them."

Another look passed between them that made Mist wrinkle her nose. She'd spent so long seeing the black dragon in a very specific way. Imagining them now as not only someone who actually bothered with mates, but had been that way with Emriel, was *weird*. Weirder than the times Eega disappeared with Papi for days on end sometimes. No, Mist didn't want to think about that. It ruined any desire she had to sneak away with Aven.

"So," Pryn said, snapping Mist out of her stomach-roiling thoughts, one finger pointed at Emriel. "You are—" she pointed at Mist. "Her sister. And—" she pointed at Fennicks. "—*their* mate?"

One corner of Fennicks' lips pulled up into a crooked smile. "Was. She *was* my mate."

Pryn licked her lips. "I see. And she's the one that shifted in the market."

"Did no one explain any of this to you?" Anyvath asked, tilting her head.

"No one bothered to tell me anything," Pryn said, cutting a glare at Mist. "Everyone preferred lying to me."

"I'm sorry, kid." The regret marring Fennicks' face was stranger than their flirting with Emriel. "I'd have told you if I could."

Pryn nodded before turning a sharp look back to Mist. "How long has Aven known about all of this?"

Mist took a shuddering breath as Fennicks and Anyvath's stares skittered over her skin. "She's always known about me. From the first day we met."

Fennicks rolled their yellow eyes. "I knew it. Rielnor always played it off as speculation, but I knew you told the kitty cat."

"Mist wasn't raised to hide what she is," Emriel snapped. "You weren't either. Once upon a time, you weren't a coward."

"That's enough," Anyvath said, resting a hand on Fennicks' tense forearm. "You left the flight. Your opinion of our choices has no bearing."

"Why did Rielnor make that decision?" Dev asked, drawing all the dragons' attention to him. "Yunaii is the only place I've seen dragons hide what they are—what they're capable of."

Fennicks glanced at Pryn, who waited as intently as Dev for the answer. With a deep sigh, they sat up, their big hands falling into their lap.

"Rielnor took the flight from Estellias a long time ago. To protect us. Things were degrading between the Elementals and their political factions. It was coming time for the dragons to choose a side."

"And as soon as we did, things were sure to boil over." Anyvath's long face pinched with sadness.

"So, you chose to leave instead?" Dev asked.

"They ran away." Raw bitterness crept into Em's voice. "My egg-layer tried to stop Rielnor. They fought for leadership of the flight, but—"

"But she lost," Anyvath said, dropping her gaze to the burning kindling in the fire. "And we nearly lost Rielnor in the aftermath. Your egg-layer is one of the fiercest dragons I have ever seen. Her wrath was frightening."

"Still is," Mist murmured. Eega's intense blue eyes, her scarred body. She had frightened Mist as a child. She was the callouses and steel to Papi's soft face and warm hugs.

"Then, you came to Yunaii," Pryn said. "To what? Hide? Why lie about being shifters when living amongst shifters?"

Anyvath shrugged one shoulder. "It wasn't intended. Upon our arrival, your ancestors did not remember what we were. It had been generations since they'd set eyes on a dragon. Humans fear us. Elves don't understand us. We barely fit in amongst shifters. The customs that shaped your people never defined ours the same way, not when we live as long as the Elementals. When the people of Yunaii didn't fear us or remember us, we chose a simple existence."

Emriel blew a breath through her nose. "You chose to lessen yourselves and be as useless as house cats."

Instead of rising to her bait, Fennicks smiled almost cheerily. "We took a break, Emriel. Perhaps you should think about taking one for yourself. It would do you some good."

"Are things so bad in Estellias?" Pryn asked.

"There isn't all out war," Em said, picking at her nails. "But Elementals are dying on both sides."

"What about everyone else?" Pryn glanced at Mist almost accusingly. "Aven has talked about going there for ages. If you knew about this, why wouldn't you discourage her? Make her realize staying in Yunaii is safer."

Mist's spine straightened as her nostrils flared. "For one thing, I cannot make Aven stay or go anywhere. Secondly, Elementals don't care about shifters or elves or fairies. They don't make a difference in a fight between a tornado and an earthquake. And thirdly, most of the conflict is through sneaking and backstabbing and manipulation. The rest of Estellias is just going about their lives, hoping the king will remember their needs again one day."

"That doesn't mean it's safe there." Anger shone in Pryn's darkening eyes. "I should have known you were just manipulating her into going home with you. Anything to get what you want, where you want it, right *Feather*? Never mind if it gets her killed."

"Watch that tongue," Emriel hissed, leaning forward. "Or I'll rip it right out of your mouth."

Fennicks rounded on Emriel, their large shoulders blocking the space between her and Pryn.

"Put a hand on the kid and we'll have round two right here."

Anger crackled as they stared at each other, unblinking, chests rising harder with each breath. Mist glanced at Anyvath with wide eyes, silently preparing for the inevitable snap. Emriel wasn't one to back down from a challenge. Mist knew it. Anyvath knew it. Her gaze flicked between the two of them as claws drew from her nails.

With a frustrated exhale, Emriel pushed to her feet and stomped towards the riverbed. Mist could barely believe it. Fennicks watched her go, blinking rapidly as if *they* didn't understand what had happened either.

Maybe Em was too tired to fight, though that had never stopped her before.

Beside Mist, Dev carefully replaced each item Willa had given him before tying the satchel shut. Without so much as a glance at the rest of them, he followed Em into the shadows, hands resting on the hilts of his swords. Mist could easily imagine the look of disgust on Emriel's face when she turned to find the elf in her shadow.

"Thank you," Pryn whispered to Fennicks.

They nodded in reply before settling back, raising up one knee to rest their forearm upon. Despite their attempt at looking relaxed, confusion lingering in the lines of their face.

"Just so you know," Mist said, fighting to keep her voice neutral. "I can't go home."

Pryn's brows furrowed in a silent question.

"My egg-layer let me leave. She set me free from my bloodkin's duty. But if I go home, I have to decide which side I'm on."

"And if Aven goes without you?"

An ache clenched Mist's chest at the thought. "No one will pay her any mind. One Qinawe girl will be of no consequence to anyone."

Pryn's jaw worked back and forth as she ground her teeth. "You're just going to let her go."

And there it was. The question cracking Mist's heart apart. Aven said she feared losing her, that Dia'veh had set them on a path to be together. Mist wanted to believe it. Aven's words the night before had stitched part of her back together, but what could Mist really offer her? Uncertainty outside of Yunaii and loneliness inside of it. Estellias could give her everything she wanted and Mist couldn't stand in the way of that.

She drew in a deep breath, fighting back the pain welling inside her. "If that's what she needs me to do, then yes. I will let her go."

CHAPTER
Twenty-Eight

Aven

Aven's heart pounded as she helped Kanai drag the ton beast down the cliffside. The hunt had been thrilling. The way Dinon and Kanai moved, like they were two halves of a whole, slipping through the shadows, driving the massive, bull-like creature straight to Aven's hiding spot. She'd seen the whites of its eyes, had moments to dodge the large, cloven hooves that flailed and kicked. It had lowered its head and tried to ram her, but Aven had slipped beneath the tangle of horns, slinking this way and that, slashing at hindquarters taller than her, all for a chance at its blind spot. When her teeth sank into its throat, she'd almost purred. It was perfect.

Getting the thing back to camp was another matter. She contemplated letting it splatter against the rocky ground more than once, but then Mist wouldn't have a full belly and after all the flying, she needed to eat.

Kanai used his powerful jaws to drag the beast along the goat path, while Aven and Dinon alternated pulling its thick legs and shoving its dead weight. It was all worth it, though, because the camp drew closer. She made out five bodies around the fire and two more at the water. With a great deal of grunting and growling, they brought the beast to the edge of camp.

Mist's excited exclamation summoned the purr Aven had swallowed down.

"Well done," Anyvath said with an appreciative look. "I didn't think you'd actually bring one back."

"Please tell me we're going to cook it," Pryn said, her eyes wide as streaks of white shot through her hair.

"We'll cook enough for you and the elf," Emriel said, striding from the darkness. "I'm assuming my shadow doesn't eat raw meat either."

Dev materialized from the black with his nose wrinkled and mouth pulled into an odd look of disgust. "I most certainly do not."

***

A blue glow shone over the shore as everyone settled on their bedrolls with full bellies. Stars winked in the black as the sound of falling water lulled Aven towards sleep. She pressed close to Mist, whose warmth radiated like the fire, leaving her cozy and content.

Kanai, Dinon, and Willa all fell into rounds of grooming; licking their fingers, wiping blood from their faces. The mannerisms of animals on two-legs was strange for even Aven to wrap her head around. The dragons lazed by the fire like tired cats, eyes drooping and bellies bulging, especially Mist, whose head kept bobbing against Aven's shoulder as she fought to stay awake.

"Thank you, darlings" Anyvath said with a satisfied sigh. "The meal was most appreciated."

Kanai used a claw to pick at his teeth. "I'm glad. Any way we can be useful, let me know."

"Regale us," Fennicks said with eyes half-closed. "Tell me how your cub ensnared a dragon. I remember Rourke being a dreamy-headed thing, but not a cat-lover."

Kanai smiled, but it was Dinon who spoke first, eyes shining fondly.

"I'm sure Nya's fierceness caught his eye. I used to follow her as a cub, just to see the mischief she'd get into. Her red hair was a beacon in all the black and brown here. It was never hard to spot her in a crowd or catch her up to mischief. She had a way about her. All the lynx loved her, even though nothing impressed her."

Fennicks stretched out on their bedroll. "Apparently dragons did. Can't blame her, though. Rourke had all of Anyvath's ridiculous color, plus a perfect face, a snarky mouth, and unmarked canvas for a body."

Emriel raised one eyebrow, as a strange scent overtook her. "Sounds like you were a fan."

A wicked grin spread across Fennicks' face. "I would have let him give me a few scars."

"Well, unfortunately for you, my Nya won his heart." Kanai licked a smear of blood off his hand. "That kit of yours seemed quite smitten when we met."

Anyvath released a motherly sigh. "He was. Your cub inspired many arguments, but I should have known. He had a curiosity about him. He never quite fit at the roost."

"Why was that?" Mist asked through a yawn.

"Because he was like you," Fennicks said, pointing in her direction. "His pop was a human."

"Really?" Mist perked up, curiosity lighting in her eyes. "Who was his father?"

A smile slipped across Anyvath's lips, the kind Mama got when Papa went on some passionate tirade. "That's for me to know."

"Honestly, you and my egg-layer." Emriel stretched, her fingers flexing towards the sky as her shoulders popped. "I'll never understand the interest in humans. They're messy, loud, judgmental—"

"Blessed, hard-working, loving," Mist finished. "Maybe you should spend some more time with them."

"I've spent my fair share," Em said, her eyes widening to emphasize her words. "I know Eega has a soft spot for your Papi, but that doesn't change facts. They also think too highly of themselves, being Sholindrea's blessed and all."

Mist waved a hand as she looked back at Anyvath. "Do you know where Rourke and Nya went?"

Kanai scratched at his beard. "Aye. Last I heard, they were in Estellias."

That drew Emriel's attention. "Really? And what are they doing there?"

"Apparently my kit agrees with you." Weariness crept into Anyvath's voice. "Rourke felt the Elementals needed dragon allies."

"And when he went, Nya decided to go too." A frown furrowed Kanai's heavy brow. "It's caused many a sleepless night, wondering if they're safe, praying that Nya hasn't tackled things she can't handle."

Dinon flashed fangs in a feral smile. "If anyone can hold her own in an Elemental war, it's Nya. She was never satisfied with just claws and teeth. She learned archery from the Qinawe, daggers from the Tribouin, and could stalk and hunt with the best of the griffins."

"I remember her," Willa said as she laid on her belly. "She often came to see my flock leader. They were inseparable."

"Aye, they were," Kanai sighed. "Two bottles of explosive mischief ready to go off at any moment. It's a shame. Yliva has changed since Nya went away. I think losing her forced your flock leader to grow up."

A gleam of mischief lit in Willa's eyes. "I think Nya kept her carefree."

"Perhaps," Kanai said, stretching out on his side, his tail flicking back and forth. "She kept me young. Ever since she left, I've felt the ache in my bones. Time is coming for me."

"Nonsense," Dinon said with a frown. "You have years left as pride leader. Your mother led for generations."

"I do not have her wisdom. Just my muscles. I'll not hold pride leader as long as she did."

Aven touched Kali's fang. "Could you tell me about her? The moons are almost full."

"Tomorrow, little sister." Kanai looked up at the sky, silver light reflecting across his eyes. "We'll dance and I'll tell you of Kali. Tonight, we rest. Sansia will be here before we know it."

Dev bobbed his head in agreement. "I'll take first watch. Pryn can take second."

"I'll take third," Aven offered, glancing down at Mist. Her head had gone limp, her lips parted as she breathed deep. The day had caught up with her fast, tenderness slowing her movements since making camp. She wasn't back to full strength yet. Hopefully, a night's sleep would help her blood repair the damage of the last two days.

***

Aven awoke to someone violently shaking her. She jerked upright, world spinning as she blinked against sleep and confusion. Darkness filled her vision until her eyes adjusted to the blue light of the moon, bringing Pryn into focus beside her.

"Your turn for watch," she whispered.

Aven nodded as she forced herself onto her knees, every part of her heavy and sluggish. The urge to bury her face into the warmth of her blankets was overwhelming. Only the crease in Pryn's brow stopped her. The way her mouth pulled into a thin line said she was judging Aven for not hopping right up.

"Alright, I'm up," Aven hissed. Her legs shook as she ambled towards the river, cursing each rock that tripped her up. Any other time, she was nimble as a bird leaping from branch to branch.

Grumbling to herself, she knelt at the bank, scooped a handful of icy water, and splashed it against her face. Once. Twice. She blinked rapidly as sleep washed away, leaving her eyes cold and aching. As she pushed back to her feet, she realized Pryn lingered in the shadows.

"Why are you here?"

Pryn glanced at the waterfalls spilling from high above. "Sorry. Am I not allowed to stand here?"

Aven blew a sigh through her nose. "That's not what I meant."

A solemn laugh rasped from Pryn's throat. "I think I'm here for the same reason you are."

Aven bit the inside of her cheek, not giving in to the bait. She wouldn't give Pryn the answer to her question.

"You're not the only one with something to prove," Pryn said, watching the churning water.

"Am I supposed to feel bad for you?"

That earned a sharp look. "You know, I pitied you once. I wanted to help you. Look where that's gotten me."

"The same place you were before me?" Aven asked. "Still a part of your people, with a Chosen to love you, and a place of your own?"

Pryn wrapped her arms around herself. "You don't know anything about anything. You think it's easy, playing the Tribouin daughter after I taste freedom on Fennicks' back? You think I look forward to having a Chosen picked for me by my Papa instead of by my heart? You're not the only one with troubles, Aven, and caring about you only brought more down on my head."

"I didn't ask you to challenge me." Kali's rage had been so quiet today, but now it seared beneath Aven's skin, summoning claws that had already tasted flesh tonight.

"I just wanted to give you a home."

Aven cursed as a different kind of ache blossomed behind her eyes. She would not cry. Not over this. Not over Pryn. Never again.

"I didn't want your home."

"I know," Pryn said, chewing on her bottom lip. "But I thought you at least wanted me."

Aven turned away, hoping to hide the tears pooling over her lashes. How? How did Pryn still know how to cut to her heart, even when her place in it had been taken by someone else?

"We were never meant to be, Pryn, and I'm sorry for that. I never should have let there be anything between us. Things would be easier for you if I hadn't wanted someone to care about me so badly."

Sand shifted as Pryn stepped beside her. "I don't want to get it, but I do. I don't have a place anymore except with the other riders. Being the best helped me carve out something for myself since my people have lost faith in me. I'll do anything to keep that."

"Even almost kill me?" Aven shouldn't have said it, but she couldn't take it back.

"If we're being honest, I was as surprised as you were." Pryn looked at Aven, her eyes round and sincere. Not a hint of yellow or gold shone in them. "I had no idea Fennicks was going to do that. I swear. I tried to turn back for you, but then I saw Dev and Topaz dive and I knew you'd be okay."

A bitter chuckle erupted from Aven's chest. "That does not make it okay. Mist is still hurting, and I really thought I was meeting Dia'veh for a moment there."

Pryn ran her hands up and down her arms, sorrow weaving through her oh-so-familiar scent. "I'm sorry."

Aven eyes widened. "What?"

"I know." Pryn wrinkled her nose. "But I'm sorry. I should have said it sooner. I'm sorry for Fennicks and...I'm sorry about what happened between us."

"Really?"

She bobbed her head, lips pursing in a look of irritation. "If it counts for anything, I let you win."

A real laugh slipped from Aven. "You did not."

"You're good," Pryn said, touching the hilt of the needle-like blade at her waist. "And you—you *might* have won on your own. But, when I saw how hard you fought to not lose, I realized I'd made a mistake. I couldn't make you be with me, so I threw the fight."

Aven blinked repeatedly, conjuring the memory of their challenge. Everything was blurred, laced with anger and anguish, distorting so much of what she remembered. The sounds of their weapons clashing over and over rung in her ears. The look of heartbreak on Pryn's face, the horror of the bystanders as they realized Aven's fear. It was hard to recall anything but desperate moments.

"I never wanted to force you to be with me." Pryn sighed and looked back at camp. "And—I hate to say it, but Mist doesn't want to either. I hope maybe...you two's story will end better than ours."

With that, she bowed her head and retreated to her bedroll. Aven stood rooted on the riverbank, waves of shock rolling over her. Of all the things she expected on this trip, this moment was not one she'd ever imagined.

***

The next day was the same as the first. Emriel and Dev led everyone along the canyon, swooping around curves and over rocks in a streak of shining scarlet, with Willa flitting around them like a bird chasing a hawk.

Aven chattered to Mist about the hunt with Kanai and Dinon, reliving every heart-pumping moment. She couldn't wait to go out again. Hunting as a member of their pride felt almost like returning to Mama and Papa's cave after a long day. She finally fit in.

Throughout the day, her gaze scoured the desolate, rocky terrain. Each time something moved, she leaned in the saddle, straining to make out if it was on four legs or two. They passed over herds of ton beasts, making their way from prickly plants full of water to scrub brushes and tiny saplings, picking leaves from the plants until the branches laid bare. Scattered boar milled about too, though they had the sense to run when the dragon's shadows passed overhead. Aven watched them go, searching for any sign of a Soulless camp.

Of course, to no avail. If they were about, they had the sense to stay hidden.

Not long after midday, the peaks of the mountain range broke through the haze of sun and dust. They seemed impossibly far away, but the sight meant they had a day or two more of flight before reaching Shard's Port. It all depended on the dragons.

Emriel kept a grueling pace, stopping only once for everyone to guzzle water before she launched into the air once more. Not long after the break, Mist began lagging, her head drooping, tongue lolling out of her mouth. Aven was ready to call for help when a gust of air caught Mist's wings, buffeting her out of the canyon. A look back revealed Fennicks and Pryn behind them, the dragon's black wings creating a current for Mist to sail upon.

"Ride by our wing for a while," Pryn shouted.

Aven nodded. Surprise was becoming a welcome friend on this trip. Next thing she'd know, Dev and Willa would fall in love, Fennicks and Emriel would make up, or an actual Tibri merchant would be waiting at the port to take her far from Yunaii.

That last part was the least likely of them all, but Aven couldn't help daydreaming as they continued their trip.

***

Konia and Levia's full, shining faces found them all gathered around their second campfire, gorged on fresh pork and roasted prickle plants coated in spices and pig fat. There'd been no bank to settle on this time, so they camped near the ledge of the canyon where everything bathed in silvery moonlight.

"So," Aven said, finishing her last bite. "Tell me about Kali."

Kanai looked around at their packs, searching for something. "Dinon, we'll need a beat for tonight's dance."

A smile spread across the younger lynx's face, his eyes gleaming in the firelight. Willa perked up at his side, excitement showing in a vibrant grin.

"Are you really going to dance?" Fennicks asked from where they lounged on the ground. They'd chosen a lithe body tonight, with a soft round face, wide eyes, and curly black hair.

"It is how we remember our elders," Kanai said, standing up. "A problem your kind is not plagued by, I know, but it brings the pride together."

Dev cocked his head to the side. "We have no instruments."

"You have your hands!" Willa launched over the fire, wings buffeting her leap so she could land almost in his lap. She grabbed Dev's wrists and brought them together in a loud slap. "Your people must take some joy in music, yes?"

He looked at where she held him before raising his gaze to her face. "We do. On occasion."

Aven grinned, relishing the joy catching her up in its wave, bolstering her heart until she itched to jump around too. She cast a look at Mist and found the pink of her eyes brightening with curiosity.

"Clap," Willa commanded Dev. "Let those hands do more than promise death. Though I'm sure they have *other* skills too."

Dev's ears pinkened as he ducked his head. With some hesitance, he brought his palms together once. Twice. On the third clap, Dinon joined him, bringing their clawed hands down against their thighs. Together they created a soft tempo that Kanai swayed back and forth to. At Aven's side, Mist picked up the rhythm, clapping along as her head bobbed back and forth.

That's when Kanai launched into a simple tune, reciting a time when Kali had rallied the pride to bring down the leader of the ton beasts. She'd led twenty lynx to the peaks of the cliffs, driving the beasts long and hard until the largest ton turned its twisting, gnarled horns upon Kali. In a moment of unbridled ferocity, she brought down the creature almost on her own.

"No lynx can bring down a ton by themselves," Fennicks said, with one arm slung over their eyes.

"Kali did!" Dinon cried, leaping up as their palms increased the beat. Their energy drove Aven to hers, leaving her bouncing from foot to foot as Kanai launched into another song.

This one told of Kali and her mate, Naito, and the love they'd borne one another. Naito had been the breeze that stoked Kali's fire, pushing her to always strive for more. Though the words Kanai sang were loving and soft, Dinon kept a fast beat, luring Willa to twirl and leap like a leaf in the wind. One pass around the fire had her reaching out for Mist, who clasped her hand and let her guide her into a spin. They moved gracefully on their toes, as if Sholindrea's pull did not weigh them down. They left Aven feeling as clumsy and heavy as a rock tumbling down the cliffs.

The songs went on and on, and before Aven knew it, she was one of the few not dancing. Emriel swayed her hips. Anyvath skipped in a circle with Kanai, their arms linked around each other at the elbow. Even Pryn had been sucked in by Willa's excitement. Aven couldn't blame her. The griffin's energy was infectious, and eventually, she turned it on Dev. His clapping never ceased, but she began circling him, brushing against his arms, or his back, coming so close a stranger might have thought them lovers. Not once did Dev send her away, even when she planted a gentle kiss on his cheek. With every song, she drew him in a little more.

Only Fennicks remained unmoving, though they tracked every move Emriel's body made. Their yellow eyes turned to molten gold as she gave in to the tempo, sweat beading over her skin.

Free of Willa's grasping hands, Mist came around the fire and offered her own to Aven. The light in her eyes and smile on her lips brought back the night at the Temple; to the press of her soft lips and the warmth of her body. Their hands clasped together and Aven found herself spun around, then drawn into the circle of Mist's arms. They swayed one direction, then the other, before they twisted again. Stars spun overhead as embers danced in the air. Aven lost herself to Dev's clapping, Kanai's words, and the stomping Dinon now used to keep the beat. She came into Mist's body, their hips moving together. The stars streaked as they twirled around and around, leaving Aven breathless and light. She tried focusing on Kanai's words, on the stories of Kali, but more and more all she saw was Mist's full lips, her teeth flashing in one of her perfect smiles, and wisps of her white hair streaming through the dark like fairy light.

Aven chased the heat of Mist's body, coming close enough to almost brush their mouths together, before she got a cheeky grin and was sent off into another spin. She didn't mind. Aven was drunk on the happiness bursting in her heart. A Soulless could have walked into camp and she would have died with a smile on her face. For the first time in her life, she was a part of something. A piece of a whole. Even though she had to return to the Matriarchs' ire in a few days, even they couldn't take this moment away from her.

CHAPTER
Twenty-Nine

Aven

They flew along the canyon for the next two days until it veered away from the mountain range. After that, Emriel led them as close to the foothills as possible before making camp another night. Again, Aven hunted with Kanai and Dinon, and again tales of lynx or griffins drifted around the fire until everyone fell asleep. Each night Aven snuggled into Mist's warmth, filling her nose with the scent of rose and vanilla while the stars watched over them. She could almost imagine them on an adventure together instead of a hunt for a murderous Soulless.

Flying over the mountains was even harder than soaring through the canyon. The range climbed into the sky, forcing the dragons to strain for the clouds, leaving Aven and the others with chattering teeth and frozen fingers. Thankfully, Mist's downy feathers were the perfect place to bury her aching extremities.

Emriel announced their arrival by banking into a series of circles until she disappeared beneath the clouds. Fennicks followed suit, with Anyvath and Mist bringing up the rear. The cool puffs of white kissed Aven's cheeks one last time before they burst through the coverage and Sansia seared her eyes. She squeezed them shut as she looked away, tightening her legs to warn Mist of her temporary blindness. It took a good bit of blinking before the black spots in her vision faded away, leaving Aven with her first actual glimpse of the ocean.

Gold and blue stretched across the horizon, shimmering like flecks of molten light. Sansia was just disappearing beneath its line, sending a streak of yellow across the surface of the water, leaving the sky painted in vibrant, fiery colors.

Aven could hardly settle her gaze on one thing as she looked from the waves to the clouds cutting through the patches of color, then followed the motion of the water to where it rippled against sandy, white beaches. She'd just caught the faint glimpse of a dock extending far beyond the shore, when Mist jerked back into the clouds, nearly unseating Aven in her haste.

"Whoa!" she yelled. "What? What is it?"

Mist yowled, head swiveling around once before focusing on climbing into the sky. They were nearly vertical now, the strength in Aven's legs and the curve of her saddle the only things keeping her from plummeting down to Sholindrea. She chanced one look back, searching for what drove Mist to flee.

That's when she saw the plumes of black smoke. There were dozens of them, all rising from the docks, the surrounding buildings, and the handful of ships. Little remained untouched, and she imagined only one culprit could be responsible.

The Soulless had razed Shard's Port.

***

Emriel led them far enough away to dive safely for the peaks of the mountains. From there, they flew as close as they could, skimming over rocks and trees, before finishing their approach on foot. Night fell just as they just made it to the rolling hills overlooking the beach.

They didn't risk a fire once Sansia gave the sky over to the moons. It was impossible to tell if the Soulless were still at the port, so they couldn't risk bringing scouts down upon them. An orange glow shrouded the skeletons of charred buildings. Nothing moved. No sounds rang out. Save for the crackling embers and ghostly smoke shifting eerily.

"So what do we do now?" Pryn asked.

Emriel stood with one hand braced against the tree they'd hidden beneath. "We need to know what's going on down there."

Fennicks lingered at her side, once more in the warrior's body that had defeated her. "This happened recently. Those fires would be out if they did this before the attack in Yunaii."

She nodded her agreement, gaze darting back and forth, undoubtedly searching for hints of movement.

"I can accompany you on a recon mission," Dev said.

Kanai braced his forearm against another tree. "Dinon and I could slip in and out with none the wiser."

"No," Anyvath said with a stern look. "Better let us go. We're impervious to fire and most Elemental attacks."

"Agreed." Emriel checked both of her daggers before she looked at Fennicks. "You, Mist, and I will go and check things out."

Aven lunged for Emriel, protests spilling from her lips to join everyone else's. "If you think Mist is going down there without me, you've lost your dung-flinging mind."

"Why am I to stay here?" Anyvath asked.

"I can help you," Dev protested. "I am soul-called to help you."

Emriel waved her hands, hissing for them to shush, but to no avail.

"Shut it!" Kanai said, stomping into Dev and Anyvath's space with fangs bared. "Honestly, do none of you understand stealth? No wonder she doesn't want you along."

Dev's shoulders snapped back while Anyvath glowered.

"It's not that I don't want your help," Emriel said. "But in case things go wrong, Anyvath is the oldest, strongest, and largest of us. She can carry the most riders and travel the farthest without tiring. No matter what happens, someone has to get back and warn Yunaii."

"And me?" Dev asked, brow furrowed.

"You just annoy me," Emriel said with a wicked grin. "And I don't need you hacking at Soulless. The priority is information and getting out alive."

Dev's nostrils flared as fire ignited in his eyes. It was the look he'd worn after being called blood-seeker.

Willa seemed to recognize it because she laid a hand on his shoulder as she tucked in close. "We'll need you here if things go sideways. Dia'veh's power is with those flashy swords of yours. If Soulless find us, you'll be here to show me how good you really are with them."

Frustration ticked in Dev's tightened jaw as he gave a curt nod. "If I see any sign of fighting, know I will not wait for some signal that you need aid."

"You underestimate me, elf," Emriel said, turning her attention to Aven.

"You're not taking Mist down there without me."

Emriel took a menacing step forward. "No faith I'll keep my bloodkin safe?"

"Absolutely none."

"I've watched over her since long before you even knew she existed, little kitty." Her hands rested on the hilts of her daggers, prompting Aven to grip the handle of her hatchet.

"Back off, Em," Mist said, stepping between them. "Let Aven and me talk."

"Give her a good swat, will you?" Emriel said, moving towards Fennicks. "I don't have time to keep your pets in line."

The familiar fire welled in Aven's chest, but for the first time, it didn't take claws slicing into her palms to push down Kali's instincts. After days of sinking into her skin and giving into the freedom of hunting, Aven's mind held strong and clear.

With a tug on her wrist, Mist led her into the shadow of the woods, slipping between trees and under low-hanging branches until Aven could barely scent the rest of their group. That's when Mist rounded on her, white hair gleaming in the speckles of moonlight breaking through the canopy.

"Please stay here." Desperation punctuated each word.

Aven took a step forward, hands slipping over Mist's forearms. "How can you ask me to do that?"

"Because keeping you safe will distract me from helping Em." Mist's lips quivered as her eyes flitted between Aven's. "You'll be safe with Dev and Kanai. That's what I need so I can focus."

Aven hated to admit that if the roles were reversed, she would feel the same way. "I don't want to sit here wondering if the Soulless are hurting you."

A soft smile slipped across Mist's face. "I know. I wouldn't either. But I'll be with Emriel and Fennicks."

"One of them called you useless and the other tried to kill you."

"Fair," Mist said with a cringe. "But Em won't let them hurt me. She's a foul-mouthed pain in my backside, but she also practically has a death wish when it comes to protecting our bloodkin. If it comes down to it, I'll be back before she is."

Aven sighed as she nodded. She couldn't be childish or selfish, not with so much danger lingering nearby. "Okay."

Mist swallowed hard. "Promise me if things go wrong that you'll take care of you. I know you'll protect everyone—that's who you are, but please, protect yourself too."

Aven slid her hands up Mist's arms and over her shoulders, reveling in the softness of her skin until she cupped her round cheeks. "Promise me the same."

"I promise." Mist pressed her face into Aven's palm, her eyes slipping shut. "We never talked about it, you know."

Aven's heart skipped a beat. "About what?"

Mist tapped a finger against her lips. "I haven't stopped thinking about it."

Longing sizzled beneath Aven's skin. The last few days had been a blur, but each night, when they'd cuddled together, Aven had wondered. What would happen if she brushed her mouth over Mist's crown, trailing kisses along her cheekbones, following the line leading right to her lips? Fear had held her back. Aven didn't trust herself to stop if Mist returned the kiss. It had been hard enough to stop in the Temple.

Now, with the savagery of the Soulless burning nearby, the threat of tomorrow never coming had her heart pounding. The memory of plummeting to her death with so much left unsaid surged through her thoughts like a raven screeching a warning.

That wasn't a moment she wanted to relive. No more what-ifs.

Aven pulled Mist's face to hers, lips parting in anticipation. The moment their mouths touched was like an explosion in her chest. Heat tingled through every part of her, coiling and pulsing, amping up when a sigh slipped from the perfect, stunning, amazing girl in her arms. Mist kissed her back with a ferocity to match the heady rush of the hunt, tasting salty-sweet. Her fingers traced searing lines along Aven's neck, nearly undoing her control. The only thing that kept her from sinking to the forest floor was the knowledge that Emriel's saucy mouth would shriek to the sky above if they were discovered.

They kissed until Aven couldn't breathe. Then Mist burrowed into her neck, squeezing her in a hug tighter than any Papa or Mama had ever given her. Their bodies pressed together, fitting so perfectly that Aven couldn't help thinking of Dia'veh's words once more.

I sent her to you.

If there was ever a way for the Maker to convince Aven to believe, it was by creating Mist and the blessing of her friendship. Maybe they knew that. Maybe they'd always known that's what Aven needed. This was the Creator of the world, after all. Was there anything they didn't know?

Aven rested her chin on Mist's shoulder, breathing in her flowery scent. She could spend the rest of her life smelling roses and vanilla and never grow tired of it. Just a whiff sent her heart racing.

"Be my Promised." Aven hadn't meant to whisper those words. They had barely begun bouncing inside her head before slipping over her tongue.

"What did you say?" Mist's eyes went wide, her body impossibly still.

Of all the reckless things she'd done, three little words left Aven more terrified than facing down a snarling dragon. She swallowed the lump rising in her throat. It was too late to go back now. "I want you with me. Always. And if you'll have me, I—I would do that. I would promise myself to you. I'd be your Chosen."

Mist drew in a shaky breath. "Where would we go?"

"Anywhere," Aven said, stroking a thumb over her cheek. "I'll go anywhere with you. It doesn't have to be Estellias or Yunaii. I'll live on a deserted island, just you and me, if that's what you want."

Tears welled in those shining, fuchsia eyes as Mist touched her forehead to Aven's. "I'm afraid. I don't want to hold you back. I don't want to be a regret."

"The only thing I'd regret is not being with you. I've tasted being a part of a pride, and no one can take that from me. But if you weren't here, experiencing these moments as I do, I'd just be missing you the whole time. Even when I'm enjoying the hunt, I'm thinking about bringing it home to you. When Kanai is sharing his stories, I'm drunk on dancing with you. Everything I have is already yours, even my joy. I want to give it all to you."

Mist pressed against Aven's forehead, eyes squeezing shut as tears flowed down her cheeks. Her scent was a muddy mess Aven couldn't make sense of, but those tears ripped at her heart. She coaxed Mist to look up with touches along her face and jaw, desperate to see her eyes once more.

"It's okay if you don't feel the same way. If I can just be with you, that's enough. We don't have to—"

"I want it," Mist sobbed. "I want all of it. I want you. I want us. I want to be your Chosen, your friend, your everything. Whatever you need me to be."

"So why are you crying?" Aven asked, touching their noses together.

"Because I always planned to let you go, to help you get your dreams and then step aside for you to live them. I never wanted to trap you."

Aven wiped at her tears. "Those were daydreams, Mist. Hopes of being part of the Qinawe, of leaving Yunaii, of being accepted for who I am. I wanted all of those things to bandage the hurt inside me. I chased after them so I could escape how sad I've always been. But you—"

She pressed a quick kiss to Mist's lips, finally getting the reaction she wanted. A smile and open eyes glistening with tears and joy.

"You're the real dream. You care about me, accept me, follow me, complete me. You're everything I've wanted and everything I needed." There was only one way left to say it now, one way to make her understand. "I love you, Mist. I've loved you for a while now, but I was too scared to say it."

Mist leaned in for another kiss. "I love you too. I've loved you since the moment I met you."

"Does that mean you accept?" Aven's heart leaped into her throat, pounding like Dinon's feet when they'd danced. She'd meant what she'd said. It was okay if Mist didn't feel the same way. Being her friend was better than not being in her life.

Mist pulled her in for a bone-crushing hug, lips pressing against Aven's neck. "I do. One day, we'll challenge each other. When the time is right."

"You mean when Soulless aren't trying to kill us and everyone we love?"

A chuckle rumbled in Mist's chest. "If we wait for that, we might never get to the challenge. Let's just say, one day when death isn't literally close enough to smell. A quiet day, someplace peaceful. It doesn't matter if it's here or Estellias or somewhere we've never been. But I'd like my Papi to meet you first."

Aven squeezed her. "Of course."

Mist drew back again and brushed a few strands of hair from Aven's face. "You're my Promised."

"And you're my Chosen."

CHAPTER Thirty

Mist

"Can you please stop grinning like a giddy fool that just got named the next king of Estellias?"

Emriel sighed. She stood with her back pressed against a tree. One of the last between them and an expanse of tall grass surrounding the port town.

"Being king of that mess would not make me this happy," Mist said, sliding from one shadow to the next, avoiding twigs or leaves that might give her away.

Fennicks threw a wicked grin at Emriel, their gaze dragging from her booted feet to the crown of her orange hair. "You grinned like that the first time I—"

"Nope. No, thank you." Mist jammed a finger in each of her ears. "I'll stop smiling. I promise."

"You," Emriel poked Fennicks' chest. "Get your mind out of my pants. And you," she pointed at Mist. "We get it. You're excited to live like some two-legger with your precious kitty, but it's time to focus. Be disgustingly happy when there's not dead people nearby, huh?"

Mist slipped her lips into an obvious frown as she thought about what the Soulless had done. She'd seen it firsthand, and was about to again. Those who lost their lives deserved her respect. Thinking about Aven right now was inappropriate.

Her *Chosen*.

Mist pressed hard on her nail beds. There was a time and place for everything. Soft, lovey thoughts didn't belong here, not when the putrid smell of burning flesh wafted so thick she tasted it on her tongue.

She fell in step behind Emriel and Fennicks, slipping through patches of darkness like living shadows. When all that remained was the open field between them and the burning buildings, Emriel crouched in the tall grass, prompting Fennicks and Mist to do the same.

"Can you do something about the beacon shining on your head?" Fennicks asked, jerking a thumb at Mist's white crown.

She touched the strands falling over her face, gleaming like moonbeams in the night. Probably a good idea to not screech their arrival to every Soulless nearby. A memory conjured quickly. She'd once found a trapped octopus on a beach. As her fingers drug over her scalp, she imagined the fathomless ebony of its ink, until her hair absorbed every splash of fire or moonlight.

"We get in, we scout, we get out." Em pulled her hood over her own bright head. "Don't engage if you see a Soulless. We're here for information, not to fight them. The Summoner could have done this on her own, but until we have proof, we assume she's not alone."

With that, they darted into the grass, doing their best not to rustle it much. The razor-sharp blades sang whenever they rubbed together and each touch made Mist cringe. In the night's silence, every sound was like a throat-rattling shriek.

The rush down the hill brought them quickly to the first charred building, smoke and heat stinging Mist's eyes. Fire still crackled deep inside, embers glowing brightly in the dark. It looked like someone's house, perhaps a fisherman's, since a half-burned canoe laid nearby. Her heart hoped the owner had made it out before the blaze, but her nose couldn't deny the smell of burning hair coiling through the smoke. Many of the houses would probably be the same.

Mist touched a bent forefinger to her head before flattening the hand over her chest. A silent prayer slipped through her thoughts, begging Sholindrea to guide these people's souls to Dia'veh's peace. *May their suffering be replaced with comfort and love.*

Emriel inspected the blackened wood before leading them deeper into town. Each home and building was the same, burned, falling apart, smelling of death. Every soul got a prayer from Mist. It was the least she could do.

Ocean waves crashing over rock grew louder as they went until the strip of dock finally came into view. The wooden planks were old and twisted, well-trodden. They made a pathway out into the water where the skeletons of burned boats peeked through the undulating surface. Only at this distance did a single ship appear, bobbing at the far end of the dock. Mist almost missed it. One lone lantern rose and fell as the ocean rocked the vessel like a babe.

"That must be the Soulless' ship," Emriel whispered.

"Are you certain?" Fennicks asked, crouching in the shadow of a dilapidated shed.

"No, but they've taken to stealing merchant vessels and pirate ships in hopes the Estellian navy won't notice them slipping off their island."

"Clever," Mist murmured.

"Do we sneak on board?" Fennicks looked around. "Still no sign of the bastards anywhere. It'd be a stroke of luck if we sank them in their sleep."

Emriel shook her head. "That would be way too easy. I'm sure they're holed up in one of these buildings."

Mist watched how the ship bobbed and swayed, tethered to the dock by only a few ropes. "Would it be a good or a bad thing if we pushed that thing off the dock?"

Fennicks' brows rose. "Look at you, kitling. What a viciously clever idea."

"But that'll trap them on the island. Right? With us."

Emriel ran her thumb over the pommel of her daggers as she surveyed the ship. "They've burned any easy resources here. The only thing left for them to do is go for Yunaii. The mountain range and wastelands are unforgiving. If we send their ship off with whatever food or supplies they left behind, it could hinder them. Without flight, we might beat them back."

"But we still don't know how many there are," Fennicks pointed out.

"They couldn't possibly fit more than three dozen bodies on that thing," Em said.

Fennicks tsk'd. "That's a lot of Soulless."

"The flight can handle them."

"You know what Rielnor will say." Worry creased Fennicks' thick brow, pinching the scars creeping from their hairline. "Emriel, that could turn into a bloodbath."

Mist hoped Rielnor wouldn't let that happen, but his anger at the roost still shook her insides. To keep the flight free of the fighting, he just might let the shifters be slaughtered.

"Let's get on that ship and see what we find," Emriel said. "If the Soulless aren't there, we'll check the buildings and then get out of here."

***

Getting close to the dock was easy. The gnarled remains of the buildings left plenty of places to hide. It was rushing down the dock that sent Mist's heart into her throat. *Stay with Emriel and Fennicks.* She was safe with them.

The farther out they went, the more the dock bobbed and swayed. Mist's head swam. At times she couldn't make out the ends of the boards, leaving her stomach rolling. She had to focus on her steps. *Keep them light. Keep them soft. We're almost there.*

Emriel's pace never slowed as she reached the ship. She simply leapt from the dock, going higher and farther than seemingly possible, to crash into a netting of ropes hanging from the crow's nest. Fennicks followed suit. Mist inhaled as she bolstered the muscles in her legs before jumping. Her body soared over the water, and for a moment it felt like flying.

Emriel caught her arm and dragged Mist into the netting. Burning seared her fingers as they slipped over coarse ropes, but once her feet found purchase, the three of them crept down to the deck.

No scouts milled about or snoozed by the wheel. The ship lay quiet. Abandoned. Mist snorted at the arrogance of the Soulless. They had no fear of someone tampering with their only escape off the island.

Emriel moved for the stern while Fennicks went the opposite way. Mist lingered by the door to the captain's quarters, listening for Soulless. When they both returned without incident, she sighed in relief. So far, so good. They searched everywhere, inspecting private quarters, places where the crew slept, storage areas. Nothing. Fennicks found barrels of water and provisions below deck, but not in significant amounts. Either they'd unloaded what they needed, or they intended on stealing.

"Nothing interesting," Fennicks said as they reconvened on deck. "Do we send this thing to the merfolk?"

Emriel stared at the ocean, a few wisps of orange hair dancing in the breeze. A troubled look marred her round face.

"You look worried," Mist said.

"This is too easy. I'm missing something."

"Well." Mist scanned the ship for anything of value. "Will taking their ship hurt us?"

Em frowned. "I don't think so."

"Will keeping it?"

Her lips twitched. "Not in any way I can think of. The worst they can do is load up and leave again."

"Is there anything they could take from Yunaii that could hurt us?" Mist braced against the ship's railing. "Or hurt Estellias?"

The question sent a tick clenching in Emriel's jaw. "Possibly. If they catch a dragon, their Mimics could study them. Learn how to take our shapes. *That* could be disastrous."

"Sounds like a good reason to sink this dung heap," Fennicks said.

Emriel nodded her agreement, so they got to work. With no knowledge of ships, Mist followed Em and Fennicks' lead. They raised the anchor, disabled the rudder, ripped the sails, damaged everything they could think of. Once it was done, they leapt back onto the dock and untied the ropes. For a while, the ship just bobbed there, drifting little by and little, until it moved far enough away that there was no getting it back.

"Great," Fennicks said, rubbing their hands together. "Now let's finish this."

***

The search took longer than any of them liked. Weariness crept into Mist's bones as they went from house to house, sniffing the air, looking for tracks in the mud. Konia and Levia had traveled across the sky before they came upon a large building untouched by the fires.

Emriel held a fist in the air, halting everyone's meandering. When she darted for the charred remains of a fish shop, Mist reluctantly followed. She'd avoided the place in their searching, its reek of rotten meat curdling her stomach.

"They must be in there," Emriel whispered, attention darting over the two-story building. No light shone in the windows, but someone could still watch from the shadows.

Claws extended from Fennicks' huge hands. "Let's burn it down."

"We should probably check first," Mist said. "Make sure the people who live here aren't holed up inside."

"I don't smell shifters."

"I can't smell anything from here but dead fish. There's no way you can either." Mist held Fennicks' glare, even against their low growl. She was right. The risk was too high to assume only the Soulless were inside.

Emriel slunk out of the fish hut, motioning for them to follow. "Let's be quick. In and out. I don't want the elf crashing in here with swords drawn because we were gone too long."

"That'd be a sight," Fennicks said with a chuckle. "All hyped up, ready for glory, and all he finds is a shack of fish guts and barbecued people."

"Well, that killed my appetite for the rest of the week," Mist said.

"Noted." Fennicks crept towards the building. "Bring up rotten fish when Mist is being a disrespectful little s—"

"Shut it!" Emriel hissed. She had ducked beneath the casement of a large window, moving on fingertips and toes. Her head popped up to peer inside, before ducking back

340

down. Mist knelt beside her as she did this over and over, moving from one end of the casement to the other.

"How many?" Fennicks asked, crouching against the wall. Their warrior body was too large to fit beneath the window.

"Fifteen, maybe twenty."

Mist's heartbeat ratcheted, beating so hard her ears ached. "Soulless?"

Emriel nodded. "I think so. The two closest are definitely Mimics."

"What are those?" Fennicks asked, touching the glass with a clawed finger. Large black objects lay against the adjacent wall in a perfect line.

"I can't tell," Emriel said.

Mist blinked a few times, pushing her eyesight to sharpen, brighten, focusing in on the balls of metal. Light glimmered across their pitted surfaces, each one no bigger than a curled-up cat. One section on each shone silver, a clear line of separation between the light and dark ore.

"What do you see, bloodkin?" Emriel asked, pride gleaming in her eyes.

"They look like—" Mist frowned. She blinked a few times, letting her eyes adjust back to normal. "Cannon balls? Big cannon balls."

"There were no cannons on the ship," Fennicks said.

Mist pressed against the beds of her nails, fighting back the twitchy feeling rising up. "So, what are they?"

"Let's take one." Light shone in Fennicks' yellow-eyes as they looked down the building.

"That's reckless even for me," Emriel said. "Let's go with your other plan and burn down the building."

"But what if they have hostages in there?" Mist asked, pressing harder on her nails.

A shadow fell across Em's face. "Soulless don't take hostages."

"They were going to take me. They planned to kill me, but they were going to draw it out. What if they've got people inside for the same reason?"

"Then we'll be doing them a favor." Emriel looked away from the window, gaze roving over the ruined town. "The Soulless have been here for hours, if not days. If they've got people inside, death is a release they deserve."

Horror pushed bile into Mist's throat. She wanted to argue against the haunted look on Emriel's face, but she'd been fighting the Soulless since before Mist was born. The mantle of Eega's fight had fallen to her long ago.

"Dia'veh blast it all." Emriel looked around. "Where in Sholindrea's name is that brainless lizard?"

Mist glanced at Fennicks' empty hiding spot and gasped. She hadn't heard a single step. Had they gone for fire or—

"The cannon balls!"

Emriel and Mist sat up, peering into the large, darkened room. It opened all the way to the second-story, with a raised platform on the end opposite two double doors. Some kind of meeting hall, perhaps. Bodies lay scattered in groups of two or three. None moved, their faces and limbs imperceptible in the splashes of moonlight. Mist checked every shadow for some hint of Fennicks, though she had no idea how they intended on getting inside.

"Soulless cursed fool," Emriel said, attention fixing on a swath of shadows.

Mist peered as something small crawled across the floor. She had to push her eyes again, straining to make sense of the body slowly coming into focus. Little arms, short legs, hair pulled into braids. The girl from the bathing pool. Fennicks had shifted back into a child.

"Why?" Of all the shapes to take. Why a child?

"Because I like my mates as dramatic as me," Emriel grumbled.

Mist cast her a questioning look before staring back at Fennicks. They'd gotten close to the cannon balls. Just a little more and they'd be able to swipe one.

The darkness shifted, pooling together, growing solid. Something came down on Fennicks' back before materializing into a boot, then a leg, forming into the body of a Soulless.

Emriel cursed as a Shadow pinned Fennicks' to the ground. She didn't stop to plan, probably didn't even think. Metal shrieked as she drew a dagger and brought the pommel against the glass. Silence shattered as the shards spilled over the floor, raising shouts of alarm from those inside.

Em leapt through the window, second dagger sliding from its scabbard as she ran for Fennicks. It took Mist's stunned brain a moment to catch up. Then she vaulted through the casement, chasing after her sister.

Firelight blazed to her right, scorching and filling her visions with spots. Her eyelids slammed shut but the damage was done. She hadn't put her vision back to normal yet. One little spark was like staring into Sansia. Tears streamed down her cheeks as something clamped over her ankle.

"What do you have there?" a female voice asked gleefully.

"The dragons came to play," a male said from Fennicks' direction.

"That we did," Emriel sneered.

Mist rubbed at the ache in her eyes. She had no time to be blind. The pressure on her ankle had tightened. A hand, maybe? One of the Soulless. Blinking through the pain, she kicked with her other foot and something crunched, followed by a howling curse. With more blinking and rubbing, her vision finally cleared.

Emriel had tackled the Shadow and buried one of her daggers deep in his gut. Her focus locked on her prey, leaving her blind to the two Soulless sneaking up behind her. Light glinted off their drawn steel, gleaming deadly in the firelight. Mist screamed a warning, feet carrying her across the room. She'd never reach her in time.

A cannon ball smacked into a gray-skinned Mimic, driving them back as they grabbed at their bloody face. Fennicks stood by the wall, two more cannonballs in hand. The second Soulless skidded to a stop, their wide eyes focused on the metal balls.

"Are you all impervious to fire like us?" Fennicks asked, their childish voice eerily repulsive.

Emriel yanked her dagger from the Shadow with a sickening squish and faced the room of angry Soulless. Mist stood right in the thick of them, at least four or five at her back, with over a dozen to her left and right. Their black and gray skins reminded her of moonlight, all monochrome and colorless. Each one wore black, save for one familiar white-skinned face.

"I hoped to see you again." Ukila tilted her head as she stared at Emriel. "Thank you for coming to me."

"Sorry, hot pants. We'll have to reschedule this date."

Ukila's gaze flicked over the room before settling on Mist. "I can take her as a dance partner. What do you say, hatchling?"

"Sorry, sweets." Emriel angled her foot against one of the cannon balls. "I don't share."

Her hips twisted, leg rearing back, before coming down in a kick that sent the ball flying. Ukila's eyes widened as gasps whooshed through the room. Mist had just enough time to register the ball headed straight for a Mimic with a fistful of fire, before Emriel was running for her.

"Go, Vhis!" she screamed as feathers burst over her skin.

By the time she came close enough to touch, her body had elongated, neck twisting around, wings reaching for the ceiling. One bump sent Mist sprawling onto her back, grabbing for purchase as wood creaked.

The wall at Fennicks' back exploded beneath black wings and scaly legs. The ceiling collapsed, slipping sideways, fractured supports reigning from above. Mist ducked her face against Emriel's neck as muscles bunched beneath her. They launched upward, following Fennicks who crashed through the ceiling like a bull. More debris crashed around Mist's ears, scraping her arms, leaving her skin raw and stinging. The cool night air was a balm as they broke free, shooting straight for the freedom of the stars.

Emriel didn't slow to right herself. Her body arched upward, aiming for the moons, before careening back down, heading straight for the forest. Fennicks flapped beside them, one massive foot clutched around something between their claws. Mist thought they'd maybe snatched a Soulless, but spotted no sign of limbs flailing about.

"Did you steal one of those balls?"

Fennicks roared in reply, their mouth full of teeth stretching into a dragon grin. The sight tore a laugh from Mist's throat. She much preferred reckless, playful Fennicks to the one that tried to kill her.

Emriel did not agree. She shrieked her fury at the black dragon, weaving into their path over and over as they sped for the forest. After the fourth or fifth time, Mist threw one leg over Emriel's side and slid off.

For a few thrilling heartbeats the black sky held her aloft, air whipping her face and pulling at her hair. She closed her eyes and breathed, completely weightless, but she couldn't indulge long. An itch slithered beneath her skin as feathers pushed out first, then wings. She angled her body, carefully extending to catch gusts of air. It buffeted her back up as she settled in her dragonskin.

When she landed, Aven ran straight for her, eyes wide, hatchet out. In one smooth move, she swung into the saddle, her weight settling perfectly. "Go, go, go! They're coming!"

Mist whipped her head around and sure enough, Soulless streaked through the tall grass. Air rushed past her head as Willa launched, followed by Anyvath with Kanai and Dinon.

Pryn was climbing into Fennicks' saddle when Dev went to Emriel, his face like a thundercloud.

"You underestimate me," he said in a snide voice, glaring at Emriel. "It is *impossible* to underestimate you!"

CHAPTER
Thirty-One

Aven

The next two days were a blur. Aven spent so much time looking over her shoulder, searching for signs of the Soulless. Fear convinced her they'd materialize before her eyes, even above the icy mountain range. No matter how hard she convinced herself that they were safe in the sky, her heart still pounded, keeping her awake even when sleep pulled at her eyelids.

Despite barely resting at Shard's Port, Emriel kept a grueling pace, only stopping when they cleared the mountains. Even then, they ate a quick meal of salted pork and cheese before taking off again. No one complained when they flew through the night and straight on the next day. Emriel's constant vigilance left everyone anxious. Only when Sansia fell again did Kanai insist they rest.

"We'll be done for if the dragons fall out of the sky," he said once his feet met rock.

Aven silently agreed. Plummeting through the sky with no dragon wings to save her was something she hoped to never experience again.

His logic still met Emriel's stubborn mouth as she laid on her pack, eyes heavy and listless. "You'll be done for if thirty Soulless catch up to us."

That seemed all the snark she had in her. It wasn't long before she was snoring, drool sliding down one cheek. Fennicks and Anyvath weren't far behind her, though they stayed in their dragonskins.

Once everyone ate, Dev and Aven took first watch. There'd be no singing or dancing. Not even a fire to keep them warm. Pryn went right to Fennicks, curling up near their leg, fear bittering her scent. Aven couldn't blame her. Scouting for Soulless from a dragon's back was a far different thing than fleeing a murderous hoard.

"Go rest," Aven whispered to Mist, who lingered nearby, her eyes dull and heavy-lidded.

With a weary sigh, she handed over a satchel holding whatever Fennicks had stolen from the Soulless, before stumbling to Emriel. There was no grace in the way she flopped down beside her sister, settling with their backs pressed together. It didn't take long for her breathing to slow as she drifted off to sleep.

"Wake Dinon and me for second watch, little sister," Kanai said. "You will need rest as well."

Aven agreed, and they were off, settling on Mist's other side, creating a barrier of body heat.

Dev already stood guard, hands on the hilts of his swords, with attention locked on the horizon. Willa snoozed at his feet, her griffin body curved around him protectively.

"Think they're out there?" Aven asked, coming to stand at his side.

"We would be dead if they were."

She flinched at the anger simmering in his voice. They were the first words he'd spoken since they'd fled the port.

"They can't be as fast as we are though." Whether that was for himself or for her, Aven didn't know. She'd never bothered with lying to herself, but this seemed a good time to try it. "Soulless can't fly."

Dev's nostrils flared as he looked at her. "A Mimic could, depending on what Sholi power they stole. Shadows do more than move through darkness, they manipulate light and a lack of it, but Mimics—my father taught me they steal souls of Sholi and take their power. If a Mimic got an Air Elemental's soul, they could travel through the skies." He glanced down at Willa, who cooed in her sleep. "If they stole a shifter's, they could grow themselves wings."

Aven shivered. Not just from the night's chill, but from the thought of someone stealing her soul. Would she be bottled up, only let out when they needed her power? Shoved into Kali's fang for them to both be used against their will?

"What is that thing?" Dev asked, jerking his chin at the satchel in Aven's hands.

She reached inside and gingerly lifted it for him to see. "It's the metal ball Fennicks stole from the Soulless."

"May I?"

Aven handed it over and turned her attention to the barren wastes. Large expanses of rock and dirt stretched on and on, scattered with bushes and prickle plants. Sparse saplings that refused to die swayed in a stubborn breeze, the few leaves left on their branches straining to break free. Rock formations stood in the distance, their tall cliffs and flat tops illuminated in the moonlight. Nothing moved and the wind carried only scents of the occasional pig or snake. Not like what she'd smelled in Yunaii's market after the attack.

"This is some sort of explosive," Dev said.

Aven took the ball back when he offered it and returned it to the satchel. "That's what Mist said. She thought maybe an odd sort of cannonball."

One corner of Dev's mouth pinched. "I do not think it is meant as a projectile. That bit of silver metal is soft. Almost pliable. If inserted improperly into a cannon, I do not believe it would maintain structure against the explosive force one produces."

"What is it then?" Aven asked.

"I am unsure, but I believe Truthseeker Gaelin will aid in finding answers."

"Let's hope we can get it to him."

Dev nodded, his attention slipping back to keeping watch. With nothing else left to say, Aven did the same. She searched for signs of approaching enemies, sniffing for hints of copper or acrid death. Her heart thudded in her ears, spiking bolts of pain through the sides of her head. As the night crept by slower than stars shifting through the sky, dread pressed down on her. All she had left was hope in the dragons and that the Maker watched over them.

Dia'veh, get us home. Please. Please help us save our home.

***

They reached the river the next morning. Aven could have cried. Her forehead and scalp burned from so much exposure to the sun. She'd never resented Sansia like she did each time her brows twitched. They couldn't hide in the shade of the canyon yet, thanks to the swollen river filling the gorge, but it meant they were getting close to the dam. Then, they could fly in the cover of rocky walls.

Thankfully, the dragons all seemed replenished. Anyvath and Fennicks stayed right on Emriel's tail, and Mist used every chance she could to ride the currents from their wings. Willa did the same, cruising in close until it felt like they were their own little flock. There was no diving in the water or flitting about, searching for nesting gifts. If it was up to Emriel, they would fly through the night again. Her focus was locked on getting everyone home as quickly as possible.

Sansia was heading for the horizon when Aven spotted the dam far ahead. They were so close. By morning, she would see Mama and Papa's faces again. She could tell them she had a Chosen, that she and Mist were Promised. She could already imagine how their eyes would light up, how they would hug Aven and then Mist. It didn't matter if Yana didn't want Aven amongst the Qinawe. She returned with something better.

She glanced back the way they'd come, again searching for signs of the Soulless. There wasn't so much as a cloud of dust. Maybe crossing over the mountains had slowed them considerably. She'd heard of no specific passages used by traders. Even Tibri flew over the range. Maybe the thing that kept Yunaii so isolated had bought them some time.

Of course, whatever time they had would go into more shifter debating. Hopefully, Kanai's testimony about the danger would spur the other leaders to fight back. Yunaii was their home, and whatever the Soulless were planning had to be stopped.

She sighed over the thought of convincing the Matriarchs and Elders to fight. That was going to be a mess. But it was a mess she would deal with tomorrow, with dragons, lynx, and elves at her side. Her people would not be slaughtered, even if they seemed determined to let that happen.

Aven waved at Kanai as the dam drew closer. If nothing else, it was time for the dragons to eat and drink. They had been flying nonstop since morning. The grove at Sholindrea's feet seemed the perfect place to rest.

As she turned to get Dev's attention, a strange *thok* echoed through the canyon. Aven frowned, looking for the source just as Pryn screamed.

"Look out!"

Mist banked right, almost slipping into a full spin. Aven grabbed hold of the saddle, her legs tightening. She couldn't see what happened, but a dragon shrieked over the din of rushing water.

They circled around in time to see Emriel plunge into the river. Aven didn't have to speak. She crouched, leaning forward. Mist dove. Fennicks did the same, approaching from the other side. Willa touched the water first, swooping in from nowhere, her clawed feet reaching for Dev. His gaze was locked on Emriel, hesitating until water sloshed against his face, the threat of drowning forcing him to release the saddle. With an eagle's screech, Willa yanked him up, her wings straining as she shot for the edge of the Lighe river.

Emriel flailed, her splashes and screams echoing against the rock. A hole cut through her left wing, but from what? All Aven had heard was the strange sound. Blood pooled in the water body, purple droplets flinging outward each time she moved.

By the time they got to her, she had shifted, her sallow face bobbing, hands barely reaching for help. Fennicks dropped both forelegs into the river, dragging through the waves with clawed feet held wide. They closed around

Emriel's torso and legs before hauling her up, climbing up as fast as they could.

Another *thok* sounded, and Aven shouted a warning. Fennicks veered left, tucking in their wings as Mist did the same. A large metal bolt shot between them with frightening speed.

That's what had taken out Emriel's wing.

Aven tracked its path back to the dam and her stomach dropped. Three strange machines stood upon the bridge. They almost looked like massive crossbows, only these things didn't shoot arrows. They shot metal spears big enough to pierce dragon scales.

Manning them were half a dozen Soulless.

"Land!" Aven screamed as they loaded another bolt.

Mist shot for the bank, aiming for a spot where large rocks jutted out into the water. They were just tall enough for minimal cover from the dragon-killing weapons.

As soon as they landed, Aven leapt from the saddle. Mist needed to shift. It was the only way she'd fit behind the rocks. As feathers turned to skin and wings vanished beneath shoulder blades, Aven ripped clothing from her pack before searching for the others.

Fennicks had landed not far upstream and was already shifting. Their massive body was too big of a target. They shrank in on themself, molding into the lithe body from the summit. Lean muscle, black hair, pale skin. Between their powerful arms and Pryn's, they hauled Emriel to Aven and Mist's hiding spot. Both of the dragons had shifted into clothes, Emriel in the same form-fitting breeches and top she'd worn the entire trip, while Fennicks had grown themself scaly armor covering their limbs and chest.

Rocks rumbled when Anyvath crashed down beside them.

"Is Emriel alright?" Kanai asked, shoving Dinon from the saddle and behind the shielding boulders.

Before Fennicks could answer, Anyvath whirled for the bridge, jaw dropping open. Fire welled over her tongue and shot in a stream of blazing heat towards the dam. Shouts went up, but Aven didn't risk looking to see if she'd hit her target.

"Tuck your wings!" Fennicks ordered. "Before we lose them too."

Anyvath hissed but did as commanded. Her wings folded against her body, her head and chest nestling behind the rocks, leaving her hindquarters and tail fully exposed. There was no way she would fit her whole self, but she didn't abandon her dragonskin or her fiery blast. Her head raised and dropped over and over, undoubtedly checking for the next attack.

Aven turned for Emriel and found Dev and Mist at her side. Her breathing was evening out and color had returned to her cheeks.

"Can you stand?" Mist asked, her voice trembling.

"Just—" Emriel drew in a deep breath, leaning back against Mist's chest. "Just a moment."

Another *thok* sounded, and Anyvath whipped her tail with a snarl. The sound of metal on scales rang before the bolt plunged into the water.

"They're not going to stop," Kanai said. "We need to get out of here."

Dev walked to the edge of the river and gazed at the bridge. "Three of them are coming."

"What do we do?" Aven tugged at Kali's fang, grasping for strands of a plan. "It took a squadron of Linseen to stop one of them."

"And a dragon," Mist said.

Aven glanced at Dev as he peered around the boulder. "How much time do we have?"

His shoulders stiffened as he ducked for cover. "The ballistae are being loaded once more."

Mist looked to the elder dragon. "Anyvath can't deflect them all. We should make a break for it, try taking off out of range."

"Those things will tear flesh just as easy as wings," Fennicks said. "We need a distraction."

What kind of distraction could get them out of this? Three Soulless approached, probably Mimics since they hadn't moved into the shadow of the rock. That meant who knows what kinds of powers. Aven pressed Kali's fang tip against her finger. Maybe some reckless anger was just what they needed.

Dev watched Willa crouching nearby, her eagle eyes darting back and forth.

"Now seems as good a time as any to show you my *swordsmanship*." He drew one of his blades, gazing at the weapon as Willa stared. "All of you go. Get out of range and fly for Yunaii. I will distract the Soulless."

Aven felt like he'd slapped her. "You can't."

"I can. I am soul-called." A crooked smile lit his face, changing him into someone Aven didn't recognize.

"I saw what the Summoner did to the Linseen. A whole squad and she ripped them apart."

"They were not soul-called."

Willa bound towards him, chittering her anger. Dev just grinned like she was a yowling cat begging for food.

"Go," he said, running a finger along her feathered face. "Help them escape."

Her sharp beak snapped at his hand and she planted her hindquarters in the dirt.

"If you stay, she stays," Kanai said with a sigh.

Dev's amusement vanished. "No. I am protected by Dia'veh."

"And she'll have my protection," the pride leader said. "I'm no Maker of the world, but my claws will do a fine job."

Dev shook his head. "You will both die."

"I won't let them," Emriel said, finally on her feet. "After all, aren't you supposed to be watching my back? I gotta stick around so you can do that." Dev's protests died beneath the hand she slapped over his mouth. "Anyvath, hold them back with your fire."

The rainbow dragon immediately released a blast, eliciting shouting from down the river and another round of ballistae. She ducked just in time for the bolts to soar over her head.

Emriel nodded her approval. "Fennicks, get the Tribouin and the cat out of here. Mister Whiskers, Little Bird, the elf, and I will hold them long enough for you all to get away. We'll meet you in Yunaii."

Aven didn't need her nose to know Emriel was lying. No matter how good she was, they wouldn't all make it back. Confidence couldn't deflect metal spears and soul-stealing power.

"There's just one problem," Fennicks said.

Emriel rounded on them, her blue eyes blazing. "I swear if you're about to complain about carrying anyone but the kid—"

"Well, we both know who I'd rather be riding me," Fennicks said with a flirty grin. "But no. I was going to say, the only problem is I can't carry Pryn and Dinon."

"Why not?"

Fennicks' arm sliced through the air, their hand slamming into Emriel's jaw with a crack. She crumpled without a sound, falling into Fennicks' waiting arms.

"What are you doing?" Mist shrieked, grabbing for her sister.

"Someone who doesn't fancy themselves a martyr needs to stay and I'm not feeling like dying today." Fennicks hefted Emriel over their shoulder. "If it all turns to a steaming pile of crap, I'll get us out. Promise."

Aven stared at Fennicks, her body numb all the way down to her toes.

"We don't have time for you all to marvel over me. Mist, take your bloodkin and get as far away as you can. As soon as she wakes up, she's gonna rush back here to die."

Mist looked between Emriel and Aven, mouth hanging open.

"Go," Aven insisted, mustering a boldness she didn't feel. "Get out of here. You know how she is."

"You all need to go," Kanai said. "Now. That fire only made them cautious."

Mist snapped out of her stupor and turned her back to the group. With shaking hands, she yanked off the clothes Aven had just given her and shifted. As soon as she was done,

Fennicks threw Emriel's limp body over Mist's back and secured her with a rope.

"Tell Rielnor to get you dragonskin for clothes," Fennicks said as they tied the last knot. "You're old enough."

Mist cooed sadly as she turned to face them. None of this made sense. Only days ago, Fennicks had tried to kill them. Now, they were trying to save everyone.

"Go!" Fennicks smacked Mist's hindquarters like a horse, startling her into a leap that didn't quite lift her in the air. Her head swiveled to Aven, fear shining in her eyes.

"Anyvath will take her! Now go!"

Aven touched her heart. "I'll see you soon. Get your sister out of here."

With one last hesitant look, Mist broke into a run, heading up the river as fast as she could. Another *thok* rang out, followed by a second. Aven shrieked, fear driving her feet forward, only for Kanai to catch her around the middle.

"Mist is fast," he said. "She'll be fine. Now get on Anyvath. It's time for you to go, little sister."

Despite Aven's wriggling, Kanai hauled her to Anyvath's side, where Pryn and Dinon climbed onto her back. She belched searing fire, tail whipping back and forth as they all mounted. Aven lingered on the dragon's foreleg, looking back to the ones staying behind. Fennicks, with their lips pulled into a devilish smile. Willa, her attention only on Dev, who looked resigned and angry. Then Kanai.

Aven grabbed the pride leader's forearm in a tight grip. "We'll see you soon."

His lips twitched, gaze moving towards the dam. "If you ever meet my cub, tell her I miss her."

Aven's stomach twisted. This wasn't happening. Kanai and the others had to get out.

He gave her a gentle push, urging her to settle on Anyvath's scaly back. Pryn had taken the saddle, so Dinon sat between her and Aven, their arms wrapped around Pryn's waist. The best place for an inexperienced rider. This was sure to be a bumpy ride.

Anyvath shot another blast of fire, and from her back, Aven saw the approaching Soulless dive for cover. The dragon waited long enough to deflect two more bolts with her scaled tail before breaking into a run. She kept her wings tucked against her sides, head low, spurring Aven to push Dinon and Pryn down as well. Anyvath's body was a big enough target. No need to give the Soulless more things to aim for.

Up ahead, Mist had launched into the air, shooting like a streak of light, aiming for the clouds. Something uncoiled in Aven's chest at the sight. At least Mist was safe. She would get home to Yunaii and warn the leaders of what was coming.

As Anyvath bounded over rock and mud, Aven looked back. Helplessness on dragonback would end her one day. Willa flew for the dam with Dev on her back. Fennicks and Kanai had shifted, but the three Soulless held their focus. With an ear-shattering roar, the dragon released a stream of fire before leaping for the approaching enemy. The way they landed, at least one creature fell beneath their black claws.

Anyvath's muscles tensed, giving Aven just a moment to brace, and the world lurched. Her teeth knocked together from the power of their launch. Nothing could rival pure dragon strength.

Anyvath clawed through the air, wings pumping, body snaking up and down, muscles bunching beneath Aven's thighs, nearly unseating her as they climbed. Wind pressed against her ears as Dinon bounced around, arms scrabbling for purchase. As they slipped sideways, Pryn's arm shot around their middle, pulling the lynx against her back. Aven followed suit, wrapping her own around Dinon's other side and gripping Pryn's hip as tight as she could. Hopefully, that would keep them all seated and safe.

Another roar sounded. Aven strained her neck to see, hair whipping in her face and sticking to her sweaty skin. Kanai had reached one end of the dam. His massive paws slashed at a Soulless, who danced backward to avoid disembowelment. Fennicks squared off with the other two Soulless. Their tail whipped around as blasts of soul-stolen fire licked over their scales. If those Mimics had swiped Elemental power, maybe their attacks would be useless against the dragon.

On the other end of the dam, Dev and Willa moved in a shockingly seamless grace. Aven had never seen a soul-called elf in battle, but now she understood. Shadow and fire parted around Dev, who used his body to shield Willa from each blast as his swords caught blow after blow from two different Soulless. Metal clanged over and over, but his strength held and his speed countered each strike. He moved effortlessly, ducking under one blade before launching a flurry of moves she could barely follow. Each time his attention switched between attackers, Willa moved at his back, beak snapping and talons slicing through flesh. They were flawless.

If not for the final Soulless, the one Kanai barreled towards. They'd turned their ballista with a metal bolt ready, taking aim for Dev with frightening precision. Aven screamed a warning, but rushing wind ripped it away as Anyvath's body curved upward, dipping into the clouds. The *thok* echoed as cool white filled her vision.

"Go back down!"

She got no reaction from Anyvath. No shift in flight. No twist in her neck. They remained lost in the stinging vapors. Helpless. Useless. Hidden while their friends possibly died.

Dinon looked from left to right, pupils pinpricks in a circle of terrified yellow. Together, they strained to see through the surrounding mist. Desperate for a glimpse of the ground.

As the clouds parted and their flight leveled out, Aven swallowed a horrified gasp.

Willa was down. Aven couldn't tell how bad it was, but she wasn't moving and one wing bent unnaturally. Dev stood between her and the Soulless, moving with a ferocity she didn't think possible. Kanai was almost to them now, drawing the attention of the Soulless at the ballista.

"Willa is hurt!" Aven called to Anyvath. "We have to help."

The dragon's neck curved, surveying the scene as they sailed over the dam.

"Anyvath, please!"

Her pace slowed, hesitation driving her lower. Fennicks had made it to the end of the dam, belching blasts of fire at one Soulless, and another, fending off attacks with swats of their tail and swipes from their wings. Desperation edged each attack. They must have seen the bolt hit Willa.

Anyvath's wings beat twice, lifting them as Fennicks reached the others. She'd nearly drawn them into the clouds when a wail of pain ripped from Dinon.

"No! Kanai's hit!"

Aven leaned to the side, looking around wings and limbs. She needed a glimpse. A hope. To hear him call her *little sister* one more time. The pride leader had to be okay.

The bridge was slipping away. All she could make out was red pooling beneath the cat's unmoving body. Something snapped inside her, a pain so raw she felt weightless. Lost. Her head swam, unable to make sense of it. Kali's son. He still wasn't moving. The Soulless had turned away from him, advancing on Dev.

The elf had abandoned the fight as he dragged Willa's now shifted body towards the edge of the bridge. He hefted her into his arms, running now. But the way she hung limp, her wings lifelessly tangling around his legs—it was bad.

"They're not going to make it." Aven pounded a fist against Anyvath's side. "Please! We have to go back."

She didn't acknowledge them. She didn't look back. Anyvath's wings pumped, pulling them farther and farther away. Her decision was made.

"You're killing them!" Dinon screamed. "Please Anyvath!"

Fennicks crawled across the thin bridge, crushing ballistae with their weight. Kanai was almost within their reach. Dev was at the edge of the bridge. His foot planted on the stone parapet as water rushed through the spillways. Was he going to jump? Even if he leaped far enough to not crash into the bottom of the dam, the fall would be fatal. No one could survive that.

"Anyvath! We could still save them!"

Fennicks rose on their hindquarters, roar shaking the air. Their wings beat. A mighty gust flattened Soulless to the bridge, knocked over the last ballista, and Dev launched. The blast sent him and Willa careening far from the dam, leaving Fennicks and Kanai behind. Their bodies angled for the water as Anyvath veered around a bend in the canyon. Rock was the last thing Aven saw as Dinon's heartbroken screams rang in her ears.

CHAPTER
Thirty-Two

Mist

"How could you?" Dinon screamed. "You left them. They're dead because of you!"

Anyvath stood expressionless in the face of their rage. Even when Dinon got close enough to strike her, anger spitting and hissing, she still didn't rise. Everything shrieked in her face undoubtedly already played in her mind. It did in Mist's.

She sat by the prayer pool in Dia'veh's Temple, knees hugged to her chest, imagining what she might have changed. Maybe if she'd lingered, she could have grabbed Willa. If Dev wasn't protecting her, he might have saved Kanai. Or maybe Mist could have gotten Kanai out, brought him to Ifera for healing. The scenarios replayed over and over.

Aven stared glassy-eyed at the water, squeezing Kali's fang, as tears slid down her cheeks. Mist wanted to comfort her, but no words could make it better. Just like when her friend Adair's father had died. All Mist could do was be a silent source of strength.

That would not be enough when Emriel woke. She lay unconscious on the Temple's cushions, her jaw an ugly purple. Fennicks had hit her harder than Mist realized. Possibly harder than they'd meant to. That's what it took to save Em from herself. What would she say when she found out Fennicks' confidence and swagger had failed them?

They'd all waited as Sansia rose, taking turns watching the horizon, Pryn especially. Her vigil on the Temple's steps had not ended yet. Her hope Fennicks might finally appear hadn't died.

Rielnor had been waiting for Mist when she arrived, as if he'd known something was wrong. Together, they'd carried Emriel inside.

When Anyvath appeared without Kanai or Willa, Rielnor hadn't said a word. He'd gone to retrieve Yliva, his mouth set in a thin line. There'd been no peace from then on. The flock leader's silent tears joined Dinon's, which eventually turned to rage. The lynx sobbed, screamed, pleaded. No one had the heart to reprimand them. Eventually Yliva went outside, standing beside Pryn, still as stone, watching the sky.

Rielnor stood by the Temple's entrance with arms crossed as Dinon railed in Anyvath's face. It stretched on and on, until their voice rasped and cracked. It had to end. Sooner or later, the pride had to know Kanai was not coming back.

A bubble of mourning trapped them inside the stone walls. Outside, life went on as usual. Tribouin fed their families. Qinawe went for their morning hunts. Linseen began patrolling. None the wiser of the heartache inside the Temple. Everyone inside waited, but for what, Mist wasn't quite sure. For the Soulless to come kill them all? For the shifters to decide to fight? For Emriel to wake up and save the day with a flick of her daggers and a sarcastic comment? It all seemed like distant daydreams and nightmares.

Mist tensed when a groan slipped between Em's lips. Time for the bubble to pop. Everyone stilled as she pushed herself up, gingerly touching her jaw.

"You dung-eating, egg-stomper. Why in the torment did you hit me so hard?"

Mist shifted onto her knees as Emriel looked around the Temple. Searching. The scowl she'd awoken with slipped away. Her gaze moved from Dinon's red, swollen face, to Anyvath's silent pain, to Aven's tear-streaked cheeks. Then she looked at Mist, anger flaring in her eyes.

"Did that coward seriously smack me and then scuttle off to the roost?"

A shadow fell across Em's face. Rielnor had approached, standing over her like a shroud of doom.

One look at him put out Emriel's fire. "Where are they? Whiskers? Little Bird? The elf?"

Rielnor's eyes flicked to Mist before he shook his head.

Mist laid a hand on her sister's shoulder. "They didn't make it."

Em jerked away in an attempt to rise, but her body wobbled until she toppled over. "They're just not back yet."

"They're dead, Emriel." Aven's voice was cold. Lifeless. She didn't bother turning. She just continued staring into the water. "I saw it."

Em blinked in the ringing silence, tears pooling over her lashes. First one. Then another. Her breathing grew ragged. Tremors spasmed up her arms. Then she doubled over, strained wheezing racking her body as her forehead touched the ground.

"Kit." Rielnor crouched, putting his hands on her shoulders as a sob shuddered through her.

"No." Emriel whimpered. "Vhis isn't dead."

"Emriel."

"No!" She fell onto her bottom, cheeks splotchy and wet. "They're not dead."

Rielnor's mouth quivered, his eyes glistening. "Vhisari is powerful, but even they cannot hold against that many Soulless alone."

Mist recoiled at the use of Fennicks' true name, instead of the one Pryn had given her racing dragon. *Vhisari.* She'd always wondered what it was.

"You're wrong!" Emriel screeched, rising on shaking legs. "I'll find them. You'll see."

"Emriel no." Rielnor barred her way. "You need to rest."

"Please lie down," Mist said, standing as well.

"No. I'm getting Vhis." She pushed into Rielnor's chest, her balled fists pounding on his scars. "Move, you oaf. Get out of my way."

Rielnor clamped onto her wrists. "Vhisari did not sacrifice themself so you could go flying back to death."

"What do you know?" Emriel sneered, clawing at his hands. Mist tried grabbing onto her, but she flailed all over, yanking, kicking, ramming into the flight leader. There was nowhere to seize without hurting her or getting hurt.

"Your recklessness has harmed enough people. Now stop!" A roar slipped into Rielnor's voice, rattling the candle holders nearby.

Emriel immediately went still, hair falling over her face, chest heaving with quiet sniffles. Her sorrow thickened the air, drawing Mist closer. No words could make this better, but she had to try. She'd almost pulled Em into a hug, when something snapped in her.

"No!" Em's mouth clamped onto Rielnor's fingers, teeth chomping so hard he yelped. His surprise left him open for a punch to the face, then a kick at his knee. He hit the ground with a grunt.

Em barreled for the exit before Mist could react. Scarlet feathers rushed over her skin, body slipping through the corridor before red streaked above the glass ceiling. Shooting towards the Lighe river.

Mist offered a trembling hand to Rielnor. "We have to stop her."

He let her pull him up, his scarred face twisted with fury and pain. "I will bring her back. Until I return, Anyvath is in charge of the flight."

Dinon snorted. "That's a poor decision."

Rielnor didn't spare the lynx a glance. He just fixed Anyvath with a cool stare, waiting until she nodded in compliance. As soon as she did, he stormed out the door of the Temple to chase after his kit.

***

Waiting for Rielnor was almost worse than what came before his departure. Mist tried keeping her mind busy, but images of him flying back, bloody and without Emriel plagued her every thought.

Dinon had at least gone quiet. They sat with Aven by the pool, sometimes rocking, sometimes as still as stone, tears rolling down their cheeks. Both of them just sitting there quietly spurred Mist to action. She sought out Ifera in hopes of getting them something to eat.

One of the doors to the Priestess' quarters was open, so Mist tentatively knocked before peering inside. The room was simple but not sparse. Potted plants took up every spot sunlight touched, covering the floor, hanging from ropes against the walls and by windows. Mist could almost imagine she'd stepped outside. A large, round bed was to her left, where even more plants hung overhead. To her right was a simple chaise, with bookshelves lining the walls on either side.

Gaelin sat on the chaise, the metal ball Fennicks stole in one hand and a book in the other. He didn't look up at her knock. His brow furrowed as he read, eyes obviously darting over information on the page as he searched for answers.

Ifera sat on a mat on the ground, legs crossed, hands on her knees. Her eyes were closed as her lips moved, whispering to herself or Dia'veh. Mist couldn't quite tell. Sorrow shone in the lines of her weary face.

Another knock had Ifera's golden eyes sliding open. "How can I help you, young Mist?"

"Aven and Dinon haven't eaten since we got back. I was hoping—"

"I'll warm some broth for them. Start simple," the Priestess said. "Look there for some flatbread I made earlier. They can have that as well."

Mist did as commanded, locating a round wooden box with layers of bread inside. She hated to take from them, but promised herself she would bring back food in trade. As she gathered up the box, Ifera warmed broth over the fire pit against the wall adjacent to the double doors. Once it was ready, Mist scooped two bowls and, balancing them on the lid of the bread, carried them out for Dinon and Aven.

"Drink this," she said, kneeling beside them. "You need to fill your stomachs."

"I feel sick," Aven murmured.

"That's normal." Mist set a bowl next to each of them before opening the box of flat bread.

"I keep seeing his puddle of blood on the bridge. Why can't I think about anything else?"

"We should have been down there." Dinon said in a flat voice.

Mist put a hand on each of their shoulders and tugged. Not hard. Just enough to draw them in. Neither resisted. They collapsed against her, faces pressing into either shoulder as they let go. Aven's body shuddered, violent sobs shaking through her so hard she shook Mist too. Dinon was quieter, softer, like the possessing anger had finally leeched away. Their hands pinched her back, clutching at her like a lifeline. Mist just held them tight, stroking their hair, squeezing now and then.

"Kanai wanted you both safe."

They lifted their heads to find Anyvath standing over them.

"Don't," Dinon said through clenched teeth.

She ignored the command, instead falling into a crouch. "You are young. You do not know these kinds of choices yet. Kanai was a leader. He knew what it meant to come on this mission, and he knew what it meant to stay. You may hate me, but I did what he wished."

"He stayed for Willa and she didn't make it," Aven said. "He died for nothing."

Anyvath tilted her head, a sigh slipping out of her. "If we all perished, then perhaps he died for nothing. But you are both here and that is something. Kanai did not die feeling like he accomplished nothing."

"You don't know anything about him," Dinon hissed, wiping at their cheeks angrily.

"It is easy to understand a kindred spirit."

Tears well in Mist's eyes as she scraped her nails over the imprint on her pendant's armlet. Dinon didn't want to hear it, but sadness filled Anyvath's voice. Her eyes were gray, the luster of her usually rainbow skin gone. The vibrance of her shifted form had faded to a ghost of its normal beauty.

"I have lived a long life, darlings" Anyvath said, her doe ears drooping. "I have seen friends fall to time, blade, and worse. Your hearts are shattered, but do not steal Kanai's bravery from him. Nor Dev's or Willa's. They did what most could never dream. Walking to one's death with weapons raised and teeth bared is—" She licked her lips, a single tear slipping down her cheek. "When you've seen as many break and run as I have, you could understand. Kanai made a choice only leaders can make. Hate me if you must. I will not hold that against you. But if I put you at risk trying to save him when he was already lost..." She shook her head. "When my time finally comes and he and I meet once more, I'll not face his rage over risking your lives."

Mist's chest cracked open. She hadn't meant for it to happen. Aven needed strength right now, but she couldn't help it. Her vision blurred as control fled in the face of Anyvath's sorrow. It was so like Eega's. And Papi's. All those back home who chased death instead of running from it.

Someone kneeling down drew Mist's face from Aven's shoulder. Ifera settled on her knees, a single candle in her hand. She touched the water in the pool, catching a droplet that she rolled between her fingertips.

"Might I pray for you?"

Dinon nodded heartily, but Aven tensed against Mist's chest.

"I don't want to pray today."

Ifera turned sad eyes on her. "I understand. It is too fresh. Loss is the greatest destroyer of our connection to Dia'veh."

Aven swallowed hard as she looked at the water. "Why would Dia'veh let this happen?"

Ifera tilted her head. "You speak of death as if it is a punishment."

"It is."

The Priestess shook her head, a sad smile curving her lips. "Child, death is part of nature. It is as natural as birth, as breathing, as living. Fearing it will get you nowhere. It always catches up eventually. Facing it head on and claiming every moment before it arrives gives you more power than fearing it ever will. Your friends claimed the ultimate power. You should not disparage that."

"Our people believe we return to what we came from." Dinon dipped their hand in the water and lifted a palmful, letting it drip drop through their clenched fingers. "Our bodies return to Sholindrea and our souls return to Dia'veh."

Aven watched the water drip. "It doesn't matter. You're still gone."

"Be sad for that loss," Ifera said, waving her hand over the candle, making its flame dance. "Saying goodbye is never easy. The hurting only fades with time. Try to seek the joy found in knowing they completed their journey and earned their peace. Death is not a punishment or an end. It is the beginning of something new. For them and for you. Their soul has taken a new turn and yours must now follow a separate path."

She turned golden eyes on Aven, her gaze traveling over the circle of Mist's arms around her. "But trust in our connections. We are bound through love and grace. Nothing is forever, even paths diverging. What brought you together will lead you to cross paths again."

Hunger drove a desperate look to pass from Aven to Mist. A hunger for Ifera's words to be true, laced with fear. It sparked in the wobble of Aven's mouth and the crinkle of her eyes. She had only just accepted that Dia'veh did more than create and survey like some sort of bored, eternal thing. What words could give her what she ached for?

"You don't have to believe any of that right now," Mist said, resting her chin on her shoulder. "Today, let's focus on what all of them accomplished. They got us back here. We can save Yunaii from whatever the Soulless are planning."

Aven didn't look satisfied, but she still nodded weakly. "We just need to figure that out."

"I believe they intend to destroy Yunaii entirely."

They all turned to find Gaelin standing on the other side of the pool, holding the metal ball before him.

"Did you figure out what that thing is?" Weariness lingered in Aven's voice, reminding Mist the day was almost over and she hadn't eaten. With a pointed look, she pushed the bowl of cooling broth into Aven's hands and stared until she took a sip.

"I have a few theories," Gaelin said. "May I have that candle, dear one?"

Ifera obliged, walking to his side and handing it over. Gaelin set the ball and candle down before withdrawing a small, curved blade from his vambrace.

"What are you doing?" Mist asked, putting the other bowl of broth in Dinon's hand.

Gaelin held up a finger before carefully running the blade over a section of silver metal that shone against the craggy iron of the rest of it. A chunk the size of a fingernail peeled away like butter.

"Why is it so soft?" Anyvath asked with a curious frown. "I have never seen metal cut that way without heat."

Gaelin analyzed the piece stuck to the tip of his blade. "If my theory is correct, this is a soft metal that is highly reactive to both fire and water."

"Dear one." Ifera rested a hand on his forearm. "I admire your studious and thorough mind, but might I beg a faster explanation?"

His silvery gaze flicked over all of them before he gave a slight nod. "Of course. Please, forgive me." He carefully scraped the metal onto the ground before slicing the small piece in half. "Watch."

He lifted the first half to the candle. It ignited in a flash of bright yellow flame.

"It's explosive, like we thought," Aven said, taking a bite of flatbread.

"Yes, but observe this." Gaelin scooped the second half with his blade and flicked it into the prayer pool.

Bubbles fizzed as white smoke rose. Mist leaned forward curiously just before the metal flared and caught fire. "What in Sholindrea's name?"

Gaelin returned the blade to his vambrace. "I believe the metal to be the source of ignition. The ball is either filled with this substance, or with a more explosive powder meant to cause a great deal of damage."

"Enough damage to do what, though?" Mist asked. "I didn't see enough of those balls to destroy all of Yunaii. It's too big. How could they—"

"It reacts to water," Aven said, staring at the pool, rubbing her finger back and forth over the tip of Kali's fang. "Could the blast destroy rock?"

Gaelin frowned. "Perhaps. I would need to conduct tests outside of the canyon to know its efficacy and power."

She drew in a shuddering breath. "Do you think enough of them could destroy the dam?"

Dinon and Mist gasped as Ifera's eyes widened.

"If the dam were to fail, Yunaii would be flooded," Gaelin said matter-of-factly. "An effective form of extermination."

Aven dropped her head into her hands with an exhausted sigh.

"But what about the dragons?" Mist said, looking at Anyvath. "The Soulless came for the dragons and most are on the roost. The wave wouldn't affect them."

"Destroying our source of food and allies would undoubtedly cause Rielnor to lead the flight somewhere new." Anyvath gazed up at the darkening sky, as if she could see the roost through the Eilawi's leaves. "We are vulnerable whilst traveling. No guaranteed sustenance, hatchlings forced to make the journey, and the unknown of our reception by strange Sholi. It would destabilize the flight and leave us vulnerable."

"So that's their plan. Drown, hunt, and kill every shifter they can." Mist shook her head, overtaken by the same exhaustion no doubt washing over Aven. Days of this. Days of fighting and hurting and healing, with little rest in between, and no hope of rest in the future. The Soulless already held the dam. Their attack could come at any moment. A tidal wave could very well wash over them that very night.

"We need to evacuate the canyon as soon as possible," Anyvath said, pushing to her feet, attention already on the door. "I must go to the flight. Dragon wings will ensure everyone's escape. Thudan and I can rally them until—"

"They're coming!" Pryn shouted, running through the doorway, her wide eyes shining bright yellow. "Rielnor and Emriel are back. And they're not alone!"

CHAPTER
Thirty-Three

Aven

ven jumped to her feet, head buzzing as they all ran for the door. Mist's hand remained clasped within her own, even as Dinon cut them off, leading the mad dash outside. Cool night air brushed their skin and they all skidded to a stop on the Temple stairs.

Emriel flew ahead, winding around like a snake. Only when Aven noticed Rielnor hissing and swiping at her with his wings, did she understand he was herding his kit. He struggled to keep her from darting back as he cradled something against his belly—clearly something precious.

Still, the flight leader drove her down. The way she collided with the ground sent pebbles bouncing over rocks and tree roots like frightened bugs. Rielnor landed more carefully, touching down on his hind legs as his wings fluttered, his tender movements so like the day he snatched Aven and Mist out of the sky.

Yliva half ran, half flew to the flight leader with arms outstretched—reaching for gray wings dangling from his claws.

Willa.

Rielnor brought his feet down and carefully deposited his prize on the ground. As his talons moved away, a mixed cry of relief and fear ripped from Aven.

Dev sat on his bottom, dripping wet, with Willa clutched to his chest. She wasn't moving. He wasn't blinking. Aven ran for them, skidding over rocks and dirt when she reached their side.

Yliva knelt down, her trembling hands hovering, as if she was afraid to touch them. Willa's head lay limp against Dev's chest, her lips blue and face pale as death. One of her wings bent at a horrible angle, forcing Aven to look away. Not soon enough to miss the jagged edges of protruding bone.

"Is she?" Yliva whispered.

"She's breathing." Dev's voice cracked. "She's breathing."

Aven swallowed a lump swelling in her throat. By the Maker. It had been a whole day since the dam. Had he clung to her all this time? In the river? Both of them were dripping, icy water pooling in the surrounding dirt.

"Let her go, Dev," Ifera whispered, appearing on his other side. "Let me help her."

"I can't." His eyes clamped shut as he began rocking. "She'll drown."

"No," Yliva said, finally laying hands on him. "You kept her alive. Now let us save her."

He shook his head, renewing his tight grip around her limp body. "I told her. Why didn't she listen? I told her she would die."

Aven choked back a sob and forced herself to kneel. "Dev. You have to let go or she will die. She's frozen and still bleeding."

His eyes snapped to Aven's face, the boy she knew lost beneath terrified eyes and a trembling mouth. "Kanai. And Fennicks—"

"I know." She gently took hold of his wrists. "We can't help them. But we can help her."

He hesitated before his grip went slack. Gaelin immediately snatched Willa up before carrying her into the Temple. Ifera and Yliva fell in step behind him, speaking in hushed voices. The flock leader whispered something about the damage to Willa's wing, and Ifera's voice sounded grim as they disappeared inside. Pryn lingered in their wake, still staring at the sky as if Fennicks might appear.

Dev remained dripping in the mud, his eyes unfocused even when Mist threw a cloak over his shoulders and began rubbing some life back into him. "They're going to help her."

"You saved her, Dev," Dinon said in a hollow voice. They almost looked a bit disappointed.

They must have been hoping Rielnor saved Kanai.

Aven blew out a quick breath, angry that every time she thought she had no tears left, something proved her wrong. Just thinking his name brought Kali's sorrow screaming through her body. Heat flashed, followed by icy cold. It felt like she'd never stop shaking.

"We have to go back."

Aven found Emriel on two legs once more, her pleading eyes fixed on Rielnor, who had shifted as well. Sansia's dying light glinted off their vibrant hair, highlighting them like actors in a play. Rielnor, the scarred monster. Emriel, the trembling child.

"Absolutely not," he said. "Look at all they have done. I will not risk it."

Emriel stomped towards him. "They have Vhis!"

"What?" Dinon gasped, making her whirl on him. "What about Kanai?"

Her lips wobbled as she shook her head. That one motion crushed Dinon all over. They'd seen Kanai go down, saw the blood, but one jerk of Emriel's chin confirmed the truth of their loss. The pride leader of the lynx was dead.

Emriel ran her hands over her scalp, pulling at her hair with blanched fingers. "The Soulless. They have *Fennicks*. I saw. Those things chained them up and threw them over the dam. They're just hanging there like a piece of meat. The Soulless will leave them there to starve if we don't go back. Or worse. If they realize we're not coming—"

"We are not going," Rielnor said. "It is obviously a trap."

"I don't care! I'm going to save Vhisari. You have to help me." Her manic energy calmed as she laid both hands on Rielnor's arms. "Please, Eewa. This is Vhis. I know I'm a disappointment, but Vhis has always been there. Always followed you. They wouldn't hesitate to save you."

Rielnor crossed his arms. "Yes, they would. They would know not to waste lives trying to save me. They would look after the flight."

Emriel screamed in his face, wheeling away as her fury echoed to the darkening sky. It was chorused by birds screeching from among the Eilawi tree's branches. Their ominous wails bleating like a funeral's march.

"Please! Please help me, Eewa." She dropped to her knees, back curving as she laid her face on the ground. "Please. I have to save them."

Soft footsteps preceded Pryn rushing to Emriel with outstretched arms. She went down to her knees and laid over Emriel's back, hugging her shoulders like they'd known each other a lifetime. It was so simple and tender, their shared grief for Fennicks shaking their bodies as they cried.

"Rielnor," Anyvath said, stepping closer. Aven had almost forgotten she was there. "There is something you must know."

He blew a breath through his nose before turning his gaze on her. "What's that?"

She lifted her chin, unblinking beneath his stare. "Truthseeker Gaelin has revealed a potential plot to destroy the dam."

Rielnor's head fell back as he looked at the sky, his arms falling to his side. "To the torments with us all."

***

All Aven wanted to do after that was sleep. Her head hurt, her stomach ached, waves of nausea kept rolling through her. She needed to eat, but couldn't choke down more than a few bites. Not when the fate of Yunaii was debated over like the weather.

Rielnor hadn't left the Matriarchs a choice in coming to the Temple this time. From what Mama said, he'd practically snatched the three women from their beds and dragged them to the meeting. That he'd sent Anyvath for Mama and Papa had surprised them both, but Aven was grateful. After everything, seeing them stride into the Temple had nearly sent her to her knees.

They all now sat in a large circle around the prayer pool. Aven, Mist, Mama, and Papa were next to Gaelin. Rielnor, Anyvath, and Thudan sat on their other side. Then the griffins, led by Yliva. Pryn with the Tribouin Elders. Dev with Commander Senwe and Zoli. The three Matriarchs. And three new lynx, who sat pensively with Dinon. News of Kanai's death had not been well-received. The older lynx looked like abandoned kittens.

Ifera remained with Willa in one of the back rooms so Yliva could attend the meeting. Aven guessed she also didn't want to distract the Matriarchs from the problem at hand.

Emriel strode around the outskirts of the circle, swinging her daggers in loose circles. She was letting the leaders speak. *For now.*

Once Gaelin finished explaining every bit of news and speculation, he looked at Rielnor with raised brows. "This is everything we know. Now it is time for each of you to decide a course of action for your people."

"You want us to evacuate on the possibility the Soulless will destroy the dam?" Matriarch Revari asked. "You have no other proof than that little hunk of metal."

Gaelin dipped his chin in acknowledgment. "You are not wrong. We cannot know for certain what they intend. We would need eyes on the dam and the surrounding area."

"It wouldn't be a bad idea to send someone," Emriel said, spinning her dagger as she circled past the Tribouin.

"It will take too long." Rielnor shot a glare at her. "If blowing the dam is their plan, a scout will not make it there and back before a tidal wave washes away every man, woman, and child in this canyon."

"Is there a chance the attack at the dam was revenge?" Elder Jywe asked, looking at Emriel with cold eyes. "*You* killed the Soulless in the market, and your account is that you potentially killed more at the port. Perhaps this Summoner's intent was to punish you for killing her people."

Emriel turned on her tiptoe, head tilting like a snake. "If she wants me, she'll bleed everything I care about first. Unfortunately for you, I made the mistake of protecting this dung hole out of the kindness of my misguided heart. If it's revenge she wants, then a tidal wave won't be enough. She'll come for heads. Maybe some hearts. Probably an army of dead shifters she can ship back home." Emriel crouched before him and flashed her teeth in a feral smile. "Either way, you die."

Blood drained from Elder Jywe's face, and that seemed to satisfy her. Emriel stood once more and continued her pacing.

"I wish my kit was wrong," Rielnor said, eyeing her as she passed. "But the Soulless' nature is not of mercy. Their intent is revealed. If it is not the dam, it *will* be something else."

"So, we begin evacuating everyone from the canyon," Commander Senwe said. "As soon as possible. Tribouin and Qinawe need to be the highest priority. My kin reside in the canopy of the Eilawi tree and the griffins can fly to safety."

"And then what do we do?" Matriarch Yana asked. She'd laid her staff down beside her, but kept her hands folded in her lap as if she still cradled it beneath her palms.

"Yes, my dear egg-warden," Emriel said, rubbing an imaginary blemish from her dagger. "Please enlighten the class on what we do once everyone is evacuated."

"Em," Mist said through clenched teeth. "Please."

"See, here is the problem." Emriel slid her dagger back into its sheath and whirled on them. "What comes next? We leave all those people to Sansia's mercy, waiting for a tidal wave to destroy their homes? No shelter. No food stores. We'll serve them to the Soulless like fattened pigs."

The leaders shifted beneath her glare as she reversed her circle, walking close enough she could drag a hand through someone's hair as she passed.

"Are we assuming they'll break the dam and call it a day?" She rubbed her hands together and smiled. "Good job, boys! No need to make sure we got those pesky shifters." Emriel's eerie laugh sent a shiver down Aven's spine. "They could have let us pass over that dam yesterday, but they didn't. They wanted blood. And bodies. They're not letting anyone off this island alive. We're too useful dead."

Aven looked to Rielnor, waiting for his rebuttal. Would he shut her down once again? Undermine her desire to fight?

Emriel gave him no chance. She stopped behind the Matriarchs and looked down her nose at them.

"Will you wait on those cliffs for the Soulless to slaughter you?" Her gaze moved to the Tribouin. "Will you?"

"We could leave," said Matriarch Hanawi. Beneath her usual fire, an acrid smell burned. Not the bitterness of fear. This was something else. Soul-shaking terror. "Our people once migrated with the herds. Yunaii has been our home, but we need not remain."

Emriel nodded as she continued walking. "Of course, but then, the Soulless razed the port. Sank every ship. Killed every trader. So—perhaps you could survive here on snakes and rain water, but that's not what your people have trained for."

Elder Dasoln glanced at Rielnor. "Could your dragons not assist?"

A satisfied smirk slipped across Emriel's lips. "Yes, flight leader. Could they not?"

Rielnor's mouth thinned, but he didn't answer.

"I didn't think so. You see, he's only here because he feels guilty. He lost a dragon and got a lynx killed because he wouldn't listen to me. Once that guilt fades, he'll take the flight and leave. Flight first, right, Eewa?"

"One day, I'm going to feed your insolent tongue to you," Thudan said, leaning forward.

"Good boy. You keep yipping at your master's feet."

"What is it you want?" Commander Senwe asked.

"Don't indulge her," Thudan growled.

But the door was open. Aven already knew what Emriel wanted, and though it was hard to admit, she wanted it too.

"We need to attack." Emriel surveyed everyone present. "We need to kill them before they kill us. Take back the dam. Hold it. Make sure they can't hurt anyone else on this island."

"And, of course, save your mate," Rielnor said. "Let us not hide factors since we are laying ourselves bare."

Emriel shrugged as if Fennicks was an afterthought. "That too. But you know I wanted to attack before they took a hostage. Or—" she glanced at Dinon. "Killed the pride leader."

"Your intentions are true," Gaelin said in a low tone. "I must protest against using the pain of the lynx to get what you desire, though. *That* is not truthful."

"Don't worry, Truthseeker," Dinon said, glancing at the older pride mates, all varying in age. "The lynx have already decided what they want."

Aven stiffened as she turned to him. "What's that?"

"The pride has committed to a hunt," one of the older lynx said. A white mane framed his dark brown face—an elder even to Kanai. "Tomorrow, we will avenge our pride leader."

"You will die," Dev said softly, staring at his hands.

The lynx all regarded him with varying degrees of pity as Zoli gripped his shoulder.

"Many might," Dinon said, gaze sliding to Anyvath. "But we will not flee from death. We will claim the blood of those who killed Kanai. They can stand against a few, but our pride's hunters are many."

Anyvath glanced at Rielnor before she closed her eyes, her head dipping into a bow. "I will help you."

Rielnor and Thudan both jerked their attention to her, but she refused to meet their eyes.

"You know I'm coming too," Emriel said. "Nothing like killing Soulless in the morning. Best way to start the day."

Mist shook her head, even as Aven silently agreed. The Soulless had done heinous things. They would do more if left to their own devices. They would come for everyone in Yunaii, even the children. They'd spared none at Shard's Port.

"The griffins will assist you," Yliva said, sitting straight-backed on her knees.

"The flock would be more useful in the evacuation," Rielnor said.

"Perhaps." She met his stare unflinchingly. "I can commit some to that cause, but many of my flock already desired vengeance after the attack in the market. I was able to argue against it, but now—" Yliva glanced at the back wall, where Willa fought for her life behind the doors. "One of our flock will never fly again." She turned back to the leaders, avoiding looking directly at Dev. "Wilella's wing was too badly damaged. It had to be removed."

Mist gasped and grabbed Aven's hand, tears welling in her eyes. All around the circle, those who traveled to the port reacted similarly. Even Emriel's brows knit together in a pained frown. Cheerful Willa, who fluttered and leaped and danced. Fearless Willa, who floated through tree branches and attacked Soulless head-on. Aven couldn't imagine her not bouncing around with a grin on her face, flitting through the air like a flirty little fairy.

Dev stared into the pool, his face schooled into the icy mask of a soldier.

"This loss, and the loss of our friend and ally amongst the lynx, has left my people resolute," Yliva said. "Tomorrow, we will hunt with the lynx."

Aven squeezed Mist's hand, drawing her attention. She needed her understanding, even as Aven sorted the words in her head. This was a fight she couldn't walk away from. Not for a place amongst the Qinawe or a chance to stay safe. Kanai had accepted her on his hunt. Mist gave her a place in her heart, but she had the strength to fight back thanks to Kali, who deserved vengeance for the death of her cub.

Mist's gaze moved over Aven's face, and a soft smile graced her lips. "We're going, too."

Aven dropped a soft kiss on her cheek. What did she do to deserve this girl?

"I hoped you'd say that," Emriel said. "I have a use for you two."

"So not only will you rise to conflict with anger," Hanawi began. "Now you seek violence when the bond needs you."

Mama stiffened. "You have never needed nor wanted my cub before. You will not judge her now for risking her life to keep us all safe."

"You have failed your daughter, Tomen," Elder Jywe said, staring at Papa.

"Why?" Pryn asked in a soft voice. Both Elders looked at her, their eyes wide. "Soulless are coming to kill us all. Why aren't any of you proud Aven wants to protect us?"

"Because she seeks bloodshed at every turn," Elder Dasoln said, glaring at Pryn. "Even her Matriarchs see it. She allows herself to give into baseless instincts."

Pryn straightened, meeting him glare for glare. "Will you not draw your weapon if Soulless come for the evacuated? Will you let us die?"

He put a hand on her shoulder, his mouth thinning in a sad smile. "It is more complicated than that. You need not worry yourself. Your father and brother will keep you safe. Your Elders will keep you safe."

"You know what, kid?" Emriel said, batting Dasoln's hand away. "You stick with me. *I'll* keep you safe and you can stab anyone that gets past me."

Pryn tried hiding her smile, but by the looks of frustration on the Elders' faces, Aven guessed they saw it anyway. She didn't know whether to be impressed or frightened. Pryn and Fennicks had been a dangerous team. She didn't want to imagine the trouble this pair could get into.

"This hunt will not end how you hope," Rielnor sighed, deep and loud. "But I will not interfere with Anyvath or Mist lending their assistance to the lynx."

"Come on, flight leader." Emriel crossed her arms over her chest. "You can do better than that."

The look he threw at her reminded Aven of the ones she got after sassing Mama. "I cannot ask the flight to go on this hunt. Many of them left Estellias to be free of conflicts such as these. The Soulless came equipped to kill dragons. I will not put them in the line of fire. What I can offer is a commitment to aiding in the evacuation. With dragon wings, we will get more people to safety, faster."

Emriel opened her mouth to undoubtedly argue, but Yliva cut her off.

"We understand your feelings, flight leader. Thank you for allowing Anyvath and Mist to join us."

"The Linseen will assist in the hunt as well," said Commander Senwe. He glanced at Dev and Zoli before putting a hand over his heart. "Our peace has been destroyed. Many of my kin have felt the Creator summon us to action. The soul-called will fight with you."

"We can always count on the elves to embody Dia'veh's ideals." Emriel's narrowed eyes cut a cool look at Rielnor. "Thank Sholindrea *some* have not forgotten the ways of the Creator."

CHAPTER
Thirty-Four

Aven

Aven didn't know when she dozed off. She'd kept her eyes open long enough to hear plans for the evacuation. Then things blurred, and the next thing she knew, Mama was shaking her awake.

"Time to get up, cub."

She blinked rapidly, urging herself not to drift off again. It was so tempting to give in to her heavy body.

"The lynx prepare to leave," Mama said. "The dragon, Anyvath, has offered to carry you and Mist so you can rest on the journey."

"Journey?" Aven rubbed at her eyes. How much had she missed?

"To the dam, my girl," Papa said, holding out a cup. Aven chugged it down, the icy water like a kick in the face.

She looked around, overwhelmed by the bodies rushing everywhere. Most, she didn't recognize. Mist slept on the cushions beside her and Gaelin made his way through the room, talking to elves clad in armor, lynx milling about on four legs, and griffins who hadn't shifted yet. The Matriarchs and Elders were gone.

"How long was I out?"

"Not long enough." Concern showed in the lines of Mama's brow. "You must rest on the flight there. Do not go into this hunt exhausted."

"Yes, Mama."

"And take this." She pressed the handle of her axe into Aven's loose palm.

"I have my hatchet."

Mama's eyes were wide, almost fearful. "A second blade might be useful. You've practiced with two."

Aven ran her fingers over the curves of the axe's handle, a pit forming in her stomach. "What if the Soulless come for you? You'll be defenseless."

"We have plenty of weapons, cub." She closed Aven's fingers around the polished wood. "You worry about you. And Mist. You two come back safe."

Mist. She still slept at Aven's side, lips parted, her face peaceful. That she survived on these precious moments of rest was a marvel. If only she could stay in the Temple and recover. This fight wasn't the place for her, but Emriel's plan relied on the tiny racing dragon no one ever rooted for. There'd be no sneaking away or keeping her safe. Not that Mist would let them. As soon as she woke, she'd be on their tail, anyway.

It hurt to disturb her. Aven rubbed Mist's arm, murmuring her name, coaxing her from whatever dreams she'd escaped to. Yet she still jerked up, eyes sharp and alert, as if she expected an attack. Her gaze shifted over those rushing around the Temple before she relaxed.

"Time to go?" She stretched her arms, tension leeching away with a yawn.

"Yes," Papa said, offering her water as well. "We brought your pike from the cave. Though from what I heard of your sister's plan, I'm not sure you'll need it."

"She doesn't think much of me as a warrior," Mist said. "I can't say I blame her."

Mama fixed her with a stern glare. "Then you be extra careful. These things will not hesitate, so neither can you."

"I won't." Mist's face smoothed, any humor gone from her eyes. "We will both be back before you know it."

Papa touched each of their faces as his lips trembled. "You had better. Do not make us come looking for you."

Aven nuzzled into his hand. "We won't. We've got too much to celebrate to botch this thing."

"What do you mean?"

Aven glanced at Mist, raising her brows in a silent question. It felt so inappropriate to think about their relationship, but just in case, Aven wanted that moment she'd dreamed of. Mist took her hand, a nervous smile pulling across her face as she looked at Mama and Papa.

"Aven asked me to be her Chosen."

Aven grinned and squeezed her hand. "We're Promised!"

The joy in her parents' eyes shone brighter than Sansia gleaming on the horizon. Mama's teeth flashed as an excited yelp slipped from Papa's lips. Both of them crashed into her and Mist, their arms wrapping tight around them, squashing them all together in a hot, messy hug that brought tears to Aven's eyes.

"I am so happy for you, my girl," Papa said, kissing her forehead. "Both of you. You deserve this. You deserve all the happiness in the world."

Mama covered their joined hands with her own, her dark eyes raw with emotion. "Mist, you are everything I ever hoped for my cub. You complement one another the way two people should. I am so proud of you both."

Aven's lips trembled as she looked between her parent's faces. "Thank you. Both of you. I know you two think you let me down, but you never did. You never will. You taught me to be strong, and you showed me that love is so much bigger than anything else."

That brought more tears and more hugging. Aven reveled in every moment, every touch, trying to ignore the pit in her stomach that this could be the last time.

But it couldn't be.

She glanced at the prayer pool out of the corner of her eye. It was too much to step into the water. She couldn't with all eyes upon her. Many here were devoted to Dia'veh, but that didn't make her feel any less silly as she thought a simple prayer.

Please keep my family safe. That's all. Please don't let this be our last hug.

***

They were heading for the Temple's entrance when Ifera touched Aven's elbow. "Willa wishes to speak with you."

The urge to flee into the woods blossomed from Kali's soul. So many goodbyes and heavy conversations. Each one hollowed Aven out. Left room for more pain. But running wouldn't solve anything. She couldn't let these feelings rule her anymore.

With a silent nod, Aven followed Ifera, slipping through one of the single doors, revealing a room big enough for a bed, a collection of tree-sized plants, and three candles on a small table.

Willa lay on her side with a light blanket, knees pulled up, one arm under her head. Aven tried not to stare at the bandages at her back covering the stump of her amputated wing. Her pain had to be immeasurable.

She held out a hand so Aven went to her, falling on her knees by the bed. Willa's fiery eyes were heavy and unfocused. Ifera must have given her something so she could sleep, but her grip remained strong.

"How are you?" Aven asked, afraid to speak above a whisper.

One corner of Willa's mouth perked up. "Not bleeding or drowning, so, you know, better?"

It felt wrong to laugh, but the sound still slipped free. "What do you need?"

Willa squeezed her eyes shut, face pinching before she opened them again. Some of the fogginess had cleared. "Don't let him become a blood-seeker."

Aven squeezed Willa's hand. "Dev won't. He's too good."

"Fool boy thinks he'll avenge me or something." She inhaled sharply as if a bout of pain had suddenly hit. "There's too much avenging. Even the flock leader. Strength of mind, not blades. It's not our way."

"I hear you," Aven said, some of her own anger dimming.

"Poor, pitiful Willa," she said, nostrils curling with disgust. "I'm not a sad little victim for you all to cry and rage over. So, *don't.*"

What Anyvath said echoed in Aven's memories. *Don't steal their bravery.* Kanai and Willa had claimed their fates and now everyone spoke of them like victims of the Soulless instead of warriors who faced them unflinchingly.

"I'm sorry. This hunt? Do you want me to stop it?"

Willa blinked as if she considered it. Then she gave a faint shake of her head.

"No." Her unscathed wing flexed, and a hiss of pain slipped between her teeth. "If a ton beast stomped a lynx in a hunt, the pride would bring it down no matter the cost. Same for the flock. Just—don't use me as an excuse to ruin yourselves."

Aven nodded quickly. "We won't. I promise."

"Finish the hunt. Kill the Soulless." Willa squeezed her hand, nearly crushing her fingers. "Then life goes back to normal."

Whatever normal was. Aven didn't know what awaited her in Yunaii after this was over. She'd gone against the Matriarchs. Publicly. She had no idea where she would land after the hunt ended.

"I won't let this consume them," Aven said. "They'll come home whole."

Willa's gaze flicked between Aven's eyes, her soft mouth curving into a frown. "You come home whole too."

***

After bidding Ifera and Gaelin goodbye, Aven found Mist waiting with a change of clothes and a plate of food. She'd already dressed in what she said was dragonskin armor that would shift with her. Aven didn't want to think about where spare dragonskin came from.

They scarfed down their food while Aven changed into a pair of billowy pants, the material stretchier than she was used to. The top was of the same material. It wasn't armor, but hopefully, if she had to shift without warning, her clothing wouldn't be completely shredded. Once dressed, she strapped on her hatchet, Mama's axe, and a quiver of arrows. Claws weren't her only weapon, and the hunt had a plethora of those. At least a few of them needed blades.

Finally ready to go, they strode out of the Temple. Anyvath awaited, scales glittering in the moonlight and horn tips adorned with metal caps that were sharp and jagged. Emriel waited in her soft, feathery body, as usual choosing speed over strength.

Rielnor turned away from Dev and Pryn, who stood at Emriel's side.

"Flight leader," Mist said, bowing her head.

"Watch yourselves out there." He looked her over, taking in the black leather she'd molded from her dragonskin clothes. "Soulless don't fight like most. Their lives are not their priority. They worship death. Theirs and anyone else's."

Aven frowned. "Do we even know who sent them after the dragons?"

Rielnor's eyes cut away as the same bitterness often hovering around Hanawi melded into his ice-cold scent. "No."

"Don't lie," Aven warned. Now was not the time for word play and games. "Who sent them?"

Mist stiffened as Rielnor's face darkened. For a moment, Aven expected a threat or even a blow. His gaze flicked to her hand as it drifted to her hatchet, but eventually, he released a sigh.

"Just hope you never trifle with the master of the Soulless. They are not an enemy simple shifters can stand against. That's a battle for immortals."

Aven swallowed her own sigh at the vague answer. Maybe one day she would get a clear response from a dragon.

"Mist," Rielnor said, scars on his face pinching when he frowned. "Are you sure about this? You have never chosen violence before."

Her back straightened as she stared up at the flight leader. "This is the right thing to do. I think you know it. Even if you disagree."

"You both have your Eega's fire." Rielnor glanced back at Emriel, his large hands clenching into fists. "It will one day be the death of me."

Mist reached out to him, nearly jerking back once or twice before touching his arm. Rielnor whirled to face her, surprise brightening his eyes.

"It's not her fire, flight leader." Mist met his gaze unflinchingly. "It's Dia'veh's. What is a greater show of love than serving each other?"

Another sigh slipped free before Rielnor pulled away. "May Dia'veh protect you."

"And Sholindrea receive us," Mist said, dipping her chin. Rielnor did the same before walking towards the Temple. Aven didn't miss how he looked back at Emriel or how sorrow overwhelmed his timeless scent.

Once he was gone, Aven peered over at Dev. "Ready to hunt?"

"I hope you are," he replied, motioning for Pryn to climb up on Emriel's back. "This will end with no feasts. Just death."

Willa's worried face flashed behind Aven's eyes. *Don't let him become a blood-seeker.* She needed to make Dev remember himself. Not the soldier or the dragon rider, but the boy that began slipping out since the Soulless' first attack.

"Lighten up," she said, clambering onto Anyvath's spiny back to settle behind Mist. "Keep being such a storm cloud and I'll start pelting you with sticks and rocks, too. We all know that gets you going."

He shot her a glare, but Aven could have sworn a fissure cracked in that horrible mask. He'd almost smiled. It was a start.

Both dragons tensed, gathering their feet together before leaping into the air. Aven's heart rose into her throat, a mix of buzzing thrill and the usual fearful jolt washing through her. Flying was almost second nature after all this time, but Anyvath was a new level of power. It took just a few wingbeats and they'd reached the canopy.

Aven glanced at the ground where little fires moved through the night. The evacuation had begun. The Tribouin lands glowed with yellow light as their people rushed to pack anything they could carry. The Qinawe were much the same.

Somewhere down there, Mama and Papa were helping people get out. It didn't matter they'd always been outcasts, they'd be some of the last to leave, especially if there were still children in the canyon.

The thought left Aven anxious, but her family most likely felt the same. They watched Anyvath crest over the cliffs, knowing Aven rode for a fight most had the good sense to run from.

Once they'd risen above the canyon walls, the pride of lynx appeared, flanked by a flock of griffins. Even in the moonlight, their vibrant crests and patterns of color shone brightly. Each one unique in their markings. Linseen rode on the magnificent birds, clad in green and tan armor, all carrying bows, arrows, and scimitars. Commander Senwe led them all into battle, Dia'veh's call claiming his soul before the rest of his people. Aven wished Zoli had remained behind, where his gentle heart could help with the evacuation, but he rode beside his leader with the same steely look Dev wore.

Anyvath caught up with the flock, bellowing an earth-shattering roar, and the shifters answered in kind. Yowls, screeches, and howls from the Linseen echoed to the night sky. Aven grinned and belted a call as well, Kali's fang heavy against her chest.

The hunt had begun.

***

Anyvath and Emriel landed far enough from the dam that the Soulless wouldn't see their approach. They'd flown as fast as they could, racing Sansia's approach. Soon her golden light would streak across the sky, chasing away any hope of surprise.

They touched down just as the sky lightened. A plateau of reddish rocks cresting high above the canyon walls provided a safe hiding spot for them to wait. Aven, Mist, Pryn, and Dev quickly dismounted and unloaded their gear, leaving the dragons to shift back to two legs.

Once Emriel and Anyvath joined them, it was time to recon and await the pride's arrival. The flock had stayed with them on the off chance they encountered Soulless along the way. They had a better chance of surviving an ambush together.

"Anyvath, keep watch with the elf and the girl." Emriel gazed up at the towering rocks sheltering them. "Mist, Aven, let's see what we can of the bastards."

Aven raised her eyes and gulped. It was not going to be a fun climb. Especially without wings or claws. An even worse fall if she slipped.

"Don't worry," Mist said, looping an arm around her waist. "I'll catch you if you fall."

"Deal," Aven said with a grin. "Try not to stare at my butt too much or you might slip. I can't have my safety net too distracted."

"You're no fun." Mist laid her head on Aven's shoulder, her eyelashes fluttering playfully. "That'll be the only thing worth looking at."

"For Sholindrea's sake, shut up," Emriel said, already clawing her way up the rock. "I will throw myself off of here if I have to listen to your flirting the whole way up."

The smile Mist flashed dazzled and Aven tried to fix that in her mind as she climbed. One foothold there, one ledge here. She made each move carefully, letting claws dig out from her nail beds to help her grip. Emriel kept the path as clear as possible, never pulling too far ahead and always pointing out suitable spots to grab. The farther they went, the more Aven considered begging Mist to carry her the rest of the way, even if that risked the Soulless spotting them. Climbing rock was not like going up a tree.

When they finally crested over one of the lower ridges, Aven shimmied up and laid panting, face down against the rock. Dust kicked up her nose, but she didn't care. Going back down would be even worse.

Rock crunched under Emriel's boots as she crawled across the ledge, making her way to the other side. After a few more deep breaths, Aven followed. Her muscles twitched horribly, but she did her best to move quietly.

The dam was a distant sight, but she could make out the shape of Sholindrea's carving. Sansia's light illuminated her crown of hair, gleaming over the rocky curls. It was said the

Great Mother had hair like a sunset, shifting from golden yellow all the way to navy blue. Aven could imagine all her glory. She surveyed the canyon with that gentle, beckoning smile. It chased away any hint that blood had been spilled over her walls.

"What do you see, bloodkin?" Emriel asked, crouching down.

Mist strained her eyes as she lay on her belly. "They've set up more ballistae."

"How many?"

"At least ten." Mist tapped her finger on the rock. "Eight on the bridge and one on either side of the canyon."

Emriel scowled. "Anyvath won't be much good to us. What about the explosives? Any sign of them?"

Mist shook her head, her brow still furrowed. Aven didn't know how she was seeing anything from so far.

"Em. I see Fennicks."

Emriel's jaw tightened as she stared at the dam, her body quivering. Were it not for the ballistae, she very well might have leaped from the rock and flown for the other dragon.

"Promise me something," she whispered.

What in Sholindrea's name could make her sound so soft? And young. A hint of fear swelled in her scent, making Aven's nose itch.

"No matter what happens out there, bloodkin, promise me you'll get Vhis. I know I should be more worried about the dam but—Vhisari matters more."

Mist sat up with a curious look on her face. "Don't take this as me asking you to choose sides but, you do know Fennicks tried to kill me. Not a day before you showed up in the market. Aven and I were almost splattered in front of half of Yunaii."

Emriel shook her head. "Vhis didn't try to kill you."

"How do you know?" Aven asked. The constant insistence Fennicks was not what they appeared had her instincts flaring. More secrets. Always more secrets.

"Vhis wasn't trying to hurt you." Emriel tore her gaze from the dam to look from Aven to Mist. "They just did what I told them to do."

"You what?" Only Mist's hand on her arm kept Aven from leaping for Emriel's throat. "You told them to attack her?"

"*No.* Don't be intentionally obtuse." Emriel dropped both knees to the rock, her palms flattening over her thighs. "I told Vhis to put Mist out of commission because the Soulless had arrived. I didn't want them to stumble over her. I figured she was safest burrowed deep in that little hole with your family."

Aven glanced at Mist. Clearly, her sister had given in to sleep deprivation or madness. That was the only way she could think sending Fennicks after Mist was a good idea.

"Why in Dia'veh's name didn't you just talk to me?" Mist asked. "Why is it always stabbing and maiming with you?"

Emriel waved a hand. "Words get nothing done and if I came to you, Rielnor would have known I was in Yunaii before I wanted him to."

"Right, of course." Mist shook her head. "You needed to trap him first."

"Bloodkin," Emriel said, sorrow giving way to a flash of anger. "You don't want to be involved in Eega's and my fight, then fine. Don't be involved. But keep your judgment to yourself. Everything I'm doing is to save lives. Everyone helping me is focused on saving lives. Saving Vhis is—"

She looked back at the dam, the spark guttering out. "It's the first thing I've done for me in centuries. All I'm asking for is your help. If not for them, then for me."

Aven thought back to all the little moments during their trip to Shard's Port. How often she caught Fennicks staring at Emriel, their jabs slowly turning to words of affection. Mist had told her that what was between them was over, but the desperation in Emriel's voice told the truth.

"For what it's worth," Emriel said with a shrug. "Vhis saw Rielnor and the elf on their tail. They knew my egg-warden would never let one of Eega's kits die. He hasn't let her go and Rielnor knows she'd never forgive him if any of us died in his charge."

Mist's shoulders drooped. "Is that the only reason he's been kind to me? An obsession with Eega?"

"No." Emriel's gaze softened as she fiddled with one of her golden rings. "Despite how insufferable he is, he's sometimes a good man. And you're kind of hard not to like."

"Really?" Mist brightened, a hint of a smile creeping up her face.

Emriel wiped her hands on her blue breeches before moving back the way they'd come. "Yeah. It's the most annoying thing about you."

A full grin spread across Mist's lips. "That's the nicest thing you've ever said to me."

"Well, keep being insufferably nice," Emriel said, throwing a leg over the ledge. "And help me save Vhis. I'll never ask anything else of you. I promise. I'll stop hounding you about fighting with our bloodkin. I'll let you live your life. Just help me."

Mist glanced at Aven, her brows raised. All these revelations. Aven didn't know how long it would take to sort out everything she'd seen and heard since Emriel arrived. It was such a mess. But there was one thing Aven could understand, and that was Emriel's desperation. If it was Mist dangling from the dam like fish bait, Aven would make any deal or bargain. It wouldn't matter. As long as she was safe.

Aven met Emriel's wavering stare and nodded. "We've got your back, Em."

CHAPTER
Thirty-Five

Aven

A dust cloud in the distance announced the approach of the lynx. They moved fast across the rocky landscape, but not fast enough. The Soulless would spot them long before they got near the dam.

"Time to work, kids," Emriel said, sheathing her freshly cleaned daggers. Her gaze went to Mist, who watched the dam from the edge of the cliff. "You got your part down?"

Mist nodded without looking away, her shoulders raised and tense. They'd argued for so long over her part to play. It meant leaving them all behind, and it was killing her.

"We're going to be okay," Aven whispered, bumping Mist's shoulder with her own.

"Last time I heard that, Kanai died and Willa lost a wing." She turned frightened eyes on Aven, her chin wobbly. "You've never fought a Soulless before."

"Nope," Aven said, flicking her thumbnail against the edge of Mama's axe. "But I've fought Mama. I'd rather face them over her."

That got the desired smile.

"Fair."

Mist glanced back at the dam before pressing a tentative kiss to Aven's lips. Fear lingered behind the soft touch, dimming the excitement welling in Kali's soul. Soon Aven would dig in with claws and blades, but first Mist needed to know tomorrow would come.

"I'll see you soon." Aven pressed a palm to her cheek, fingertips sliding into the silky hair behind her ear. "I won't be reckless. I promise. *You* worry about you. Watch those wings of yours. They're a pretty bright target."

Mist nodded before leaning in for another kiss. This one firmer, needier. Aven responded by pulling her close, indulging in her body's warmth as long as possible. When they parted, even Sansia couldn't keep back the chill that rushed over Aven's skin.

Mist cast a look at Anyvath, Dev, and Pryn, as if memorizing how they looked. Then her gaze settled on Emriel, and she held out a hand.

"Don't get yourself dead. Okay?"

Emriel pulled her into a fierce hug, cradling Mist's head like one might a baby's. "I'll do my best. Thank you, bloodkin."

Mist pulled out of her arms, backing up to the edge of the cliff. A smile slipped across her lips, despite the hollow look in her eyes. She stared at Aven as her arms stretched out to her sides and she tipped backwards into the canyon.

A chuckle slipped from Emriel as Aven ran for the gorge. "Drama runs in the family."

Aven couldn't disagree. Mist, Em, Rielnor. She could only imagine what their egg-layer was like. She peered down at the Lighe and caught a flash of white feathers diving into the water. Mist was off. Hopefully safe. Aven didn't know whether to be grateful or anxious about her departure, but she couldn't dwell. Mist had her job. Now the rest of them had to go to work.

***

Emriel made a slight change to the plan, as if needing to one-up her sister's dramatic flair. She'd originally intended to drop upon the bridge from the clouds. Send the Soulless scattering. But with the ballistae replaced, she wasn't taking the chance.

So instead of rushing the dam, or sneaking up on them, Emriel strolled her way across the wastes as if heading to the market for some bread.

On the other side of the canyon, Anyvath crept towards the opposite end of the bridge with Pryn nestled between her tucked wings. Her hissing and growling echoed over the water pouring through the spillways. It got the desired result. As soon as she drew near, the Soulless turned the bulk of the ballistae on her, leaving only two pointed at the sky.

Aven flanked Emriel, her weapons drawn, with Dev at her side. His lack of complaint left her unsure if she should be concerned or confident about this plan. He tracked every bit of movement, but his gaze kept flicking back to the bridge. Was his mind on the present? Or was he reliving the last time they were here too? Could he see Kanai's blood pooling over the rock? The stain still lingered in splotches where he'd fallen.

And kneeling on those horrible red marks was Fennicks.

Aven didn't need her nose to recognize them. Beneath a layer of bruises and dried blood was the warrior's body she'd come to know. She imagined the black dragon fighting to their last bit of strength. Then, when their claws left them captured, they tried escaping with blades. The mottling of purple and blue all over their face and chest told the tale. As did the heavy black manacle around their neck. It pinched so tight that fresh trickles of blood seeped with each breath.

It wasn't the chain keeping Fennicks on their knees. A white-skinned Soulless stood behind them, fingers curled in their hair and a knife resting against the hollow of their throat. One slow tap of the blade stopped Emriel at the entrance of the bridge. The creature was close enough for an arrow, but only if Aven could draw before she slit Fennicks' throat. She itched to unsling the bow across her back, but that would certainly draw the ire of the Soulless dotted across the bridge. Two manned each of the ten ballistae, and two more with skin as black as ink flanked the woman holding Fennicks.

"Ukila," Emriel said almost pleasantly. "You waited for me. So sweet."

A wide, unsettling grin stretched across the Summoner's face. "I was hoping my bait would bring the big fish."

"Well, here I am," Emriel said, raising her hands. "So, what's the play?"

Ukila stroked Fennicks' hair, practically glowing when they jerked away from her, anger simmering in their yellow eyes. If it wasn't for that manacle around Fennicks' throat, the chains pinning their arms, and the bloodied cloth pulled tight across their mouth, Aven imagined they'd have turned claws and fangs on the Soulless already.

"You know, I was going to gut this one," Ukila said, petting Fennicks again. "But then I remembered you crashing through glass to save them. I realized we could work on getting even."

"How boring," Emriel said in a dull voice, but Aven didn't miss the faint tremor in her hands. "You keep promising we'll dance, but every time, one of us either already has a partner or has to run. I'm starting to think you just like making a girl empty promises."

Ukila slid her knife along Fennicks' collarbone, gaze locked on Emriel. She no doubt searched for any flash of weakness. Any sign that killing Fennicks would hurt her.

Anyvath was not so controlled. She growled from the other end of the bridge, keeping her body low, protecting her chest and wings. Ukila threw a look at the dragon before yanking Fennicks' hair and baring their throat.

"Back off lizard!" Her shout echoed, eliciting another snarl. One of the ballistae clicked ominously as a Soulless prepared to fire.

"Let my dragon go!" Pryn's voice was like iron. Hard and cold. Aven could barely make out her face, but the threat was clear. She and Anyvath were ready to pounce.

Ukila's brows rose as she grinned at Emriel. "Is this one really so important?"

No answer came. It was hard enough for her to stand indifferent to the pain twisting Fennicks' face. If it was Mist, Aven would have already launched across the bridge and gotten them both killed.

Anyvath roared as more ballistae clicked, her hot breath wafting across the bridge. The smell of ash and blood wove through the mist of the rushing water. It nearly sent Aven to all fours.

Ukila stared into Anyvath's eyes as she hauled Fennicks up by their hair. Despite their height and bulk, she shoved them towards the parapet, forcing the dragon into a cutaway in the stone. Their feet slid as they balked, pushing back from the open air.

"If that thing attacks, this one gets a taste of flying without its wings."

Emriel flashed a bright smile. "Chains won't stop them from growing wings."

"This kind will." Ukila caressed the black metal. "You think we'd come to fight dragons without all the proper toys? The Mimics assured me these will trap any shifter. They took over a thousand souls to craft, but it was worth it. No matter how your flight mate snarled and raged in my care, I never saw so much as a fang."

Aven glanced at Dev, swallowing down the fear and nausea rising up her throat. That wasn't possible, was it? Could the Soulless make things to block the power Dia'veh gave them? From the look of horror on his face, she feared Ukila wasn't telling stories.

Anyvath hissed and took a step onto the bridge. Her head snaked this way and that, tongue licking at the air. Ukila didn't hesitate to give Fennicks a slight push in response. Pebbles tumbled over the edge of the parapet as they wobbled, fighting to keep their balance. It was enough to halt Anyvath in her tracks.

"Don't make me toss my plaything." A pout warped Ukila's deep voice, making Aven's skin crawl. "You already stole my fun with the hatchling."

Emriel took another step onto the bridge, making the Summoner grab the back of Fennicks' tattered shirt.

"Oh, let it go. I keep telling you I'm more fun."

"I plan on having you too." Ukila moved Fennicks closer to the edge. "But first you'll pay for killing my brothers."

Emriel threw back her head and laughed. "That's why you're mad? You should have trained them better, then maybe they wouldn't be dead."

Ukila's face darkened, rage lighting in her eyes. As her fist balled against Fennicks' back, Aven threw another look at Dev. His arms tensed, the tips of his swords rising slowly. Any moment now.

"This started as just a job. I hope you know all the blood that spills today is on your hands."

Delight slipped across the Summoner's face as she gave a hearty shove, sending Fennicks careening over the edge. Their muffled cry was drowned out by the rushing water, disappearing just as they did. Aven had to hold herself back from running for the parapet. Out of instinct or emotion, she wasn't sure, but not moving felt heartless. Even if it was part of the plan.

Ukila threw a triumphant glare at Emriel. It turned to confusion when their eyes met. Her pale brow furrowed.

"I'm surprised," Emriel said, lowering her hands to her daggers. "You never asked *where* the hatchling was."

Ukila cursed as she ran for the parapet. Just as she leaned over, a mass of white feathers whooshed past her, sending her careening onto her bottom. Water sprayed over them all, dripping from Mist's ivory wings.

Aven couldn't hold back her whoop of excitement. Mist streaked towards the clouds, Fennicks clutched tight against her feathery chest. She was absolutely magnificent. Practically glowing in the morning sun.

"Fire!" Ukila screamed. "Bring them down! I want them both."

"To the torments with that." Dev spun one sword before rushing the Soulless manning the nearest ballista. They were so focused on lining up their shot that one lost an arm before even realizing they were under attack.

Emriel moved towards Ukila like a lynx, stalking over the rocks with daggers drawn.

"No running this time."

Ukila leapt to her feet as Emriel attacked. Their blades clashed, but Aven spared no time to look. Her attention settled on the other ballista pointed at the sky. As she raced for it, Anyvath's roar shook the canyon, a fiery blaze overtaking the other end of the bridge.

The two Soulless manning Aven's target were waiting when she drew near. One worked on aiming for Mist, while the other stepped into her path. She skidded across smooth rock, bracing for the strike. This one had gray skin. A Mimic. Her nostrils flared, scenting for anything that might give away his stolen power. She caught a faint hint of crackling lightning as the wind shifted around them.

An Air Elemental. He'd killed an Eilawi.

Aven tried not to think. Panic would get her killed. The Soulless' curling fingers flicked outward, and a gust knocked her off her feet. Her back slammed against rock, forcing the air from her lungs, but instinct kept her going. Keep moving. That's what Mama would say. She rolled, getting her feet beneath her. Her hands gripped the hilt of her hatchet, and she didn't hesitate. Her arm whipped through the air and released the weapon, sending it careening for her attacker.

It didn't surprise her when a wave of his arms stopped the hatchet midair. That was fine. The look of shock she craved came when the arrow she loosed hit with a quiet thud. Not in the Mimic, but straight between the eyes of the Soulless aiming for Mist. They collapsed without so much as a gurgle.

Just like that, she'd made her first kill. Aven waited for a sick feeling to overtake her. She'd prepared herself, expecting this moment to be horrifying. Awful. Shock nearly slowed her when warmth blossomed in her chest at Kali's triumphant roar.

There was no time to process or celebrate. As soon as the Mimic snapped out of his stupor, he sliced his arm through the air. Her hatchet spun back with full force. Aven tracked it and dodged, air whizzing by her face as she tilted to the right. She regretted losing her weapon already, but Mama's axe still laid heavy against her palm.

She chanced a quick glance at the sky. Mist had reached the clouds, her body arcing back the way they'd come. Her job was to get Fennicks home, and Aven could have kissed Emriel for assigning that to her. She was safe.

Another blast slapped against Aven, nearly knocking her down once more. She managed to dive beneath the worst of it, curling herself towards the rock into a sloppy roll. It brought her that much closer to the Mimic, who had to dance back when she sliced at him with her axe. The surprise in his eyes made her purr. If he thought she'd die easy, Aven would show him. Navya's cub had better plans.

Metal clanged at her back. Aven turned in time to brace a hand against Dev as he parried a swipe from a sword and then deflected the jab of a spear. Both of the Soulless from his ballista had abandoned the weapon, hacking and slashing at him in a perfect dance. Aven rose with her back to him as she waited for her own Soulless to attack.

"Move with me," Dev shouted over another clang. "Stay close."

Aven nodded. That was fine with her.

***

Fennicks' incessant wriggling forced Mist to land. She touched down on the river bank as she considered dumping them on their bottom. Lucky for Fennicks, Papi had taught her better manners.

She released her death hold, and Fennicks stumbled away, fussing through the gag tied around their mouth. They cast a pointed look with narrowed yellow eyes, so Mist turned away and willed the change.

It was strange remembering to shift not only her body, but the dragonskin Rielnor gave her. Not unlike the metal and jewels she wore, but still different. It sank into her when she pushed feathers through her skin, but now it emerged, draping over her until she told it what to do. Once she'd fitted it against herself in black leather armor and boots that reached her thigh, she turned to deal with Fennicks.

Approval shone where irritation usually did. They bowed their head as she untied the gag and worked on unraveling their chains.

"Not bad," Fennicks said once their arms were freed. They rubbed at their bruised wrists, hissing when she touched the manacle around their throat. "We need to go back. The corpse bitch has the key."

"No way," Mist said, dropping her hands to her sides. "I promised Em I would get you out."

Fennicks made a deep, disgusted growl. "Of course you did. Why do all your bloodkin chase death like gold?"

"Hollow words, considering why I had to save you."

A smile peeled across their angular face. "Right. No one can steal the glory."

"That's not what I—"

"It doesn't matter." Fennicks scanned the canyon as gray clouds shifted, casting a shadow across their strong nose. "We have to go back. Not just for the key but to keep your bloodkin alive. That freak of nature will blow the dam with herself on it if it means taking Emriel with her."

"I take it you heard their plan. Do you know why they haven't blown it yet?"

Fennicks nodded. "Body count. They knew someone would come. They'll wait until there's enough shifters on the dam before making everyone go boom."

"Aven is still there." The world tipped sideways as Mist's knees wobbled. She had to shift. Get back to the dam. Save Aven. Her skin itched as her eyes moved to the sky. "You're no good to anyone without a weapon or dragonskin. So just wait here."

Fennicks' triumphant smile dropped as they stalked after her. "Torments take you! If you try leaving me behind like some fresh hatchling, I'll–"

"You'll what? Glare at me?" Mist lifted her chin, but it still wasn't enough to make them eye-level. "You can't shift. You've got no weapons. And you're as colorful as a field of flowers with all those bruises. Stay here. Rest."

"You think I'll rest while Emriel is in danger?"

"What is going on with you and my sister?" Mist's eyes widened as she blurted out the question. It wasn't her business, but Emriel would never give her an answer. "You two are so...*confusing*. You hate each other. You want to hurt each other. You'll die for one another. I don't understand."

The sharpness of Fennicks' face softened, and beneath all the anger and sarcasm, someone appeared who—

maybe—loved her sister. "You're still a kit. Fresh on your first mate, and a mortal one at that. One day, you'll understand. Dragons aren't heartless or apathetic. We burn. Burn with love, hate, desire. And we *never* forget. Not the ones we love or kill, and never the ones we've lost. You know why Rielnor won't fight anymore?"

"I don't know what that has to do with anything."

"It's everything. Rielnor is tired. Tired of burning, of losing, of hurting. A millennium of loved ones lost makes you tired. Losing the one who stood by you through the ages makes you want to quit everything and be the animal many think you are." Fennicks' gaze slid to the water as their brow furrowed. "Emriel reminds me not to quit."

"Even though you act like you want to stab her sometimes?"

That drew a strange smile across Fennicks' lips. "In some shape or form."

"Ugh." Mist squeezed her eyes shut. Nope, nope, nope. She walked right into that one.

"You deserve that, you know," Fennicks muttered. "For making Pryn watch you and Aven together."

Mist flinched. She deserved *that*. Even if Pryn caused the end of that relationship, it still had to hurt.

"Now," Fennicks said, waving a hand at her. "Let's go save all those fools before they get themselves blown up."

Mist put a hand on their broad chest. "Uh-uh. I will go save them. You will stay here."

"Oh, come on! We were bonding. It was going so well. Don't leave me here!"

"You're just going to distract everyone," Mist said, backing up until her feet touched the water. "Emriel, Pryn, Anyvath. They won't be able to focus on protecting themselves if they're protecting you. Plus, you'll just slow me down. You're not exactly light in that body."

Fennicks raised their hands, fingers twitching as if they wanted to choke her. The anger in their eyes and the twisting of their face was indescribable. For one moment, Mist thought they really might lay hands on her.

That's when a shadow fell over them. Mist froze. Fennicks' eyes went wide. A roar shook loose boulders, sending them careening down the cliffs to slap against the water. Ringing filled Mist's ears as Fennicks wheeled around. Their hand rose protectively, shoving Mist into the river. She splashed a few steps before catching herself to brace for an attack.

When she raised her gaze above Fennicks' head, shock rattled through her.

****

The hunt had almost reached the dam. Aven could make out a mass of shaggy bodies racing her way while griffins streaked through the clouds. She just had to keep the ballistae from shooting them down, just a little longer.

Dev stayed with her, moving like lightning as he blocked Soulless attacks with his sword or body. She'd never seen anything like him before. Fire attacks fizzled to sparks before reaching him. Streaks of light blotted out the Shadows' dark blades when they came near. The way he moved was unnatural, as if he knew how the Soulless would attack before they did. If this was what it meant to be soul-called, then Aven believed. Dia'veh was here. Watching over them.

Anyvath and Pryn had been driven off the bridge by a round of ballista fire, but that didn't stop them. The dragon scrambled over rock and cliff face like a spider, digging her claws in wherever she could, snapping her massive jaws at anyone careless enough to get close. Pryn fired arrows from her back, whooping each time she made a hit. Together, they held most of the attacks, keeping the swarm from overrunning Aven and Dev.

Near the middle of the bridge, Emriel and Ukila still clashed. Each time Aven spared them a glance, a new cut shone on Em's arm or Ukila's leg. For every punch she saw land, the other repaid with a kick. Bruises and blood dotted their bodies as they went back and forth between the parapets, chests heaving, sweat pouring down their faces.

What worried Aven most were the two Shadows flanking Ukila. They circled their leader, driving Dev off any time he got close. They never raised their wispy black blades to Emriel, but how long that would last? Each time Aven clashed with the air-using Mimic, she imagined turning back to find Emriel skewered by their shadowy weapons.

Dev now danced with a black-skinned Soulless who stepped in and out of what darkness she could find. Sansia had risen high enough that only a small shadow lingered beneath the parapets. The Soulless used them to slip from sight, forcing Aven and Dev to continually shift their focus. Between her and the Mimic, it was getting harder to keep tabs on Em, but Aven would march herself to the torments before she let Mist's sister die.

It was time to tip the scale and save Emriel's ass. *Again.*

The Mimic stood between Aven and Ukila. She drew in a deep breath and loosened her grip on Mama's axe. She'd spent enough time studying and reacting. It was time to end this.

When the gray Soulless swiped with their arm, Aven didn't brace. She'd learned his pattern: gust, sword slash, spin, gust. The dance steps only varied slightly. This time she charged, summoning Kali's strength to battle through the attack. She nearly lost her footing. Rocks slid beneath her feet, but Kali was stronger. Aven's body was tempered by years of practice. She raised her axe and brought it down on the Mimic's shoulder. He howled as blood sprayed.

The Mimic jerked back, nearly yanking the axe from Aven's hand. Without it, she'd have only her bow. Panic kept her clinging to the handle, slicing it deeper as he wrenched away. The sight of his half-severed torso nearly undid her, but he raised his hand as blood spilled over his lips, eyes burning like coals. Aven brought her arms up, but the blast never came. She looked just in time to see Dev spin, his sword arcing up, before bringing it down on the Mimic's neck. She didn't wait to see his head fall away. Her stomach already churned.

The Shadow didn't grant a reprieve. At the sight of her dead comrade, she dipped into a slip of shadow and vanished. This wasn't new either. Aven raised her axe, waiting, nostrils flaring. It was the coppery smell that gave the woman away. It slithered through the air, announcing her reappearance.

Aven caught the blood scent and dropped just as a blade whizzed for her head. She would thank Mama for the years of hunting. It had just saved her. Instinct dropped her to one knee, and then she kicked with her other leg, catching the Shadow right above her shin. A sickening crack sang with the woman's shriek of pain. She buckled over, and Aven didn't hesitate. This one was hers. Her axe hacked through the Soulless' spine, paying back the life of the Linseen warrior felled in the market.

With both their enemies down, Dev and Aven turned eyes on the Shadows guarding Ukila. Their inky black faces twisted with a feral rage, reminding Aven of snarling lynx.

The thought had her spinning around, searching for any sign of the hunt. Relief washed over her when she found Dinon standing at the end of the bridge with fangs bared. The pride stalked behind them, growling and hissing.

The hunt had arrived.

Yliva drew first blood. They never saw the griffin coming. She dropped from the sky, her steely gray wings gleaming in Sansia's light. Her talons ripped into a Mimic attacking Anyvath with streams of water.

Aven looked back to the Shadows, hoping they saw the triumph in her eyes. She wasn't expecting the smiles slipping across their lips. Were they so eager to die? Or did they crave the violence about to fall upon them?

"Let us finish this," Dev said. He held out a hand, Aven's hatchet gripped in his fist.

"Yes," she said, reveling in the feel of it back in her palm. "Let's."

CHAPTER
Thirty-Six

Aven

$\mathcal{S}$hifters descended upon the bridge in a wave of claws and talons. Their fury ripped into the Soulless, intoxicating Aven's senses. Her nose filled with their anger, hot and burning, tempting her to abandon weapons in favor of slashing and biting. She shoved down the desire and clung to her training. *Qinawe are not animals.* Mama's lessons rang over and over in her ears as she parried sword strikes and blocked bone-shearing swings. Today she was in control, not Kali.

As Dinon led the charge, a mass of Linseen dropped from the swooping griffins, their scimitars flashing in Sansia's light. Commander Senwe led them towards the ballistae, ducking and hacking his way through Soulless.

When Zoli's feet touched the bridge's bloody rock, he glanced between his people and Dev, concern blazing in his eyes. The sight of Ukila's shadows pulled him from the ranks of the Linseen, tempting him into the circle Aven and Dev made around the Summoner.

The Shadows disappeared at his approach, leaving Ukila's back exposed. She and Emriel continued their match, sweat and blood gleaming on their skin. Their blades clashed over and over. Neither gave any ground.

With two elves to lend their aid, it was time to tip the scale of this fight.

Dev went first, charging in with swords raised, while Zoli did the same from the other side. Their merciless movements allowed Aven to hang back. She needed to study this dance, to study Ukila.

The Summoner either heard or sensed the elves, because she landed a well-placed kick to Emriel's gut and turned to catch Dev's blades with her own. Excitement shone in her eyes, twisting her face in a way that turned Aven's stomach. Her mouth was too wide, her skin too stretched. She looked more animal now.

With a surprising burst of strength, Ukila shoved Dev's swords up and swiped for his midsection. She might have cut him in half if he didn't move with the momentum of her thrust, curling into a backflip that took him out of her reach. Zoli dove in while Dev soared, parrying her next attacks with one scimitar and then the other. The distraction allowed Dev to slide into a roundhouse that connected his boot to her chest.

"Cute," Ukila sneered, rubbing the spot he kicked. She glanced at Emriel, who was now on her feet, then looked from Zoli to Aven. "Well, this is just unsporting. Where is your honor and all that?"

"With Kanai," said Dev, lifting his bloody swords.

"Who?"

Aven imagined clawing the joy out of her eyes. "The lynx your people murdered."

"Is it really murder in a place like this?" She released a soft, lilting laugh. "Your friend lost a fight he shouldn't have picked."

Emriel wiped at the purple blood dripping from her nose. "*This* is a fight *you* shouldn't have picked."

"Oh, sweetheart," Ukila said in a husky voice. "I've already won."

Dread shivered through Aven's limbs. What did that mean? The lynx and griffins harried the Soulless, herding them into the waiting scimitars of the Linseen. Anyvath was destroying a ballista with her massive teeth, tearing into the wood like flesh. Pryn had run out of arrows, but she remained in the saddle, riding out the wrenching of the dragon's frenzied motions. What did Ukila see that she did not?

Emriel didn't waste time searching for meaning. She flipped one dagger, holding it so it curved along her arm as she ran at the Soulless. Her slash nearly caught Ukila across the ribs, but she danced aside just in time, right towards Dev's waiting swords. He swung once, twice, but again Ukila slipped away, towards Zoli's waiting strikes. As Aven watched, she realized this was a new dance. A new game. Had she been holding back the whole time? A sheen of sweat gleamed on her forehead, but no sign of exhaustion showed.

Ukila effortlessly moved between Dev, Zoli, and Emriel, blocking their blades, landing kicks and punches where she could. Aven waited for an opening, reluctant to break the flow between dragon and elves. They moved seamlessly. One went for the strike while the another retreated. Then Dev and Zoli came in for deadly blows together, only to be driven back again.

Ukila had definitely been holding back. But to what end?

Aven scanned the bridge again, searching for something amiss. A Mimic using Earth to crack the dam? A Shadow going for a kill they'd never expect? Her eyes continually roamed from bridge to spillways, to the banks upstream.

That's when she saw them. The Shadows. They were up the river, hefting a collection of metal balls towards the rushing water. All it would take was a toss. With the spillways overflowing, it wouldn't take long for the explosives to float beneath the bridge.

The Soulless would blow the dam with everyone on it.

"Emriel!" Aven screamed, running for the cliff. No way she made it before those things hit the water, not without wings. "Yliva! Anyvath!"

Ukila's delighted cackle rang in Aven's ears. She had her victory. No way the dragons could save them all. The lynx. The Linseen. Zoli. Dev. They would all be caught in the blast.

She had reached the end of the bridge when a scream sang over the chaos. The sound stopped Aven in her tracks. Its horrible echo nearly halted her heart as well. Aven whipped around, dreading to find who they'd lost this time.

Ukila had Emriel pinned to the parapet, a knife buried deep in her shoulder. Dev ran for them, but nearly skidded into the blade of a Shadow when it winked into his path. Only Zoli's quick tackle saved him from being impaled.

Aven looked to the explosives, then back to the bridge. Ukila pressed close as she slid a hand over Emriel's glistening forehead. Aven could only imagine the look of sick pleasure on the creature's face. She twisted her blade in Em's shoulder so slowly, no doubt reveling in each scream she forced out.

Dev was pushing to his feet, Em's name spilling from his lips. Her face was so pale. The pain sent her eyes rolling back in her head. Aven threw a desperate look at the bank. Would Ukila's Shadow really throw the explosives with her and the other Soulless still on the bridge? The one not blocking Dev had come close enough to toss the balls into the water.

Aven would never reach them, no matter how fast she ran, but she could save Emriel.

Decision made, she spun back around, intent on running for her friends. She barely made it a step before her gaze moved over the edge of the parapet, landing on a sight she could barely believe.

***

Mist had never flown so fast. Not in the races. Not when she'd swooped in to catch Fennicks. Never had so much been on the line.

As she rounded the last bend and the dam came into view, she realized she still wasn't fast enough. Chaos had erupted on the bridge, bodies flailing, wrestling, and slamming against one another. Blasts of fire shot from Anyvath and a Soulless. Metal shone as it hacked through flesh.

Aven's screams ricocheted against the rock.

Mist desperately searched to know what ripped such an awful sound from her throat. She found her on the end of the bridge. Her terrified face pointed to Dev. He moved with a speed she didn't think possible for an elf—aiming for Ukila, who bent Emriel's head back, exposing her throat for a killing slash.

Mist pushed every muscle to the point of burning pain. She had to get to Em. She wasn't losing Em to this mess. Light bounced off Ukila's blade as her arm raised. The blow would do more than sever skin.

A roar rumbled, its force propelling Mist forward, nearly sending her into a tailspin. Only practice in the races kept her in control. She'd learned to use the power and strength of larger dragons to move faster than her wings could manage.

Just a little farther. The spray of the spillways now cooled her skin.

"Emriel!" Fennicks screamed. "No!"

Green crept into the corner of her vision as Rielnor cut for the bridge like a hurricane's blast, pushing Mist closer and bringing Fennicks near enough to leap from his back. With a horrible crunch, they collided with Ukila, sending them both tumbling away.

Before Mist could land, the flight leader's massive feet clawed at the rock, grasping for the Summoner or Shadow, any Soulless he could get ahold of. His body blocked her way, forcing Mist to zoom past the bridge. He deserved a chance at Ukila anyway. He'd come to end this fight, and she was happy to oblige him.

Mist had just banked into a turn when movement on the shore caught her eye.

A single Shadow stood on the rocks, arm pulled back, metal ball clenched in their fist. With a powerful throw, the explosive sailed into the air. Aiming for the dam. Mist threw herself into a dive, wings tucked close, Sholindrea's pull dragging her down. The river rushed towards her as she tracked the ball's path. Her legs strained, reaching, grasping. It smacked into her outstretched feet barely a tail length from the water.

Too close!

She flapped her wings, correcting her direction away from the river and back into the sky. What to do with it now?

Where would it be safe? She curved back towards the ground, aiming for Aven.

She was already racing towards Mist. "We have to stop them! Everyone needs to get off the dam."

Mist dropped the ball at Aven's feet before launching away. This ended now. A roar burst from her throat, calling to dragon and griffin as she aimed for the Shadow. They had two more explosives in hand. She wasn't close enough this time to catch them. The balls slapped against the water and immediately began to spin and smoke as the current pulled them towards the dam.

"Run!" Aven screamed. "Everybody off the bridge!"

Yliva cut through Mist's path, her claws reaching for the Shadow. They must have seen her coming because they threw as many explosives into the water as they could, before the griffin fell on them with a sickening squish of talons on flesh.

That left Mist to focus on the explosives. She had to do something. Anything. Smoke stung her eyes as she dove into the cool depths of the Lighe. There had to be a way to stop them from reaching the dam.

She summoned webbing between her toes and cut through the water with hearty swipes of her tail. The current nearly towed her into the spillways, but her focus locked on fragments of a plan. She needed to get all the explosives together. That meant making her own current, something stronger than the river.

She shot through the water with her wings and feet, curving her body until her back ached. One circle. Then two. Then three. Each time, her speed increased. The water yielded. Soon the cyclone caught her up, propelling her faster and faster until the pull of the river fell away.

If she got lucky, she could bring all the explosives to her instead of the dam.

***

Zoli barreled towards his people as Aven ran for Fennicks and Dev went for Emriel. Neither had moved at her shouts. At the other end of the bridge, griffins took to the skies as lynx ripped their way towards the riverbank, felling any Soulless that tried stopping them. Anyvath launched off the rock, her wings straining as she rose into the sky, taking Pryn and at least two Linseen with her. Commander Senwe was shouting for his people to run, ignoring the way Zoli tugged at him, trying to save him.

Rielnor growled from his perch, his long neck arched as he surveyed the river. Whatever he saw had him leaping for the sky, the power of his wings shoving Aven to her knees.

When she finally reached Fennicks, it took all her strength to roll them onto their back. Blood dripped from their open mouth, but after a few tense moments, their chest rose and fell.

Thank Dia'veh!

"Wake up!" She pushed at their muscled shoulders. "Come on! The dam is gonna blow. You have to move!"

They groaned, but they didn't rise.

"Vhis, please."

Aven turned to find Dev standing over Fennicks with Emriel in his arms. She reached out her unbloodied hand, grasping for Fennicks with shaking fingers.

"Vhis!"

Fennicks' yellow eyes snapped open. One look at Emriel's face had them rising to their feet, their own hand taking hold of hers.

"Go!" Aven said, pushing at Dev. "Run."

He didn't need to be told twice. This was why he'd been called, to save Emriel's life. Without a glance back, Dev ran for the cliff with Fennicks limping behind.

Aven scanned the bridge, searching for any other stragglers. Even the Soulless were running now. The ones who could walk, anyway. Their comrades' bodies littered the bridge, as well as a few lynx and at least one Linseen. Aven considered running for them to see if they lived. No one got left behind on a hunt.

That's when she noticed Ukila. She'd fallen not far from Fennicks, her black hair splayed around her head, fingers twitching as her eyes fluttered open.

To the Torments. How was she still alive?

Aven slipped her hatchet into its loop on her belt and hefted Mama's axe. It was foolish. She should let the explosives take the creature out, but Aven couldn't risk it. What if she survived?

Someone called her name, but Aven ignored them. This was for Kanai. For Willa. And for everyone who died in the market. She couldn't even lie to herself. The desire to see blood run filled her with excitement. Kali's place inside her keened for it.

Ukila was sitting up when Aven's shadow fell over her. She didn't seem surprised. Her fingers rubbed at her bloodied temple as a sigh slipped from her lips.

"Come on then. Have at it."

"You lost," Aven whispered.

Ukila looked up through her lashes, her face so alien to Aven. Not a shred of fear or remorse lingered in her black eyes. "I won long before any of you set foot on this dam. This was just a bit of fun."

Aven tightened her fingers around the axe's handle. No more talking. Ukila was playing mind games. Those bombs would blow any minute. She wanted Aven here when they did. She raised the axe, gaze locking on the Summoner's neck.

The bridge shook as a dragon's screech rang in her ears. Aven could barely scream before a clawed foot wrapped around her middle.

"No!"

Ukila's look of triumph seared into Aven's mind as a Shadow winked into the space beside her. They snatched the Summoner into whatever void the creatures moved through, whisking her to safety. Then the bridge fell away as the grip on Aven's middle pulled her up, away from the bloodstained rock.

A wail ripped from Aven's throat as she looked up. Rainbow scales. Massive wings. Pryn peered over Anyvath's side, sorrow in her blue-tinted eyes. They soared downriver before circling back, heading for the bank where many had gathered to watch the whirlpool forming at the mouth of the dam. Smoke from the explosives circled as they fell into its current.

At the heart of it was a streak of white, moving so fast through the waves Aven almost didn't understand what she was looking at.

Mist.

She was pulling the bombs away from the dam. But that meant they were drawing closer and closer to her, their smoke and sparks blurring everything at the center of the vortex.

"Anyvath! Drop me!" Aven screamed, kicking and clawing against the dragon's foot. "Save Mist!"

All she got was a roar as they continued aiming for the riverbank.

"Pryn!" Panic pulled searing tears from Aven's eyes. Not again. This wasn't happening again. "Save her! Not me."

A deeper roar sounded, so loud it shook Aven's bones. Rielnor dropped from the sky, crashing into the whirlpool with so much force it sent a towering wave in every direction. His green body cut through the water, deepening the cyclone, exposing the muddy river bottom, before he shot into the air once more. Each of his feet clenched tight, and billowing smoke trailed in his wake. A glance at the Lighe revealed all hints of the explosives gone. Rielnor had snatched them all.

Now he flew for Sansia in a shroud of water, smoke, and sparks. He'd nearly reached the clouds when he curved his body and launched the explosives into the air.

Aven crowed with excitement. He'd done it! Rielnor had saved the dam, Mist—*everyone*. No matter what Ukila said, they had won. Anyvath joined her whoops of joy, veering to meet Rielnor in his descent.

Beams of light curved around him, glinting off his wings and scales in a halo of gold, as if Dia'veh themself smiled at what he'd done. Aven could just make out the tired relief in Rielnor's emerald eyes when the sky exploded.

His howl of agony drew tears to her eyes. She would never forget the sound. Fiery chunks of metal rained from the clouds, ripping through Rielnor's wings and back, sending a shower of blood towards the ground. It splashed hot against Aven's face. She nearly gagged at the heat of it, until Rielnor plummeted towards them.

"Anyvath!"

This time the rainbow dragon responded, veering for her flight leader as he wailed his suffering. He curled in on himself, his wings in tatters. Aven didn't know how they would stop such a massive beast from crashing into the earth.

She wriggled against Anyvath's hold, peeling herself free of the curled toes keeping her aloft. Anyvath would need every claw. Aven's heart hammered as she wrapped herself around the dragon's foreleg, ignoring Mama's voice in her head, calling her a twice-cursed fool.

It took everything to keep from retching when Anyvath spun. The sky went down, the ground went up, and wind whipped against her face. She nearly lost her grip. Only pure instinct kept her glued to the dragon's leg.

A mass of green scales careening towards her had Aven squeezing her eyes shut, bracing for impact. Anyvath collided with Rielnor, sending Aven scrabbling for purchase as she slipped. For one horrible moment, she was floating, trapped between their massive bodies. As Anyvath dug her claws into his legs, his sides, anywhere she could get purchase, she slowly drew Rielnor close. Aven collided with the green dragon's side and grabbed with her own claws. She hated tearing into him, hated every whimper and growl of pain. But he would live. She would live. It was better than the alternative.

More horrible spinning had Aven pressing her face against Rielnor's bloody side. They had to be close to the ground. Soon her feet would touch sweet blessed rock and this would all be over. Their descent was slowing, growing jerky and uneven as Anyvath's wings strained to save them all.

When Aven felt Rielnor touch the ground, it took a few deep breaths before she could pull her face from his side. Shouts of relief rang out. Pryn called her name. Her whole body shook as her stomach churned.

It was Mist's voice that drew her to reality. Aven blinked through the haze, and there she was. Wide fuchsia eyes and tears sliding over her round cheeks. She was real. This was real. Aven collapsed into Mist's waiting arms with a sigh. They'd survived.

Aven

A ven sat on the hard rock, grateful it was beneath her instead of spiraling out of reach. She could have sat there all day, despite the ache in her tailbone.

All around, leaders were taking stock. Commander Senwe had Zoli lining up the Linseen squads. The ones that could line up, anyway. The injured were still being gathered from the bridge. Yliva presided over the griffins and lynx, her calm demeanor soothing the pain of those lost in the hunt. No one Aven knew, but the yowls of sadness still pulled at her heart.

It wasn't done. Ukila, had gotten away.

That was a fight for another day, though. Anyvath and Dev were somewhere nearby, pleading with Rielnor to push through the pain so he could shift. Then he could be transported to Ifera and her salves. Aven didn't have the stomach to look at his ruined body yet. The way blood had sprayed like rain told her it was bad. Mist sat with Emriel, who needed to get back as well. Her shoulder was a ruined mess thanks to Ukila's twisting knife.

No matter where Aven let her mind wander to, she kept retreating to the simplicity of the Lighe river rushing into the dam. Its waves pouring over the spillway soothed the nausea in her gut.

Rocks crunched nearby just before Dev sat beside her. "Are you well?"

She drew a deep breath through her nose and nodded. It was all she could muster. Her throat was raw from all the screaming in the battle.

Dev's eyes narrowed, but he kept his disbelief to only a look. "Fennicks has been freed of their collar. As soon as Rielnor shifts, we will depart for Yunaii."

"And the dam?" Her gaze flicked to its rocky expanse.

"Yliva and Senwe are leaving sentries under Zoli's command. We will have at least some warning should the Soulless return."

Aven nodded again, continuing to stare at the river. Dev's gaze lingered on her, tension radiating like a cloud. She wanted to tell him to take it away. The scent of his worry burned her nose.

"What?" she finally croaked.

"It is fine if you are not—*okay*. Hunting is not like killing." His gaze moved to the water. "A hunt yields sustenance, furs, and sustainability for your family. Killing Soulless...that is bringing ourselves low, even if it is for the good of others."

Aven pulled her knees to her chest, swallowing hard against the pain in her throat. "I don't know what concerns me more—that I took lives today or that I'm actually okay with it."

"I know this feeling." He made a sound somewhere between a laugh and a sigh. "I imagine for someone taught to avoid violence at all costs, it can be frightening."

"Is there something wrong with me?" Aven asked. "Maybe Hanawi is right. Maybe I do have a warring heart."

"No more than I am a blood-seeker." The word came out without its usual bite or bitterness. His familiar stillness had returned, as if the anger possessing him had drunk its fill. "You do not seek the fights. You let your body be a shield to the world and its innocents. If you are at peace with this, then do not entertain the shame. My people would hail you as one of the most dutiful."

Aven looked at him. Really looked. From his pointed nose and ears, to the sweaty curls stuck to his brow, and the thin line of his mouth. His seriousness had always put her off kilter. It had made her feel unsure, until their days of travel and it became a comfort. When the storm of rage had claimed him, she'd missed his calm presence.

"How are you?" Aven asked, bumping him with her elbow.

Dev looked down at his hands in his lap, one thumb rubbing over the other. "I am not well, but I will be. I failed Willa. I saved Emriel. I have done what I can."

"You didn't fail Willa," Aven said. "She's alive because of you."

"She is also forever changed because of me." He reached into a pouch at his belt and produced a white rock that glittered in the light. "I indulged in a dalliance instead of focusing on my calling. The cost was high and it should've been me who paid it."

Aven shouldn't have smiled. She knew it, but her lips still curved. He cradled the little stone from Willa so preciously, his bloodied fingertips stroking over its bumps and curves as if it were her.

"Don't steal Willa's power, Dev. She'd claw your eyes out for that."

A laugh rumbled out of him, soft and real. It was a beautiful sound. "Yes. She would."

Aven watched him tuck the rock back into his pouch. "So, what happens now? Do you and Willa make a nest and live happily ever after?"

"Doubtful," Dev said, glancing at the sky. "This call has been answered, but my time of serving has only just begun. Dia'veh willing, I will be summoned again soon."

She didn't expect the hollowness that blossomed in her chest. "You're not soul-called to Yunaii anymore."

He shook his head. "I will leave when I am called again. I cannot refuse. Someone might die if I do."

This was a burden she knew he could never live with. Some elves might one day turn away, take hold of their own fate, but not Dev. He was too good. Too selfless. She glanced towards Rielnor, who had tried so hard to run from the call to fight. It made sense now why he'd chosen Dev to be his rider. They were cut from the same cloth.

It was time to go. The flight leader had finally shifted, his normally reddish face pale and sweaty as he leaned against Fennicks. Blood dripped over his bare shoulders in rivulets of purple and navy. Even the tiniest movement had him cringing. Between his injuries and Emriel's they were a horrible sight to behold.

A boom echoing in the distance stilled all progress. Elves froze, griffin screeched, lynx yowled. The sound ricocheted off the walls of the canyon, sending pebbles cascading into the river.

"What was that?" Pryn asked, lifting her bow.

Aven pushed to her feet, straining to see past the dam. Another boom sent rocks tumbling from the cliffs, accompanied by a pained roar. Far in the distance, she realized what she'd thought were clouds, was actually puffs of white smoke billowing from the horizon.

"Is something...burning?"

Dev rose beside her, his head cocked curiously. Somewhere behind Aven, Yliva ordered her flock to the air. They were just soaring over the dam when a dragon veered around the bend and collided with the cliff face.

Anyvath gasped. "Thudan!"

The spike-covered dragon pushed against the canyon, wobbling through the air like a baby bird, his leather wings bloody and black. His neck lagged and when he finally reached the dam, his massive body scrambled onto the rock as if he could go no further.

Aven ran for him, ignoring the protest shaking her bones. By the time her feet crossed onto the bridge, he was shrinking in on himself, plated armor giving way to shredded skin. Anyvath reached him first, collapsing to her knees as he laid panting on all fours, blood dripping from his mouth. Mist was not far behind, and soon a small crowd gathered around, all waiting with nervous energy for him to speak.

"Thudan," Anyvath whispered, touching his jaw with trembling fingers. "What is it? What's happened?"

"It's burning," Thudan gasped before giving in to a bout of coughing. He stunk of blood and soot, his body blackened by ash. "Yunaii is on fire. The Soulless are burning everything."

Gasps of horror slipped around Aven as her world stilled. *I won long before you set foot on this dam.*

She turned towards the plume of smoke, Ukila's words ringing in her ears. This is what she had meant. Blowing the dam was her fun. Burning Yunaii and everyone in it was her plan. Maybe even from the start.

The sick feeling welled back up, forcing bile into Aven's throat. *Mama. Papa.* They were there, in the thick of it. She had to get to them.

Aven didn't think. Her feet just moved, carrying her towards the parapet as a cry tore from her ravaged throat. She didn't even mean to call out for Mist. It was instinct. Like breathing. The one person she could always count on. Her claws dragged along the rock as she pulled herself up, her attention never leaving those horrible, billowing clouds. Could anyone still be alive? They were so far away, but the smoke reached so high. Another cry for Mist. Then she leaped. Screams rang out, fear and terror jolting through her friends as she fell.

No. Not fell. As she waited. The water drew closer and closer, but sure enough, a flash of white feathers streaked past her. Mist would always come.

She drew in a breath as their bodies aligned, Mist's wings held out wide as she hovered, air from below buffeting her up towards Aven. They came together seamlessly. Aven bent into position, knees resting where Mist's wings burst from her back, feet settling along the line of long feathers. Once she was nestled into place, Mist tucked in her wings and dove.

Wind whipped at Aven's face, nearly wrenching her into the air. She had to flatten down, her fingers buried deep in clusters of feathers. They were almost to the bend in the canyon when Mist's wings beat hard, shooting them around the curve, nearly turning sideways to keep from careening into the cliffs.

Yunaii was so far. How would they ever make it in time? Tears burned her eyes as Aven imagined Mama and Papa, helpless and alone as Soulless descended upon them. Would she find them in the cave? The woods? Mama would go down fighting. Papa would be with the Qinawe, protecting those who had never even looked at him.

They were never going to make it, no matter how fast Mist flew.

A dragon's roar rumbled. Aven whipped around, tears ripping from her cheeks. Anyvath and Fennicks soared behind them, wings beating hard, carrying Dev and Pryn. The dragons snaked through the air, straining, legs clawing with each flap.

Mist veered up, catching a draft that pulled them out of the canyon. They rode it until she could hover on Fennicks' wing, letting their power pull her along. Pryn peered up at them, her eyes wide, but her mouth pulled into a determined line. Her chin dipped into a nod, and Aven returned the motion.

No matter the outcome, this was a race they would win or lose together.

***

The closer they got, the less Aven could see. Sansia was setting, but that wasn't why. Clouds of smoke swirled, carrying embers and ash that coated her skin and her eyes. They were so dry. She kept blinking to summon tears, something, but nothing helped. Every bit of her was coated in dry, grimy ash, even her throat. Hacking coughs ripped from her throat as they flew, leaving it raw and aching. By the time they drew near the vast opening of the canyon that housed Yunaii, Aven could barely see or speak.

Inferno raged in a whooshing roar beneath her. The Eilawi tree's canopy was fully engulfed and the forest she'd birthed was being steadily overtaken. Black clouds of smoke blotted out sections, making it impossible to tell how much remained. The sight of her home on fire cracked something in Aven's chest that might never heal.

"Look!" Pryn screamed. She pointed to the cliffs, through the plumes of smoke and fire, to what could only be a battlefield. Screams crept over the roars of the blaze as the clang of metal joined the awful chaos.

The evacuees were under attack, just like Emriel had warned. Her understanding of Ukila and the Soulless sent a shiver down Aven's spine. They should have listened to her from the start.

A dragon's shriek pierced the din and Mist dropped away from the others to avoid being crashed into. The creature plummeted, its wings ripped to shreds. Anyvath and Fennicks wailed as its dark body disappeared into an ashy cloud. Aven looked up to the floating rock that held the roost and found an orange gleam overhead as well.

This was an extermination.

"Go help the people on the cliffs!" Aven screamed over the commotion. "I'll see if anyone was left behind."

Pryn's face paled beneath the ash streaked across it. "You can't go down there! The fire is out of control."

"My parents could be down there." Aven could imagine them ushering every soul from their burrows or tents, putting everyone before themselves. "I have to be sure."

"Not alone!" Dev called out. He didn't wait for Aven's protests. One moment he sat on Anyvath's back, the next his nimble feet carried him across the length of her back. Before Aven knew his intent, he'd jumped for Mist.

He hit with enough force to drop them lower, nearly unseating Aven and sending himself into the inferno. As Mist righted herself, Aven threw every curse she knew at Dev, not stopping even when he settled into the spot behind her with a wide grin on his face.

"Have you lost your Dia'veh-loving mind?" Aven didn't care that he looked as pleased as a kitten with its first kill. She was ready to slap the look right off of him. "You almost missed!"

"You made it look fun," Dev said with a shrug. "Now stop wasting time. If anyone is down there, they will not last long."

Aven's nostrils flared, searing air stinging her nose. He was right, but by Sholindrea was he getting an earful when this was all done.

She looked up at Pryn, whose terror left streaks of white in her hair. "Stay with Fennicks! Let the dragons do the fighting."

Pryn didn't look like she needed to be told twice. Fennicks growled in reply, as if issuing their own reminder to be careful. Anyvath echoed the sound before heading for the cliffs with teeth bared and talons extended.

Aven watched them disappear into the swirling haze. *Dia'veh, please. Please watch over them.*

"Time to go," Dev said, wrapping his arms around her waist.

"Hold on tight." Aven leaned forward, and that's all Mist needed. Her wings drew in and they dropped.

What came next was a mix of falling and flying. Mist's navigation through flaming branches and collapsing trees was a miracle. She wove this way and that, blasting through pockets of searing heat, before veering into places where the fires barely burned. How she could see was beyond Aven. She could barely make out Mist's neck, let alone the forest beyond. Only when the Lighe came into view, could she orient herself.

Mist dropped straight into the water, submerging all three of them. Aven reveled in the cold soothing her heated skin before eventually kicking for the surface. Blazing air blasted her face as soon as she burst through. Once they had all pulled up on the Temple's side of the river, Mist shook herself off and Dev checked his weapons.

"Where to first?" he asked.

Aven glanced at the Qinawe's section of forest. It was fully engulfed in flames. If anyone remained, they were already dead. Hopefully, Mama and Papa had realized the impossibility of staying there.

"We'll check the Temple," Aven said. "Gaelin and Ifera were coordinating the evacuation from there. If the attack began before they were done, they'll still be inside."

She got no arguments, so they ran for the stone building. Destroyed and burning market stands laid around the base of the Eilawi tree as embers and ash reigned from above. A blanket of darkness hovered overhead, pierced only by bright spots of orange and yellow. With little left to burn, much of the tree's roots laid unscathed. Their massive forms hovered behind shrouds of gray, growing clear only when Aven was right on top of them. Each time she wove around something familiar, the pit in her stomach grew heavier.

When the Temple's form appeared through the haze, Aven's sigh died on her lips. Statues laid in pieces around the entrance. The carvings on the walls were cracked and destroyed. Shards of glass glittered on the ground, catching sparks like razor-edged jewels.

And the dead clustered at its entrance, blocking any way to get inside.

Dev swore when he saw them. Qinawe with wounds in their guts. Tribouin missing limbs. Lynx. Griffins. They clamored around the opening to the Temple, pushing and clawing against whatever blocked their way. No door stood in the entryway. There had never been one, and Aven couldn't see any kind of barricade.

"Dia'veh protects the Temple," Dev whispered.

"There must be survivors inside." Aven pulled the hatchet and axe from the loops on her belt. "We have to help them."

Dev scanned the Temple as he pulled out his swords. "The dead means the Summoner is here."

"Watch your back."

Mist hissed as she took the lead, approaching the writhing corpses with her head down and wings raised. Ready to pounce. Aven and Dev walked on either side of her, both of them on guard for any sign of Ukila.

A lynx turned on them, his eyes dull and mouth spattered with blood. Something had pierced the shifter's side in a blow that had hopefully brought a quick death.

"Do not hesitate," Dev said over Mist's back. "He is already gone. There is nothing you can do for him."

Aven nodded, grateful for his words. All her instincts balked at turning her blade to the lynx. Kali's sorrow clawed free, bringing fresh tears as the cat approached, even when its fangs bared in a deadly snarl.

Mist moved first. Her wings fluttered, and she took an extended leap that brought her down on the dead thing's back. It didn't so much as yowl as she tore into it.

That drew the horde upon them. They shambled from the Temple, silent and horrifying in their dismemberment. Those without claws reached with grasping fingers, straining to rip flesh with torn fingernails. Aven had to swallow down a heave of vomit as they fell upon her.

They weren't alive. She couldn't save them. All she could do was set their bodies free. With Dev at her side, she went about the grim work. Mama's axe sailed through necks and elbows while Dev hacked away at any sharp part on the lynx and griffins. Each splatter of chunky red ooze and every thud of limbs left Aven fighting to keep it together. This was a nightmare brought to life. A pointless nightmare. Even with little left but torsos and legs, the ruined shifters still crawled towards them as they approached the Temple, possessed by a need to bite, rip, and destroy.

As the crowd of standing dead grew thin, Aven finally made out the Temple's entrance. A lone shadow stood in its arch, their pale hands held in front of their chest.

"Ukila!" This time, Aven sank into Kali's swelling rage. Claws brushed her palms as fangs pricked her lips. The Soulless would pay for what she had done. To the shifters. To Yunaii. It was time for her blood to run instead of theirs.

Aven ducked past the bodies between them before stalking towards the Summoner. The axe and hatchet were heavy in Aven's hands, but she was ready. She'd almost had her before. This time, she wouldn't hesitate.

Ukila never tried to run. She simply stood in the doorway with that freakish smile on her face, fingers twitching and moving all the while.

Aven wrenched back the arm holding her hatchet and let it fly. It should have landed square between the witch's eyes. Instead, it bounced off and went veering to the side, as if a sword had swiped it away.

Ukila threw back her head and laughed. "Your Maker protects all. Not just the ones you like."

A snarl furrowed Aven's brow. "Come out here, you blood-seeking coward."

The Summoner tilted her face, loosing a few dark strands of hair from the knot holding it back. "Not yet, little one. I'm still eradicating vermin."

Aven looked over the archway, searching for something, anything, that could end this. Maybe Mist could slam the entrance with her body and bring it down on top of the Soulless. Would Dia'veh allow that? They wouldn't actually be striking Ukila.

As Aven considered tackling the Soulless and dragging her out by her hair, someone else took the initiative. A feral roar echoed inside the Temple, and a cat like Aven had never seen stalked through the corridor. Its body was a wash of tan and cream, with faint golden stripes all over. Fangs smaller than a lynx's bared in a still terrifying snarl as it approached. Ukila wavered, seeming torn between standing her ground and running. She pulled a blade from her belt and slashed at the cat, only for it to be knocked back just as Aven's hatchet had. The massive feline almost smiled.

No claws came out when it reached her. Instead, the cat's head bumped Ukila like a lynx might its cub. The impact backed her up. One step. And another. She was nearly out of the entryway before she planted her feet and pushed. That resulted in her body being knocked backwards, flinging her onto the steps before the Temple.

A grin twisted Aven's lips. However, the cat had superseded Dia'veh's power, it didn't matter. Ukila was hers now. She cast a grateful look at the striped beast and found its golden eyes fixed on her.

Golden eyes. Like Ifera's. She'd claimed Qinawe blood. Did she carry the soul of this strange cat? Perhaps the Priestess of the Temple had the power to remove people from its veil of protection.

Ukila was on her knees when Aven drew near. "This feels familiar."

"I just wish you could suffer like they did," Aven said, lifting Mama's axe.

The Summoner's fingers twitched and flexed. "Let's burn together, shall we?"

The ground rumbled as something big lumbered behind Aven. She turned in time to see the corpse of a fallen dragon approaching, its torn wings dragging over the ground as fire welled between its jaws.

CHAPTER
Thirty-Eight

Mist

Mist lunged as the dragon's carcass spewed fire. Her wings curled around Aven's body, tucking her close as they rolled over rocks and soot. She tried not to worry about how hard they'd slammed together. Anything was better than the alternative. The heat of the blast would have left nothing in its wake.

The abomination growled as Mist rose on shaking legs, her heart splintering into a million pieces. She didn't want to do this, but Aven could do nothing against a dragon. Neither could Dev. With an angry chitter, she whipped her tail towards Ukila, who had rolled away as well. This only ended one way. Aven looked where she pointed and nodded. The Soulless was hers. The dragon was Mist's.

Another growl rippled over the roar of the forest fire. Ukila was gearing the beast up for another blast, but Mist's flightmate would not be used this way. She launched with a vicious screech. A few powerful wing beats had her claws digging into its throat, but no cry of pain followed. Just globs of thick purple blood slid over her feet as an acrid smell filled the air.

Mist sprang back, arching into an airy somersault before launching at the thing's face. Her claws dug deep just as Ifera leapt for the dragon's side. Gaelin came sliding in nearby, dodging beneath a swipe of claws as he aimed for its chest. Mist wanted to howl at them to stay back, but they'd never listen. The best thing she could do was take the corpse down as fast as possible.

More ripping and tearing left the dragon's face ruined. Yet still, its throat gleamed with the spark of fire. Mist beat her wings, carrying herself up and over to land on its neck. Maybe if she severed its spinal column. If it couldn't lift its head, then it couldn't aim its fire. She hissed in disgust as her teeth connected with dead flesh, clotting blood oozing over her tongue. It took everything she had to hold on as Ukila made it flail about, its claws lashing at Ifera and Gaelin as they attacked from below.

One hearty toss of its head sent Mist sailing into the air. With her lungs on fire, it took longer to right herself than it should have. Once she leveled out, she shot for the corpse again as its claws raked over Ifera's hindquarters. Her awful yowl pulled a roar from Mist and a shout of fear from Gaelin. All sense of self-preservation left him as he ran for the tan and white cat, jumping between her and another slash of claws. Mist collided with the thing, praying she had enough strength to knock it away from the elf.

Stiff flesh gave way, and Mist fell with the abomination. It hit the ground with a boom, its body rolling over itself, wing bones snapping. Mist tried throwing herself off, but skidded over the ground, rocks tearing at her sides. A shadow fell over her and she had seconds to pull her wings in as the dragon's bulk rolled over her.

***

A pained squeal stopped Aven in her tracks. She tore her attention from Ukila, horror chilling her bones as the mangled body of the dead dragon rolled over Mist.

"Aven!" Dev screamed, knocking her sideways as his sword caught Ukila's.

She stumbled before finding her feet, axe still somehow in her hand. She looked once more at Mist, who laid curled in a ball, unmoving save for a few labored breaths. Everything in Aven screamed to go to her. Check on her. Touch her. Then the shadow of the dead dragon moved in the fiery shroud beyond. Ukila still willed its ruined body to fight.

The only way this would stop was with her death.

Aven touched Kali's fang, summoning every bit of strength the pride leader offered. Her throat burned, her eyes stung, and moving her limbs was like wading through mud. But she had to end this. Mist needed her.

Metal clanged over and over as Dev caught a flurry of blows, matching Ukila's speed with skill. The way he moved frightened Aven, his body almost impossible to track as he dipped beneath the swing of Ukila's sword or danced back from a kick.

She rolled the handle of Mama's axe, sinking into all the times they'd faced off. The steel in Mama's eye, the brush of a breeze against her skin, the weight of familiar weapons. Moments in time, born and now gone in a fiery blaze. Everything she'd known, everything she loved about Yunaii--just gone. Reduced to embers, smoke, and ash.

Aven's stampeding heart slowed as a chilling calm washed over her. No more games. No more slacking. She *wanted* Ukila dead.

She raced towards the Soulless, axe raised high. Of course, Ukila countered, her second blade catching Aven's attempt at slashing through her back. Her strength rivaled a dragon's. She knocked Dev's sword aside and Aven's axe, before turning into a spinning kick that sent him sprawling.

Aven didn't wait to move in. She'd studied Ukila on the bridge. The monster didn't understand the thing she faced. Diligence, honed by Mama, patience tempered by Papa, and ruthlessness brought out by Kali's fire. They melded together in Aven, leaving her thirsty for victory.

Ukila's two blades swung in tandem. One came down in a chop, then the other, before she popped one sword tip up at Aven's face. A desperate, sloppy move. Aven caught the attacks with the handle of her axe, dancing through a series of strikes and parries she'd practiced for years. Her muscles took over, blocking and attacking, testing and reacting until Aven realized she was now being studied.

That just wouldn't do. *Time to shake things up.*

Dev provided the chance when Ukila slashed through his attack, forcing him backward. Aven's mind blurred with fear as Kanai's sad smile flashed behind her eyes. The last one he'd given her. Over her dead body was Ukila taking Dev, too.

A hiss slid between Aven's teeth as she abandoned her usual chopping motions in lieu of popping her axe back and forth, straining for one goal. Just one moment. When Ukila brought her own weapon down in a similar motion, Aven grabbed her thin wrist and twisted. The blade's length jerked to the side and her chest jutted out from the force jolted through her arm.

This was it. Aven rechecked her grip on the axe and brought it clean into Ukila's breast. Bone crunched. Something squished. A wheezing gasp of surprise escaped the pale woman. Her eyes went wide, pupils drowning in a sea of black. Aven studied every detail of her face. She didn't want to forget.

"Enjoy Dia'veh's torments," she whispered. "You evil bitch."

Aven yanked the axe free with another sickening squelch. Her knees buckled, blood slipping out one corner of her mouth. From her other side, Dev approached, both swords in hand. He gazed down at her, his mask of neutrality in place.

He touched the edge of his sword to the back of her neck. "Rest, Ukila. May whatever brought you into Sholindrea take you back. I pray that you find peace with them."

Ukila bared her bloody teeth, chest heaving with every rattled breath. "And I pray that when she finds *you*, elf, that even death rejects you."

Aven threw a confused glance at Dev, but the furrow in his brow held no understanding either. With a sigh, he raised his sword before bringing it down in a clean sweep. Aven didn't look away, even when Ukila's head tumbled free of her shoulders. Nothing washed over her. No relief or sadness. Instead, a hollow emptiness snaked inside her, latching on to anything it found. There was no sense to any of this wanton killing. Ukila had done so much, hurt so many, and for what? Nothing. For her head to roll like a rock tumbling over the cliffs. So much useless death. Aven would never understand.

***

Mist's body throbbed, pain twitching through places she didn't know could hurt. Every feather and bone she willed away left her skin stinging. If only she could ease the aches as well. With a weary breath, she rolled onto her hands and knees before lifting her head.

Just in time to see Ukila lose hers.

Her death brought only emptiness. Killing brought sorrow. Killing brought victory. But the death of a Soulless brought nothing. They had ended Ukila's violence, but not the aggression of her people. The rest were still out there. Destroying lives and homes. It would never stop.

Not unless we do something.

She cringed at how the thought sounded so much like Emriel's voice. It made her want to disagree, but she couldn't. This couldn't happen again.

"Mist!" Aven's voice arrived just before her hands. They grasped at Mist's back, her arms, her face. Searching. "Are you okay? Can you move?"

She sat back on her heels and mustered a nod. "I don't feel like it, but I'm alive."

"Feeling something is better than nothing."

Mist gave a begrudging nod and let Aven pull her to her feet. She would try to appreciate the bruises, even if she hurt all the way down to her bones.

Dev approached, streaked with soot and blood. Cuts laced up his arms and across one cheek, but he was in decent shape.

"Where are Gaelin and Ifera?" Mist asked, looking around. Confused silence hung as they peered through the smoke clouds and ash falling like rain. A blanket of muted darkness hung over them, muffling any noise save for the roar of the fire.

Mist backtracked over her fight, searching behind the tree's massive roots and under shattered market stands. They had to be somewhere. The corpse of the dragon loomed nearby, its black, misshapen form like a hulking monster beyond the smoky haze.

"Ifera!" Aven called. "Gaelin!"

"Here!" came a soft voice closer to the tree. Mist followed the sound, stepping over broken wood and weaving around abandoned layers of cloth. Her feet trudged through piles of ash until coming to thick, slippery puddles beneath a crown of jagged timber.

Ifera was there on her knees, wrapped in a sheet of dirty fabric she must have found after shifting. Gaelin lay sprawled across the ground with his head in her lap. Mist could almost imagine he was resting, if not for the smell of blood hanging over them. She didn't know if the scent was what drew her into a run, or the way his hands lay motionless at his sides.

He couldn't. Not the stark, awkward Truthseeker.

Mist collapsed beside them, barely noticing when Dev and Aven did the same. One look at Ifera's face told them all they needed to know. Tears left streaks through the soot on her cheeks as her lips shook with repressed sobs. There was no running for her salves or dragging him into the Temple. She just sat with him, her trembling hands caressing over his jaw and cheeks, tracing lines Mist guessed she knew by heart.

It hurt to drag her eyes from Gaelin's face. Mist didn't want to blink and miss even one flutter of his eyelids. It took a single glance to see the truth of his injuries. Dragon claws had sheared through his plate armor, slicing deep into his chest. The metal bought him time as his warrior heart clung to every single moment, but death loomed with each rattling breath.

"What can we do?" Aven whispered. "I can run to the Temple—"

"No." Ifera's chin wobbled. "Just sit with us. Please."

Aven glanced helplessly at Mist. After all the fighting, this was a battle none of them could win. How was it ending like this?

Mist's vision blurred as she laid a hand on his shoulder. "Gaelin. C-can you…can you hear us?"

His eyes fluttered open, their silver sheen dull and tired. "Ifera."

"I am here," she said, taking his hand when Aven lifted it for her. "I am here."

"S—sorry." A gurgled cough rasped over his lips. "So sorry."

"No," Ifera said, kissing his fingertips. "You have nothing to be sorry for, dear one. You saved my life."

"I can't." He gazed up from her lap, fighting for each breath and sound. "Can't leave you. Here."

"Oh, beloved." Ifera pressed his bloody hand to her cheek, leaving red streaks over her skin. "I will be fine, Gaelin. Don't worry for me. Please. It's okay. You can—let go."

A tear slipped down his cheek as he smiled sadly. "Find me."

"I will, my love." Ifera's fingers grasped at his face and lips, sliding over his eyes that had fallen shut. Her body rocked back and forth, even when Aven and Mist wrapped her in their arms. They couldn't hold back the sorrow possessing her, rooting them all beneath fire and ash. "I will find you again. I will find you. I will find you."

***

As Aven flew to the cliffs, she found no words for how she felt. Resigned. Exhausted. Heartbroken. None of them were right. It was like someone had hollowed her out, scooped up every bit of energy and emotion, and left a shell behind.

That's what watching Ifera cling to Gaelin had done. She'd chanted over and over that they would be together again, long after he'd taken his last breath. The mantra kept her on the brink of soul-shattering sobs, the kind that people heard and never forgot.

Aven almost wished for those. Ifera's desperate assurances had been so much worse.

They hadn't left him behind. They couldn't. Even though Aven's people returned their dead to Sholindrea, Dev said that's not what elves did. So, they carried Gaelin's cold body with them as they approached the evacuees' camp and hoped no more enemies awaited.

Gaelin and Ifera had kept a handful of survivors alive in the Temple, Dia'veh's power the last line of defense as dead shifters tore apart anyone left alive. A few griffins, a Linseen and a handful of Tribouin had made it inside, but no Mama or Papa. Their absence chipped away at Aven's empty husk, threatening to take that as well.

With the griffins' help they got everyone out of the canyon. Mist touched down on the outskirts of what had been a battlefield upon their arrival. Now—now Aven didn't know what to call it. Refugee camp? Sanctuary?

Graveyard.

Everything stunk of death, its coppery tang mingling with the smell of fear, and the kinds of wounds that made soldiers go pale.

The Soulless had been merciless.

Dev and Aven slid to the rocks, their weapons raised in case of attack. The sounds of battle had died away, but the inferno's storm whistled and roared even up here. Visibility was better, but they might not be hearing the sounds of struggle.

The sight of Pryn running for them brought something to life in Aven. Her weapons were sheathed, and golden pride shone in her eyes. She didn't stop her mad dash, instead colliding with Aven and Dev, nearly knocking them over with the force of her hug. Blood clung to her too, but her relieved sigh was enough to drop their guards.

"You made it!" Pryn threw a tentative smile at Mist. "Thank the Maker."

"Not all of us." Aven looked over her shoulder to where Gaelin's body was being removed from a griffin's back.

Pryn pressed soot-covered hands to her lips, the gold in her eyes fading to black. Aven felt like a beast for snatching away her joy.

"Fennicks?" Mist asked, having shifted back to two legs. "Anyvath?"

"They're okay. They turned the tide," Pryn said, pointing back the way she'd come. "The dragons were caught completely by surprise. The Soulless went for their nests and hatchlings before attacking the evacuated people."

A shuddering breath slipped from Mist, but Aven couldn't bear to look. Her tears would send another crack through her broken pieces. She almost didn't want to ask the next question burning in her head, but she had to know.

"My parents," Aven whispered. "They weren't down there."

Pryn's shaking fingers grasped Aven's shoulders. "They're here. They made it out."

She looked up sharply, her dry eyes going so wide they hurt. "W-what?"

"Your mother saved the Qinawe from being wiped out." Pryn pointed towards the tattered tents and shelters shrouded in smoke. "She was amazing. You should have seen her."

When Aven started running was a mystery. Her feet carried her through the swirling gray clouds, dodging bodies appearing beneath the haze. People gathered dead, saw to wounded, repaired what they could. Aven didn't care about any of it. She searched every smeared, bloody face, needing a glimpse of Mama's black eyes or Papa's full smile. They were here somewhere, but it was hard. Soot covered everyone's sweaty skin, blurring features and skin colors. They all looked the same now.

"Mama!" she called out, spinning amongst a small crowd she'd wandered into. Tired eyes gazed back at her. Defeated faces. "Navya!"

"Aven?"

Another turn had her facing them. Mama. Papa. She stood amongst the gathered injured, a gash across her bicep and her lip split open. He rose from the place he crouched, the person he tended forgotten as he stared at Aven.

Mama's lips parted in a silent sob. "My cub."

Aven was in their arms before she realized any of them had moved. First Mama's came around her, before Papa squeezed both Aven and Mama to his chest. Their smells. Their warmth. Their voices. Everything familiar and good wrapped around her, and finally something shifted inside. She wasn't completely empty. The place they held in her heart was still full and beating. With them here, the sorrow could not drown her.

She could have stayed there forever, but the moans of pain around them demanded they couldn't. Aven drew out of their arms and looked around, searching for familiar faces amongst the injured. She'd fought to keep this very outcome from happening.

"What can I do?" Aven asked.

"There's plenty." Papa rubbed his blackened hands against his dirty pants. "Dress wounds. Help people find family members. Sort through the shelters. The Soulless did everything they could to destroy not only us, but any provisions we'd set aside. The next few days are going to be rough."

"Mist!" Mama said, walking past Aven with outstretched arms. Papa followed in her wake, both of them catching Mist up in the same heart-filling hug they'd given Aven.

"Where are the others?" Aven asked when they parted.

"Dev went to get a report from the Linseen who stayed behind. Pryn is helping her people."

Aven blinked in surprise. "They're listening to her?"

"Elder Dasoln and Elder Jywe died in the attack," Papa said with a sad sigh. "They did their best and stood between the Soulless and their people. Without Elders or anyone else that's ever stood in battle, Pryn is easily filling the void. I cannot imagine it will go on for long, but for today she gives her people what they need."

A smile slipped across Aven's lips. Pryn no doubt loved every second of it. Bouncing between the part of dutiful daughter and champion dragon rider had been the hardest part of her life, at least before their failed mating challenge. Aven hoped she could bring those two parts of herself together now.

"What of the Matriarchs?" Mist asked, scanning the injured nearby.

Mama's lips twitched as she glanced off to where the dead were being gathered. "Hanawi and Revari survived."

"Yana?" A breath caught in Aven's throat.

"Dead," Hanawi said, approaching from behind them. Revari was at her side, the blade of her axe stained red. "She died as a shield to the helpless."

Aven hated her relief over this news. She wasn't happy the old woman was gone, but now she'd never have to look into those hateful eyes again. Nor would Ifera.

Disgust twisted Hanawi's sour face into something new. Something cold. "Try not to smile. Yana's death changes nothing."

Revari gave the other Matriarch a sideways look. "It changes some things."

"This is not the place for such a discussion," Hanawi said, speaking with more bite than ever before. Perhaps without Yana to cow her, the anger simmering inside her was free to lash out.

"Nothing can be made official," Revari said, looking at Navya with a calculating look. "But with Yana gone, a new Matriarch must be named."

"Not now," Hanawi hissed.

Aven's gaze slid between the two women. Resignation showed in the lines of Revari's face, while Hanawi's was wrought with frustration. All around, Qinawe had gone still. The uninjured watched beneath masks of dirt and grime, the whites of their eyes showcasing their fear.

"Our people want Navya," Revari said. "She served well. She saved lives. All I have spoken with have requested it."

Hanawi's eyes rolled with derision. "It is not a decision that should be made right now."

"It is not a decision *we* can overrule," Revari said. "Matriarchs lead and teach, but most importantly serve the people. If they choose her, then that is the will of the bond."

"Yana's body has barely gone cold!" Hanawi whirled on the Matriarch, tears gathering in her eyes. "Loss is heavy and fear is in control. We must take time to discuss this, as a people, when our dead are given to Sholindrea and the injured are able to speak."

"You are not wrong," Mama said, her expression cool and calculating. She stood with her shoulders thrown back and chin raised. The picture of a Qinawe Matriarch. "The people must be allowed to speak. Until then, I will serve as best I can. There is much pain to be soothed. My Chosen and I are here for as long as we are needed."

Words of gratitude and love floated from the surrounding Qinawe. Some reached for Mama, some even laid hands on Papa, as if touching them could siphon some of their strength.

Hanawi's gaze moved over the Qinawe, her eyes a wash of sorrow, anger, pain. Aven scented it as much as saw it. The power she coveted was slipping free. With Mama among the Matriarchs, she would never be the leader Yana was.

"Does she threaten you so much?" Aven asked. After facing Soulless and the dead, she was done with pretenses.

Hanawi threw back her braided hair as she straightened. "Navya is no threat to me, cub. She is a threat to the bond. *You* are a threat to the bond. Your warring heart has no place amongst us."

"Her warring heart saved all of you," Mist said, putting a possessive hand on Aven's shoulder. "She fought at the dam."

"She should have been here," Hanawi said, idly touching the bone in her ear. "If she had, some might not have died. She *chose* to go seeking a fight that need not have happened."

"The dam would have been destroyed." Mist stepped past Aven, trembling with anger. "It was all we could do to keep the Soulless from doing so."

"And yet either way our home is gone and our people are dead, so tell me what was the point of it?"

"We might never know," Mama said. "To debate what might have been is pointless. They might have destroyed the dam before we could evacuate everyone. They might have blown it in time to save our home from the fire. All we know is the Soulless had no intention of letting any of us live. If Aven took the life of even one, it saved the lives of those they meant to take."

"It is not her willingness to defend that is the problem." Hanawi pressed a hand to her forehead, looking more like a mother debating her child than a woman of equal intelligence. "She seeks battle instead of waiting for what might come. She will infect those prone to admiration and the young. She will change what our ways mean to us."

"Maybe they need to change," Mist muttered, crossing her arms.

Aven looked again at the gathered Qinawe. Some did stare as if she were someone—powerful? Wondrous. Like she'd probably looked at dragons for the first time. Hanawi wasn't wrong. She would change them.

"Don't worry, Matriarch." Aven spat the last word. "I won't be able to corrupt the bond because I'm leaving Yunaii."

"You have said that for many turns of the moon," Revari said, tilting her head.

Aven took Mist's hand and cast a desperate look her way. "I've flown to Shard's Port. We know we can make it now. There's something I need to do. A request I need to see through."

Confusion twisted Mama and Papa's faces while Mist's brow furrowed. Her mind was swirling. Then her eyes widened with understanding.

"Kanai?" Mist whispered, drawing a nod from Aven. Her gaze went to the sky, before settling on their audience. "We're going to Estellias to find Kanai's cub, Nya. She deserves to know what happened. To him, to the pride, and to Yunaii."

"Are you sure?" Aven asked, squeezing her hand. "You don't have to come with me. I can find you after."

Mist sighed as her eyes focused on the flames spreading across the forest. "You're my Chosen. Where you go, I go. My bloodkin will want me to choose a side when I return, but what happened here has already shown me what I have to do. This cannot happen again. Not here. Not in Estellias. Not anywhere."

Bitter fear slipped into Papa's scent as he looked at Mist. "Will that not put you in danger, dear girl? You said the Eilawi care not for shifters, but dragons are another matter."

"It could, but I will give my bloodkin a chance to tell me their intentions. Then I will decide how *I* can help." Mist's eyes grew unfocused, as if she were remembering something. "I'm old enough now. I will find a way to serve Dia'veh in this. *My way.*"

Another bit of the hollowness slipped away, replaced by a burning Aven couldn't put into words. She didn't know she could love or admire Mist more, but here she was, completely lost by how this ethereal girl loved *her*.

"We'll figure it out together." Aven pressed a kiss to her cheek, hoping this was the beginning of putting herself back right.

The smile on Hanawi's lips told her it wasn't going to be as easy as she hoped. The harrowing triumph in the Matriarch's eyes was so much like Ukila.

"If you intend to leave, you must surrender the pride leader's fang."

Protests erupted all around them. Not only from Mist or Mama or Papa. Even Qinawe around them balked and gasped, some declaring Hanawi wrong for making such a claim.

Even their defense couldn't ground Aven's spinning head. The fang. Kali's fire. Kali's strength. Without her, Aven might not have survived this day. How could she get through the healing her soul needed now that the fighting was done?

Hanawi waved a hand, silencing all but Mama. "Kali entrusted herself to the bond. We have a duty to ensure she goes to Dia'veh's peace. Perhaps not today or tomorrow, but it is a promise made when a Sholi chooses a Qinawe. We cannot follow through if you take her soul from Yunaii."

Aven touched Kali's fang. The lynx had been there for so long. Life without her was a distant dream. She had shaped Aven almost as much as Mama or Papa.

"You're not wrong."

"Aven no," Mama said, both hands wrapping around hers and the fang. "Kali left herself to you. She chose you. Hanawi is wrong about this."

Aven looked to Revari. The woman didn't like her, but their flaring tempers connected them. Of all the Matriarchs, Aven held begrudging respect for her.

"It's on you to settle it."

Revari's thin brows shot up. "You will yield to my decision?"

Bitterness tasted like bile in Aven's throat. "I didn't put it on you just to spit on your judgement."

Another flare of shock washed over the Matriarch's face. She absently stroked the bone thrust through the shell of her ear, her eyes darting over the watching Qinawe. The way she hesitated sparked a hope that she might be fair and unemotional.

"Aven."

The sound of her name coming from the Matriarch stoked the fire welling in her chest. To even be acknowledged as such was a show of respect. She'd never earned her place or her name, but Revari gave it anyway.

"I do not know you." Revari thumbed the blade of her axe. "That is my failing. In a different time, I might have come to admire you as well. You have the best of our people coursing through your veins. What you did today is nothing short of a miracle."

Mist squeezed Aven's hand as a tremor shot through her body.

"The problem is that I do not know your character well enough," Revari said, closing her eyes, as if regret weighed them down.

Hanawi had no such problem. A triumphant sneer stretched across her face as Revari took a deep breath.

"I am sorry, Aven, but I cannot know that you will do right by Kali. I should know. It's my responsibility to know. I want to believe you will, but you must understand that the best resolution is for her soul to be sent on to Dia'veh. Now."

"What?" Hanawi gasped. "Now?"

Revari shot a glare at her fellow Matriarch. "*Yes. Kali did not entrust herself to either you or myself. Or Navya for that matter. Our people's promise must be upheld, and this is the only way I can ensure that it is.*"

It took Aven a moment to remember how to breathe. Revari might as well have put a fist to her gut. It took everything to stay upright, to not double over and sob. If her audience of Qinawe had not been staring she might have fallen to her knees.

Only the strength she was about to lose kept her back straight and gaze steely. There was nothing left to say. No feeling to indulge. No argument to make. Aven had said she would yield to Revari's decision. She would prove the Matriarch right if she didn't.

Her vision blurred as she lifted the necklace over her head. The tears saved her from seeing Hanawi's horrible face or the sorrow in Revari's. Bidding Kali goodbye should have been a moment far down the road, something to be done in private. Instead, she cradled the fang in one shaking palm, already missing the pride leader's love and strength.

What would she do without it?

"Thank you, Kali," Aven whispered, touching the fang to her forehead. She could almost hear a whine of sorrow in her ears. The way her chest heaved as the words slipped out couldn't only be her pain. Nothing had ever felt like this. Not when the forest burned. Not when Kanai fell. Not when Pryn betrayed her. Not when the Matriarchs denied her. Her legs could have been cut from beneath her and it would not have dulled the twisting ache hollowing her throat. Every breath rasped through her and she knew without a doubt that Kali's soul mourned as much as her own. They were supposed to be together forever, until Aven's dying day. Released to Dia'veh together, to face the Make side by side. Kali intended it. Aven craved it. A bond and strength never meant to be severed.

A stifled sob shook Aven's lips as she gingerly deposited the fang in Revari's outstretched hand. Without another word, she turned her back on her people, and left behind the shattered pieces of her soul as she walked away.

CHAPTER
Thirty-Nine

Mist

Mist had always found the ocean soothing. The waves rolled and crashed, birds screeching overhead. Creatures emerged from its cool depths to splash and snap at fish. As the salty breeze toyed with her hair, she drew in a deep breath, not unlike the one she'd drawn after first setting foot on the Din Shard housing Yunaii. It was hard to believe she was leaving, finally returning to the cool lands and shaded forests of Estellias. A lifetime ago she'd planned to never go back. Now she couldn't wait.

The eerie port town lay beyond, its skeletal buildings proof this place had once teemed with life. Hopefully, the spark her present group struck remained in its old bones. Perhaps it could come back. For the port, for Yunaii, for the shifters.

Many of them bustled about. Mostly dragons, mingled with a few Linseen, lynx, and a single griffin with her Klesian elf. Dev and Willa strolled through the sand, heads tilted towards each other as Mist assumed they said their goodbyes. There had been so many lately.

Aven stood far down the dock, eyes locked on the horizon. Saying goodbye to her parents and Kali's soul shattered something inside her. Her smiles didn't come as easily, and the flight to the port had been devoid of her cheerful chatter. She needed time so Mist wouldn't rush her, but each day it went on a piece of her broke as well.

"You ready for this, bloodkin?"

Emriel stepped through the sand, wiggling her bare toes like a child. Her spirits had carried them all this way. Unlike Aven, she had gotten everything she wanted.

"Ready as I'll ever be." Mist gazed past her sister, towards the dragons milling about on two legs and four. Dozens of them. They ate, drank, snoozed in the sun. They had a long journey back to Estellias. A lone figure stood in the mix, his green hair blowing in the ocean's breeze as he surveyed those he'd once commanded.

"Did you say goodbye to him?" Mist asked, nodding her chin towards Rielnor.

"Not yet." Emriel's nostrils flared as a line pinched between her brows. "I doubt he'll care. I'm not exactly in his good graces."

Mist fought the urge to roll her eyes. "Don't be that way. He's not angry with you. You're not the one who took the flight from him."

"I might as well have."

"Come. I haven't said goodbye yet either." Mist looped an arm through Emriel's, giving her no chance to protest. If dragging her was what it took to clear the air with Rielnor, that's what Mist would do.

He didn't regard them as they approached, not even when they stopped before him. His gaze followed the dragons in various forms of preparation, as if cataloguing each one.

"Rielnor." His eyes snapped to Mist's face. Accepting he no longer held the title of flight leader had been hard. Speaking his name out loud still sent a wobbly feeling through her stomach. "I wanted to say goodbye, and thank you. For everything. You took me in, protected me. I owe you a great deal."

"You owe me nothing." His deep, rumbling voice comforted something fragile inside her. She would miss it when they were gone. "Just take care so it was not all for nothing."

Mist resisted the urge to stare at his shoulders. Fresh scars crept over each one, his back a ruin of healing red skin.

When Emriel's silence stretched on, Mist pointedly bumped against her hip, earning a glare worse than a Soulless' smile.

"For what it's worth," Emriel said, drawing out each word like they stuck to her tongue, "I'm sorry you've decided to stay."

"Someone should remain and restore Yunaii. The mother tree and some of her children survived. With proper care, there is hope for the future." He didn't quite make eye contact as he spoke. "The lynx have no pride leader, the Tribouin face great change, and the Matriarchs are in transition. Yliva and I are all that remain. Though I am a dragon without a flight, I can still lend my knowledge."

Mist's heart wrenched. "I'm sorry."

He raised a dark green brow. "You have nothing to be sorry for. It was not you who took advantage of my weakened state."

"Yes," said an unfamiliar voice carrying an all too familiar scent. "Let's make sure our grumpiness is directed at the right dragon."

Fennicks appeared at Rielnor's side. No, not Fennicks anymore. *Vhisari.* The black dragon had claimed their true name when they claimed the flight. Their yellow eyes and hair were the same today, but their features were new, as usual. Their clothes molded to a tall, muscular body, but not one as formidable as the form they'd used to defeat Emriel in battle. Long black hair veiled a beautiful face, with chiseled cheekbones, a soft chin, and a delicate, kissable mouth. Perhaps their first face at last, but Mist might never know.

"There is no anger, Vhisari." A sigh crept into Rielnor's words. "Just sadness. I wish you all the best, but I fear the worst awaits you."

"You're still welcome to come," Vhisari said in a softer voice. "You will always have a place in my flight."

"My place is here today." Rielnor gazed at the three of them, brows pulled into a fond look. "Perhaps I will blink, and this coming war will be over. Then we might fly together again."

Vhisari looked ready to argue, but Emriel laid a hand on their arm. A shake of her head had resignation taking over their face. With a sigh, they offered a hand and Rielnor took it, grasping Vhisari's forearm in a tight grip.

"You have prepared for this. Just watch your back. Do not put blind trust in the Elementals. They lie as easily as they speak truths."

Vhisari nodded before going to continue preparations. Taking the whole flight across the ocean required planning, just like Anyvath said. She never ventured far from Vhisari, and they listened to her advice in a way Mist never expected. Their arrogant energy had been replaced by a mantle of concern.

"Emriel," Rielnor said softly. "Mist."

They both straightened. Gazing up at his scarred face left Mist feeling like a child.

"What is coming will shape you both." He looked between their faces. "Do not let it break you. Remember to take things for yourselves. Serving as a soldier or voice of Dia'veh does not mean you must deny yourself joy. Or love. Or peace. Watch over each other and your other bloodkin."

"Eewa." Emriel sniffled, her steely facade nearly crumbling. "I am sorry for how it all turned out."

His lips twitched into a smile with an impressive lack of bitterness. "No, you're not. That's what I love about you, kitling. Never change. You will be a force to be reckoned with. Do not let your eega's fight destroy you."

"Do you—" Emriel paused, glancing at Mist. "Is there anything you want us to tell her?"

"Tell her I still live. And still wait should she grow weary." He gave them each a fond look, before pressing a kiss first to Emriel's brow and then Mist's. "Take care, bloodkin."

Without a backwards glance, he walked away, a swath of new scars slashed across his coppery back. Mist studied each mark, hoping to see them again one day. He passed by Thudan as he headed for the hill overlooking the port. The spikey dragon looked at the flight one time, before following

Rielnor. He would not leave him, and that comforted Mist a little.

Someone would be watching over the elder dragon.

Emriel roughly cleared her throat as Dev and Willa approached, their fingers interlaced. If Rielnor and Thudan were leaving, that meant their final goodbye had come.

"How's it, little bird?" Em asked. "I hope you bedded him good. Broody, angry elves aren't the best traveling companions."

Willa's face pulled into a mocking look, her pink lips parting with some snappy retort.

"I require no bedding to be pleasant," Dev said, his humorless tone unable to distract from the flush in his long ears. "I take great joy in knowing I am no longer responsible for keeping you from maiming, scarring, or killing yourself."

"Hey," Emriel bristled. "I only have one new scar, and I think it's pretty awesome. Vhisari hasn't given me that many good ones. They've got their work cut out to do better than Ukila."

Dev indulged a dramatic eye roll. "*Dragons.*"

Willa stepped between them, her fingers toying with a white rock he'd hung around his neck. "Thanks for the dance, elf. And the save. If Dia'veh has you pass through again, there will always be a spot for you in my nest."

She yanked at their joined hands, tugging him flush against her. He had the skill to avoid it, Mist had seen him fight, but Dev yielded, dropping his head as Willa rose on her toes. Their lips crashed together, devouring with a passion that pushed Mist to look away, while trapping her attention all at once. When they parted, a soft smile graced Willa's face. Her rosy cheeks glowed, as her eyes lazily opened, perhaps returning from some private memory.

Mist sighed, aching to pull Aven into her own arms. Everyone deserved to be touched like that—looked at like that. Dev's fiery gaze followed Willa as she walked Rielnor's path, her good wing tucked over the place her other had once been.

"You gonna make it, elf?" Em asked, clapping him on the shoulder. "Did you say bye to the old man?"

He raised one brow as his gaze lingered on where she'd touched him. "Of course. I did not reserve such a parting for a place like this. Too much needed to be said."

"Good," Mist said, glancing back at Rielnor. How much did this hurt him, watching even his rider leave him behind?

Dev followed her gaze, admiring the dragon he'd once spent so much time with. Regret lingered in his eyes, but he seemed to shake it off. "I must find Ifera. I am to accompany her safely to Dia'veh's Temple on the mainland."

"How is she?" Mist asked in a soft voice. Aven's silence was rivaled only by Ifera's. After committing Gaelin's body to Dia'veh, she'd often been found staring at the sky with a contemplative look on her face, as if she might find him amongst the clouds.

"She speaks in riddles I do not understand," Dev said. "My study of Dia'veh's laws is not as astute as that of the sword. She speaks of souls moving beyond Dia'veh's peace, but I know nothing of it. I believe she seeks answers from the Priestesses on Din'Sha."

I will find you. That's what Ifera had said.

Mist looked out at the ocean, longing to dive into its depths and call out to Dia'veh. Was it possible? Could a soul be found once it fled its body?

She would search for those answers one day. For now, there was still so much to do. Dev and Ifera would be escorted west to the shattered lands of Din'Sha, then the flight headed east to Pri'Av. The continent housed the most powerful kingdoms in Sholindrea.

"Dev, if you're ever in Estellias, you can find Aven and me in Tem'bria. It's a village to the south. The door is always open and we have plenty of food to spare." Mist smiled as she thought of Papi. Aven would finally meet him. And Adair! What would her childhood friend make of her?

Dev bowed his head, probably to hide the curve in his lips. "I will remember that. For now, take care."

He walked off without another word, sparing a few glances at Willa's retreating form. It was a shame. Elves usually mated for life. Griffins did not. Mist hoped he wouldn't suffer too much from this parting.

"Oh, before I forget," Emriel said, patting down her pockets, face scrunched as if she'd lost something important. "I have something. I know it's here somewhere. Ah!"

She dug into her back pocket, one eye pinching shut as her tongue flicked between her teeth. Whatever it was must have been very interesting. She was having too much fun keeping Mist in suspense.

Eventually she held out a closed fist, grinning like she'd just brought down a ton beast. When her fingers slowly uncurled, Mist choked on a gasp.

Kali's fang lay cradled in Em's palm.

"What? How?" Mist snatched it up, every bump and groove so familiar. Aven's scent even still clung to it. Desert flowers. "Where did you get this? Did the Matriarchs change their mind?"

"Oh, Great Mother, no. Those judgy bags of air are probably still seething that it's gone."

Mist stared into her sister's dancing eyes. "Then how?"

Emriel threw a pointed look at Vhisari, who fussed at a young dragon nearby. "Dinon was quite vexed that the Matriarchs had Kali's soul. They sent their regards, by the way. Says to tell Nya hello if you find her. We have apparently been awful influences on the baby cat, because they went tattling to Vhis. Next thing I knew, they'd hatched a scheme to get the fang back."

"You mean steal it?"

"Stole. Reclaimed. You can pick whatever word you want. The lynx said those hags had no right to decide anything for their pride leader." Her grin widened. "And so of course our dear sweet Vhis had to have some fun along the way."

Mist squeezed her eyes shut. "They didn't."

"Oh, they dropped right on top of Hanawi. Gave her a good fright. Then snatched up the fang and flew off."

"Was that really necessary?" Mist imagined the other Qinawe's terror after everything they'd been through.

Hanawi was a sour old beast but even her fear brought no cheer.

Emriel shrugged. "I think so. Everyone knows Vhis and Aven aren't exactly pals. No one will ever suspect. Vhis enjoys playing the bad guy."

"I've noticed," Mist muttered. "I'm starting to think they were in on everything from the beginning. Even your challenge to Rielnor."

A twinkle lit in Emriel's sky blue eyes. "Vhisari has been with me since the beginning. Rielnor always favored them over me. We both knew they had a better chance of becoming my egg-warden's number two."

"Which made them the most likely person to accept your challenge in Rielnor's place?" Mist finally saw the lengths she would go for her cause. "What if Rielnor had accepted the challenge?"

That got another shrug as Em admired Vhisari. "I was ready to win. I'd trained. If Rielnor accepted, I would beat him, and if he let Vhis fight, then I would let them win."

"Either way, Rielnor lost the flight's respect."

Emriel nodded. "Vhisari is not who you think, Mist. They just play the parts given to them."

"All to save Estellias?" She still couldn't wrap her head around it. Vhisari held such disdain for Mist's loyalty to her home. Or had that been an act?

"It's not about Estellias," Emriel said, taking hold of Mist's shoulders. "Estellias is just a battlefield. It's the most powerful kingdom in Sholindrea. Ensuring Estellias' survival protects the world."

Mist frowned. "From the Soulless? Have their numbers grown that much?"

Emriel blinked a few times, her jaw working back and forth before she released Mist. "You figure out how you want to serve Dia'veh, and then I'll tell you everything. For now, the less you know, the safer you are."

"What does that mean?"

Mist only got a shake of Emriel's head before she sauntered towards Vhisari. A momentary pause halted her trek as she pointed to Aven's still figure on the dock.

"Go give that thing to her so she stops moping. There's work to be done." She'd almost reached Vhisari, who'd stopped their fussing to stare at Mist.

"Tell your pet not to worry," Vhisari shouted. "Dinon will let her mummy know in a few days where the fang is."

Secrets. Always more secrets. At least returning to Estellias gave her a chance to ferret them out. No matter what it took. She threw a grateful look at Vhisari, who dropped their chin before returning to their task.

For now, she had a smile to deliver. Mist broke into a run, kicking up sand before leaping onto the dock. Her feet pounded over the rough wood, just like the night they snuck onto the Soulless' ship. She tried ignoring how everything swayed beneath her, instead focusing on Aven's growing form. Almost there.

Of course, the sound of her steps drew Aven's attention. She turned, confusion and concern lighting in her deep brown eyes. When her gaze landed on Mist, she jumped into a lazy run, padding up the dock as resignation washed over her face.

"What is it?" she asked. "What's wrong?"

Mist drew in a few breaths, taking a moment to steady herself. She didn't want to miss any part of this moment. Aven stood in a halo of yellow gold, looking like a fabled Ayferi–mysterious creatures basked in light, sent to Sholindrea by Dia'veh themself.

"Mist?" Fear shook Aven's voice.

She couldn't hold off any longer, not if Aven was scared. Mist closed the distance and took her hand. Aven didn't fight, even when Mist uncurled her clenched fingers, leaving her palm raised to the sky.

Confusion rose in Aven's eyes as she looked at their joined hands. She didn't have to speak her questions. They hung in the air, as clear as the ocean's waves beneath their feet.

Mist wrapped her slim fingers around the fang, concealing every inch of its stark surface and the beaded necklace attached to it. She wanted to revel in the moment, when it touched Aven's skin and she realized what she had.

What she earned. Not just the fang, but Dinon and Vhisari's loyalty and their friendship. Aven might have lost her people, but she had found better ones.

In one, smooth motion, Mist deposited the fang in Aven's upturned hand. At first, she stared, blinking rapidly, lines creasing her brow. Her fingers didn't curl around the precious gift, the sorrow didn't flee from her eyes. She just stared.

"What?" Her voice cracked, still hoarse from screaming over the clash of weapons and breathing in smoke. "H-how? Where?"

Mist closed her hand around the fang. "Dinon sends their love."

Aven's soft lips parted, releasing a shaky breath that turned to a sob. "I can't."

"Yes," Mist said, squeezing Aven's fist with both her hands. "You can. You deserve it."

"I gave it up."

"Listen to me." Mist traced Aven's jaw, thumb skimming the corner of her mouth before sliding up her cheekbones. "Kali entrusted *you* with her soul. Not Hanawi, not Revari. She saw something in you that none of them could. Kanai saw it too. He trusted you to do right by her, even when his end was near. This belongs with you. If you don't trust me, them, or even yourself, then we'll let Nya decide. She can choose what to do with her grandmother's soul."

Aven stared at their hands, breathing hard. She wanted this, craved it. Mist couldn't blame her. Kali was strength. Shifting was freedom. Even if she had already taken those things for herself, nothing replaced the power Dia'veh granted.

Mist knew when acceptance washed through Aven. Her smile shone brighter than Sansia, crinkling her eyes and pinching dimples in her cheeks. Tears glistened over her lashes as she clutched the fang to her chest, a choked sigh of relief slipping between her lips. She might have gone to her knees had Mist not caught her in a hug, pressing so close together nothing stood between them. And nothing ever would.

As long as Mist could end every day seeing that glimpse of perfection, everything would be okay. No matter what the Soulless plotted, or Emriel schemed. If Mist and Aven were together, they were going to win.

The End

Dev will return soon.

And you will see Aven and Mist again.

Acknowledgements

I could write a book purely for the thank you's I owe. I don't think I would have made it this far without the people who supported me all these years. First is my husband, who is not a reader, but has spent countless hours listening to me talk about my books and offering ideas on how to make them better. Fennicks in particular owes their complexity to you. I'll never forget the car ride where I lamented not knowing where Fennicks fit and you said to give them the role of mastermind. Everything clicked into place in that moment and I owe that to you.

Of course, my daughters deserve a ton of thanks too. The four of you are my pride and joy. I'm so grateful to be your mother and I'm even more grateful that you are the first people in a room to declare that I wrote a book and that I draw my characters. Your pride gives me the confidence to step out of my comfort zone and offer my projects to the world.

Then there is my sister, who has read everything I've ever written and tells anyone who will listen that my books are better than Tolkien. That's a nice compliment sis, but definitely not. I appreciate how much you believe me though. You and Dad. You've both watched me scribble and type for years, and no matter what I've done, you've pushed me to do more, try more, to always keep going.

My dear friends Diana, Serena, and Eva. You've listened to the ramblings, you've read the words, and endured hours of fretting and self-doubt. Diana in particular, you've been on this journey with me since college and that doesn't feel real. I still remember sitting in the computer lab beside you as I frantically typed away a million ideas. The fact that you've read some of the roughest bits of my writing makes me cringe and smile all at once.

My Grandmas both helped push me to where I am. Thank you for always believing in every crazy, creative idea I ever threw at you both. I dreamed of Grammie reading this book, but no matter how hard I tried, the words just did not finished it in time. Grandma, I hope I'll be able to put a signed copy in your hands in just a few months.

I also owe a lifetime of gratitude to Jamie Dalton. Were it not for Project Author I might have used fear and doubt to procrastinate for another decade. You gave me hope and the desire to follow through. Thank you for taking a chance on little authors like me and for giving your time out of the kindness of your heart.

My biggest, sappiest thank you goes to a group of people that I have never met, but have been essential in this book ever seeing the light of day. The Veggie Patch. I'm sure I just got a lot of raised eyebrows with that one, but let me explain. Sam, Liz, Justin, and Jaysan are members of my writing group, the Veggies. They are the best of the best, a group of people that remind me every time I read their work that I still have a lot to learn.

Sam Crook could give an intriguing voice to a rock. You are that writer who could probably never use dialogue tags and the readers would still know who was speaking. The way you personify every character in your books is pure magic.

Which speaking of magic, Elisabeth Wallsworth paints pictures with words the same way I do with brushes. I am envious of how beautifully you bring your scenes to life with just a few, poignant phrases.

Justin Corriss is a master of dialogue in a way I will never be able to achieve. Your work is poetic and clever, with threats, insults, and compliments woven into a tapestry of words that make me question my intelligence sometimes.

Lastly is Jaysan Charlesford, who blends storylines together in a way that my brain sometimes cannot comprehend. Your work is intriguing and impressive, while sometimes befuddling, but in the kind of way that authors want for their readers. You make people think and I admire that greatly when measuring your work against my explosions and in your face fight scenes.

Each of the Veggies has taught me so much and supported me even more. The cheerleading, the feedback, and sometimes the threats from Sam and Justin to get my projects done, has helped keep me on track. I'm so glad I found each of you and I will be forever grateful that you are my friends, critique partners, and honest people to bounce ideas off of. I would not be publishing this book if it was not for the four of you.

The last thank you is to my readers. Thank you for giving me a chance. Thank you for loving my characters. Thank you for stepping into Sholindrea. I hope you found a home here and I hope you will stay a while. Sholindrea is a place I wanted to make for anyone and everyone, with heartfelt stories set against magical backdrops. I can't wait to see you again in the pages of my next book, but until then, Aven and Mist will keep you company on the arid cliff tops and sleepy forests.